Borderlands
Lake Aeternus
Water Keep
Windlash Mountains
Plains of Thayer
Noble River
Westland Woods
Two Prongs River
Westland
Terra ne Staric
Aster's Bay
Sea of Eternal Sorrows
Uncharted Territory South

FARWORLD

LAND KEEP

BOOK TWO

J. SCOTT SAVAGE

SHADOW
MOUNTAIN

To Robert C. Martin,
December 4, 1936–January 26, 2009.
Uncle Bob knew the power of laughter,
and shared it freely with everyone he met.

And to Orin Voorheis
who exemplifies what it means to be
a true hero every day of his life. You rock!

First printing in hardbound 2009.
First printing in paperbound 2013.

Library of Congress Cataloging-in-Publication Data

Savage, J. Scott.
  Land keep / J. Scott Savage.
    p.   cm. — (Farworld ; bk. 2)
  Summary: Having discovered that his destiny is tied to that of Farworld, Marcus, despite his growing power over water, struggles with physical pain and inner doubts as, with the help of his companions, he tries to complete the quest to find the other elementals that will help destroy the evil force of the Dark Circle.
    ISBN 978-1-60641-164-3 (hardbound : alk. paper)
    ISBN 978-1-60907-331-2 (paperbound)
    [1. Foundlings—Fiction.   2. People with disabilities—Fiction.   3. Magic—Fiction.
  4. Fantasy.]   I. Title.
  PZ7.S25897Lan 2009
  [Fic]—dc22   2009025673

Printed in the United States of America
Edwards Brothers Malloy, Ann Arbor, MI

10   9   8   7   6   5   4   3   2   1

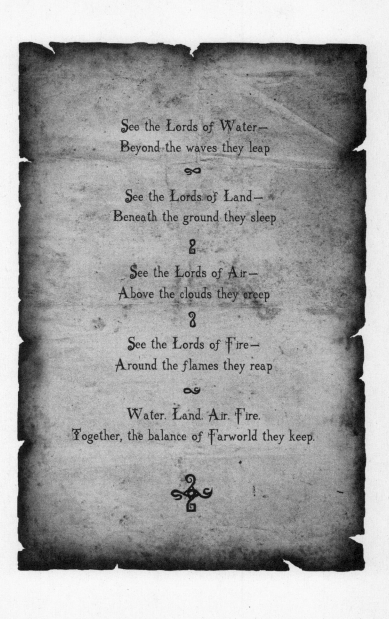

See the Lords of Water—
Beyond the waves they leap

See the Lords of Land—
Beneath the ground they sleep

See the Lords of Air—
Above the clouds they creep

See the Lords of Fire—
Around the flames they reap

Water. Land. Air. Fire.
Together, the balance of Farworld they keep.

CONTENTS

PART 2: LAND KEEP

PART 3: RETURN

PART 4: BATTLE FOR THE CITY

KEEPERS OF THE BALANCE

Aster's Bay

They came in the impersonal darkness of early morning, before the sun painted the sky, before the street peddlers began setting up their stands—at least an hour before even the farmers outside the city walls would arise and start another day of toiling in the fields. They came at a time when those wakened by their coming could pull their heads back under the blankets and try to return to a troubled sleep.

Jaklah had been waiting for their arrival—dreading the sound of hoofs on the cobblestones late at night. At the first high-pitched whistles of the snifflers, the skin on the backs of his arms prickled with fear. He lunged out of bed and pressed his face to the window, where the pale, orange moon illuminated the buildings below and a pink crescent gleamed just above the horizon.

In the distance he could see the riders coming. The creatures at their sides were only shadows in the dark. But in his mind he could envision the six spiked legs, the clacking mandibles, and worst of all, the gray skin that turned into—

"Don't do it," Kelthan whispered from his bed across the small room. "Don't run. It'll only make it worse."

"What do *you* know?" Jaklah snapped at his older brother, his voice sharp with terror. He turned back to the window and his stomach knotted. They were closer now—the snifflers just visible in the moonlight. "You didn't even try."

In the darkness, Kelthan was silent, perhaps stung by his brother's accusation, perhaps just in thought. At last he spoke. "What good would it have done? If they catch you, they just make it that much more painful. And if they don't . . ."

Jaklah knew all about what happened to the ones who ran. There was only one place the Keepers didn't dare follow and that was for good reason. The thought of where he would have to go, what he would have to face, raised cold flesh all over his body.

"It ain't fair!" He slammed a fist on his hay-filled mattress. "I was just getting good."

"The Keepers of the Balance don't care 'bout that. Least not for people like us."

Sweat burned Jaklah's eyes, and he wiped it away with a shaking hand. He could hear the horses snorting and whinnying outside. And was that the sound of boots coming up the stairs?

"Does it hurt? If you . . . let 'em take it?"

"Yes." Kelthan's answer was instant. "But I've talked to folks who've run. They say fighting against it is like swallowing hot coals. The blood still burns inside you weeks later."

Jaklah tried to imagine the agony of fire under his skin. Before he could finish the thought, someone pounded at the front door. "They're here!" he gasped.

His pa's heavy footsteps echoed across the kitchen floor. The front door swung open with a squeal of unoiled hinges. Beneath the sound of men's voices, the *cheeee-cheeee-cheeee* whistling of a sniffler sounded like metal on a grindstone.

"I'll fetch him," his father said from the other room, and Jaklah's self-control snapped. Shoving open the window, he crawled over the sill. His feet found the small ledge just below.

The latch on the bedroom door jangled. "Jaklah, Kelthan. Open up!" his father shouted, the fear in his voice obvious.

Jaklah looked back to see his brother pressing his shoulder against the door, and hesitated. If he ran, the Keepers could make it real bad for his family.

Tears dripped down Kelthan's cheeks, but his teeth were bared as he strained against the door—fighting his father's greater strength. "Run," he whispered, his eyes glistening. "Run!"

PART I

Lost and Found

ONE MAN'S TREASURE

ASCADE?" Kyja leaned across the gunwale of the sailboat, searching the sluggish brown Noble River. The boat's trim bow knifed silently through water that smelled of fish, mud, and slime, but there was no sign of the Fontasian.

Sunlight peeked over the eastern horizon, and one by one, the dawn chimes raised their tiny purple heads, breaking into song. Still asleep in his net hammock, Marcus rocked fitfully and began moaning. He was having the nightmare again. But if she woke him, he'd only deny it and grump all morning about not getting enough sleep. She supposed he'd tell her when he was ready about whatever had been haunting his dreams for the last few weeks.

Leaning further over the side of the boat, she tried again. "Cascade, where are you?"

She'd told the water elemental to come back before Marcus woke up. They'd reach the end of the Noble River in only another day or two. And still there was no sign of Land Keep. They might have to bribe someone for information, and to do that, this plan needed to work.

Several large air bubbles gurgled from the depths of the river, and a pair of dark eyes appeared beneath its murky surface. Kyja gave a tiny yelp and jerked back into the boat, thinking it was Cascade trying to scare her.

But a moment later, the eyes rose out of the water—bulbous and gray on a pair of swaying green stalks. The stalks were attached to a round, fleshy face, nearly the same color as the river. The creature's body looked as if someone had taken a bunch of leftover parts from other animals and slapped them together—a short, pudgy torso covered with blotchy green warts, webbed feet nearly as long as the body, and a neck that rose so far into the air that the creature's head seemed constantly in danger of toppling over.

"A throg," Kyja sighed, smiling at her earlier fright. To think she had mistaken *that* for a water elemental. Cascade would be highly insulted if she told him. The idea made her smile even wider.

As though reading her thoughts, the throg opened its broad mouth so its entire head seemed to split in half and croaked, "Cascade, where are you?" in a booming voice that echoed across the water's surface. Marcus moaned and rolled over in his hammock.

"Hush," Kyja whispered to the throg, trying to shoo it away with one hand.

But the creature paddled happily alongside the boat, croaking "Cascade, Cascade, Cascade. Where are you? Are you?"

Kyja groaned. Now she'd done it. Throgs were copycats— imitating any sound they heard until something else drew their attention. If she didn't chase it off, it would wake Marcus for sure. Stretching to her tiptoes, she managed to get her fingers into the water and splash at the Throg's big, gray eyes. "Go away!"

"Go away!" the throg repeated, raising its voice so it sounded almost exactly like Kyja. "Away. Away. Away."

"Ohhh!" Kyja grimaced. She looked around for Riph Raph, hoping he could blow a fireball in the throg's direction to scare it, but the skyte was off somewhere—probably hunting fish and bugs for breakfast.

Kyja leaned so far toward the river, her feet actually left the deck. She cupped a handful of water to throw at the creature that was still happily chanting, "Away, away, away, away." At that moment, the boat bumped against a sandbar, bouncing sideways like a cork. Kyja's arms pinwheeled, trying to catch the edge of the boat, but she was too far off balance.

"Help!" she squeaked as she went over the side. She gulped a quick mouthful of air and closed her eyes, dreading the inevitable splash of lukewarm water that would leave her feeling bedraggled and soggy all day. Instead, a firm hand caught her shoulder.

Opening her eyes, she saw a blue-tinged face that looked no older than sixteen or seventeen, topped by spiky, white hair. "Did you *want* to go swimming?" Cascade asked without a trace of humor in his voice. "It seems odd to bathe at this time of morning, but I'll let you drop if you like."

"Of course not," Kyja said, trying not to look as embarrassed as she felt. "Put me back in the boat." She hoped Marcus hadn't seen the whole thing. He'd tease her about it all day if he had.

"Very well." The Fontasian blinked his curious, sea-green eyes and lifted her onto the boat with seemingly no effort.

Once her feet touched the polished wood deck, Kyja glanced at Marcus. He was still asleep, thank goodness. "Where were you, anyway?" she asked as she yanked her robe back into place and straightened her long, dark hair.

"You asked me to find what was at the bottom of the river," Cascade answered, floating through the water at the exact same pace as the boat.

Even though they'd been traveling together for over three months, it was still strange to watch the elemental rise out of the water. For one thing, he never got wet. His hair looked white and frothy like the foam of a fast-moving river. But there were no drops in his hair, and it never plastered against his head the way Kyja's did when she went swimming. And for another thing, he didn't emerge out of the river—he formed *from* it.

Though his blue-robed torso, arms, and head appeared completely solid, Kyja could see that the rest of his body disappeared as soon as it hit the water, as if he didn't exist from the chest down. He could appear whole when he wanted to, but he seemed to take great delight in rising without warning from the river or suddenly morphing into a puddle of water.

Kyja took a deep breath to steady herself. "So what *did* you find?"

The Fontasian reached into his robe and pulled out a handful of brown goop leaking slowly through his fingers.

"Mud?" Kyja rolled her eyes. "You took all that time to bring back a handful of *mud?"* Cascade was every bit as difficult to understand as Zhethar, the frost pinnois, had predicted. She could never be sure if the water elemental was teasing her or just being his annoyingly logical self.

"Not *just* mud," Cascade wet his fingers in the river and waved his hand over the mud. Kyja's view of the glop expanded until it was like she was peering into a miniature forest. A dotted yellowish blob oozed toward a tiny green, tree-like shape. A larger blue blob came into view and made straight for the smaller one. It opened what looked like a mouth. But as the blue blob was about to eat the yellow blob, a spark of light shot out from the tree. A second later, the tree sucked up both the blobs and swam away.

"There is a wide variety of plant and animal life within," the water elemental explained.

"It *is* interesting. I was just hoping there might be something more *unusual* down there. Maybe something a little prettier?"

"I see." Cascade nodded. He returned the mud to his robe and pulled out an item that glittered in the morning sun.

Kyja's eyes widened at what she thought might be jewels until the terrible smell hit her. "Yuck," she said, realizing the glittering came from light reflecting off the scales of a dead fish. "That's disgusting. Throw it away."

Shrugging, the water elemental tossed the fish into the river.

Kyja wrinkled her nose. When she asked Cascade to find what was under the water, she'd imagined sunken treasure—not mud and dead fish. But she knew from experience that the Fontasian would refuse to look for treasure if she asked outright for it. Water elementals didn't understand the concept of doing things for others without getting something in return. Half the reason Cascade had agreed to join Marcus and Kyja was to learn more about what they called "caring."

"Did you find anything that doesn't stink?" she suggested, wondering if water elementals even had a sense of smell.

Cascade tilted his head. "It would be odd to find something on the bottom of a river that didn't smell like the bottom of a river."

"I don't mind if it smells like a river," Kyja said. "Did you find anything that's pretty and doesn't smell like a . . . a dead fish?"

The Fontasian reached into his robe again and pulled out a rock. "This doesn't smell like a dead fish."

"Arghh," Kyja growled, sure Cascade was teasing her. "You search the entire river and come back with mud, dead fish, and rocks!" But as Cascade began to drop the rock into the water, something glinted brightly.

"Wait," she called. "Let me see that."

Cascade handed her the rock, and she turned it slowly in her fingers. Flecks of metal shimmered on its surface. "This looks like gold," she murmured.

The water elemental nodded. "It does have a larger than normal amount of that mineral within it, giving it a shiny appearance. You may keep it if you like."

"Really?" Kyja's eyes lit up, but then narrowed with suspicion. "Why would you give me something so valuable? What do you want in return?"

Cascade frowned. "Humans have an odd idea of value. The mud contains a wealth of plants and animals. It is rich in nutrients. The fish is a source of energy. The rock simply *is*." He shrugged. "It shines, but so do many things."

Understanding dawned on Kyja. She and Marcus had managed to sell several more of the trill stones on Ert—*Earth,* she corrected herself; she'd been working on pronouncing the name. But Earth money was no good on Farworld. They would need information soon, but had nothing to bargain with to get it. If the Fontasian didn't value gold, having him bring it to them might be a way to fix that.

"Do you have any more shiny metal?" she asked, thinking how surprised Marcus would be when he woke up to discover they were rich.

"Of course." The Fontasian reached into his robe and pulled out

. . . an old boot. Its leather was mostly eaten away by fish and time, but a brass buckle gleamed dully through a mossy coating.

Kyja pretended polite interest. "Anything else?"

As Cascade reached into his robe again, Kyja wondered how he could store so many things in there. Was it some kind of water magic, or did he just have a lot of really big pockets?

"Oh," she gasped as the Fontasian held out something that glittered in the sun. This time it wasn't a dead fish or even a rock with flecks of gold. It was a beautiful necklace covered with dozens of gems.

"Can I hold it?" she asked.

Cascade offered her the gorgeous piece of jewelry, and Kyja held it up to the light. The sun's rays reflected off the gems in a rainbow of colors. It had to be worth . . . well, she didn't know how much. But a lot.

Looking quickly into Cascade's unreadable eyes, she tried to assume the shrewd attitude that had helped her get the best deals in the marketplace back when she'd lived with the Goodnuffs. "I guess since this is made of more rocks, you wouldn't mind if I kept it?"

Cascade roared with laughter. "Splash and spray! What kind of a fool do I look like?"

Kyja's face went red. Cascade had been tricking her all along. Now that she thought about it, she remembered seeing the elemental wearing a gold medallion on occasion. "You said you didn't care about gold," she complained.

"I do not," the Fontasian agreed.

Kyja shook her head, gripping the necklace tightly in her hand. "Then why would you care if I kept this?"

The Fontasian looked confused. "Because of the workmanship that went into it, of course. The stones themselves are only rocks.

But the time taken to create such a piece is of great value. I would no more give it to another than I would give the boot."

"The boot? You think that rotten old boot is worth as much as the necklace?" Kyja didn't understand Fontasians at all. Were the other elementals this odd too? "What if I trade you my boots for the necklace?" she offered. "They're in much better shape than that old one."

Cascade held out his hand for the necklace. "I have no need of boots."

"Fine, then," Kyja huffed. She gave back the necklace. "What are you going to do with it?"

"Nothing."

She watched in horror as Cascade tossed it over his shoulder, where it quickly disappeared into the slow-moving water. "I have no need for the necklace, either."

"Ohhh!" Kyja cried, clapping her hand to her mouth. "If you weren't going to keep it, why not give it to me?"

The water elemental tilted his head, an odd half-smile on his face. "You have nothing I want."

Kyja balled her fists, unable to believe how selfish he was. "You are such a . . . such a . . ." She tried to think of a word bad enough to encompass so mean an act. Suddenly, she remembered a word Marcus had used on Earth when a man nearly hit them with his car. "You are such a . . . *jerk!*"

From behind her came the sound of loud laughing. She spun around, eyes blazing.

Marcus was awake.

CHAPTER 2

WATER MAGIC

"WHAT ARE YOU LAUGHING AT?" Kyja growled.

"You really think you can teach him to care?" Marcus grinned. "It's not in his nature." He swung his left leg out of the hammock and, gritting his teeth, lowered his right leg to the deck. But as soon as he put weight on it, his right leg buckled, and his laughter died at the sharp burst of pain spiking up his hip. He would have collapsed to the ground if he hadn't grabbed a rope.

"Let me help." Kyja set the gold-flecked rock on the deck and started toward him.

"I'm fine," Marcus snapped, though it was clear to both of them he wasn't.

Kyja bit her lip. "Is it worse today?"

Balancing on his left leg, Marcus leaned down and picked up the staff Kyja had found for him in the Westland Woods. When he'd first left Water Keep, he'd been able to walk without it. True, it was slowly and for only a minute or two at a time, but for those few minutes, he'd felt . . . whole. Over the last few months, though, his leg had grown worse, until now he could barely move it without feeling like shards of glass were rubbing together inside his muscles.

"It's this crazy hammock. It's like spending the night in a fish net. And the way this boat rocks, it's amazing anyone can walk at all."

"If those bags under your eyes get any bigger, you can curl up in them," called a taunting voice from above. Riph Raph glided out of the sky and landed on the prow of the boat. Clutched in one of the skyte's talons was a half-eaten fish, which he quickly popped into his beak and crunched with obvious delight.

Marcus scowled. "Be quiet, bird brain."

Riph Raph cocked his head and picked a bit of meat from off his beak with the tip of his dark blue tongue. "I wasn't the one squawking in my sleep."

Marcus stiffened. He'd been dreaming again. That explained the pain. It was growing worse every day but was especially bad after the recurring dream.

"Leave him alone," Kyja said, giving Riph Raph a dirty look.

Marcus turned away and stared out at the river.

What neither he nor Kyja had been willing to discuss—at least so far—was what his worsening condition might mean. When Master Therapass revealed to them who they really were and the role they were prophesied to play in saving each of their worlds, he had suggested that Marcus's health might in some way be linked to the health of Farworld. After they defeated the Summoner and obtained the help of the water elementals, his leg and arm both felt stronger, as though Farworld was in less danger. If that was the case, his increasing weakness could only mean the Dark Circle was growing in power. Farworld was at greater risk than ever.

At least Marcus still had his magic. Leaning against the gunwale, he focused on the muddy, slow-moving water. Little by little, the pain in his arm and leg eased away as the power of water magic flowed through his body. Beneath his gaze, the river seemed to clear several feet down, as though he were looking into an aquarium. Cascade had taught him that one of the greatest strengths of water magic was the ability to see more clearly—that a powerful wizard could use water magic to see great distances and even through obstacles.

Marcus wasn't that skilled yet, but in the water he could easily make out several fish large enough to provide breakfast for Kyja and himself. *Seeing* was only the first part, though. Next he had to convince the water to help him. This was the part of magic he struggled with the most. Growing up, he'd read lots of stories about magic. In them, all you had to do was wave a wand and say some special words. Once you mastered the trick, it was yours to use however you wanted.

But here, he'd quickly learned, magic wasn't like that at all. In order to perform even the most basic spells, you had to convince the elements your need was worthy. The elements could choose to help you or not. To force them to obey your will was to use black magic, which ultimately corrupted whoever touched it.

Fortunately, he was only using water magic this time. When a spell involved more than one element, it was especially tricky, because the elements didn't like working with each other. Focusing on the fish, he pictured himself eating breakfast. He imagined how the food would provide energy to his body. He knew words weren't necessary to communicate with water, but he still found it easier to concentrate if he made up a little poem for his magic.

"Fish for breakfast is my need," he whispered under his breath. "Grant me this that I may feed." As though pulled by an invisible line, the fish Marcus had been looking at turned and began to swim toward the surface. The closer it got, the faster it swam, until the river water lifted it up and tossed it, flipping, into Marcus's hand.

Holding tightly to his breakfast as Cascade guided the boat toward shore, Marcus beamed at his improving skill.

But Riph Raph wrapped his tail around his legs and crowed, "That must have been a stupid one."

CHAPTER 3

SECRETS

WHAT ARE WE SUPPOSED TO DO NOW?" Marcus asked as he and Kyja finished eating their fish. They sat in a small grassy meadow at the edge of a thick forest. "We're nearly to the Sea of Eternal Sorrows, and I haven't seen anything that looks like it could be a land elemental."

"I guess we keep sailing," Kyja said. "Riph Raph says Aster's Bay is only a few miles downriver. Maybe they know something about Land Keep." She looked at Cascade to see if the water elemental had any suggestions, but he sat a few yards away, staring out toward the sailboat as it bobbed at the river's edge.

It was impossible to tell what the he thought of their conversation or if he was even listening to them. He could talk for hours, asking all sorts of random questions about humans and why they acted the way they did. Then he'd go silent—like he was now—for hours.

"Hmmph," Marcus snorted. He peeled a piece of meat from the fish and chewed it slowly, intentionally ignoring Riph Raph, who watched for bony scraps from a tree branch overhead. Apparently food hadn't fixed whatever was bothering Marcus. "I don't know why you even try asking Cascade. He hasn't told us anything new for weeks. For all we know, he lied about the land elementals being near the end of the river. Land Keep could be hundreds of miles from here."

"Why would I lie to you?" Cascade asked without turning his head.

"Who knows why you do anything?" Marcus rubbed his sore hip. "Maybe to laugh at us. You said you were going to help us find Land Keep, but you won't even tell us if we're close."

"I don't blame him for laughing," Riph Raph said to Marcus. "Your looks do that to everyone."

"Maybe he *can't* tell us," Kyja said.

"Of course he can. He just won't," Marcus said.

Kyja shook her head. They'd had this same argument a hundred times as they sailed down the river. From what Kyja could see, Cascade was willing to answer any questions he could. But there were certain subjects that, for some reason, seemed to be off limits. It was frustrating, but she didn't think he was being intentionally mean.

"What if there's some kind of water elemental rule we don't know about?" she asked.

"Great. Take his side." Marcus pulled a fishbone from his mouth and threw it into the grass.

Cascade turned his head to watch Marcus with the same slightly amused expression he'd worn while studying the creatures in the river mud.

"I'm not taking anyone's side," Kyja said. But was she? All her life she'd tried to see the best in other people—even when they didn't seem to deserve it. Maybe it was because she'd grown up without magic. If she got offended every time someone made a mean comment about her or looked at her strangely, she'd have been angry all the time. She thought Marcus had probably experienced the same things with his disabilities. But where her experiences made her more likely to believe people, his seemed to have made him even more suspicious of others' motives.

What if he was right though? Cascade had told them to look near the Sea of Eternal Sorrows. He'd provided them with a boat and helped Marcus improve his water magic. But his reasons for helping them were never clear. He'd told them before they even started their journey down the Noble River that he was coming along mostly to satisfy his curiosity. What if that curiosity included seeing how she and Marcus reacted to frustration? He seemed to take a special interest in their disagreements.

Kyja took a deep breath and turned to Cascade. "You told us we'd find the land elementals where the Noble River meets the sea, and we're nearly there."

"I suggested following the Noble River as one possible course of action," Cascade said with a small shake of his head.

Marcus waved a hand. "See, this is what I'm talking about. We've been following the same smelly river for nearly three months, and now he tells us it's a *possible* course of action. What's another possible course of action? Jumping off a cliff?"

"Not a bad idea," called down the skyte.

"That would be a course of action," Cascade said with annoying good humor. "Although not one I would recommend."

Kyja seized on his statement. "You *did* recommend we sail down the river. So it must mean we're going in the right direction, even if you can't tell us that."

Cascade said nothing, but he didn't disagree, either.

"All right, so you can't tell us if we're close," Kyja said. "You *would* tell us if you could, wouldn't you?"

The water elemental's look of amused interest was replaced by one of confusion. "You ask me to tell you something based on facts neither of us possesses. That makes no sense."

Marcus rolled his eyes, but Kyja worked on controlling her temper. Cascade wasn't trying to make them angry—at least, she didn't *think* he was. Water elementals were incredible at analyzing information and forming conclusions, but concepts like caring, imagination, and guessing seemed impossible for them to understand.

If she couldn't get Cascade to answer her questions directly, maybe she could approach the problem as a puzzle for the Fontasian to solve. "If Marcus and I discover the location of Land Keep on our own, you won't interfere, will you?"

"No," Cascade answered at once.

"And it *is* possible for us to find it?"

"Yes."

This was working. "Do you think Marcus and I will discover the location by ourselves?"

"I believe the likelihood is small."

Kyja's shoulders slumped, but Marcus seemed to hear exactly what he'd been expecting. Kyja bristled at his know-it-all expression. He'd been getting grumpier and grumpier this entire trip, as if all of their problems were somehow her fault. "Do you have a better idea?"

"This whole thing is a complete waste," he muttered.

"Speaking of waste," Riph Raph said, "how about you stop letting the rest of that fish go to waste and give it to me? Or are you going to hog it all yourself?"

"You already finished your share." Kyja frowned at Riph Raph. Then, turning to Marcus, asked, "Do you think your dreams could have something to do with us finding the land elementals?"

Marcus's face went red. "What dreams?"

Kyja swallowed. "I know you've been having bad dreams. I've heard you moaning at night. Don't you think it might be more than a coincidence that as we get closer to Land Keep, you've started having nightmares?"

"I don't know what you're talking about," Marcus said, his jaw tightening. "I told you, it's just the hammock. It's uncomfortable."

Kyja got up and gathered the remains of the fish—almost half of it was left—onto a large green leaf without looking at Marcus. "I won't ask you to tell me about it until you're ready. But it's not a good idea for us to keep secrets from each other."

"Really?" Marcus glared at her. "Then when are you going to tell me where you keep taking the food?"

"What?" Now it was Kyja's turn to feel her cheeks grow hot.

Marcus pushed himself to his feet, leaning heavily on his staff. "Don't you think I've noticed how you've been sneaking into the woods with the leftovers after all our meals? You talk about secrets like you don't have any of your own. But you're worse than Cascade."

The water elemental was watching the two of them argue as if observing an especially good match of Trill Stones. Her stomach knotted, the food she'd just eaten burning. She hadn't meant to keep a secret from Marcus, exactly. She just wasn't sure how he'd react if he knew what she'd been doing.

"That's what I thought," Marcus said. Leaning on his staff, he turned and stomped off into the trees.

"Wait," Kyja called. "I'm sorry. I should have told you. Come back. You don't know what's in those woods."

But Marcus was gone. When Kyja turned to look for Cascade, he had disappeared as well.

CHAPTER 4

The Visitor

KYJA WATCHED MARCUS STOMP into the woods, torn between the desire to bring him back and the realization that it was probably better if she let him go. Obviously he didn't want to talk to her right now. He'd been struggling with something for weeks, and she didn't think it was just the dream, or even Land Keep. Something else was bothering him.

Something bigger.

"Let him go cry in the woods," Riph Raph said, looking in the direction Marcus had disappeared. "He's the biggest baby I've ever seen."

"He is not. He's in a lot of pain. And you're not making things any easier with all your insults."

"He doesn't want anyone to make it easier. He wants people to listen to him whine, and you're doing a great job of that." Riph Raph flapped his pointed blue ears. "You didn't used to let him push you around all the time. I think you're getting soft."

"Hush," Kyja said. She wasn't thinking just about Marcus. She was thinking of herself, too.

She'd never had a lot of friends. If she was being honest with herself, she'd never had *any* friends except Riph Raph before meeting Marcus. When she'd needed someone to turn to, the Goodnuffs had always been there for her, but now the Goodnuffs were gone—killed by the Dark Circle. And while Riph Raph was willing to hear her out, talking to a Skyte wasn't the same as having a conversation with a person.

When Cascade had agreed to join Marcus and her, she'd thought there would be three of them to help make decisions. But trying to have a discussion with a water elemental was like talking to your own reflection in a stream. Half the time she wasn't sure if he was even listening.

Which left Marcus. He was the only person she could confide in, the only person she could share worries and compare ideas with. Lately, though, talking with him was like gathering spear fruit. No matter how careful you were, eventually you made a mistake and got jabbed by a long, painful thorn.

"Are you going to eat that fish or let it rot?" Riph Raph asked, licking his beak. "I'd be happy to finish it for you."

Kyja realized she was still holding the leaf with the remains of breakfast. "No. I'm going to . . . do something else with it."

"Fine!" Riph Raph flew off in a huff.

Balancing the fish-filled leaf in one hand, Kyja walked into the trees, headed in the opposite direction Marcus had gone. Shiny little blow flies circled the food, moving about on jets of warm air that left faint rainbow trails in their wake. Kyja shooed them away.

Was it because of the way Marcus was acting that she'd begun sneaking food? Could this be her way of looking for another friend?

She didn't think so. It certainly hadn't given her anyone to talk to. She didn't even know for sure if she was feeding an enemy or a friend.

Somewhere deeper in the woods, leaves crackled. Kyja stopped and stared. He was out there somewhere, but she'd managed to spot him just twice.

The first time was almost a month ago, late in the evening. Marcus was already in his hammock, and Kyja was getting ready for bed when something caught her eye near the edge of the river. For a moment she thought she'd seen a bird or one of the many throgs that left the water at night. The only thing on the bank was a spindly-branched tree. Then the tree had moved, and Kyja sucked in her breath as something tall turned and disappeared into the woods.

The next time had been early in the morning. Kyja now suspected that he'd let her see him on purpose, specifically showing up shortly before dawn and after sunset, when Marcus was asleep. After the first sighting, she'd had a hunch about who it might have been—although she'd had no idea how he could possibly be there. The second time, she recognized him for sure and realized he had to be following them.

Her first reaction had been fear. What if he was trying to catch them? But if he'd wanted to hurt Marcus and her, he'd already had plenty of chances to attack.

Her second reaction had been to wake Marcus. But she knew how he'd respond if he learned who was out there, and something about the creature made her feel sorry for him. He looked even more bedraggled than the last time she'd seen him—and hungry.

Instead of telling anyone, she'd begun leaving him scraps of food. She was sure Cascade knew about what was going on—the water elemental didn't miss much. She'd made sure to keep Riph Raph away;

he wouldn't approve. But until today, she'd had no idea Marcus was aware she was up to something.

At the base of a knobby-looking tree, Kyja stopped and set the leaf on a flat rock. She knew from experience the creature wouldn't come as long as she remained. Calling out to him didn't help. Still, she crouched by the tree, searching the woods and wondering where he was hiding.

Cupping a hand above her eyes, she slowly scanned the trees and bushes. She was about to give up when a soft breeze carried a scent she was very familiar with—horses. At the same moment, something moved off to her right. Kyja spun and saw a man in a long red robe. He sat astride a powerful-looking, white horse. He too, was cupping a hand over his eyes, searching the woods.

At the same time Kyja saw the man, he saw her. Both of their eyes widened in surprise. Then the man jerked his horse's reins and shouted, "Over here!"

CHAPTER 5

MELANKOLLIA

MARCUS CONTINUED HIS FIRM PACE—clasping the staff with his good right hand and what little strength remained in his left—until he was sure he was out of sight. Then he stopped and nearly collapsed. His right leg trembled so badly he felt like a tightrope walker balancing on a high wire in a heavy wind. Pain raged from his ankle to his hip, and he ground his teeth together to keep back tears.

Around him, insects buzzed and birds he'd never seen on Earth cheeped and sang. The river might not have smelled the best as it slowed and widened, nearing the end of its journey to the sea, but the soil it carried created a lush landscape of trees and flowers that filled the air with a hundred different perfumes.

Gasping for breath, Marcus paid attention to none of it. What was he doing here? Life had never been easy on Earth. He'd spent most of his time dreaming of what he would do once he finally got away from foster families and the boys' schools. But back then, no one had expected anything of him. Depending on who you talked to, he was either disabled or a freak. Most of the families he'd lived with were happy if he just stayed out the way.

But in Farworld—if Master Therapass was to be believed—Marcus was supposed to be a hero—like Arthur drawing the sword from the stone. What a twisted joke that was!

"I'm happy to pull out your sword, but if I let go of my staff, I'll fall down. And even if I do get the sword out, I'll never be able to use it."

Kyja was naïve to believe Cascade would lead them to Land Keep. But she was even more foolish to believe Marcus was the great hope of her world. What if, by some miracle, they did manage to gather all four elementals? What then?

Say they did open a drift so he could come completely into Farworld instead of this halfway jumping that made him sick if he left Earth for more than three or four days at a time. He'd still be a cripple. As soon as he came through the doorway, the Dark Circle would attack him and finish the job they'd started when he was a baby.

Sighing, he looked around to make sure Kyja hadn't followed. He knew part of the hopelessness he felt came from the almost constant pain he was in. It was hard to stay positive when every morning he awoke wondering if this would be the day he tried to get up and found that, even with the staff, he could no longer stand. If the Dark Circle was trying to wear him down, they were doing a good job of it.

But the real source of his frustration and anger was the black kernel of doubt growing inside him. He couldn't—or wouldn't—allow himself to remember all of the dream he'd been having for the last few weeks—small fragments were all he could recall. But he awoke nearly every morning with a growing feeling that failure might not be the worst he could do.

He still remembered what Master Therapass had told him about his fate being tied to that of Farworld. The words of the legend were burned into his memory. In the first version, Marcus saved Farworld—*He shall make whole that which was torn asunder. Restore that which was lost. And all shall be as one.*

But there was another ending, one the wizard had seemed reluctant to share. Marcus remembered the sadness in the old man's eyes as he'd said, "In the other ending—the ending spoken of only in the quietest of whispers around fires late at night—the child joins the forces of darkness, and Farworld is destroyed."

That was the fear Marcus couldn't admit to anyone—not even to Kyja. His magic was growing even as his body was failing. But what if the weakness in his body wasn't a result of what was going on in Farworld at all? What if, instead, it was just an outward sign of what was happening inside him? The one thing he was sure about the dream was that in it, instead of becoming Farworld's savior, he turned into its ultimate destroyer.

That would explain why he and Kyja hadn't seen a hint of the Dark Circle since they left Water Keep. They weren't attacking him because they knew that he was going to do their work for them.

Somewhere off to his left, Marcus heard the sound of branches snapping. Kyja had come looking for him after all. He'd go back, but not yet. Not until he could pull himself together. Nearby, he saw a tree with a gnarled trunk and branches that grew straight out like spokes on a wheel. Vines covered with fuzzy, light purple leaves hung down from the branches. It looked like a mix between an umbrella and a weeping willow, the perfect place for him to gather his thoughts.

Hobbling through the thick grass, he pushed his way through the vines and lowered himself gingerly to the ground. As he leaned his head against the trunk, he saw the leaves had left a powdery residue on his fingers and cloak where he'd brushed against them. He sniffed the back of his hand. The light purple dust had a soothing smell to it—like vanilla and the pages of old books. He stretched out and closed his eyes.

He'd been rude to Kyja, and maybe even to Cascade as well, although he doubted the Fontasian was even capable of being offended. Marcus knew he should probably apologize.

On the other hand, he thought, breathing in the relaxing aroma the tree gave off, *shouldn't they have been a little kinder to me as well?* It wasn't like he didn't have his own problems. Neither of them understood how it felt to have something as simple as walking across the deck of the boat or leaning over to put on your boots become a major endeavor.

A gentle wind blew the purple leaves against his face like a caressing hand, and he suddenly realized how much he'd been eating fish lately. How many times did you have to eat fish for breakfast, lunch, and dinner before you got completely sick of it? Until this very minute, he'd never realized just how much he hated fish.

With his eyes still closed, he reached up and ran his hand along one of the tree's long vines, remembering a blister that had sprung up on his right palm a few weeks earlier from the constant friction of the staff rubbing against it. It was an especially painful blister, and it had burned like fire when it finally burst. Did Kyja have blisters on *her* hands? Cascade certainly didn't. But did anyone ask how he was feeling or offer to put a cool cloth on his palm?

An incredible feeling of sadness washed over him. The soft leaves felt good against his fingertips, and the touch actually seemed to cool the spot where his blister had been. It was as if the only one who even understood him was . . . *this tree?*

The thought seemed crazy, and yet the more he touched the vines, the more he realized it was exactly right. The tree was kinder than any person he knew. It really understood him—actually encouraging him to release his sorrows. It was a good tree, an understanding tree, a kind tree.

Riph Raph certainly wasn't kind. He'd been a major pain since the first time Marcus laid eyes on him. In the past, it had seemed like the two of them gave each other as good as they got. Teasing was kind of like a game. But as Marcus lay in the shade of the tree, feeling the cool leaves wash back and forth across his body, he realized the skyte's taunts were terribly mean. Almost unendurable. How could he have put up with them for so long?

A tear rolled down his cheek, and another, as it occurred to him his trials were worse than anyone else's. Hugging the vines to his chest he rehearsed all the terrible things in his life—bad colds, hangnails, even occasional b-bad b-breath.

Pressing his face against the tree's rough bark, he began to sob— hot tears dripping down the trunk. Now the vines were doing more than brushing against him. They wrapped themselves around his arms, legs, and body, enfolding him in a cocoon of warm comfort. A single leafy creeper entwined itself lightly around his throat.

In the distance, Marcus heard more branches cracking, and something that sounded like the whinny of a horse. But what did that matter compared to the time he'd had to go to bed with no dinner for fighting with his foster brother?

Closer by, the stomping hooves of several horses sounded, and men called out to each other. A voice inside Marcus's head warned him that something was wrong. But another voice whispered, "It's not your problem. Don't worry about what happens to anyone else. Your feelings are the only ones that matter."

"That's right," Marcus sighed. "Only my feelings matter." He didn't need to worry about anyone else. Except that . . . not worrying about anyone else meant—

A scream jerked Marcus alert.

"Kyja!" His eyes flew open. What was he doing? It felt like he'd been pulled from a deep dream. He found himself lying flat on the ground, leaves binding his arms and legs together. He tried to jerk his right arm free, but the vine around his throat tightened like a cord. The tree had been playing with his emotions while it carefully wrapped its branches around him.

He was trapped.

CHAPTER 6

CAPTURED

FOR A MOMENT KYJA COULD ONLY STAND, mouth hanging open, as the man on the white steed charged toward her. She had no idea who he was, and her first thought was that the stranger must have her confused with someone else. Even as he took a coil of what looked like silvery rope from his mount's saddle, she was sure he'd pull up and stop once he realized his mistake.

It wasn't until a familiar blur of blue wings plummeted from the sky, forcing the horseman aside, that she realized she might be in actual danger.

"Run!" Riph Raph shouted. He banked, shooting a quick succession of small, blue fireballs at the horse. The flames deflected harmlessly before getting anywhere near the rider, but the distraction gave Kyja a chance to turn and race into the trees.

Something snapped behind her, and Kyja turned her head to see the entire silver rope flying high into the sky, as if it had a mind of its own. Blazing points of light crackled from both ends as it twisted and looped, narrowly missing Riph Raph, who dodged and rolled in the air. A second later, it coiled into a loop and dropped into the horseman's hand.

A branch slapped against her face, and Kyja barely avoided running headlong into a tree. The silver cord cracked again, slicing through the branch as cleanly as a knife blade. Why was the man chasing her? Was he part of the Dark Circle?

Kyja ducked under some low-growing bushes and pushed though a bank of reeds. Muddy water splashed beneath her feet, and she thought maybe she had lost the horseman. Her hope quickly vanished when another rider appeared out of the reeds in front of her. She skidded to the right, returning to the woods.

"Call the snifflers!" the horseman shouted.

Riding parallel to Kyja, the second man put a black, crescent-shaped instrument to his lips, and a series of high-pitched whistles cut through the air. Some distance away, another set of whistles answered.

"Halt in the name of the Keepers!" the first man called.

"Leave me alone!" Kyja screamed, panting for breath. As she leaped over a log, the rope cracked again, and something bit at her ankle. She stumbled as white-hot sparks shot from the rope, but the light bounced harmlessly off her leg, and the whip returned to its owner. Behind her, the man gaped in surprise.

The rider to her left cut across Kyja's path. Grabbing a small sapling, she used its trunk to spin to the right as her feet slipped in the dead leaves. She didn't see the third man—crouched and hiding in the bushes—until he lunged forward and swung a thick branch at her.

A burst of pain filled Kyja's chest as she fell to the ground.

"I've got her!" the man shouted, dropping his branch. He wrapped an arm around Kyja's neck, and she instantly sank her teeth through his thin robe and into his flesh.

"Ahh!" the man screamed. "She bit me."

The whistling sounds were growing closer, drilling into Kyja's brain and increasing her panic. She struggled, stomping on the man's foot and almost breaking free before she was yanked nearly off her feet by a hand that twined itself in her long hair.

Gasping with pain, she turned to see a mounted figure with shoulder-length, white hair. Unlike the other riders, he wore a silver robe with a pair of golden scales sewn over the left breast. His dark eyes looked dead to Kyja as they bored into hers. "Bring the snifflers. This child is in need of balancing."

———◆———

Marcus tried to kick his legs, but the tree's hold on him was too tight. The purple powder felt sticky now, like glue, bonding the leaves to his skin. He tried to gasp, but he couldn't draw any air. He couldn't breathe, couldn't call out.

"Over here," a man shouted from somewhere nearby. Marcus heard Riph Raph snarl, and Kyja screamed again—this time clearly in pain.

"No!" Marcus roared soundlessly. He looked up at the tree, remembering something Cascade told him when they first started their trip. "Water is one of the most powerful forms of magic because there is water in nearly everything." What was the tree but fiber and water?

Drawing on all his anger, he called upon the water to run out of the branches and leaves of the tree. He couldn't speak, but this time he didn't need to; he had no problem communicating the serious-ness of his situation. Like a storm cloud breaking above his head, a downpour of water crashed over Marcus. The branches which held him tight as ropes a moment earlier withered to dry twigs before his eyes as the moisture was sucked out of them. Leaves crackled like tiny bits of paper and washed away beneath the torrent.

Behind him, Marcus heard a long, low groan like a spike being pulled from a block of wood. He turned to see the tree lean precariously to one side. Shriveled roots as thick as his arm wrenched from the ground, ripping up huge clods of water-soaked dirt. It was coming down.

Grabbing his staff, Marcus rolled across the swampy ground. Bone-dry twigs stabbed at his arms and face. Another groan, and the tree began to fall. It crashed straight toward him, as though still trying to get at its lost prey. Rolling to the side, Marcus watched as the dead tree thudded into the muddy grass, bounced once, then sank into the very water that had been sucked out of it.

"Let me go!" Kyja cried in the distance.

Marcus jabbed his staff into the ground and yanked himself to his feet. He could hear more voices now, not far away.

"Hold the girl!"

"Grab her hair. She bit me."

Unmindful of the trees and bushes slapping his face and tearing at his cloak, Marcus limped toward the sound of the voices as fast as he could. At last, he rounded a deadfall of old trees and branches and saw a group of five men. Two were on the ground, trying to keep a grip on a struggling Kyja. The other three were still on their horses. Four wore dark red cloaks with some kind of symbol embroidered on the front. The fifth man's also had the symbol, but his cloak was silver.

"Bring the snifflers," he shouted. The two on horseback turned and rode into the woods.

Marcus started toward the men, but a cold, blue hand closed around his arm. "Stay back," Cascade whispered. "There's nothing you can do for her."

CHAPTER 7

RESCUE

WHO ARE YOU, CHILD?" The man with the black eyes stared at Kyja. His jaw muscles twitched and bunched beneath the skin of his pale face, as though he had a mouthful of serpents.

Kyja tried to turn away from his demanding gaze, but the man twisted his fingers in her hair, forcing her to look at him. A gasp of pain escaped her lips. "Hannah Montana," she said, remembering a name she'd seen on Earth.

The slap came so quickly she didn't realize what had happened until the side of her face exploded with pain. Tears gushed from her right eye.

"There is something very strange about you," the man whispered, running the tip of his tongue over lips the color of uncooked liver. His eyes darted back and forth across Kyja's face, as though looking for a clue hidden in her features. "You speak strangely. Where are you from?"

Kyja touched a hand to her throbbing cheek. Who were these people? What did they want with her? If they were part of the Dark Circle, would they be asking these questions? Wouldn't they already know who she was?

"I'm from that way," she said, pointing upriver.

The man raised his hand, and Kyja pulled back, expecting another blow. Instead, he lifted a gold chain that hung from his neck. At the end of the chain was the same symbol sewn onto the front of his robe—a pair of balanced scales. "Do you know what this is?"

For a moment Kyja considered lying, not wanting to give the man any more information than she had to. But she knew he would only hit her again, and her eye was already beginning to swell closed. She shook her head silently.

"No?" The man's eyes narrowed as he dropped the necklace into his robe. "You've never heard of the Keepers of the Balance?"

Again, Kyja considered pretending that she had. But what if this was some kind of trap? What if she said yes and he asked questions she couldn't answer? Better to say nothing at all until she understood what was happening. She could see movement out of the corners of her eyes. Several men gathered around her—their horses stomping and snorting—and the whistling sound was closer. But she couldn't turn her head to make out what was happening. Although Riph Raph hadn't shown himself since his useless fireball attack, she knew he was somewhere near.

She swallowed. "I think you've made a mistake. I'm not from here. There was a fire in my village, and my family was killed. I'm trying to find my . . . my grandmother."

"Really?" the man said, his voice softening a little. "How unfortunate. Of course, if we've made a mistake, we will let you go at once." For a moment, Kyja let herself hope that she might get away before they discovered Marcus. "What village would that be?"

"N-Northwoods," Kyja stammered, trying to come up with a name that sounded feasible.

"N-northwoods," the man repeated. The corner of his mouth rose into a mirthless grin, and she knew he was toying with her. "Do all the little girls in N-northwoods lie as much as you?"

Kyja dropped her eyes.

"She is immune to the lash," said a voice to her left.

"Is she?" The man holding Kyja pulled her head back until she was looking almost straight up. "Well, let's see what the snifflers think. Perhaps after they finish with her, she'll be more disposed to tell us the truth." With that, he released her, shoving her backward onto the ground.

———◇———

"Let go of me." Marcus tried to pull himself from Cascade's grasp. His body still buzzed with the powerful water magic that had raged through him when he attacked the tree.

The water elemental shook his head. "It would be a mistake to let them discover you. You would only end up captured along with Kyja."

The man in the silver robe yanked Kyja by the hair. Marcus's right hand squeezed the head of his staff until his knuckles went white. "So you just want to stand here and watch?"

Cascade's expressionless eyes studied the men surrounding Kyja. "For the moment."

"Who are they?"

Gradually, Cascade released Marcus's arm. "They call themselves

'Keepers of the Balance.' They are even more powerful than they appear."

The man hit Kyja—the sound of his slap echoing sharply across the woods—and Marcus lurched forward, his teeth clenched. "If you won't do anything, I will."

Again, Cascade stopped him. "I do not believe she is in serious danger at the moment, but she could become so if you persist in interfering."

"What do they want with her?" Marcus growled. His own pains had disappeared. His hand itched to hit the man in the silver robe the same way he'd hit Kyja.

"They are seeking someone else. Once they discover that she is not—" Cascade stopped and looked into the trees. "We must retreat at once. They are coming."

"Who?" Marcus followed the elemental's gaze. He couldn't see anything, but the whistling he'd been hearing for the last few minutes was growing louder. The sound echoed strangely in his head, making his stomach churn in a way that reminded him of being back in the unmakers' cavern.

"They will smell us," Cascade said. He faded from sight, and a dark puddle of water appeared where he'd been standing. That would have been a great trick to learn for Marcus, but according to the Fontasian, only water elementals could morph into water. Careful to make as little noise as possible, Marcus followed the small trail of water as it flowed deeper into the woods.

Near the side of a large bolder, Cascade reappeared. "Snifflers sense magic," he whispered, when Marcus reached him. "They are creatures of . . . Shadow."

"Shadow?" Marcus asked. How could a creature be made of shadow? Or was shadow a place? Before he could get an answer, the whistling grew to a shrill crescendo, and three creatures appeared out of the woods. Marcus stepped involuntarily backwards.

The creatures looked like crickets as big as German shepherds. Each had long, insect-like heads with glittering, bulbous eyes and claw-like mandibles that snapped open and closed near the fronts of their mouths. They had bent legs with spikes all along the lower half. But instead of two large back legs like a cricket or grasshopper, they had six—two on the front, two on the back, and two that stuck straight out from the sides. Instead of jumping, they moved with an odd shuffling hop—like spiders.

Something about their bodies made Marcus think of the unmakers again. It was hard to focus on the insects for long. Their shiny, grey shells seemed almost to be in motion—as if they weren't shells at all, but some kind of liquid.

"What are they?" Marcus asked, his lips pulling down in disgust.

"The Keepers call them snifflers." His face tightened as though the very sight of the creatures offended him. "The Keepers use them as servants, but they are not of this world."

"Not of this world?" If they weren't from *this* world, then where . . . ? But the creatures were moving now. One of them hopped toward the edge of the clearing, spooking the horses so their riders could barely keep them from bolting. Another landed beside the silver-robed Keeper, who ran his hand across its back as though petting a dog.

The third jumped straight toward Kyja.

Marcus leaned forward, ignoring Cascade's whispered warning to hold back. What was it doing? How could Cascade say she wasn't in danger? Releasing Kyja's hair, the man in the silver robe pushed her backward. She stumbled, falling at the feet of the creature.

"Look out," Marcus gasped under his breath.

Seeing the sniffler, Kyja scrambled to her feet and tried to run. Something rose from the sniffler's back. At first, Marcus thought they were wings. But as they separated and flicked through the air, he realized they were feelers or tentacles. And they weren't just coming from the creature's back, they were coming from underneath it as well, and the sides. Several even emerged from its mouth, like strands of greasy, gray spaghetti. The whistling that had stopped briefly now rose to a frantic pitch.

One of the feelers darted forward and attached itself to Kyja's arm with a wet smack. Another wrapped itself around her leg. Kyja screamed and tried to pull free of the quivering strand, but three more twisted around her wrist, pinning her arm. With a high-pitched squeal, the sniffler opened its mouth impossibly wide and dragged Kyja toward it.

"No!" Marcus screamed. Cascade grabbed his wrist to hold him back, but Marcus instinctively used air magic, buffeting the water elemental the same way he'd knocked aside the stick in Master Therapass's magic lessons.

At his scream, the men on the horses turned. "Over there!" one shouted, pointing in Marcus's direction.

With a shout of fury, Marcus gripped his staff and flung a blast of air magic at the man in the silver robe. He'd done it before, using air to knock away the Thrathkin S'Bae, Bonesplinter. But this time, something went wrong. Trying to attack the man on the horse was like slamming his head into a brick wall. The Keeper didn't move, but Marcus was thrown to the ground with dizzying force. High-pitched whistles filled the air.

"Look out!" Cascade called, and Marcus turned to see a sniffler leap toward him. He held out his staff, and dozens of wavering feelers attached themselves to it. Even more wrapped themselves around his arms and legs, dragging him across the ground toward the creature's gaping mouth. With horror, Marcus saw that each of the feelers ended in a mouth of its own—complete with lips, teeth, and even a glistening, gray tongue.

Fire burned across his arms and legs where the tiny suckers attached themselves to his skin. It felt as if they were worming their way right into his body. He tried using magic to knock the creature off, but that seemed to excite it even more. Suckers attached to his neck, his head, and one even tried to squirm inside his mouth.

Slowly being dragged toward another sniffler, Kyja saw Marcus. Her eyes widened with fear. She tried to shout, but her words were drowned out by the sniffler's whistles.

Struggling with the sniffler, Marcus saw something race through the trees. Too tall to be Cascade, it loped through the woods in long, ground-eating strides. It looked almost familiar. Distracted by Marcus and Kyja, the man in the silver robe didn't see the figure until it emerged from the trees and launched itself at him.

With a cry of surprise, the Keeper fell from his horse. The long-limbed figure leaped across the clearing. Dropping his shoulder, he rammed into the side of the sniffler, and the creature's whistles turned into a scream of pain. The sniffler's feelers released Kyja, raising up to protect itself.

Agony burned every inch of Marcus's body. "Jump!" he yelled to Kyja. "Jump!"

Kyja turned, and Marcus felt the inside-out twist of being pushed from Farworld back to Earth. The figure heard him as well. It turned to look at him, and just before Marcus was pulled out of Farworld, he recognized the face.

It was Screech.

CHAPTER 8

ANSWERS

MARCUS WASN'T SURE THE JUMP was going to work. He felt Kyja pushing him toward Earth, felt the familiar tugging in his stomach. The sniffler tugged back as though it wanted to go with him, not releasing his body. But it wasn't just a physical hold. The creature had formed a deeper connection with Marcus—one that tore at his insides the way the unmakers had torn as they tried to suck away his magic.

Kyja was part of the connection too. For a moment he could see through her eyes, feel her panic, as she struggled to break free. She was still on Farworld wrestling with the sniffler. She was trying to send him to Earth, but it was much more difficult this time—like lifting a boulder. And she was afraid—afraid that if she pushed any harder . . .

Like a bad radio signal, her thoughts faded from his mind. Unable to resist the sniffler's pull, he felt himself being dragged back to Farworld. Kyja pushed again. Being caught between their two forces was like being trapped in the gears of a powerful machine. He tried to cry out but couldn't. Kyja pushed harder, and something ripped inside him. Pain flared through his body.

For a moment he seemed to be made of glass, his skin shattering into a million pieces, his insides flowing out. He wasn't on Earth. But he wasn't on Farworld, either. He was caught between the two in a strange, gray world of shadows and mist.

"Marcus?" Kyja's voice floated to him out of the darkness.

He tried to answer but his voice barely carried past his lips. He squinted his eyes, trying to make out anything through the billowing fog. Did he even *have* a body here? He felt as if he were floating. But he wasn't alone. He could hear a wet, snuffling sound in the distance, as though something was searching for him.

"Where are you?" Kyja called.

When Marcus answered, it was with his mind. "I think I'm hurt. The sniffler did something to me."

"Marcus? I can't see you." Kyja's voice seemed to be fading, while the fog grew colder against his skin. The sound of whatever was searching for him grew closer. Panic filled his mind. What if Kyja left him here alone?

"Push me to Earth!" he shouted in his mind. "Or pull me back to Farworld, but do it quick. Something's coming."

A menacing shape rose from the darkness—hungry eyes gleaming. Before it could reach him, Marcus felt a strong shove, and he was falling again. At the last minute, he remembered to reach out for Kyja and Riph Raph. When he opened his eyes, he was lying on a grassy field in front of an old-fashioned-looking, two-story building.

"Thank goodness," Kyja cried running to his side. "Are you all right?"

"Uggh," Marcus groaned. "That was so weird. It was like I got caught between worlds for a minute. Only there was something else there. Maybe it was the creature trying to come over."

"I could hear you, and I couldn't . . . I was afraid that . . ." Kyja wiped at her eyes.

"I think I'm okay." He sat up slowly. His muscles felt like someone had hit him with a baseball bat. Clearly they were back on Earth. The air was warm and damp, and the sun was either just rising or setting. He could never quite get the time changes right when they jumped. "Where are we?" he asked, rubbing his eyes.

"Harahan School." Kyja pointed to letters carved into the front of the building.

"School. Great. I don't even have my math book." He dropped back onto the grass. His head pounded, all of his joints ached, and he thought he was running a fever. "What were those things?" he asked. "Those snifflers?"

"I've never seen them before."

"It felt like they were trying to get inside me." He looked up at Kyja, remembering the odd sensation he'd had of seeing through her eyes for a moment. Had it been real, or just the stress of breaking free from the sniffler? "Did you feel anything strange when they attached to you?"

Kyja paused for a moment, then shook her head. "The suckers were disgusting." She rubbed at the red welts the snifflers had left on her arms. "But nothing else. Maybe because I'm immune to magic."

That made sense. "Cascade called the men 'Keepers of the Balance.' Are they part of the Dark Circle?"

"I don't think so. They didn't seem to know who I was. But I saw a man with the same symbol on his robe enter Terra ne Staric just before I escaped. He was riding with the high lord."

A large, blue insect buzzed through the air, landing on the top of Kyja's head. For some reason, Riph Raph always changed into a different creature when he jumped to Earth, perhaps because there were no such things as skytes here. Several times he'd turned into a chameleon—quite disturbing, since skytes hated being called lizards—and once, he'd come over as a chicken. This time he was a dragonfly. It seemed to suit him.

"Whatever snifflers are," the dragonfly said, "they've got powerful magic."

Marcus nodded, remembering what happened when he'd tried to knock the man in the silver robe off his horse. "It can't be a coincidence that they arrived right before the Thrathkin S'Bae attacked the Goodnuffs' farm and that they nearly captured us now that we're getting close to Land Keep."

They both sat in silence, considering what that might mean. Then Marcus remembered how they'd managed to escape the Keepers. "Did you see who knocked the sniffler off you?"

Kyja nodded slowly.

Marcus remembered thinking he'd seen something escaping the unmakers' cavern just as Zhethar, the frost pinnois, smashed the entrance to dust. At the time, he'd assumed it was his imagination. "Screech must have climbed down the ledge you discovered while the air was filled with dust. Somehow he tracked us. Could he have been following us all along?"

"Maybe." Kyja averted her eyes.

Understanding dawned on Marcus. "You *knew* he was there, didn't you?"

"I thought you'd be upset if I told you," Kyja said softly.

"Upset?" Marcus clenched his fists. "You thought I'd be *upset?* He nearly killed me. He enclosed you in a block of ice. He was going to feed us to the unmakers. Why didn't you tell me?" Another thought occurred to him, one almost beyond belief. "Tell me *he's* not who you've been sneaking food to."

Kyja's cheeks went red. "He looked hungry."

"I can't believe this!" Marcus shouted, his voice bouncing off the school building. "How could you feed that . . . that *monster?* It's one thing to give our cloaks to homeless people, or our money to poor kids. But Screech might have snuck up and killed us while we slept."

"He didn't," Kyja said, her voice rising as well. "If he'd wanted to attack us, he could have. But I don't think he wants to harm us. He let me see him on purpose, twice."

"He serves the unmakers. Why else would he follow us if not to kill us, or at least capture us and take us back?"

"I don't think he works for them anymore. I think we helped him escape. Maybe he's grateful."

"Hah!" Marcus gave a scornful laugh. "I'll bet he's just waiting for the right chance to bring us a thank you card. Sometimes you have to use your brains instead of your emotions."

Kyja turned away. Marcus realized he'd hurt her feelings—again. "I'm sorry. That was a dumb thing to say."

"You've been saying a lot of dumb things lately." Kyja refused to look at him.

"I know." Marcus swallowed. "I guess I've been pretty selfish. I need to remember I'm not the only one who has problems."

Kyja shot him a questioning look over her shoulder. With a rueful grin, Marcus told her all about the tree. By the time he'd finished, Kyja was giggling.

"Melankollia," she said. "They're not dangerous if you recognize what they are. Kids back home used to cut off the leaves and rub them on someone's scrolls during tests or put the powder down their robes as a joke."

"Seriously?" Marcus imagined pulling a prank like that on Chet back at the boys' school and watching the bully bawl his eyes out about having to eat peas for dinner.

Kyja nodded. "The powder didn't affect me, of course, so once I rubbed a bunch of leaves on my hands and went around touching all the meanest kids at school."

"You went to school?" Marcus asked. For some reason, it had never occurred to him that Kyja had classes too.

"I did until it became clear that I couldn't learn magic." Kyja gave a wistful sigh. "Then I was asked to leave the academy."

"Wait. You had to leave your school just because you couldn't do magic?"

"Of course. What's the point of learning spells and charms when you can't do them and they don't work on you?"

"But what about the other stuff?"

Kyja raised her hands in confusion. "What other stuff?"

"You know, math, science, writing, art, geography."

Kyja looked at the building in front of them again, her mouth dropping open with wonder. "Is that what they do here? Study those . . . other things?"

Marcus looked at Kyja as she examined the old elementary school with obvious longing. He realized how little he still knew about her world and how much he'd taken for granted. Sure, he'd had a tough time having to go everywhere in a wheelchair. But at least they hadn't kicked him out of school because he only had one good arm and leg.

"We'd probably better get going," he said. The sun was almost completely up now. Apparently it was morning. He didn't want to be found here once students and teachers began arriving. And besides, just because he and Kyja hadn't seen them didn't mean the Dark Circle wasn't still looking for them.

"All right," Kyja said, tearing her eyes away from the school. "But how are you going to get around?"

Something landed on the front walk of the school with a soft *fwump*. Marcus and Kyja turned to see a newspaper delivery boy. He looked to be about twelve or thirteen. He wore a ragged old carrier bag around his neck—now mostly empty. But it was the mountain bike he was riding that caught Marcus's eye.

"Hey," he said, waving to the boy. "Wanna sell that bike?"

CHAPTER 9

Ups and Downs

"WATCH OUT FOR THAT CAR!"

"I am—I am!" Kyja steered around the SUV that pulled out in front of them, the front wheel of the bike wobbling dangerously before she brought it back under control.

"That was close," Marcus breathed, clutching Kyja's waist in a death-grip with his right arm.

"Stop being a baby," Kyja called over the wind roaring past her face as they raced along the city street. Her long hair stuck out from under her helmet, whipping back and forth as she dodged around parked cars and pedestrians. She still couldn't believe she was riding her own Earth machine—even if it wasn't a car. Of course she'd seen plenty of bikes on her various jumps to Earth, but she'd just assumed that, like cars, they required some kind of license to drive.

"I think we should move to a less-busy street," Marcus gasped, pushing Kyja's hair out of his face as they bounced over a dip in the road.

"Fine, fine." Kyja turned right at the next street, leaning the bike so far over that Marcus squeaked in terror.

"Do you have to do that? What's the hurry?" he asked, squeezing her so hard she could barely breathe.

"No hurry. It's just fun!" Kyja said, a huge grin pasted on her face. She fumbled briefly with the gears, found the one she was looking for and peddled harder to make her point.

Her first attempts at driving an Earth machine had been a little bumpy. When she'd realized Marcus was buying the bike and that she would be the one operating it, she immediately jumped on—and just as quickly fell off again.

"You have to balance," Marcus had explained, holding out his hands to show her what he meant.

Picking the bike back up, she examined it more closely. It reminded her a little of a wheeled horse. The handles, like reins, were used to turn left and right. You put one leg on each side—resting your feet on what Marcus called *pedals*. And there was even a small saddle to sit on.

For her second attempt, she took a firm hold of the handles and gave the machine a hard push with her feet. The next thing she knew, she was lying on the grass, the front wheel of the bike spinning slowly next to the tree she'd run into.

"I'll think I'll stick to the air," Riph Raph called, buzzing over her head.

Kyja picked up the bike. It looked like a horse, but it certainly didn't ride like one. "Are you sure this doesn't require some kind of magic?"

"No magic. Just practice." Marcus had tried to hide his smile, but Kyja could tell he was laughing at her. Still, the idea of operating her own machine—one that didn't require any magic—fascinated her enough that she got back on again. This time she was more cautious, listening as Marcus explained how the pedals and brakes worked. It took several more tries—and multiple scrapes and scratches—but after a couple of hours she got the hang of it.

Now, as they turned onto a bike trail that ran along the levee of the wide Mississippi River, Kyja cut the wheel left and right, laughing with delight as the bike obeyed her every command.

"I think I almost prefer riding in a grocery cart," Marcus groaned.

"Stop fussing," Kyja called, happily looping the bike left and right across the mostly empty trail. "We're making great time. Do you think we can bring this thing to Farworld with us when we jump back?"

"I think a bike might make us stand out just a little."

He was probably right. They'd been trying to remain undercover as much as possible—avoiding anything that might alert the Dark Circle to their whereabouts. Now they had the Keepers to worry about as well. But it was still fun to imagine riding a shiny bike through the streets of Terra ne Staric. The other kids would be so jealous.

"When do you think we should jump?" she asked, hoping Marcus would say not for several days at least.

Jumping between worlds anytime and anywhere they wanted was a great benefit in their search for the elementals. The Dark Circle was limited to coming and going through the permanent doorway they'd created with dark magic. But neither Kyja nor Marcus were sure whether the Thrathkin S'Bae could track them by their jumps. And Marcus and Kyja could remain in each other's worlds only for a few days at a time. Any more than that, and they began to grow progressively sicker.

Master Therapass had explained that while they *seemed* to be completely in the other's world, half of them was actually suspended in the gray nothingness between them. The only way to recover was by returning to their own world for a few days.

Marcus pointed ahead to a large city. "That's New Orleans. I'd guess we're no more than nine or ten miles away. We're probably getting close to the city Riph Raph saw downstream on the Noble River. I think we'd better go back tomorrow morning. Hopefully someone there can give us a clue where Land Keep is."

Kyja nodded, already missing her bike. "What about the Keepers?"

"That's what I'm worried about," Marcus said. "There could be more of them in the city. We'll just have to make sure they don't spot us."

Watching a flock of birds soar out over the river, Kyja didn't see the old man that stepped up onto the levee until Riph Raph, flying just over her shoulder, shouted, "Look out!"

Kyja whipped her head around in time to see a man with a bushy, white beard carrying a fishing pole over his shoulder. He was standing in the middle of the bike path, eyes wide with surprise and fear. Kyja grabbed the brakes with both hands. The bike's back tire skidded on the loose gravel.

"Turn!" Marcus yelled, leaning away from the skid.

Kyja turned the handlebars, but she overcorrected, heading straight toward the edge of the levee and the river below. She tried to steer away, but Marcus had overbalanced the bike. Instead of turning away from the fall, they leaned into it.

"We're going over!" Marcus called, his arm like a vice around her stomach.

Kyja yanked on the handlebars with all her strength, but it was no use. The bike was tipping over, and she couldn't control it. Then, just as she was sure they were going over the side, it was as if a giant hand lifted the bike, pushing it upright again, and bringing it to a stop inches from the edge of the levee.

"That was some mighty fancy riding," the old man said, shifting his pole to his other shoulder. "Thought you two were heading into the drink for sure. Guess I surprised you there."

"You did," Kyja said, trying to catch her breath. "I wasn't paying attention to where I was going."

"Happens to me all the time," the old man said. "It's the river. Brings to mind flights of fancy. Sometimes I set out my pole and completely forget where I am for hours at a time." He held up a string of fish. "I'd better get back home and clean these." With that, he crossed the path and disappeared into the woods beyond.

Kyja glanced back at Marcus, whose face had gone an alarming shade of green. He was breathing in hard, quick gasps. "That was close," she said. "Good thing you used magic to stop us."

Marcus looked at the spot where the man had disappeared. "I don't think I did."

CHAPTER 10

ASTER'S BAY

WAKE UP." Marcus nudged Kyja, who was sleeping curled in her cloak next to the trunk of a large pine.

Kyja cracked open an eye and looked around at the Louisiana woods still wrapped in darkness. "What time is it?"

"Not sure." Marcus peered into the trees, listening for any unusual sounds.

"It's nighttime," Riph Raph buzzed sleepily at Marcus. "Go back to sleep."

"I think we should jump now."

"It's not even close to morning." Kyja sat up and rubbed a palm across her face. "Are you crazy?"

"Of course he's crazy." Riph Raph, who'd stayed up late gorging himself on mosquitoes, buried his face in Kyja's hair.

"It'll be breakfast time in Farworld. We could be at the city before lunch."

"I know you don't want to ride with me anymore," Kyja said, stifling a yawn. "But this is ridiculous. Go back to sleep."

"I can't sleep. I don't think we should stay here any longer than we have to."

"Why not? You need at least another day or two here to recover. Besides we're safe from the Keepers." Kyja pushed herself to her feet, brushed the pine needles from her clothing, and stretched both arms above her head.

"Something isn't right," Marcus said, tapping his foot against the ground as though anxious to start a race. "I didn't stop the bike, and you sure didn't. That means someone around here has magic. Doesn't that make you nervous?"

"You think the old man with the fishing pole was a Thrathkin S'Bae?" Kyja asked with a sarcastic smile. "The only ones who can use the Dark Circle's doorway use black magic. No one else from Farworld could be here."

"That's my point!" Marcus slapped his hands together, then looked around, afraid the noise might have attracted someone's—or something's—attention. Ever since they'd jumped to Earth, something had felt wrong. At first, he'd assumed it was the usual disorientation of moving from one world to another—"super jetlag," he'd come to think of it. But now he wondered if there wasn't more to it.

"You probably cast the spell without realizing it," Kyja said. "We were about to go over the side, and you panicked."

"Of course I panicked. You were driving like a maniac. But I've never cast a spell without meaning to before." He *had* felt something as they were pushed to a stop. It was the same tearing feeling as when the sniffler attacked him. What if Kyja was right? What if he'd used magic without knowing it? What might that mean? One thing he was coming to realize about magic was that it wasn't a toy. Like fire, it was a powerful tool as long as he could control it.

But if it escaped his control . . .

"Fine. I'm awake now." Kyja stomped her feet, getting the tingles of sleep out. "We might as well go to Farworld. But you have to promise we'll buy another bike next time we're on Earth."

"I promise—I promise." Marcus gripped his staff, tensing for the jump. They'd been in Farworld for just over two days. He knew he should have stayed at least two more days on Earth to fully recover, but after what happened with the bike, he'd feel much more comfortable once they were gone. "Watch out for Keepers when we arrive. They should have left by now, but there was something strange about those snifflers. I don't want to meet up with them again."

Kyja gave one last, longing glance toward the mountain bike then closed her eyes. "Here we go."

A moment later, Marcus found himself lying on a riverbank, head resting on a moss-covered rock. He'd been a little afraid that the horrible feeling of being trapped in the strange gray place on the last jump would happen again. He was relieved not to spend any more time trapped in that in-between place.

"Look who's here!" called out an amused voice.

Marcus sat up quickly and spun around, raising his staff in preparation to use magic. But it was only Cascade resting easily against his sailboat as a half-dozen water creatures of his creation dove and twirled through the air.

"I still don't understand how you know where to find us," Kyja said, helping pull Marcus to his feet. "You have no idea where we were on Earth. How are you always wherever we land when we jump back?"

Cascade waved a finger as though leading an orchestra, and his creatures rose in a graceful swirl of movement before losing their shapes and splashing back into the river. "Where else would I be?"

"Full of information, as always," Marcus said, climbing the ramp onto the boat. It was strange coming from Earth to Farworld. He had more movement in his bad arm and leg here, but the pain was much worse. "You don't happen to know if the Keepers are still around, do you?"

Riph Raph stretched his wings as though glad to be returned to his normal shape and launched himself into the air. "I'll fly up and take a look."

"No need to," Cascade said. "Despite your doubts about me, I am pleased to tell you that the Keepers of the Balance have taken their pets and returned to Aster's Bay. Between your sudden disappearance and the arrival of your friend, they seemed rather shocked. I suspect they left to report to their superiors."

"Screech is no friend of mine," Marcus said, clutching the gunwale of the gently rocking boat.

Cascade only tilted his head and smiled.

"Did he . . . get away?" Kyja stared off into the trees.

"Indeed." The water elemental nodded. "Cave trullochs are slippery creatures. In more ways than one. The snifflers were unable to track him."

"What are snifflers?" Marcus asked as the boat began sailing downriver.

Cascade seemed to be in an especially good mood this morning. He stood before the wheel of the sailboat, though he didn't need to touch it to steer, and waved his arms expansively. "I believe you already know. Snifflers are the larval form of a much more dangerous creature. They are what you might call babies."

Marcus thought for a minute. There had been something familiar about the creatures. Something that had seemed almost . . .

"Unmakers. The snifflers are baby unmakers, aren't they?"

The water elemental nodded.

"But why would anyone want an unmaker for a pet?" Kyja asked, crinkling her nose in disgust.

Again Marcus thought he might understand. "Does it have something to do with how the unmakers feed on magic?"

Instead of answering the question directly, Cascade looked out over the water. "When we first met, you accused the Fontasians of selfishness. Yet we consider ourselves to be quite fair. We take only what we need and always give equal to what we ask. Your kind is very difficult to understand. At times, you give far more than is expected—such as feeding the creature who imprisoned you. Other times, you take far more than you could possibly use but offer nothing in return."

Kyja frowned. "If you want your gold rock back, you can have it."

But Marcus didn't think Cascade was talking about them at all. He was starting to get an inkling of what the Keepers of the Balance might be up to, and he didn't like the idea—it felt far too much like something that might happen on Earth. Before he could finish piecing the concept together though, the sailboat rounded a curve and the river opened into a wide bay, and beyond that, a broad expanse of greenish-blue water that must be the Sea of Eternal Sorrows.

On a finger of land, between bay and ocean, was a city surrounded by imposing-looking walls of stone and rock. Dozens of ships were docked at a bustling harbor. North of the city, farms and clusters of small wooden houses spread out for several miles.

"Aster's Bay," Cascade said, his eyes narrowed and his brow

furrowed. "This is a dangerous place but a necessary stop if you intend to find the land elementals."

With that said, he slowly faded away, like mist evaporating on a hot day. When his voice spoke again, it came from what looked like a reflection rippling in the river water. "You took the Keepers of the Balance lightly before. It would not be wise to do so again."

CHAPTER 11

CHARMED TO MEET YOU

"A RE YOU COMING?" Kyja asked, a growing frustration in her voice.

"Sure. I just . . . did you see that?" Marcus stood at the edge of the pier and watched open-mouthed as two men loaded bushels of corn onto the deck of a heavily-laden ship.

It was the sort of activity he might have seen at any Earth harbor. But the way they were loading the boat was like something out of a fairy tale. One man seemed to be in charge of the corn. He held a leather-wrapped scythe with both hands. He raised the tool, and the heads of corn twirled into the air, using their husks as propellers. A second man snapped a leather strap between his hands; the empty bushel bounced like a rubber ball up the ramp onto the boat. Once the bushel was in place, the corn dropped neatly into the wooden basket.

"Come on," Kyja whispered, tugging Marcus by the arm. "People are staring."

People *were* staring—not at the flying corn, but at him. Some with amusement, others with suspicion.

"He's cloud-eyed," Kyja explained, cupping her hands to each side of her face, and a group of fisherman burst into laughter.

"What does 'cloud-eyed' mean?" Marcus hurried to catch up with her, his leg aching, staff knocking against the cobblestone street.

"Just that you're easily amused." Kyja glanced quickly around to see if anyone else was watching as they walked toward the city's western gate. "You're drawing attention to us. For all we know, the Keepers have told people to watch for a boy and a girl who are new in town. Hopefully they didn't notice your leg back in the woods, or we'll be spotted for sure."

Even though she was right, Marcus couldn't help gawking at everything around him. It was like walking through the middle of the most amazing special effects movie ever made. Fascinating things were all around—from the man charging admission to watch a caged mimicker turn into your worst nightmare to the group of black-cloaked women who barely came up to his knees playing strange flute music that made him feel woozy if he listened too long.

Some things he could understand. There was the man in the stained leather apron standing with his arms folded across his broad chest as pieces of meat sliced themselves off a butchered cow and he waited patiently for the dark paper that wrapped itself around them. Or the flock of chickens in the wooden crate saying things like, "What do you call two chickens chasing one another? Fowl play!"

But other things left him completely confused. Like the woman weaving red liquid into braids up to ten feet in the air like huge strands of colored glass before they disappeared with a loud pop. Or the group of young men floating hundreds of feet above a meadow, inside gently glowing bubbles. At any moment, Marcus expected a movie director to step out of the shadows. Is this how Kyja felt the first time she saw an Earth city?

Marcus picked up his pace, realizing he was falling behind again. "I knew you had magic here," he whispered. "But this is . . . I don't know. Amazing!"

Kyja gave a curt nod. "See why I don't exactly fit in? Stop staring and try not to look like too much the quinnel."

Marcus didn't know what a *quinnel* was, but he got the point and tried not to gawk too obviously. They approached the city gates— iron-bound wooden structures that looked strong enough to stop a charging elephant. Before the gates stood a pair of stern-looking guards outfitted in heavy armor.

"Just look normal and let me talk," Kyja hissed under her breath.

Marcus gave a quick look toward the sky. Riph Raph was up there somewhere, keeping an eye out. They'd both agreed it would be wiser not to have the skyte join them for the time being. A boy and a girl might be able to slip through the crowds unnoticed, but pet skytes were rare enough to attract attention.

"Names?" the guard on the left asked, looking them up and down with a bored frown. "Kailid and Yerhom," Kyja said "My brother was attacked by a cave bat. We're here to see the healer."

"Very well," the guard sighed.

Kyja raised her arm, and the guard on the right pressed a wad of something pink onto the back of her hand. She nodded to Marcus, and he did the same. The guard slapped on what looked like a wad of bubble gum. A moment later, the wad flashed dimly, forming into a different shape.

"Come, Yerhom. The healer will be angry if we're late," Kyja said. As soon as they were out of sight of the guards, she put her hand to her mouth and licked rapidly at the pink substance which was changing into some kind of symbol. Following her lead, Marcus raised his hand to his mouth.

"Don't!" Kyja cried. Marcus recoiled as she took his hand and licked the back until the pink was completely gone.

"One of the few benefits to having no magic," she said. "If *you'd* done that, you would have been covered in very painful and embarrassing sores all over your body for at least a week."

Marcus examined his hand. It looked a little shiny but showed no trace of pink. After months in Farworld, he thought he understood things. Now he was realizing how much he still had to learn. "What was it?"

"A visitor brand," Kyja said, rolling her eyes as if she was talking to a baby. "They're to help the authorities identify people who aren't from the city."

Marcus shook his head. "So what now? You obviously know a lot more than I do. How do we find Land Keep?"

"I have no idea," Kyja admitted. They studied the mass of people moving through the city streets. She suddenly stiffened. "Over there."

Marcus turned in the direction she was looking. A man in a red Keeper's robe walked with a stiff air of authority. As he approached, people moved out of his way. Obviously, he was viewed as some kind of authority figure, but his face showed none of the boredom the guards' had. Instead, he seemed to be studying the crowds, examining the faces looking away as he passed by.

"Inside," Kyja urged, pushing Marcus into a nearby doorway.

They ended up in what seemed to be some kind of shop. Shelves of odd little statues and gleaming necklaces filled the room from floor to ceiling. Behind a pitted counter of dark wood sat a fat man with a sweaty, bald head. He carved a piece of rock with a tiny hammer that glowed red and rang like a bell with each tap. As Marcus and Kyja entered, the man looked up from his work.

"What do you kids want?" the shopkeeper asked in a pleasant, high-pitched voice, and Marcus realized it wasn't a man at all. It was a large, bald woman. She set aside her hammer. "Love, maybe? Happy feet? Shiny, white teeth?"

"What's all this?" Marcus asked, ignoring Kyja's warning look.

"What *is* it?" The shopkeeper grinned showing a mouth filled with teeth so pearly they would have put an oyster to shame. "What *isn't* it? Charms for anything a boy or girl could want. Need to impress the ladies with your manliness? Try this." The woman picked up a little pin that looked like a closed fist. She slid it onto her robe, and instantly her forearms bulged. She pulled up her sleeve and made a muscle as big as a coconut. The minute she took the pin off, her arm returned to its normal shape.

"Cool!" Marcus breathed, earning a curious look from the woman and a glare from Kyja.

"How about you, little lady?" Rising from her stool, the woman lifted a glittering necklace and leaned toward Kyja as though preparing to put it around her neck.

"No, thank you," Kyja blurted, instantly stepping back. "But I've got some gold I'd like to sell." She set the rock Cascade had given her on the counter, and the woman gave a quick nod.

"Fair enough." Apparently children selling valuable stones wasn't as strange an occurrence here as it was on Earth.

"What happened to you, lad?" the woman asked as she carried the rock to a small stone table near the back of the store.

Marcus looked quickly away. "I was, um . . . attacked by a cave bat. I'm here to see the healer."

"Cave bat, eh?" the woman said. "They can be nasty creatures, all right." She put the stone onto a circle-shaped red cloth and tapped it with her hammer. "Have to say though, I've never seen marks like those on your arms left by a cave bat."

Marcus looked at the red welts left by the sniffler's suckers. They were beginning to fade, but the circles still stood out against his pale skin.

"We'd better leave," Kyja said, pushing Marcus. "We'll come back for our money later."

"I wouldn't do that just yet." The woman nodded toward the door. Kyja and Marcus turned to see another Keeper—or maybe it was the same one—walking slowly past store fronts on the other side of the street. "I don't imagine the guards noticed anything when you came through the gate. They're hungover half the time and drunk the other. But a sharp-eyed Keeper wouldn't likely miss sniffler marks, now, would he?"

CHAPTER 12

DOG DAYS

KYJA EYED THE WOMAN behind the counter and the Keeper moving slowly along the other side of the street, trying to decide which way to take her chances. "What do you want?" she finally asked the woman.

The woman rubbed her head. "I want a handsome sailor who has a lot of money and a hankering for fat, bald women. You haven't seen one have you?"

When Kyja only grimaced, the shopkeeper turned her attention to Marcus. "Is your friend always so stern?"

"More than you'd think," Marcus agreed, earning himself a dirty look.

"We're in a lot of trouble here," Kyja said. "This is no time for laughing." If this woman alerted the authorities, they'd never make it out the city gates, but if Marcus tried to use magic on her, the commotion could be just as bad.

The shopkeeper did something to their rock, and the gold oozed out of it, forming a small, gold rectangle. "Not bad. Not bad at all." She lowered her bulk onto a creaky stool and set the gold bar on the counter. "I've always found that humor is one of the best cures for trouble. I once owned a one-eyed swamp runt that could tell the most—"

"You can have the gold," Kyja said. "Just give us enough time to get outside the city walls before you tell the Keepers."

"What makes you think I'd tell those stuffed robes anything? You're in a great deal of trouble if the Keepers of the Balance are looking for you. They generally find what they're looking for. But that doesn't mean I have to turn you over to them."

"Thank you for not telling." Kyja reached for the gold bar, but the woman placed her big, pink hand over the top of it.

"Not so quick."

Kyja narrowed her eyes. "I thought you said you didn't want our gold."

"Of course I want it," the shopkeeper said. "I run a business, don't I? Show me a shopkeeper that says she doesn't want gold, and I'll show you a liar or a woman that's out of business. But I want to earn it honestly. We never decided what it is you need."

"Right now we need to get out of here." Kyja watched the door anxiously. After searching the other side of the street the Keeper would probably start checking shops on this side.

"Fair enough," the woman said, taking her hand from the bar. "I won't tell you how to run your business. River knows I have enough trouble running mine. But I can tell you that you'll be lucky to get two blocks from here without running into another one of those red-robed fanatics. Word is, they're keeping an eye out for a young girl and boy who gave them the slip."

"Oh, no," Kyja said with a groan. Their plan was coming

completely apart before it ever got started. They had no choice but to get outside the city as fast as they could and somehow continue the search for Land Keep out there on their own.

"But then," the woman said, fingering the bar of gold again, "it would make their search much more difficult if they were looking for a boy and a girl, but you two were . . . something else."

"Like what?" Marcus asked far too enthusiastically for Kyja's taste. She'd seen plenty of shopkeepers try to cheat children.

The big woman hefted herself to her feet with a loud grunt and plucked a red ribbon off the shelf. It had a small, silver charm hanging from the front that looked sort of like a tiny bone. "Here," she said, handing Marcus the ribbon. "Tie this around your neck."

Kyja watched apprehensively as Marcus wrapped it around his neck and knotted the ribbon in a bow. "Is something supposed to happen?" he asked. "I don't—*yip.*"

Without any warning, Marcus disappeared, staff, robe and all. In his place was a small brown dog, with shaggy fur that nearly covered his eyes, and a bushy tail. Kyja started forward as the dog looked up at her in surprise, then down at itself.

"Hey, look . . . *bark* . . . at me!" the dog cried in Marcus's voice. "I'm a . . . *ruff* . . . dog."

"I'm still working on a few issues," the shopkeeper said, resting her hands on her large hips. "There's the whole barking problem. And the transformation only lasts for twenty or thirty minutes at a time. Then you have to let it rest for a bit. I'm not exactly sure how many uses it's good for. But it should be long enough for the two of you to get wherever you're going." She untied the bow, and a moment later the dog turned back into Marcus.

"That was so . . . *ruff* . . . cool!" he said, picking up his staff that had reappeared along with him.

The shopkeeper grimaced. "The side effects wear off after an hour or so. At least, they're supposed to."

"I don't know," Kyja said. She was still unsure about the woman's motivations. Usually she was better at knowing what people were thinking. But today she was distracted. Nothing felt normal.

But Marcus seemed convinced. "How much?"

The shopkeeper tapped the gold with her hammer. About a fourth of the bar split off. "It's some of my better work, but as I said, it does still have a few flaws."

Kyja had to admit, the price did seem fair. She'd seen charms go for more than ten times as much, but usually they were the kind that promised to make someone fall in love with you. People were willing to pay a lot for romance.

"Done," Marcus said, pushing the smaller piece of gold across the counter to the woman and giving the rest to Kyja. "If we stand around here much longer trying to make a decision, we *are* going to get caught."

"All right," Kyja agreed. Waiting here certainly wasn't an option. For a moment, she considered offering the woman the rest of the gold in exchange for any information she might have on Land Keep or the elementals. But if the Keepers managed to track Marcus and her to this shop, she didn't want the woman to have any information that might help the Keepers—or that might get the woman in trouble.

"Don't forget," the shopkeeper said as Marcus retied the bow around his neck, "thirty minutes, tops, and you'll change back. You should start to feel a tingly sensation right before you change. Or not. It still—"

"I know," Marcus said. "Has a . . . *bark* . . . few bugs."

Kyja shook her head as Marcus changed back into the spunky

little dog. It was a good transformation. If it had been a simple illusion—like most charms—she would have seen through it with her magic immunity. But, as far as she could tell, he *was* a dog. He still limped on his front left and back right paws, but managed to move quite well.

"I wouldn't recommend going back west out the front gate," the woman said. "The guards aren't the sharpest, but they still might recognize you and wonder what happened to the boy you came in with. And they'll definitely want to know how you managed to remove your visitor brand. Try the north or east gates. But do *not* go south under any circumstances."

"Thank you," Kyja said, realizing she'd misjudged the shopkeeper. She wanted to ask about the south gate, but Marcus was already heading for the door.

"Come back anytime," the woman called. She picked up her red hammer. "But stay away from those Keepers."

Kyja was afraid that advice might be more difficult to follow than it sounded.

CHAPTER 13

FUN AND GAMES

BEING A DOG WAS GOING to take some getting used to. It was odd looking up from the level of everyone's knees. And colors looked all wrong. But the smells were amazing. *Have they been here all along?* Marcus wondered. *If so, how have I missed them?* There were hundreds of scents, thousands, and they all seemed to tell a story.

A young man walked past, and Marcus could tell not only that he'd had lamb chops and carrots for lunch, but that he'd had several servings of a strong drink that made him a little tipsy, that he worked around fires a lot—was probably a blacksmith—and that he'd kissed a female companion in the last few minutes.

"What are you doing?" Kyja asked.

Marcus realized he'd raised his nose to the air, sniffing like a, well, like a dog. "Sorry," he yipped. If Master Therapass could smell things this well as a wolf it was no wonder he'd chosen that form so often. "Where to now?"

Kyja scanned the streets. "Let's find other children. Adults ask too many questions, but kids like to tell stories, especially to other kids."

Marcus sniffed the air. "This—*bark*—way," he said and trotted off down the street with Kyja on his heels.

Turning up one street and down another, Marcus followed the scent of children like an invisible trail floating through the air. Children smelled different from adults—fresher somehow, like fun and games, while adults smelled like work and worry—serious smells. Of course, children were all over the city, but the trail he followed led to lots of them. He wasn't entirely sure *how* he knew that; he just did.

As he sniffed his way through the streets, he recognized another smell. It was a predatory smell, hungry and intense, like a tiger stalking an antelope. That, he knew immediately, was the smell of Keepers. Everywhere they'd been, the smell of fear appeared. He avoided the odor at all costs, even if it meant going out of their way and losing the trail of the children for a minute or two.

They rounded a corner, and Marcus stopped before a large stone building. This was definitely where the children-smell was coming from. He could hear their voices now—shouting and laughing from the other side of the building. Marcus began to trot that way before realizing Kyja wasn't with him.

He turned back to see her staring up at the building with . . . what? *Sadness?* Yes, he could smell sadness coming off her like a bittersweet perfume. But there were also other smells that were harder to read. Longing, anger, jealousy, and . . . even a little fear. Suddenly, he realized what this building must be.

"This is a school, isn't it? A place where they teach . . ."

"Magic." Kyja nodded, still looking up at the stark, gray building with such a subtle expression of sadness that Marcus wouldn't have been able to read it if he hadn't been a dog. "It's not nearly as big as the one in Terra ne Staric. But it is an academy."

"Then let's go somewhere else," Marcus said. "I can find some other children. We passed a houseful a little ways back."

"No." Kyja folded her arms across her chest, and Marcus caught a whiff of determination, although the fear was still there too. "We don't have enough time. You could change back to a person in less than fifteen minutes, and we've got to be out of town by then. Besides, this was the right place to come. If anyone here has heard about Land Keep, these kids will know about it." Kyja strode along the side of the building. "Come on. It sounds like they're on break right now. But lessons could start again any minute. Let me do the talking. Remember, even in Farworld, dogs don't carry on conversations. They *do* tell stupid jokes," she added with a wink. "But you should be able to handle that."

Following Kyja, Marcus wondered what exactly went on in the academy. Would it be like a normal Earth school with tests and grades? Would there be bullies like Chet and his friends, the boys who tried to beat him up at his last school? He couldn't imagine that. If he went to a school where they taught magic, he'd be too happy to bother anyone. And if he saw a bully trying to pick on other kids—

Marcus's thoughts cut off abruptly as he and Kyja reached the back of the building. Even though they were on Farworld, he'd been thinking of the school grounds in terms of the ones he was used to. Behind the building would be a typical playground—asphalt basketball courts, maybe a few tetherball poles, swings and slides for the little kids, and a baseball diamond for the big kids.

It was an image so locked in his mind that at first he thought he *was* seeing that. A group of kids about his age pushed and shoved one another as they ran up and down a long, stone-paved court. The kids wore short pants and sleeveless shirts that could have been basketball uniforms if it weren't for the glowing patterns of stripes on the shorts, and that the shirts kept changing colors as the kids jostled for position. Along the sidelines, other kids raised their hands, cheering or complaining, depending on who they were rooting for.

Then he realized there were no hoops. And no ball, either. After a moment of watching, he realized they were fighting for control of what looked like a large, spinning top. It skittered across the stone court in a zigzag pattern, staying on the ground for several feet before bouncing high into the air.

A broad-shouldered boy lunged for the top as it zipped by. It gave out an ear-splitting squeal as the boy's fingers neared it, but just as he looked like he was going to get it, a girl stuck out her foot, and the boy smashed face-first to the stones.

"Ouch!" Marcus groaned, almost feeling the boy's pain himself.

"Just watch," Kyja said.

Marcus turned back to the game in time to see the girl leap for the top as it again bounced into the air. Before she could get anywhere near it, though, two other girls, wearing green double X marks on their red shirts, hit her with what looked like a blast of air magic. The blow threw the girl twenty feet down the court. As she landed, Marcus heard a clear snap—like a tree branch breaking. The girl got slowly to her feet, tucking her bent arm to her chest.

What kind of game was this? It made football look like a sport for sissies. By the time these kids were finished, they'd all be in the hospital. The top skipped unexpectedly to the right between the two girls, but before either of them could grab it, a boy who looked to be no older than eight or nine dove between them and snatched it with a graceful, rolling grab.

Clutching the top under one arm, the boy made a mad dash for the end of the court, the rest of the kids in close pursuit. Still bucking and trying to escape the boy's grip, the top gave out three sharp whistles. *Tweet, tweet, tw-e-e-e-t.* At the end of the third whistle, the boy held the top above his head and it . . . exploded, throwing the players in all directions.

CHAPTER 14

HARBINGERS

MARCUS BARKED IN DISMAY, unable to form words to express his horror at what had happened. His mouth hung open. Where the young boy had been standing was a smoking pit several feet deep. The boy was disintegrated, and the rest of the players lay, unmoving, on the court. He couldn't believe what he'd just witnessed. What was wrong with these kids? They were all cheering and laughing as if the boy's death was just part of the game. Was that it? Was dying part of the game? This was sick.

He looked up at Kyja, who was cupping a hand to her mouth. Marcus thought he actually heard her giggle.

"Look," she said pointing.

Across the court, kids were jumping up and down, pounding someone on the back. As the crowd cleared a little, he recognized the person they were congratulating. It was the boy. The one who'd just blown up. And one of the people congratulating him was the girl with the broken arm. Only her arm looked fine now. In fact, all of the players seemed to be standing on the sidelines. But if they were over there, who were the kids on the ground?

Pop! The girl with the broken arm disappeared from the court. *Pop! Pop!* The two girls with the Xs, who were lying tangled on the flat stones, disappeared too. One by one, each of the players vanished until the court was empty.

He looked at Kyja who was openly grinning now. "It wasn't real?"

She shook her head. "It's called *Lusia.* Each player controls a magic duplicate of himself or herself. That was actually a pretty tame version. There's one where you try to keep from being eaten by a set of giant fangs."

"Lusia," Marcus whispered under his breath. He could hardly believe none of the kids had actually been injured. His heart was still pounding.

"You're not supposed to bring dogs to academy," said a small voice behind him.

Marcus turned to see a little girl with straight, red hair that hung almost halfway down the back of her yellow robe. Forgetting that he wasn't supposed to talk, Marcus opened his mouth, but Kyja quickly spoke first.

"I don't attend here. I'm just visiting."

With a snooty expression, the girl shook back her hair. "Pets still aren't allowed."

"I know, but . . ."

Bored, Marcus wandered across the field, studying the rest of the students and trying to imagine what it would be like to be one of them. Snippets of conversation intrigued him.

" . . . and I told him second water and fourth fire still won't allow a goat's tongue to translate . . ."

"So she said, 'This juice tastes a little tart,' not knowing that Laquias laced it with Ogre's Breath just that morning."

"But she says he likes her. Can you imagine? What he would see in a string bean of a girl that hasn't even mastered basic air is beyond me. So I told her . . ."

"Hey, little guy."

Marcus looked up as a boy with a freckled face knelt beside him and scratched the fur between his shoulder blades. Holy cow, that felt good! Something seemed to be shaking the back half of his body, and he craned his head around to see his bushy brown tail wagging like crazy.

"What are you doing here? Did you come to learn magic?" The boy laughed and moved his fingers to a spot just behind Marcus's left ear.

"He's not supposed to be here," said the little girl with the red hair, who'd apparently followed him.

"Go get lost in the swamp," the boy said.

Marcus knew he was supposed to be looking for clues to Land Keep. But the scratching felt so good, he thought he could just stand there all day, melting like butter. Then he heard something that caught his attention. By the corner of the building, a group of five very young children were playing a game that looked like a mix between hopscotch and jump rope.

The children stood in a circle pushing a colored symbol that hovered in the air from one child to another. Every time the symbol moved, it changed. Depending on what it turned into, the children had to do something different—jumping, spinning, sometimes very simple magic like making a rock fly through the air or creating a puff of wind. As they waited their turn, the children clapped their hands and chanted out the words to a song, just like Earth children did while jumping rope.

Leaving the boy and girl who were now locked in a heated argument, Marcus edged closer to the game so he could make out the words.

> *Ice worm, mud worm, piece of pie,*
> *Miss a turn, and you will die.*
> *Then you have to make your bed,*
> *In the swamp with all the dead.*

> *Ice worm, mud worm, piece of cake,*
> *Keepers see you make a mistake.*
> *If they do, then you must go*
> *To the city far below.*

> *Ice worm, mud worm, piece of meat*
> *Must move quickly with your feet.*
> *If you don't, you lose because*
> *Harbingers will get you with their big, big claws*

City far below? Could that be Land Keep? Marcus scratched his ear with his back paw. If Water Keep was under the water, it stood to reason that Land Keep could be underground. But what was that about sleeping with the dead? And the harbingers with their "big, big claws" didn't sound any too promising. A commotion of raised voices interrupted his thoughts, and Marcus turned to see Kyja surrounded by a group of kids her age or a little older. He hurried back to see what was going on.

One of the girls who'd been playing Lusia was eyeing Kyja with obvious suspicion. "Why aren't you in school?"

"I told you—I'm visiting," Kyja said falling back a step. The crowd moved with her. "With my aunt."

A broad-shouldered boy with a jaw that looked like the front of a bulldozer leaned forward. "Where's your brand?"

"I . . . don't need one. My aunt lives here."

"Have you been scaled?" asked someone in the crowd.

"Y-yes," Kyja stammered.

"Highbal or lowbal?" demanded the boy with the thick jaw.

Kyja hesitated.

"She's a lowbal," called the girl. "No lowbals allowed at academy."

"I'm not a lowbal," Kyja said. Things were starting to turn ugly. Marcus looked for Riph Raph, hoping he could provide a distraction, but the skyte was nowhere to be seen.

Go, he urged Kyja inside his head. *Let's just get out of here.*

"Prove it," said the girl. "Prove you're not a lowbal."

"Prove it. Prove it. Prove it," the kids began chanting. A clump of mud flew out of the crowd and hit Kyja in the side of the face. Marcus growled and felt the hackles rise up on the back of his neck.

"That your dog?" the boy sneered. "He's probably a lowbal too." The boy aimed a kick at Marcus. He tried to dodge it, but the kick caught him on his bad right leg, and a yelp of pain escaped his muzzle.

"Leave him alone!" Kyja shoved the boy backward, and he tripped on the girl standing behind him, landing on the ground with a grunt.

In an instant, the boy was back on his feet—hands clenched into fists. "No lowbal pushes me." He shoved Kyja off her feet. A blast of magic ripped a chunk of sod from the ground and smeared mud across the front of Kyja's face.

"The lowbal doesn't deserve to wear a robe," the girl hissed. She raised her hands, and Kyja's robe began to flutter and slide up past her knees. It was all Kyja could do to keep her clothing from pulling off her.

Marcus knew he couldn't do magic without giving himself away, so he charged forward and bit the girl on the ankle. As she shrieked and fell backward, Marcus jumped at the boy who was sending rocks flying at Kyja's face and body as she struggled to hold down her robe. His teeth sank into the meaty part of the boy's calf.

"Get off me!" the boy screamed. Something slammed against Marcus's ribs, and he felt his grip on the boy slipping. Another blow from one of the kids in the crowd, and he was tumbling through the air.

"Stinking mutt bit me." The boy looked at the blood dripping down his calf and onto his boot then started toward Marcus.

"Don't touch him!" Kyja tried to struggle to her feet, but several kids held her pinned to the ground. Now nearly all of the children in the school had crowded forward to see what the commotion was about.

Thinking of Chet, Marcus set his feet and bared his teeth. Just because he couldn't use magic didn't mean he couldn't fight back.

The boy pulled up his sleeve, and a second later, a blast of pain shot through Marcus's body. He tried to run forward, but his legs wouldn't move.

"Say good-bye to your dog. There won't even be enough of him left to bury when I'm done with him."

"Let him go!" Kyja screamed. She scratched at one of the boys holding her; he slugged her in the stomach. Marcus growled in rage, and a wall of red flames rose up out of the ground. Eyes wide with fear, the boy and his friends backed up against the rest of the crowd.

The kids who'd been holding Kyja released her and moved away as well. The wall that had started a few feet high continued to grow, turning from red to green. Five feet, then ten, then twenty.

"Stop it," Kyja called. "That's enough."

But Marcus couldn't stop it. Didn't even know how he'd started it. This was fire magic, and he had no idea how to use fire magic.

Then, just as quickly as it had arisen, the wall of flames disappeared.

"What's going on here?" asked a stern voice.

Marcus turned to see a Keeper staring down at him.

CHAPTER 15

WHAT YOU CAN'T SEE

W ELL?" THE KEEPER ASKED, his eyes glaring at the group. "What is all this commotion about?"

At the Keeper's stare, the crowd fell back, eyes looking at the ground or off in the distance. None dared meet the man's gaze. Slowly, Kyja got to her feet and eased her way through the other boys and girls.

"Don't make me ask again," the Keeper said, his hand going to the silver coil at his hip. "I have no time to trifle with you today."

"It was the girl," said the boy Marcus had bit. "She says she's a visitor, but she doesn't have a brand."

"She's a lowbal," the girl called.

Kyja pushed her way more quickly through the group, hoping to make an escape. The last few feet would leave her exposed, but she had no choice. Ducking her head she hurried to the corner of the building, expecting to hear the Keeper shout, "Halt!" at any moment.

"Girl?" the Keeper's eyes narrowed. "What girl?"

"There," the boy pointed to the spot where Kyja had been—then realized she was gone.

Standing out of sight of the Keeper, Kyja waved, trying to catch Marcus's attention. Finally, he noticed her and disappeared in a forest of legs.

"Where is this girl?" the Keeper roared. Several of the younger children began to cry.

"Hurry," Kyja mouthed silently.

"She . . . she had a dog," the boy whimpered, and Marcus made a break for the school wall.

"Come on," Kyja whispered as Marcus reached her. "We have to leave the city now. Where's the nearest gate?"

"I don't know," Marcus said. "I have no idea what the—*bark*—gates smell like."

"This way," called a voice from above. It was Riph Raph. "Hurry! The Keepers are already starting to gather."

Running as fast as they could, Marcus and Kyja followed the skyte as he led them through alleys and behind buildings.

"Why did you make the fire so big?" Kyja panted.

"I don't know. I didn't even mean to cast it." Marcus slipped on a patch of wet cobblestones and yipped in pain. "Maybe the snifflers did something to me. I don't seem to have any control over my magic." His dark little doggy eyes went wide. "What if I'd really hurt one of those kids? What if I'd *killed* one?"

"It was my fault," Kyja said. "I should have left when things started to go wrong. I shouldn't have let them goad me into a fight." She wondered if the snifflers had somehow taken away Marcus's ability to control his magic. Not being able to start and stop his spells could be as dangerous as having no magic at all. Maybe even more.

"This way," Riph Raph called, flying into the open. Ahead, Kyja spotted a gate like the one they'd entered, but this one had no crowds bustling in and out. In fact, there was no one anywhere in sight except for the guards. But there were lots of guards—at least ten. Why would there be more guards at this unused gate than at the main entrance?

Marcus skidded to a halt and raised his nose to the air. "Wait!"

"What is it?" Kyja glanced nervously behind them. How long before the Keepers realized where they were and what Marcus was disguised as?

"We can't go that way," Marcus said. "This is the south gate. It leads to the swamp." He sniffed at the air. "There's something out there."

"Hurry up!" Riph Raph called. "If the Keepers warn the guards, you'll never make it."

Kyja looked down at Marcus. "What's out there?"

"Whatever it is," Riph Raph said, "it can't be any worse than the Keepers."

Marcus raised his nose to the air again. "I'm not sure. I don't—*ruff*—recognize the smell. But—" All at once he began to shiver, claws rattling against the cobblestones. "I think—I think I'm starting to change."

"Come on," Kyja said, making up her mind. "We have to get outside the gate."

For a moment, she thought Marcus wouldn't follow. He whined in a very dog-like way, glanced back toward the city, then lowered his head and charged after her.

"Stop!" one of the guards called as they reached the gate. "This isn't a place for kids. Go to one of the other gates."

"We can't." Kyja looked at Marcus, who was growing more

agitated by the minute, trembling and yipping. His change had to be close.

"Why not?" the lead guard asked, studying Marcus closely. "What's wrong with your dog?"

"The mimicker's coming!" Riph Raph called from above.

"Mimicker?" one of the guards said, and they all looked toward the alley Marcus and Kyja had just run out of.

"That's right," Kyja nodded, realizing what Riph Raph was up to. "It was in a cage, but it got loose." Several of the guards withdrew their swords. Then a stroke of inspiration hit. "The Keepers are right behind it."

At the word *Keeper,* all the guards became noticeably anxious. They turned their attention away from Kyja completely. She took advantage of the moment to race through the gate. A dirt road led into a grove of tall trees with beards of long gray moss. To either side of the road, the ground quickly dropped off to a squishy-looking bog filled with a thick forest of trees and bushes. No sooner had they escaped sight of the guards than Marcus gave a high-pitched *arf* and changed back into a boy.

"Whew," he said, standing shakily on two feet. "That was close." Although he'd changed back, he still looked a little dog-like. Maybe it was the way the tip of his tongue poked slightly out of the corner of his mouth, or the way he kept flaring his nostrils as though trying to catch a scent.

"I liked the dog better," Riph Raph said from the branch of a tree.

"Definitely more friendly," said a voice from the swamp. Kyja turned to see Cascade leaning against a tree, his feet seeming to float on the surface of a puddle of scummy-looking green water.

Marcus picked up his staff, tugged the ribbon from his neck, and shoved it into his pocket. "Thanks for—*bark*—all your help back there."

Cascade ran a hand through his white hair and yawned. "You seemed to have it all under control."

"I don't suppose you have any advice on which way we should go?" Kyja asked.

"It depends on what your destination is."

Marcus scowled. "You know where we want to go."

"We want to find Land Keep," Kyja said. "But at this point, I'd be happy just to escape the Keepers."

Cascade pointed toward the south gate. "Returning to the city will lead you neither to the home of the land elementals nor toward escape."

Kyja sighed. She already knew both of those things. "How soon do we have before the Keepers reach us?"

Cascade shook his head, a slight smile on his face. "They are not following you."

"What?" Riph Raph squawked. "Of course they are." He soared into the air and returned a few seconds later. "He's right. There are at least twenty Keepers back there, but they're waiting just inside the gate."

"I don't like the sound of that," Marcus said.

Kyja didn't either. But it certainly made their choice easier. She looked down the road. It didn't appear to have been used much. Weeds grew down the middle, and the trees and plants encroached from both sides like stretching arms. There was no sign of fresh footprints in the dirt, and even the wheel ruts looked as if they had been made months, or even years, earlier.

"I suppose this road must go somewhere," she said doubtfully.

Marcus gripped his staff. "If the Keepers want us to go this way, it's a trap."

Kyja agreed but what choice did they have? "What's through those trees?" she asked Cascade, pointing to the left.

"Swamp," he answered immediately.

"That way?" she asked, pointing to the right.

"Swamp."

"Let me guess," Marcus said. "If we keep going straight we reach swamp, too."

The Fontasian merely shrugged.

"We could wait here and try to sneak past the guards at night," Marcus suggested.

"No," Kyja said. "The gates close at night. I don't want to be stuck out here after dark. Wherever we're going to go, we need to do it while we still have daylight." She turned to Riph Raph. "Can you fly ahead and see where this road goes?"

Riph Raph flapped his wings and took off.

"I still say this is a bad idea," Marcus said.

"Do you have any better suggestions?" Kyja asked.

In answer, he rammed his staff into the dirt and began heading down the road.

Three hours later, the way had narrowed until it was barely wide enough to be called a trail—a little higher than the swamp to either side of it. Kyja and Marcus could just walk side by side without brushing up against the dense vegetation that clawed for space out of the wet ground. And Kyja had no intention of touching any of the plants if she could help it.

Tall, swaying trees gave way to black-trunked monstrosities. Instead of hanging from the branches, gray moss wrapped itself around them until it seemed to be oozing out of the bark itself.

Beneath the stunted trees, huge ferns and spongy-looking reeds grew with a ferocious energy that seemed more animal than plant. She had the feeling that if you got too close, those plants would pull you into the swamp and devour you.

As the sun dropped lower in the sky, the cooler air brought out insects that buzzed around Marcus and Kyja's faces, darting about their eyes and into their mouths. If they didn't swat them away, the bugs landed on their arms and legs, feasting on warm blood until they flew sluggishly away or burst in the process.

But the worst part was the sounds. Just out of sight, groans and grunts echoed through the twilight. Every so often, the air was split by a deep-throated roar that shook the trees and made Kyja and Marcus jump. Then there were the splashes that sounded far too big to be made by fish.

"Any sign of civilization ahead?" Kyja asked, as Riph Raph glided down from the sky and landed on her shoulder.

"Nothing," the skyte said tiredly. "The sea is off to the right. Between here and there are miles of swamp. Straight ahead is nothing but the same."

Marcus collapsed to the ground and glared at Cascade. "You led us into this."

Cascade studied a bloated-looking frog at the base of a tree.

"I'm sorry," Kyja said, sitting beside Marcus. "It's my fault we're here."

"No. We've had enough of spreading blame," Marcus said. "We're in this together. But I had a bad thought awhile back. If everyone in Aster's Bay knows this road leads into the middle of a swamp, why place guards at the gate?"

Kyja shrugged.

"What if it isn't to keep people out," Marcus said, "but to keep something else from getting *in?*"

What kind of something? Kyja wondered. The thought made her shiver. "But if they want to keep whatever is in the swamp out, and no one leaves through that gate, why have a gate at all?"

Now it was Marcus's turn to shiver. "What's a harbinger?" he asked suddenly.

"I have no idea," Kyja said. "Why?"

Marcus told her about the rhyme the children sang at the school. Kyja sat silently for a moment, then said, "I've heard songs like that, but nothing about harbingers or a city below. Maybe it's just one of those things kids talk about to scare each other, like . . ."

"The boogeyman," Marcus filled in.

Kyja hadn't heard of "the boogeyman" but guessed it added up to the same thing. "We used to call it *Tem Shad,* the creature that snuck into your bedroom at night and bit off your thumbs if you were bad."

"Ouch. It wasn't a real creature, was it?"

Kyja tugged the sleeves of her robe. "I didn't think so back then." She looked at the sun that was now nearly below the horizon, giving the swamp a blood-red glow. "It looks like we're going to have to spend the night here after all. Riph Raph, can you fly back and make sure the Keepers aren't following us?"

Riph Raph, who had been nearly asleep on Kyja's shoulder, lifted his head and grunted, "Anything to get away from his complaining."

"How much food do we have left?" Kyja asked as the skyte disappeared.

Marcus rooted around in the leather bag they took turns carrying. "It looks like—" He stopped and tilted his head. "Did you hear that?"

"Hear what?" Kyja strained to listen, but the only thing she could make out was the buzzing of insects and the croaking of frogs.

Marcus pulled himself up with his staff. He stared into the trees. "It sounded like voices."

Kyja listened again. Still she heard nothing. "Are you feeling all right? Maybe the charm . . ."

"There!" Marcus pointed into the trees. "Something's moving out there. And there! And there!" He pointed into several spots of the swamp.

Kyja jumped to her feet. "What is it?" She looked where Marcus was pointing, squinting into the night, but saw nothing. Was this part of what the snifflers had done to him?

"There isn't anything," she said, trying to take hold of his shoulder.

He jerked out of her grip, spinning left and right, his face a pale, terrified circle of white. "Can't you hear them?" he cried. "They're singing the songs of the dead. They're coming up out of their graves. We have to get out of here."

Kyja looked around, almost believing he was seeing something.

"Run!" Marcus screamed. Clinging to his staff, he hobbled back up the trail. "They're everywhere!" he panted. Eyes wide with terror, he looked over his shoulder and stumbled off the trail into the swamp. Instantly, the dark water sucked him up to his knees. Marcus raised his hands, muttering something Kyja couldn't understand. Then his mouth dropped open with dismay. "My magic. It's gone."

"Come back!" Kyja shouted, pulling at his arm. "Whatever you think you're seeing, it isn't real." But if Marcus could hear her, he didn't show it.

"Harbingers!" he cried. "Look at their claws. Run Kyja. Run-n-n-n-n!"

Kyja stumbled into the water and reached for Marcus's cloak, when something jerked him into the air. "No-o-o-o!" he screamed, struggling in the clutches of some unseen creature. His staff dropped from his hands, and Kyja watched with horror as he was sucked into the trees and out of sight, his cries echoing in the darkness until they disappeared completely.

CHAPTER 16

THE SWAMP

NYTHING?" KYJA ASKED as Riph Raph landed in the branches of a gnarled, black tree that looked more dead than alive.

"Nothing," the skyte panted, resting his mud-caked wings.

Kyja yanked her sodden and stinking robes up to her knees and climbed onto one of the tree's lower branches. The bark felt slick, like the rubbery skin of a slime-nymph, but it was the only way to get out of the foul water for even a few minutes.

"Your body needs rest," Cascade said. Although Kyja and even Riph Raph were both covered in mud from head to toe, the water elemental looked like he'd just stepped out of a pristine lake. "You haven't slept for two days, and you've barely eaten. In your current state, you are far more likely to pass out from exhaustion than accomplish anything of value."

"But I need to find Marcus," Kyja snapped. She scratched at the hundreds of bug bites that covered her skin and peeled mud suckers from her arms and legs.

Riph Raph snapped a bug out of the air and scraped the dried mud from his wings with his rough tongue. "Maybe it's time to give up. There's nothing out there. Nothing but miles and miles of . . . this." He waved his tail at the hopeless morass before them.

"We *can't* give up," Kyja said. "We're the only help he has." She'd tried everything to locate Marcus, including pushing him back to Earth. But somehow, he was beyond her reach. She wouldn't believe he was dead, but the idea kept coming back to her that maybe he was. The last thing he'd heard before being carried off by whatever attacked him was her doubting him. Now he was alone, somewhere in the middle of this endless muck. Maybe injured and in pain—but *please,* alive—and she had no idea whatsoever how to find him.

Hot tears dripped down her face as she clutched his staff to her chest, running her fingers across the surface worn smooth by his hands. "Are you sure you can't find him?" Kyja asked Cascade. "I'll give you anything you ask."

"I can protect you from the animals that roam these waters." The water elemental stared down into the dark surface of the muddy water, his eyes reflecting its bleak surface. "But Marcus is beyond my sight."

"Can you at least tell me if he's . . . alive?" Kyja cried. "I thought you could see everything. I thought that was the power of water magic."

"There are places even *I* cannot see."

Kyja slammed her fist against the bark of the tree, cutting her knuckles. "Then tell me where Land Keep is. Tell me where the land elementals are so they can help me."

"I cannot."

Kyja could hear the pain in the water elemental's voice. But that wasn't good enough. *No* wasn't a good enough answer. There was a way. There *had* to be. "Where do we search next?" she asked Riph Raph.

The skyte looked up from licking his wings. "There's nowhere to look. We've searched for miles. I haven't seen any sign of him. Do you really think he's worth all this effort?"

"I won't stop." Kyja felt her eyes begin to droop, so she jumped out of the tree to wake herself up. Instantly, her feet sank into the thick goo, and the murky water rose nearly to her chest. Using Marcus's staff to probe the ground ahead, she began walking in the direction she thought she'd been headed before she stopped to rest.

"We've already covered that area," Riph Raph said, taking to the air.

"Then I'll cover it again." Head down, she blinked the sweat out of her eyes and took one step at time. She'd keep going for as long as it took. With whatever energy she possessed, she would keep searching until she found him or until finally she succumbed to the swamp herself. Half asleep, she concentrated on taking one step after another, calling out Marcus's name in a hoarse voice.

She was so exhausted she nearly walked into a figure that stepped out of the trees. With bleary eyes, Kyja looked up at the stick-thin creature with ragged clothing and too-long limbs. He was so tall the top of her head barely came to his waist.

"Screech?" Kyja asked, wondering if she was seeing things. She thought that surely she'd left him behind when they entered the city. Yet here he was, combing his long fingers through his greasy clumps of hair, looking as though he wasn't quite sure whether to stay or run.

Finally he hunched over so their eyes were nearly on the same level then ran his long tongue over the few remaining blackened teeth in his mouth. "I can help you find the boy."

—◆—

"Are you sure you know where you're going?" Kyja asked Screech for what felt like the hundredth time.

The cave trulloch looked over his shoulder and grinned. At least, Kyja thought it was supposed to be a grin. With his long, gaunt features and rotten teeth, it could just as easily have been a snarl. He stopped, broke a small branch off a tree, and lifted it to his nose. "Yes, yes," he said as though sniffing a delicious meal, then pointed with a long, boney finger. "The boy passed this way."

"I don't trust him," Riph Raph whispered into Kyja's ear.

Riph Raph didn't trust anyone—at least, anyone other than Kyja. But that didn't mean he wasn't right this time. Kyja wasn't sure she trusted the cave trulloch, either. They'd been traveling most of the day and as far as she could tell, were wandering aimlessly. Out here, everything looked similar, but she was pretty sure they'd passed the same blackened stump at least twice.

Cascade had been even more silent than normal. The longer they walked, the more sullen he became.

"Are we getting any closer?" she asked. But Screech only gave his snaggletoothed smile and pointed ahead.

"Can you tell if we're doing anything other than walking in circles?" Kyja whispered to Riph Raph.

The skyte flapped his leathery ears and blinked. "It's hard to say. Flying up there is like flying over the ocean. Everything looks the same in every direction."

As Screech waded into a thick bank of reeds, Cascade suddenly came to a stop.

"What's wrong?" Kyja asked.

The Fontasian planted his hands on his hips. "I stop here."

"Why?" Kyja asked. "What do you mean, you stop here?"

Cascade said nothing, but stood as steadfast and immoveable as a tree.

"Cascade, you said you'd help me."

The water elemental clenched his teeth.

"Who's going to protect me from whatever's out there?"

"Splash and spray!" he said at last. "Don't you understand? I can . . . not go . . . with you into this . . . this place." He spat the words as though Kyja had asked him to swim through raw sewage.

Understanding dawned on Kyja, and with it, new excitement. "It's Land Keep, isn't it? We're getting close. *That's* why you can't go any farther. Is it some kind of rule? Elementals don't go into each other's keeps?"

Cascade turned away. "I will wait here for you."

"Okay." Kyja leaned forward and hugged the elemental, whose eyes opened wide in surprise. "Thank you. Thank you for all your help. I knew you'd get me here."

"Be careful of the trulloch," Cascade whispered so silently Kyja could barely hear him. "He has reasons of his own for helping you, reasons he is not revealing."

"I'll be careful," Kyja whispered back. "Come on," she said louder, looking into Riph Raph's big yellow eyes. "Let's find Marcus."

An Unexpected Prisoner

Terra ne Staric

High Lord Dinslith heard the first faint screams even before he reached the end of the dim hallway. He paused in front of the heavy, iron-bound door. His legs trembled and his stomach curdled at what awaited him at the bottom of the long spiral staircase.

"My Lord?" The guard standing to the right of the staircase entrance stepped forward, but the high lord held out a weathered hand.

"I will be going down—alone." At least his voice didn't tremble. The guard on the left responded immediately, removing a chain with a bronze key from around his neck and unlocking the door.

As Dinslith began his descent, the thick, stout wood slab clanged shut behind him, and the high lord shivered. The air rising from the depths of the tower dungeon carried a dank cold that gnawed at his old bones with sharp, hungry teeth. But as he walked the worn stone stairs, it wasn't the cold that made his knees and elbows feel as loose

2

as the limbs of the flip-me-up dolls that entertained small children in the square.

For the last seventeen years, he had ruled as Terra ne Staric's High Lord. For the twelve years before that, he'd been chief arbiter and magistrate. Twenty-nine years he'd been part of the leadership of this city. In that time, he could count on two hands the number of people he'd sent to the dungeons. The capital of Westland had always been an island of peace in a world of turmoil.

But now, now . . .

As the cries grew louder, the steps seemed to grow more slippery beneath his feet. He coughed wetly into one fist and ran a hand along the icy wall to keep his balance as he descended into the gloomy depths. How had things come to this? In the last sixty days, he'd consigned more than a dozen—more than *two* dozen—people he'd thought of as friends to the forsaken chambers beneath the city—a city that had always stood for knowledge and understanding.

"Your Lordship?" The bone-white face that floated out of the darkness startled him so that he jerked before recognizing Zentan Dolan staring at him from beneath the cowl of his long, white robe.

"I'm sorry to call you to such a depressing and inhospitable place," the zentan said. "Perhaps it would be better if we discussed matters further in your chambers." Hands that felt too dry and smooth closed around the high lord's, and it was all he could do to keep from tugging his fingers out of the man's unsettling grip.

"No." Dinslith swallowed hard. He tried not to let the screams that bounced and echoed through the chambers affect him, but he could feel his hands bunching into fists. "These are my . . . *prisoners*." The word felt strange and out of place on his lips. "I will inspect them personally."

"As your Lordship wishes," the zentan murmured, his voice oily smooth. He bobbed his head, revealing a hawk-like face and close-cropped gray hair. When he raised his head, the cowl covered his features again.

Dinslith eyed the balanced scales embroidered in gold on the front of the man's otherwise plain, white robe before following the figure as he turned and strode deeper into the dungeon. When the Keepers of the Balance had arrived two months earlier, warning of treason within the city walls, Dinslith had nearly laughed in their faces. The only reasons he hadn't had them thrown out at once were the seeming sincerity of their leader, Zentan Dolan, and the strength of the order he represented.

The Keepers were not as numerous in Westland as they were east of the Windlash Mountains or to the northwest in the Borderlands. Most considered their odd philosophy of rebalancing magical power—taking it from the commoners and redistributing it among the influential—nonsensical drivel. Magic wasn't like water. It couldn't be poured out of one pitcher and into another.

In the past, the order had kept mostly to themselves, at least in this part of the world. Occasionally a lone Keeper would arrive, predicting certain doom and warning of the unbalancing of Farworld. Then he would leave, continuing to the next town. But lately they'd been popping up more and more. Seeing a zentan this far from his sanctuary spoke volumes about how seriously the Keepers took their claims. Dinslith had thought it wise not to offend them.

Still, he'd assumed their stay would be short. A few days. A week at most. They would discover their mistake and be on their way. Terra ne Staric was a place of learning, a place where people came seeking higher knowledge—not some far-flung village where people bowed and scraped to a zealot spouting fancy words and nonsensical symbolism.

Yet within days of the Keepers' arrival, the zentan uncovered an act of betrayal by one of Dinslith's closest associates. Trinstel Wartwood, a master wizard, had been practicing dark magic right inside the tower—an act so vile Dinslith wouldn't have believed it if he hadn't seen it with his own eyes.

He would have granted the man mercy, forgiven him based on their long years of friendship. The man was human. He'd made a mistake. But a day later, the zentan offered irrefutable proof that Trinstel hadn't been working alone. Rashden, Dinslith's personal bookkeeper, had been stealing funds.

To say Dinslith was shocked would be putting it mildly. Rashden, a mouse-like man with large ears, was not much to look at, but he was so personable and friendly that everyone who met him liked him. He was practically family. He would have become a master wizard himself in only a few years.

Within a week's time, the high lord—with Zentan Dolan's assistance—found that Master Wartwood and Rashden were working together. Worse, they were, in fact, part of a group with designs to overthrow the tower and take control of the entire city.

Walking past the rows of prison cells filled with men squatting on the cold stone floors or lying motionless on the filthy straw beds, the high lord tried to focus on the men's crimes and not on their families, who would be going hungry without their fathers and husbands.

As they neared a cramped cell on their left, a prisoner dressed in ragged, gray robes threw himself against the bars and screeched, "Heeeeelp meeee!"

Dinslith stumbled backward, shocked by the man's ghoulish appearance. For a moment he didn't recognize the dark eyes and gaunt cheeks. When he did, he could hardly believe what he saw.

"Rashden?" he said, unable to accept that this was the book-keeper he'd sent to the dungeon less than a cycle of the moon earlier.

"I beg of you," the man wailed, pressing his face into the bars. "Free me from this spawn pit!" His bony fingers clung to the iron bars like the claws of a bird. Drool ran from the corner of his mouth and splattered on the dusty floor.

Looking into his former associate's unfocused gaze, the high lord didn't think the man even recognized who he was talking to. He spun on the zentan, color rising in his cheeks. "What have you been doing to this man?" he fumed. "I gave you no permission to starve anyone."

Zentan Dolan seemed unaffected by the high lord's outburst. "I have done nothing but question him," he said, his pale brown eyes steady in the dim light. "He is *your* prisoner. *Your* guards provide him with food and water."

"Guard!" Dinslith shouted. "Have you been withholding rations from Rashd—that is, from this . . . *prisoner?*"

Immediately one of his royal guards appeared. "No, my Lord. He receives meals thrice a day, same as all of 'em."

Dinslith turned from the guard to study the prisoner, who had collapsed, weeping, to the floor of his cell, clawing at solid rock with his fingertips as though he thought he could dig his way out. What could turn a man to this in only weeks? "Not possible," he murmured.

The zentan rested a hand on the high lord's shoulder. "It is not hunger that consumes this man, but the guilt of his crimes. He is eaten by the knowledge that, because of his greed for power, he has failed his family, his friends, and his city."

Dinslith nodded uncertainly. Perhaps Dolan was right.

"Food cannot fill the emptiness that darkness creates," the zentan continued. "Only when a man forgives himself can he find peace. Only when he learns to place his own needs beneath that of others' will he discover true order inside himself. That is why I am here—to help him find an inner balance."

"The way a cave bat finds balance with a water skimmer." The voice that spoke out of the darkness was hoarse with exhaustion, but it still cut through the screams and cries with a power that caused both the zentan and the high lord to turn toward it at once. As if responding to the words, the other prisoners quieted their cries or grew silent altogether.

"Who is that?" the high lord called, thinking the voice sounded familiar, but unable to place it. He strode the dungeon hallway, ignoring Zentan Dolan tugging at the sleeve of his robe. The hallway ended in a barred door. Beyond the door was an empty, roughly circular room. At the other end of the room, another barred door fronted a cell large enough to contain a single prisoner.

Peering across the circular room, the high lord could see a bearded figure seated on the floor of the cell, but he couldn't make out the face. Dinslith tried to enter the room to get a better look, but the door was locked.

"Who is in that cell?" he asked, shaking the bars.

"Stay away from that prisoner," the zentan said, trying to pull the high lord away from the room. "He is not safe."

"Not safe for whom?" the voice asked with a tired chuckle that Dinslith could almost remember. The man slowly got to his feet. He favored his right leg as he pulled himself up. His shoulders sagged as though he'd carried a great weight for a long time, and his hands appeared to tremble as he clutched the bars. Despite his condition, he held his head high with the magisterial air of a king or warrior.

"Am I a danger to the man I instructed when he was but a

youngster, entering the tower for his first magic lessons? Whom I have stood by and stood up for ever since that time? Or am I a danger to you—*Zentan*." He spoke the title as though it stung his lips like an unripe skyberry.

With a gasp, the high lord recognized the prisoner. His eyes went wide as his mind reeled. It was impossible. This man was supposed to be dead. What was he doing locked in the dungeon?

"Therapass?"

PART 2

Land Keep

CHAPTER 17

THE END OF THE TRAIL

K YJA SMELLED IT LONG BEFORE she saw it—the stench of rotten eggs, dirty socks, swamp gas, and dead fish all mixed together. "What's that terrible stink?"

Screech only shrugged and continued pushing through the tall reeds. Riph Raph wrapped his ears around the front of his face and squinted his eyes. "Whatever it is, it's nothing we want any part of. We should have stayed behind with the water elemental. At least he had the good sense to stop going any further into this cesspool."

"Well, it can't get worse," she said, wiping sweat from her forehead with the back of her hand. Covered in muck from head to foot, she felt like a golem made entirely of dried clay and swamp gunk. The only good part was that the coating kept most of the insects away—probably because they couldn't tell the difference between her and the rest of the swamp. Her robe felt like it weighed a hundred pounds, and she was forced to scrape the end of the staff every few minutes to keep the mud from clumping.

As the stench grew stronger, the air started to take on a yellowish tinge, and Kyja's eyes began to water. It was like being trapped in a stable full of rotting cow manure. She was about to suggest they take a different route when the reeds abruptly ended and she found herself standing in front of a large, open circle of bubbling gray mud.

Obviously this was the origin of the horrible smell. Thick mist rose from the mud and hung in a dank yellow cloud above it. The air here was even hotter than the rest of the swamp. Every few minutes, a huge bubble rose from the depths of the pool, stretched several feet high, then burst with a mucus-like pop that shot foul-smelling gunk everywhere.

Screech came to a halt. "Why are we stopping?" Kyja asked.

The trulloch crossed his arms. "The trail ends here."

Kyja looked down at the gray sludge with the consistency of oatmeal. "Whatever took Marcus must have flown across to the other side. We'll just have to go around."

"No," Screech said. "He did not go across. He went down. In."

"Into *that*?" Kyja stared into the sulfurous pit. Her stomach clenched. If Marcus had gone into *that*, he was dead. Was that why she couldn't find him? Had the creatures that captured him dropped him into the middle of that bubbling mess, knowing he'd never make it out alive?

"Creatures carried him down," Screech repeated, jabbing a finger toward the mud.

"They carried him?" Kyja stepped closer to the churning caldron. There was something odd about it. The circle looked too perfect to have been formed naturally. At the edge of the pit, her staff clanked against a hard surface. Wiping away the muck, she ran her hand across a smooth stone surface nearly a foot across. A wall of some kind?

Tapping with the tip of the staff, she discovered the pool was completely enclosed by a barrier. What was it, and how did it get here?

Nothing about this made sense. Who would wall off a pool of mud and why? There had to be something she was missing. Whatever it was, Screech wasn't going to help. The cave trulloch watched impassively as she studied the steaming muck.

"You've done all you can," Riph Raph said, landing near Kyja. "It's time to find a way out."

"How many times do I have to tell you? I'm not going until—"

Kyja stopped mid-sentence. Nearly hidden by the foliage where Riph Raph was perched was a straight edge. "What are you standing on?" she asked, tearing away vines and bushes.

"What? I don't know. A rock, I guess." Riph Raph flapped his wings and tilted his head. "What does it matter?"

"No." Kyja pushed aside a tree branch, revealing a stone surface that was clearly man-made. "Look, it's not a rock. It's a wall."

It was a building of some kind—about ten feet by ten feet. The roof had collapsed long ago and the walls had crumbled away, but the floor and several stone pillars were still standing. "Look," she said, pointing out a rectangular space that faced the pool. "It's a door."

Scraping away the moss and debris, she discovered a set of stairs leading into the mud.

"Look how the stairs go into the pool. There must have been an entrance here at some point."

"Maybe there was once," Riph Raph said. "But there isn't now."

"What if there *is* some kind of opening down there? A tunnel or something?"

Riph Raph's eyes opened wide, and his tail lashed back and forth.

"It doesn't matter what's down there. You can't go into that mud. If the gas didn't kill you, the heat would. If Marcus is in that, there's nothing left of him but bones."

Kyja's heart sank. She could feel the heat coming off the boiling surface. It would be impossible to find anything inside it before she was overcome by the fumes. Regardless, she found herself pulling her robe up above her knees and tying it off to free her legs for kicking.

"No!" Riph Raph wailed. "I won't let you go. How do you even know Marcus is down there at all? Maybe it's a trick. Maybe the trulloch wants you dead for what you did to the unmakers."

Kyja paused. Was that possible? Was that what Cascade had been warning her of? She tried to read Screech's eyes, but she could sense nothing behind his scarred and haggard face. "Is Marcus down there?" she asked.

Screech nodded.

"Is he . . . alive?"

The trulloch shrugged his scarecrow-like shoulders.

It was up to her then. If Marcus had been pulled into that pit, he had to be dead. Adding her death to his would only ensure that neither of their worlds would be saved from whatever the Dark Circle had in mind. But what chance did she have on her own? Could she find the other elementals without Marcus's help? They'd been a team—pulling each other up when they stumbled, adding their own strengths to the other's weaknesses. If she knew for sure Marcus was dead, she'd find a way to go on. If there was a chance, any chance at all . . .

"I have to try," she said, tying Marcus's staff to her back with a length of leather cord. "If I don't . . . come back up, get to Terra ne Staric and tell whoever you can find that we failed."

"This is a really bad idea," Riph Raph said, eyeing the pea-soup surface. "Skytes don't swim, you know."

"It's all right," Kyja said. "I don't expect you to come with me." She walked to the edge of the pool. Heat radiated off of it. Already the fumes were making her dizzy. If she didn't go now, she'd lose what little nerve she had.

Talons latched onto her shoulder. "I always thought I'd die surrounded by little grandbaby skytes," Riph Raph said.

"Really?" Kyja asked. "I never thought you were the fatherly type."

"Maybe not," he admitted. "But it'd be better than being cooked in a soup." He closed his eyes and pulled his wings tight against his body. "If we're going to do this, let's get it over with."

Turning her head away from the toxic clouds rising from the pool, she took a deep breath, turned back, closed her eyes, and jumped.

CHAPTER 18

DESCENT

EYES CLOSED, BRACED FOR THE HEAT of the burning caldera, Kyja nearly tripped when her feet collided with a hard surface. Her eyes flew open, and she found herself teetering on the edge of a narrow staircase. In front of her, past the edge of stone stairs, was a wall of bubbling gray mud.

"Get back!" Riph Raph shouted, tugging at her shoulder and flapping his wings. For a moment Kyja thought she was going to fall, then—with the skyte's help—she managed to regain her balance.

"What happened?" she gasped. Had she somehow missed the pit? No, she was standing in it, chest-high. But the muck had retreated from her, revealing a set of curving steps running along the outer wall of the pit and disappearing into the molten soup below.

Where had the staircase come from, and what had made the mud clear away? Kyja moved a step up and the mud rose with her, covering the riser she had just been standing on. Cautiously, running one hand along the wall of the pit, she lowered her foot. The gunk retreated again. She reached toward the center of the pit, and her hand disappeared into the gray surface. Yelping with pain, she yanked her hand back. Her fingers had gone a bright pink, but the burning wall of mud stayed where it was.

"Did you know about this?" she asked Screech, who was watching her from above.

The cave trulloch shook his head.

She moved her foot forward, and another step appeared.

"I don't like this," Riph Raph said.

"It's the entrance," Kyja said. "It has to be. And it beats drowning and burning."

Riph Raph shrank against her body, looking at the gray wall with suspicion. "Who's to say we won't still do both? That stuff could collapse on us any minute."

"I don't think so." Kyja stepped down to the next riser. As her head dropped below the surface of the pit, the mud suddenly closed in over the top of them, and Riph Raph gave a squawk of terror. Panicked by the darkness, she moved back, and the sky reappeared.

"I told you!" Riph Raph said. "Let's get out while we can."

"No." She stepped forward, and again the mud closed over the top of them, turning everything black. "I think it's okay," Kyja said, her voice echoing in the darkness. The tight space gave her the unsettling feeling of being buried alive, and the air still smelled of rotten eggs, but she didn't have any trouble breathing.

"This *must* lead to Land Keep," she said, following the curving staircase downward.

"Not exactly a cheery place," Riph Raph's voice said next to her ear.

Water Keep had a wall of mist to keep people out. So it only made sense that Land Keep would have something similar. Maybe this secret staircase was designed to turn back unwanted visitors. But if so, why have the stairs at all? And if the land elementals wanted to keep people away, why send creatures to capture Marcus? And why take him and not her?

Going deeper and deeper into the pitch-black darkness, she came up with no answers. Instead, she counted stairs, trying to determine how far underground they were. Master Therapass's study in the Terra ne Staric tower was two hundred and eighty steps high. The balcony above that was four hundred and eighty. After five-hundred and sixty steps, she and Riph Raph had gone farther underground than the entire tower was tall. As she continued to descend, an unsettling thought occurred to her. What if the staircase never ended? What if it was a trap after all?

Apparently the same thought had occurred to Riph Raph. "Let's go back," he said, breathing heavily against her cheek.

"No," Kyja concentrated on taking things step by step. But she'd lost count. Was she on six or seven hundred?

"I think the space is getting smaller," Riph Raph said.

"Don't be silly," she answered. But was it? The wall felt cooler against her hand than it had when they started. But the air felt just as hot, and thicker than it had above. What if there was only so much oxygen in this bubble of protection? What if they used it all up? At the thought, her lungs began to burn, and she picked up her pace.

Once she opened her mind to fear, her imagination took over. Was the mud closing in on her? Could she hear sounds in the darkness—what Marcus had called the songs of the dead? With each breath, she tried to tell if she was still getting enough oxygen. Would she know if she wasn't, or would she simply pass out and die here, far underground where no one would ever find her?

Without even realizing it, she began running—leaping from step to step, the wall brushing past her fingers the only thing that kept her from total panic. She might have given in completely to her terror and thrown herself headlong down the stairs if it hadn't been for Riph Raph's voice.

"Look there."

What was he talking about? There was nothing to see, and no way to see it in the pitch black.

Except it was no longer black. At some point, the total darkness had given way to a murky gray without her noticing. And the mud was gone. Turning slowly, she saw she was now standing in a gently sloping tunnel more than twice her height, wide enough for eight or nine people to stand side by side on the stairs. The air had lost its sulfurous stench, replaced with a musky scent that made her think of the Goodnuffs' barn.

High up, she saw what had attracted Riph Raph's attention. It was a picture painted directly onto the wall. The image looked like one of the tiny creatures Cascade had shown her in the mud from the bottom of the Noble River. But was it *painted?* Squinting in the dim light, it seemed the picture had more depth than a painting could possibly have—as though the image had first been carved into stone and the color added later.

"Here's another one," Riph Raph called, flying several feet ahead.

Kyja followed, walking down the stairs to inspect the next image—a painting of a plant. The plant itself wasn't all that spectacular—nothing more than a stem and a couple of leaves. But the detail was amazing. It was definitely carved. You could almost believe you were seeing the real thing hanging on the wall.

The farther they moved down the tunnel, the more images appeared on the walls. Plants and animals, rocks and streams. Soon, both walls turned into continuous carved murals teaming with birds, mammals, fish, snakes, lizards, and even humans. Whoever had done this work was an incredibly talented artist. She knew the things she was seeing weren't real, yet they were so life-like she could almost smell the blossoms of the silver teardrops and hear the buzz of twilight flitters.

"Look," she said, pointing to a carving of a skyte soaring above a flock of geese. "It's you, Riph Raph."

"My ears aren't nearly that floppy," he said, tilting his head. "But it does capture the magnificence of my wings."

Kyja couldn't help laughing in delight. Moving down the hallway was like strolling through a forest. The tunnel was getting brighter, too. It took her a moment to realize the light came from constellations of glittering stars overhead. If she hadn't known better, she'd have sworn she was standing outside and looking up at a crystal-clear night sky. She could have spent hours studying the walls, but Marcus was down here somewhere, and she needed to make sure he was all right.

Still, she couldn't take her eyes from the murals as she hurried down the steps. It wasn't until she finally reached the bottom of the staircase that she looked ahead and saw what was lying on the cold stone floor in front of her.

"Oh," she gasped, her voice small and filled with shock. Her hand went to her mouth, and for a moment she let herself hope what she was seeing was only another mural. But these were no paintings. Strewn across the floor like toys left behind by a distracted child, were one, two, three, four—at least a dozen, she counted with growing horror—human skeletons.

CHAPTER 19

KEEPERS' HOLD

"ARE YOU A VIL OR A SCALER?"

Marcus looked up from where he sat with his head in his hands. A boy about his age was speaking.

"No offense intended." The boy squatted next to him, a rolled rush mat tucked under one arm. He looked younger than most of the people Marcus had seen down here. The boy must not have been here too long; he didn't have the same pasty, white complexion as the others, and still wore his own clothes, not the roughly-woven, gray robes. "You don't look like a vil—not that I would hold it against you if you were. Everyone's got their own reasons for what they do. But if you're a murderer or something, I'll keep my distance. No offense."

Overhead, the glow lighting most of the enormous cavern was fading. Soon the ceiling would turn from yellow to red and finally to a deep, midnight blue pricked by the twinkling of millions of fake stars. All across the open stone floor, people were preparing to sleep.

It would be Marcus's second night trapped here, and he knew from experience that in the morning he'd wake up with the beginnings of a pounding headache—the first sign that he needed to get back to Earth soon.

"I'm not a murderer."

"Great!" the boy said, unrolling his mat beside Marcus's. "A word of advice—stay away from the vils. Nothing here to steal to speak of, and the harbingers don't allow for no killing—less they're the ones doing it, of course. But those vils are a nasty group anyway. My name's Jaklah." He held out his arm, and Marcus bumped elbows with him—the way he'd seen these people greet each other.

"I'm Marcus."

The boy stretched out on his mat and pulled off one of his boots. "Harbingers do that to your arm and leg?"

"No. It's a long story."

"Well, Toonuk was a healer in the nother life. He might be able to get you fixed up if you ask him nice. It's good to not be the only new one here. The others say that eventually, I'll wish I'd given in, but I'm glad I ran from the scaling. How 'bout you?"

Marcus sighed. Whether they should have let the Keepers *scale* them seemed to be the only thing these people talked about. That, and what they'd done in what they called their *nother life*. "I didn't commit a crime, and I wasn't about to be scaled. I *was* running from the Keepers, but I went into the swamp looking for a place called Land Keep."

Halfway through unlacing his second boot, the boy froze and stared at Marcus. "The only people who go into the swamp are vils sent there by the Keepers and folks who run into it on their own trying to escape being scaled. Nobody goes there lest they have to. You sure you're not a vil?"

"I'm *not* a vil. I'm not even from Aster's Bay. I'm from . . . well, somewhere pretty far away."

"Ah, that explains it." Jaklah relaxed and finished pulling off his boot. "Didn't nobody tell you not to go out the south gate?"

"They did but we didn't have a lot of choice." Marcus rubbed his temples, hoping Kyja would think to send him back to Earth soon. From the time the harbingers carried him down through the long, black tunnel and dropped him here, he'd been expecting the familiar tingling in his stomach.

"We?" the boy asked.

"My friend and I. Her name's Kyja. We were together when those creatures grabbed me."

Jaklah burst into laughter as if Marcus had told an especially funny joke. "You're twisting my ear, you are. Harbingers take everybody who goes into the swamp. Less she wasn't human. Your friend wasn't a fairy or something, was she?"

Over the two days that he'd been here, Marcus had given a lot of thought as to why the harbingers had taken him and not Kyja. "It has to be because she's immune to magic. The creatures must be magical in some way that keeps them from being able to touch her. Or it could be that they can only see people that have magic. Kyja doesn't have any. "

"*No* magic? Never heard of anyone with no magic. That'd be awful. Did the snifflers do it?"

"No, she was born that way."

"No magic." Jaklah shook his head. "That's why I ran. Keepers were going to take my magic. But even *they* leave you at least a little. Guess I'd kill myself if I had *no* magic."

"That's crazy," Marcus said. "Magic is cool, but it's not important enough to kill yourself over. You just live with it."

Jaklah looked at him as if he'd spoken gibberish. "What'd be the point of living without magic? Couldn't get a job. Couldn't buy nothing. Nobody'd want to marry you or even be your friend for long. You'd be a freak."

Freak. Marcus had heard that word directed at him often enough. The more time he spent in Farworld, the more he was coming to realize that maybe Kyja had heard it just as often. Something else occurred to him—when the harbingers attacked, he'd tried to use magic to protect himself. But like a car with no gas, when he'd reached for his magic, there was nothing there. He still couldn't use it here. He'd assumed it was the harbingers affecting him. But if what Jaklah was saying was true . . .

"Can you . . . use your magic here?"

"Sure," Jaklah said. "How else'd they harvest crops and make these robes and such? Harbingers won't let you do anything that looks like causing trouble—or like you're trying to escape. But otherwise, you're free to do what you want. Guess I'd go crazy down here if they didn't."

So the harbingers weren't keeping him from casting spells. That meant the snifflers *had* done something to him, something that affected his magic. What if it didn't come back? What if his condition was permanent? If he and Kyja succeeded in opening a drift, at least she'd be like everyone on Earth. But how would he save Farworld with a broken body and no magic? The thought sent his heart racing.

"Tell me about the Keepers," he said. "What does *scaling* mean, and what do the snifflers have to do with it?"

Jaklah yawned and lay back on his mat, lacing his hands behind his head. The ceiling of the cavern looked indistinguishable from the real night sky. "The Keepers of the Balance teach that magic should be put in control of those who can use it best. About the time you turn twelve, they come to your house and scale you to see how much magic you have and how much you need. They take magic from those that don't need so much and give to those who can use more."

"Are those the lowbals and the highbals?" Marcus asked, remembering the kids who had tormented Kyja at the academy.

"Yep. Lowbals are the ones who lose their magic. Highbals are the ones who get more. Course, that's usually the leaders and families with the most money. It's all a big show, if you ask me. Just another way to keep the rest of us down."

"But how do they take your magic?"

Jaklah closed his eyes. "Nobody knows, except it has to do with the snifflers. They're the ones that suck the magic out of one person and give it to another. Some folks think the Keepers take a little for themselves, too."

That would explain why the one Keeper's magic had seemed so strong when Marcus tried to attack him. "But what if they make a mistake? How do you get your magic back?"

Jaklah was breathing heavily now, his words little more than mumbles. "Can't. Once . . . taken . . . never . . . back."

Never? The thought sent icy tendrils into Marcus's stomach. He couldn't have lost his magic forever. There had to be some way to get it back.

He was lying on his mat, trying to convince himself that his magic wasn't really gone at all, when a shout arose. "Something's coming!" cried a voice out of the darkness. All around, small lights began to appear as people rolled out of their beds.

"What is it?" a woman shouted.

"Some kind of monster," said a man with shoulder-length hair.

"Help me up." Marcus woke Jaklah, who pulled him to his feet.

Together, the two headed over to see what was happening. A group of people crowded near the entrance to the cavern. Leaving plenty of distance between themselves and the harbingers that kept anyone from escaping, they shined their lights at a lumpish figure that shambled slowly toward them.

"It's a harbinger," called a girl. "Run!"

"It's not a harbinger," said a man toward the front of the crowd. "It doesn't have any claws." But he fell back a few steps anyway.

"Can't be human," said Jaklah. "Or the harbingers would have brought it in."

Jaklah helped Marcus push to the front of the crowd. Whatever the creature was, it looked frightening. Brown and lumpy, with long, mud-caked fur, it carried a staff and had a weird lump on its shoulder that moved and flipped about with each step. It passed through the patrolling harbingers as if they didn't even exist. The creature paused for a moment, looking at the crowd of people, then turned and came straight toward him. It raised its arms as though reaching for him.

"Come on," said Jaklah, pulling him backward.

But a cracked voice said, "Marcus?"

Marcus stared at the muddy creature, and the lump on the monster's shoulder fluttered. "I told you we should have left him here."

"Kyja!" he shouted, and she ran forward, wrapped her arms around his neck, and gave him a loud, muddy, smacking kiss on the cheek.

CHAPTER 20

NO WAY OUT

KYJA, BATHED AND DRESSED in a clean, homespun robe, stood looking around the huge, domed cavern. It was still night. For the last few hours, people had pestered her with questions about how she got past the harbingers and if there was any way she could help them escape. Once they finally accepted it was only because she had no magic and that she had no way of helping them, they'd drifted off to their beds. She, Marcus, and Jaklah were gathered near the wall of one of the few stone buildings.

"What is this place?" she asked.

"They call it 'Keepers' Hold,'" Marcus told her. "But it's really just a dressed-up prison."

"So many people," she said. There had to be at least a thousand of them sleeping out on the wide expanse of stone floor. "They can't all have been sent here by the Keepers of the Balance?"

"Yes, miss," said Jaklah, who for some reason wouldn't meet Kyja's eyes. "We're all either scalers or vils."

"People running from the Keepers so they can keep their magic, or those the Keepers consider criminals," Marcus explained. "Although, I think some of the so-called criminals might just be people who spoke out against scaling."

Kyja still couldn't believe there were so many. This had to have been going on for decades, at least. "And they're all from Aster's Bay?"

"Oh, no, miss," said Jaklah. "Those of us from around here know about the swamp and the harbingers. So most just give in. But people from away know only that the swamp is the one place Keepers won't hunt you down if you run from them. They think the harbingers are just children's spooks."

"But you knew they were real. Why did you run into the swamp anyway?"

Jaklah scuffed his boots against the floor. "Figured it couldn't be any worse than being scaled."

Looking toward the cavern entrance, Kyja still found the harbingers hard to believe in. All she could see was a wide, empty space that the people kept a healthy distance from. "What do they look like?" she asked.

"Like something dragged out of the grave," Marcus said. "White skin covered with sores, moss, and toadstools. Their hair grows down to their feet, and it streams out behind them when they fly. Most of the time, they're quiet—unless you get too close. Then they start this terrible singing about death and the grave that makes you feel like you're already dead. But the worst part is the claws." He held his good hand above his head, fingers curled. "They're as long as swords and they gleam like bone."

"And if you try to leave?"

Jaklah pointed to the tunnel Kyja had entered through. "Didn't you see the bones?"

Kyja shivered. "But there has to be some way to escape?"

"No, miss. You can outrun 'em for a while. They aren't all that fast. But once they see you trying to escape, you're as good as dead."

"Why not just go back up the stairs?" Kyja asked. "If you run fast enough couldn't you stay ahead of them?"

"Every few years someone gets that idea," Jaklah said. "I guess folks go crazy once they've been stuck here long enough. Some of them even make it to the pit before the harbingers catch up. But eventually they do. Then they drag the prisoner back down before they . . ." He looked at his feet and swallowed. "Guess they want everyone to see what happens when you try to run."

Kyja thought through such an escape. You could stay ahead in the tunnel, but once you reached the spiral staircase, the harbingers could fly straight up to get you. You'd lose any lead. The thought of running blindly up all those stairs and waiting for bone-white claws to grab you made her go cold all over. "And there are no other exits?"

"Only two," Jaklah said. "A lot of the people here think one of them used to lead out. But that one's filled with rocks. Harbingers won't let you near it anyway. The other, no one knows exactly what it is. But no one's ever made it through. Vlaxson—he's the oldest here—says that once, a quick fellow managed to make it to the end of that tunnel and back without getting caught. He shouted something about a locked door before the harbingers slit his throat."

Marcus caught Kyja's eye, and mouthed the word "jump." She nodded. If you couldn't go through the doors, it was the only way out. The idea of leaving the rest of these people trapped made her sick. But maybe, once she and Marcus had gathered all the elementals, they could figure out some way to save these people.

"I think Kyja and I need to talk alone for awhile," Marcus said.

"Sure." Jaklah started to leave but then turned back, his eyes on the ground. "If you don't mind my asking, did you really jump into the pit?"

Kyja felt herself blushing. So that's why he wouldn't look at her. "It wasn't any big thing. I'd probably have jumped back out as soon as I felt how hot it was."

Riph Raph blinked his big yellow eyes. "Don't let her fool you. She'd fight those harbingers hand-to-hand if she could see them. And I'd be right behind her."

"Bravest thing I've ever heard of," Jaklah said, his voice filled with admiration bordering on awe.

Marcus grinned. "You should have seen her take on a Summoner all by herself. Guess being a freak doesn't make you useless after all, huh?"

"I, uh, no." Jaklah looked as though he were about to burst into tears, and Kyja couldn't help but feel sorry for him.

"You entered the swamp even though you knew all about the harbingers," she said. "That took a lot of courage too."

"Nothing like you," Jaklah said, but his chest seemed to swell a little anyway. Finally daring to look Kyja in the eye, he asked. "Would you mind telling me where you're from? Just in case anyone asks."

"Terra ne Staric," Kyja said. "It's in Westland, on the other side of the Windlash Mountains."

"Terra ne Staric," the boy repeated with something that sounded like fear in his voice. "It's a good thing you're not back there."

"What do you mean?" Kyja bristled. "Terra ne Staric is a wonderful city."

"Oh, no offense intended. It's just . . . that's where the zentan went."

"Zentan?" Marcus asked. "What's a zentan?"

"Not *what,*" the boy said, clasping his hands in front of his chest. "*Who.* Zentan Dolan is the leader of the Keepers of the Balance. He hardly ever leaves the sanctuary. But six months ago, he took a group of followers with him. Everyone said he was going to a place called Terra ne Staric."

"Why?" Kyja asked. She'd never even heard of the Keepers of the Balance when she lived there. Was that the man she'd seen riding with the high lord?

Jaklah wrapped his arms around himself as if the temperate air had suddenly gone ice cold. "No one knows. Some people said it was to convert the Westlanders. Others said it was to raise an army. There was a rumor that he went to retrieve a powerful artifact. But whatever it was, I wouldn't want to be there right now. The rest of the Keepers are bad enough. But the zentan is worse than all of them put together. He's terrible. He started the Keepers hundreds of years ago, but he doesn't even look old. Some people say he's not human, that he's some kind of monster. I don't know about that, but I'd rather be here a hundred times over than be *there* when he arrives."

CHAPTER 21

A DIRTY BUSINESS

WE'VE GOT TO GET BACK to Terra ne Staric," Kyja said. "The zentan had to be the one I saw with High Lord Dinslith."

Marcus couldn't help smiling at how she never backed down from anything. "Great. I'll call a taxi."

"I'm serious," Kyja said. "He's been there for four months. Anything could have happened by now."

"So what are you suggesting? That we give up on trying to find the land elementals? You said it yourself—he's been there four months. It would take us at least another month to reach Terra ne Staric. And once we do—what then? Jaklah said Dolan is some kind of monster. By now he's probably taken what he wanted and left."

"So you just want to ignore the whole thing?"

"No." Marcus rubbed his neck. He was already starting to feel the aches and pains that came from spending too much time on Farworld. "I want to get away from the harbingers and then figure out a plan." He glanced toward the creatures patrolling slowly back and forth in front of the entrance, afraid that just discussing how to get out of this prison might draw attention.

"I hate to agree with the feeble-minded one," Riph Raph said. "But I can't even see those things, and still they give me the shivers. I vote for escaping, too."

"All right," Kyja agreed. "But once we're out of here, we're going to discuss a way to help Terra ne Staric. I think there's more to the Keepers than we know. They've got to be working with the Dark Circle somehow."

"Deal," Marcus agreed. He looked to where Jaklah lay curled on his mat, and promised himself that somehow he would come back and free him. "Okay. Let's jump."

Closing his eyes, he waited for the tug that would push him back to Earth. He couldn't wait to take a breath of fresh air and see a real sky. He didn't care if it was cloudy, or rainy, or smoggy, or—

The twisting in his stomach came, and, with it, the falling sensation that didn't even bother him anymore. "Thank goo—" he started to say, reaching for Riph Raph and Kyja. But everything was wrong. The words wouldn't come out of his mouth. Weight pressed on him with unbearable force. When he tried to scream, something cold and gritty poured into his open mouth, covering his tongue, and forcing itself down his throat.

He couldn't move; he couldn't breathe. He tried to open his eyes, but everything was dark. *Help!* he screamed inside his head. *Bring me back. Bring me back!*

The tugging sensation returned, and he found himself lying on the cold stone floor, coughing and gagging.

"What happened?" Kyja shouted. "What *is* that all over you?"

Marcus opened his eyelids; something scratched beneath them

like grains of sand. For a moment he couldn't see at all. When his blurry vision returned, he went stiff with fear.

"Don't move," he whispered.

Kyja looked around. "What is it?"

"Harbingers." They were everywhere, circling around him, staring at him with their black, empty eye sockets. They waved their long claws dangerously close, their gumless teeth clacking together as they sang.

Piercing the dirt,
There comes a scream,
From the souls
Imprisoned there.

Eternity spent 'neath
The deep black sod,
Their sins from life
To bear.

Eyes that will never
See light again,
Stare through
The ghastly must.

Bodies that once
In the sun would bask,
Now gather dirt
And dust.

Marcus pressed his hands to his ears, trying to block out the song, but it seemed to be coming from inside his head.

Join us. Become one with us. Become one with the land. We can take you. We want to take you.

"N-n-o-o." Forcing the word from his mouth was like trying to push his finger through a keyhole. But once Marcus spoke, the harbingers drifted away. Except for one. It stood above him and raised its arms, starlight glinting off its long, curved talons. He waited for the blades to slice through him. Then it whirled away and joined the others and went back to patrolling the entrance to the cavern.

"Oh, that was close," he breathed.

Kyja looked left and right, trying to see the danger, while Riph Raph hunched with his wings pulled up around his head.

"Are they gone?"

Marcus nodded. "I think they knew I was up to something, but not what. They were warning me. If they'd known I was trying to escape . . . I'd be over there with rest of the skeletons."

"What happened on Earth?" Kyja asked, brushing away the fine, brown substance that covered Marcus's clothes, staff, and body.

He coughed and spit a brown stream onto the floor. "We forgot where we are. When you pushed me, I must have landed a couple hundred feet—"

"Underground," Kyja finished. "I sent you *underground*. I didn't even think of that!"

"Neither of us did," Marcus said, shaking dirt out of his robe and combing it out of his hair with his fingers.

"But then how do we get you out of here?"

Marcus hung his head. "I don't think we can."

Kyja stared at him as if he'd just insulted her. "I'm not going to leave you here."

"I don't think you have any choice. You heard Jaklah. There's no way out."

"But if you don't get back to Earth, you'll die. What if you close your eyes and I lead you out? Maybe if you can't see them, they can't hurt you."

"I don't think it works that way." Marcus took out the ribbon they'd purchased in Aster's Bay and watched the light flicker off the tiny silver charm as it swung back and forth. "Someone's bound to have tried that by now. Besides, even with my eyes closed, I can hear them singing."

"Then cover your ears," Kyja said. "You cover your ears and close your eyes, and I'll lead you up the stairs."

"I'd never make it without my staff, and you can't carry me. Besides, I can hear their song even when I cover my ears." He didn't like to give up, but he didn't see any other option. "Even if we made it part way up the stairs we couldn't be sure we'd be above ground on Earth."

This adventure had been crazy anyway. Whoever came up with the idea that two kids could save their worlds against a force as strong as the Dark Circle deserved whatever fate they ended up with.

"What about the door?" Kyja said suddenly.

"What door?"

"The one Jaklah told us about. He said there was a tunnel filled with rocks, and another with a door."

Riph Raph flapped his ears. "You mean that one that was locked and guarded by bloodthirsty creatures with fingernails that could turn us all into dog food?"

Riph Raph had a way of putting things into perspective, even if he was a flying lizard.

Marcus shook his head. "Jaklah also said the person who made it to the door was fast. I don't know if you've noticed, but I'm not exactly quick on my feet. The harbingers would be on me before I got ten steps."

"Then we'll just have to find a way to get you past them," Kyja said.

"Well, let me know when you figure it out." Marcus started to put the ribbon back in his pocket. But Kyja grabbed his wrist.

"That's it! That's how we'll get you by the harbingers."

Marcus stared at her confused, but she snatched the ribbon out of his hand.

"We'll use the charm."

CHAPTER 22

FINDING A REASON

THIS IS CRAZY," MARCUS SAID, looking at the charm. "Even the shopkeeper said she wasn't sure how many times it would work, or how long the effects would last. Besides, what makes you think a dog would be anything other than a smaller target?"

"They haven't bothered Riph Raph, have they?" Kyja asked. "The harbingers aren't looking for animals. They're looking for *people*. If Riph Raph and I can't even see them, maybe they can't see us either."

Marcus took the ribbon from Kyja and looked at the small silver charm. Did he really want to stake his life on a piece of magic jewelry he'd picked up in some store? There was still so much they didn't understand about the harbingers. For instance, if he'd really lost his magic, why could he still see them when Kyja couldn't? And how did the Keepers control them?

"It might not last long enough to make it up the stairs," Kyja said. "But I'll bet we can make it to the end of the tunnel."

"Do you have any ideas about how to get through the locked door if and when we manage to reach it?"

"We'll figure that out once we get there."

Marcus closed the charm in his hand. His options *were* pretty limited. "Let's say we do manage to get through the door. How do we know we'd be safe on the other side? Maybe it's locked for a reason. Maybe there's even more harbingers behind it. Maybe it's like a harbinger dinner party, and we're the main course."

"Or maybe it's the entrance to Land Keep."

Marcus hadn't considered that, and the thought made him sick to his stomach. "You think this whole thing is about keeping people away from the land elementals? You think the harbingers are their creations? I don't think I'd want the help of someone who could do all this."

"So what are you going to do?" Kyja threw her arms wide. "Sit here and wait to die?"

Marcus bit his lip. Kyja's plan went way beyond risky, but what choice did he have? "Let's go then." He picked up his staff and got to his feet, trying to ignore the pain that raged through his leg. "If we're going to try this, I'd like to do it before everyone wakes up and draws attention to us."

And before I lose my nerve, he thought.

Together, they crossed the cavern, passing several large gardens and the stream that provided the cavern with water. Near the mouth of the stream, they found the closed-off tunnel Jaklah had described. Boulders filled the entrance from floor to ceiling as if an earthquake had piled stones in the tunnel. As they passed by, the harbingers watched them closely but made no move to interfere.

"There it is," Kyja whispered, pointing to a large archway a little farther down. Marcus craned his neck to look at the entrance. The opening was bigger than both the tunnel Kyja had come through and the one that was barricaded. Matching symbols curved up each side of the arch and met at the top in a pair of intersecting circles.

"Do those markings mean anything to you?" Marcus asked.

"No."

As Jaklah had warned, there were plenty of harbingers protecting the entrance. "Well, here goes," Marcus said, taking the charm from his robe pocket. "If this doesn't work, tell the shopkeeper I want my money back."

Kyja looked like she was about to say something, then closed her mouth. She gestured for Riph Raph to scout ahead and the skyte disappeared into the tunnel.

A moment after Marcus wrapped the ribbon around his neck and tied it, he was looking up at Kyja and sniffing the air. "I can't see them anymore," he whispered.

"Don't say anything until we get through the entrance," Kyja said. "Just in case."

She didn't need to worry about that; Marcus was too scared to speak. His mouth felt so dry he couldn't even swallow. As they approached the tunnel, he kept waiting for the harbingers to reappear. But as they made it through the archway and nothing happened, his heart slowed back to normal.

"It worked," Kyja whispered.

"You didn't expect it to?" Marcus asked.

Kyja shrugged. "Let's just say it's good to be right," she said with a nervous laugh.

After a few minutes of walking, Riph Raph returned. "Get a move on," he said. "It's a long tunnel ending in a pair of big stone doors."

"Are they locked?" Marcus asked.

Riph Raph rolled his eyes. "Do I look like a locksmith to you? I don't even have hands. How should I know?"

"Let's go," Kyja said, breaking into a trot.

Following her, Marcus wondered what would happen if he started to change back before they got through the doors. Would he have enough warning to make it out in time? The tunnel sloped slightly downward, curving left and then right. Along the walls were images. Some were maps, others diagrams of the musculature of animals, or the structures of plant life. The beauty of the images didn't seem to jibe with the harbingers, or the things he'd seen outside. How could creatures that seemed to take such an interest in life forms of all types trap and kill people so easily?

Finally, the tunnel turned a corner and they came to the stone doors Riph Raph had described. "Look," Kyja said, pointing to the symbol inlayed in glittering gold in the center of each of the smooth stone slabs. Marcus recognized the symbol at once—a loop on one end and a square within a square on the other—the symbol for land magic.

"*See the Lords of Land,*" Kyja murmured. "*Beneath the ground they sleep.* This is it. This is Land Keep."

"Open the door," Marcus said. "I want to talk to these guys."

Kyja pushed against the slab. "It won't budge." She shoved against the other one with her shoulder, but it wouldn't move either.

"Look for some kind of secret latch," Marcus said. He began sniffing along the walls and up each door, but the smells were all so old, he couldn't make anything out. He'd have sworn that no one had come this way for years and years.

"Maybe there's a secret word," he said, and began trying all the secret words he'd ever heard of. "Open sesame. Abracadabra. Hocus pocus. Friend. Open up."

"Rotten cabbage," Riph Raph added. "Fried fish. Thirty-seven."

"What kind of magic words are those?" Marcus asked.

Riph Raph flipped his tail. "You try your words; I'll stick with mine."

"What if we knock?" Kyja suggested.

Marcus and Riph Raph shared an exasperated look.

"It couldn't hurt," Marcus said, although he seriously doubted it would be that easy. But time was passing, and he didn't have any better idea.

Taking a deep breath, Kyja made a fist, raised her arm, and pounded on the left door. Instantly a booming voice answered.

"Who wishes to enter Land Keep?"

Kyja smirked at Marcus and answered, "Kyja, Marcus, and Riph Raph."

"What do you seek?" the voice echoed off the tunnel walls.

Kyja glanced back at Marcus and mouthed, "Land elementals?" Marcus gave a quick bob of his head.

"We seek to meet with the land elementals," she answered. When there was no response, she added, "We're trying to save Farworld from the Dark Circle."

"You may not enter," the voice said.

"What?" Marcus barked. "That's—*ruff*—crazy! What do you mean we can't enter?"

Kyja frowned and put a finger to her lips. "I'm sorry to bother you. I'm sure you're really busy, and all that. But if we could just take a minute or two of your time, we'd really appreciate it."

"What do you seek?" the voice repeated.

Kyja raised her hands in a *what-now?* gesture.

Marcus coughed to clear his voice. "We seek to meet with the land elementals."

There was no response.

"To get, um, their help in opening a drift," he added.

"You may not enter," the voice said.

"Why not?" Kyja asked. But the voice didn't answer.

"Maybe it's some kind of puzzle," Marcus said. "What would you come to Land Keep to seek?"

"Land magic?" Kyja suggested.

"Great idea!" Marcus said. "We come seeking land magic."

"You may not enter."

"This is—*bark*—stupid," Marcus said.

"We come seeking tasty fish," Riph Raph tried.

"You may not enter."

"We come seeking help?" Kyja said.

"You may not enter."

It's like we're stuck in some kind of loop, Marcus thought. For the next ten minutes, they tried answering everything they could think of. Safety, protection, help, assistance, directions, training, food, the way to open the door. All of their tries resulted in the same response. It was maddening, and time was running out on his dog charm. Marcus began to grow desperate with each new failure. Were the harbingers nearby waiting for him to turn back to a human so they could attack?

"There has to be something we're missing," Kyja said as she and Marcus huddled a few feet from the door.

"But what?" he asked. Both looked back at the entrance.

"If only there were some kind of instructions," Kyja said.

"That would kind of defeat the—*bark*—purpose of the secret, wouldn't it?"

"But why have a secret at all?" Kyja slapped her palm against the cold floor. "None of this makes sense. Why have a hidden staircase if the harbingers bring everyone who enters the swamp here anyway? And why have a doorway into Land Keep at all if the harbingers won't let anyone go through it? There has to be something obvious. Something we're missing."

"I don't—" Marcus jerked his head around and looked back into the tunnel.

"What is it?" Kyja asked following his gaze.

"I'm not sure," Marcus said. "I thought I saw something move out of the corner of my eye. But when I looked, there was nothing."

He sniffed the air. There was no smell, and yet . . . Again he thought he saw movement. But when he turned, the hallway was empty. "Maybe we'd better go back."

"Okay." Kyja nodded. "We can try again later, after the charm has a chance to recharge."

Marcus took a step then yipped in fear. His body tingled all over, and suddenly the harbingers started to reappear, blinking in and out like the picture on a bad television. "It's too late!" he shouted. "I'm changing back."

"Run!" Kyja screamed. He'd never make it. He wasn't sure the harbingers could see him yet, but they seemed to sense something. There were at least three fading in and out of view with each tremor of his body. But more were coming down the hallway toward them.

"We've got—*arf*—to get in that door," he cried as his body began to shudder.

"Let us in! Please." Kyja pounded on the door. "You have to help us."

"What do you seek?" The voice was exactly the same, as if something terrible wasn't about to happen just outside the door.

"What do you want me to say?" Kyja screamed at the door, pounding her hands against its relentless surface. "You're all a bunch of fakes with your pictures and maps and stars. You pretend that you care, but you don't."

Marcus fell onto his side, his legs kicking and his body shivering uncontrollably. More harbingers were coming, staying in focus longer and looking in his direction.

Pictures, he thought. *The answer has to have something to do with the pictures.* They reminded him of the kinds of things you saw in museums and books. The kinds of things you saw in—

He had it. The kinds of things you saw in school! That's what the pictures and maps reminded him of. They reminded him of school. And why did you go to school?

"To learn!" he shouted. "We're here to learn."

At once, the stone doors groaned and began to swing inward. Dust swirled about the entrance, as though the doors hadn't been opened in hundreds of years. At the same time, Marcus's body gave one last convulsive heave, and he was human again.

As one, the harbingers turned toward him, their teeth clacking in unison. "Kill, kill, kill."

"No." Marcus raised his staff to try and block the falling claws, and something grabbed him from behind.

"Come on," Kyja sobbed. "Get through the door."

Marcus pushed his feet against the stone floor as Kyja tugged at him. A razor-sharp talon swung toward his neck as Kyja gave a hard tug. The claw struck, and for a moment he thought it had imbedded itself in his neck. Then the ribbon dropped to the floor—sliced as cleanly as if it had been cut with a pair of scissors—and he was rolling through the doorway.

CHAPTER 23

KNOWLEDGE

EVEN AFTER THE DOORS HAD CLOSED, Kyja and Marcus lay on the ground, panting and staring at the entrance—waiting for the harbingers to find a way through. It wasn't until several minutes had passed, and they realized they were really safe, that they turned and saw what was behind them.

"A tree," Kyja said, her voice filled with wonder.

"A supercomputer," Marcus said at the same time.

They looked at one another and then turned again to gape up at the majestic edifice in front of them. At the center of the room, two planes of silver-tinted glass as wide as city streets spiraled about each other, rising into the air like great, twin staircases that rose so high Kyja couldn't see the top. Starting about fifty feet up, ramps of the same silvery substance arched out from the central pillar, splitting and re-splitting into walkways—the smallest of which looked barely wide enough for two people to stand side by side. They really did seem like branches of an enormous glass tree, even more so because each branch ended in what appeared to be thick bunches of golden leaves.

Beneath the tree, sparks of yellow and blue light raced across the gleaming black floor, curved up the spirals like shooting stars, and flowed out onto the branches until they disappeared into one group of leaves or another.

"It's like electricity or data or something," Marcus whispered, watching the sparks flow up the tree.

Having seen Water Keep, with its graceful floating towers and fountains, Kyja had expected Land Keep to be similar. But this didn't look like a city at all. Unlike the buildings of the water elementals, which were constantly in motion, seemingly about to change with the whim of every wave, this had a feeling of permanence—as if it had grown over thousands of years instead of being built at all.

She searched the immense space for some sign of houses, but the tree seemed to be the only structure. *Was* it a city, then? Was this where the land elementals lived? Other than the lights, she couldn't see anything moving along any of the walkways.

"Where is everyone?" Marcus asked, echoing her thoughts.

"Look up there." Riph Raph pointed his tail at something bright and glittering floating down from the branches of the tree. At first Kyja thought it was one of the leaves, but as it came closer, she realized it was a cloud of shiny, gold particles.

"It looks like fairy dust," Marcus said under his breath.

The cloud stopped a few feet in front of them. Rotating slowly in the air, the particles swirled in a pattern that looked a little like a shimmering, tilted, figure eight.

"What information may I help you locate?" asked a tinkling voice.

"Are you a land elemental?" Marcus asked.

The cloud flashed briefly. "I am a knowledge illuminator. What information may I help you locate?"

Remembering their experience at the door, Kyja wondered if this was another trick. Choosing her words carefully, she said, "I'd like to find information about the location of the land elementals, please."

The cloud flashed again, and Kyja and Marcus found themselves gliding toward the base of the tree. "Whoaaaa!" Marcus called, holding out his arms. "It's like one of those moving walkways they have at the airport."

Kyja didn't know what a *moving walkway* was, but something seemed to push them forward, or maybe the ground itself was moving. As they reached the tree and began to ascend one of the two spirals, air blew past her face, but there was no other sense of movement—none of the friction she would expect to feel sliding across the surface of the ramp, and no sign that the floor was moving. It was a little like flying, except that her feet were still touching the floor. Whatever it was, her immunity to magic didn't seem to affect it.

"Look at me," Marcus said, turning sideways and holding out one arm. "I'm surfing."

Kyja didn't know what *surfing* was either, but she smiled a little, allowing herself to enjoy the ride as they circled around and around. Still, she couldn't shake the feeling that something was wrong.

"Not scared of heights, are you?" Marcus asked as, about a third of the way up the tree, they glided off the main ramp and onto one of the narrower walkways.

She *was* scared of heights, and looking down at the black floor far below—with no barriers between her and a fall of at least a hundred feet—made her step back from the edge of the walkway. A moment later, they slid onto a flat, round platform and came to a stop. Lying on a dais at the center of the platform was one of the golden leaves. It was much bigger and thicker than it had looked from below. In fact, now that she was up close, it looked more like a *stack* of leaves. A stack of thin flat leaves pressed together like—

"It's a book," she said, lifting up the cover. She looked up at the tree and suddenly felt a little woozy. How many leaves were there? On this platform alone there had to be at least several thousand. And on the entire tree? Millions—maybe hundreds of millions. Hundreds of millions of golden leaves, and each one a book?

"This is a library, isn't it? This whole thing is a giant library."

The golden cloud flashed. "This is Land Keep, the repository of all knowledge."

All knowledge. Kyja's head spun. She'd seen libraries, of course. The tower in Terra ne Staric had the best library in all of Westland. But compared to this, it was nothing.

"Look at this," Marcus said, pointing at the first page of the book. "It says that Land Keep was created by the land elementals as a way to share everything they'd learned with the rest of the world."

Kyja looked where Marcus was pointing and read along. There was a great deal of information on how every new piece of data was collected, gathered, and catalogued to be shared with anyone seeking knowledge. Turning the pages, she saw several diagrams of how the library was laid out.

"The flashes of light," Kyja said. "That's information being fed directly into the books. Everything new that happens is updated immediately. It comes right from the land itself, from the plants, and animals, and—"

"This doesn't make sense," Marcus said, flipping the page. "Isn't that the staircase you came down?" he jabbed a diagram with his finger, and the image suddenly came to life. A miniature spiral staircase rose from the page carrying people down to the tunnel below, the same way Marcus and Kyja were carried up in the tree.

"Where's the muddy pit?" Kyja asked. She turned the page, erasing the staircase, and another image appeared. It showed a group of fairies leading people down the tunnel and into Land Keep. In the picture, the open area which now housed all the people captured from the swamp was filled with men and women, boys and girls. The room had beautiful gardens and flowing streams. Everyone was reading and studying from the big, gold books.

Marcus pointed to the caption under the picture. "This says harbingers are little fairy creatures. That's a lie! Harbingers look nothing like that."

"Is the book wrong?" Kyja asked the knowledge illuminator. "Or did the harbingers turn into monsters somehow?"

The cloud flashed, and the pages flipped to the back of the book.

Marcus scanned the page. "They didn't change on their own. The Dark Circle changed them. According to this, the Dark Circle corrupted the harbingers, blasted the exit tunnel, and filled the pit with mud over a thousand years ago. By turning the harbingers into monsters, they made sure people would stay out of the swamp."

"They didn't want anyone to enter the library," Kyja said.

Marcus turned to the last page. "The Keepers of the Balance discovered the harbingers two hundred years ago and turned the library into a prison."

"Why would the land elementals allow that?" Kyja turned to the knowledge illuminator. "And where is everyone else?"

"There are no others seeking knowledge at this time," the cloud answered.

"No one?" Marcus said. "This is kind of creepy, like walking through a closed amusement park."

"When was the last time someone came seeking knowledge?" Kyja asked.

"Before yourselves, the last knowledge seeker arrived one thousand twenty years, seven months, six days, and two hours ago."

Marcus whistled. "Holy cow!"

"But what about the land elementals?" Kyja asked. "They must show up to make sure everything's running all right."

The glowing cloud blinked off and on, blinked again, and a third time. At last the knowledge illuminator said. "The record of the last land elementals in Land Keep dates three thousand, six hundred seventy-seven years, three months, twelve days, and nineteen hours ago. There have been no land elementals here since that time."

CHAPTER 24

THE DOORS OF ETERNITY

THAT CAN'T BE!" KYJA SAID.

"Yeah, what do you mean?" Marcus demanded of the cloud, slamming the book closed. "Where did they go?"

"I'm sorry. That information is not accessible."

"Are you saying the information isn't somewhere in one of these books?" Kyja asked. "Or that you won't show us where it is?"

The knowledge illuminator flashed. "I am unable to locate the information you requested within my base of knowledge."

"Sounds slippery to me," Riph Raph said.

"Does it matter?" Marcus looked at the millions of books spread around them. "Even if it is here, we could search for years and not find the right book on our own."

"Is there any kind of index?" Kyja asked the cloud. "A place we could look up what's in all of these books?"

"I am a knowledge illuminator. That is my function," the cloud said. "What information do you seek?"

Marcus rolled his eyes. This was going nowhere fast.

Apparently Kyja wasn't ready to give up. "Are there other knowledge illuminators besides you?"

"There are as many knowledge illuminators as are needed to serve the seekers of knowledge," the cloud said.

"Do any of the others have access you don't? Is it possible one of them could tell us where the land elementals went?"

"All knowledge illuminators share the same knowledge base."

Marcus rubbed a hand across his forehead; it came away damp with sweat. He was starting to run a fever. "We have to find a way out of here," he said to Kyja. "I've got to get back to Earth soon, and you look even more tired than I feel."

"How do we get out of Land Keep?" Kyja asked.

"There are three exits from Land Keep," the cloud said. "The first is the doorway through which you entered."

"No thanks," Marcus said.

"What about the second?" Kyja asked.

"The second exit is through the doors of eternity."

"That sounds interesting," Marcus said. Suddenly an idea occurred to him. "When the last land elementals left, which exit did *they* take?"

He was sure that information would be "inaccessible" as well. But the cloud said, "The last land elementals left through the doors of eternity."

"Perfect!" Marcus punched a fist in the air. "Take us there."

Instantly, the book they'd been reading flew back to join the others, and they were whisked backed down the narrow walkway.

"Where do the doors of eternity lead?" Kyja asked, keeping her eyes fixed straight ahead.

"I'm sorry," the cloud answered. "That information is inaccessible."

"Figures," Marcus said. "But who cares where the door goes as long as it gets us to the land elementals? I say we try it."

Kyja ran the tip of her tongue across her lips. "I don't know. The *doors of eternity* sounds sort of ominous."

"Marcus wants to see what's through the doors," Riph Raph said. "How about he goes first, and comes back and tells us how eternity was?"

"I'm not saying any of us should go alone," Kyja said. "I'm just saying we might want to use a little caution."

The walkway they were on joined with the main spiral, and once more they glided up into the tree. Soon, they were so high that the view to the ground was completely blocked by walkways and leaves.

"Hey, what's that?" Marcus asked, looking up. They were nearly to the top of the silver ramps. He pointed at something that, until now, had been hidden by branches. It looked like a huge black, upside-down pyramid. Between the tip of the pyramid and the top of the ramps was a pair of linked circles—one vertical, the other horizontal, intersecting at ninety degree angles with each other like the outside of a large gyroscope. A white platform filled the horizontal circle.

"A door," Kyja said as they came to a stop in front of the platform.

"A door to nowhere," Marcus said. He limped onto the platform and looked at the simple silver door set in the exact middle. Above it was the pyramid. Below it was the library tree. But the door itself just stood there, leading nowhere. He went to the other side, grimacing at the pain in his hip. The back of the door—or was it the front?—was painted black. Other than that, it looked exactly the same as the other side.

"*This* is the door of eternity?" he asked.

The cloud did not respond.

"How does it work?" Kyja asked.

"I'm sorry—"

"Right," Marcus said. "That information is inaccessible." He put a hand on the doorknob. It didn't feel especially warm or cold, just like a plain, old doorknob.

"Wait," Kyja said, grabbing his shoulder, "let's think about this for a minute."

"What's there to think about?" Marcus asked. His head was beginning to pound. "I don't know how the land elementals managed to leave through this, but I'm willing to give it a try to find them."

"What if it's a trap?" she said. "Let me go first."

"Why you?" Riph Raph said. "This was *his* idea. Let him go."

"Why would they trap the door?" Marcus asked. "Besides, if something happens, I'd rather have it happen to me."

"But I'm immune to magic." Kyja took his hand and stepped up to the door. "Hang on to me in case I get sucked in or something."

"Fine. But I think this is a complete waste of time. It's just another dead end," he said, looking back at the knowledge illuminator. Still, he gripped Kyja's hand tightly as she turned the knob. Carefully she pulled the door open and looked through. All they saw was the other side of the platform.

"See?" Marcus said. "Nothing."

"Maybe you have to actually enter it," Kyja said. An inch at a time, she pushed her hand into the doorway. Nothing happened. She walked completely through. Nothing.

"Great joke," Marcus said to the cloud. "Where's the real door of eternity?"

"These are the doors of eternity," the cloud said.

"Let's try it from the other side." Kyja closed the door and walked to the black side. Taking Marcus's hand once more, she cracked the door open—an inch and then two. She walked completely through again.

"Let me try," Marcus said. "Maybe it's not working for you because it's magic." They changed hands, and he took hold of the knob. He'd joked around when Kyja was trying it, but as he gripped the metal knob, his heart began to pound. What if he opened the door and some huge monster leaped out at him? What if it was a room filled with harbingers?

"Are you okay?" Kyja asked.

"Yeah." He licked his lips, took a deep breath, and jerked the door open with one quick lunge. Through the door he saw . . . the other side of the platform. "I think your door is busted," he said to the knowledge illuminator. He opened the door and closed it. First from one side and then the other. He tried knocking. He tried magic words. Every time he opened the door, all he saw was the other side.

"Are you sure you don't know how this works?" Kyja asked.

"I'm sorry," the knowledge illuminator said. "I do not have access to that information."

"Well, who does?" Kyja asked, stomping her foot. "Isn't there anyone who has more information than you do in Land Keep?"

The knowledge illuminator flashed once. "The Augur Well," answered the tinkling voice. "The third exit."

CHAPTER 25

THE AUGUR WELL

HAVE YOU FOUND ANYTHING USEFUL about the well?" Marcus asked, resting on the floor of another branch.

Kyja paged through the thin, gold book the knowledge illuminator had lain before them. "There's not a lot of information," she said. All she'd been able to glean from the sparse pages was that the Augur Well was some sort of oracle or prophet.

"It says here that land elemental acolytes went on a quest to seek the Augur Well as part of becoming full-fledged elementals. But there's nothing about what the quest was, how the Augur Well helped them once they reached it, or even if humans are allowed to search for it." If she'd come across this kind of book in the library at Terra ne Staric, she'd probably have assumed the whole thing was a myth. Then again, until she'd met Marcus, she'd assumed the elementals themselves were a myth.

"You don't have anything else?" Marcus asked the cloud. "Like maybe maps or journals from the land elementals who found the well?"

"This is the only volume concerning the Augur Well," the knowledge illuminator said.

"You really haven't given us much information on the land elementals," he said. "Just things they've done or places they've been. Do you have any pictures of what they look like?"

"I'm sorry. I do not have access to that information."

Marcus rubbed the back of his neck and groaned. "You know, you really don't have to go through that whole, 'I'm sorry, I don't have access' routine every time you don't have an answer. You can just say, 'No.'"

"What about the other elementals?" Kyja asked. "Fire and air especially. Do you have anything here about them? It would be nice to know once we get out of here."

The knowledge illuminator flashed. "No."

"Looks like we search for the Augur Well." Marcus pulled himself to his feet and leaned against the pedestal. Kyja noticed that, more and more, he was leaning or sitting every chance he got—as if standing was too painful, or too tiring, or both.

"Okay," Kyja said to the illuminator. "Take us to the exit that leads to the Augur Well."

As they glided down the spiral ramp, Kyja tried to think of how to bring up something she knew wouldn't go over well with Marcus. Deciding there was no easy way to do it, she swallowed and said, "I don't think both of us can go looking for the Augur Well."

"Huh?" Marcus frowned. Apparently the thought hadn't occurred to him. That would make this even more difficult.

"The book said that reaching the Augur Well was some sort of test for acolytes to pass before they could become real elementals.

It doesn't sound like something they'd let two people work on together."

Marcus nodded slowly. "Okay, good point. I hadn't thought of that. I'll search for the well while you and Riph Raph return to the swamp, since it's safe for you two to go back through the tunnels. If I'm not back in two days, go on without me. By now, the Keepers probably think we've both been captured by the harbingers, so you should have a pretty good chance of sneaking into the city."

Kyja bit her lip. "I don't think you should be the one to go."

"What?" Marcus exploded. "This is *my* problem. I'm the one who's stuck here. Of course I should be the one to go."

"This isn't just about you. If anything happens to either of us, it'll affect both of our worlds. We want to save both Earth and Farworld from the Dark Circle, but we can't save either if we don't open the drift. And that means finding a land elemental to help us." Kyja knew how much the rest of what she had to say would hurt Marcus, but there was no way around it. "I think I have the best chance of doing this."

Marcus glared at her, his jaws clenched. "Why? Because I'm crippled?"

"It's not just that," Kyja said, unable to meet his eyes. "You're sick. Don't you think I've noticed how flushed you are? How even your good leg starts to tremble after you've been standing for very long? Who knows how long this quest might take or what it involves. What if you have to climb a mountain or something?"

When Marcus refused to answer, she wondered if she'd gone too far. Marcus was tough. Tougher than she was, when it came down to it, and she considered herself strong. But he'd been away from Earth for too long. Whatever the snifflers had done to him seemed to have sped up his deterioration here in Farworld.

She knew how awful it felt to have people judge you for something you couldn't do through no fault of your own. But the truth was, in his current condition, Marcus wasn't up to something like this.

"What if the test requires magic?" he said at last. There was something in his voice Kyja didn't recognize. Something she didn't like. She tried to see what he was thinking, but he wouldn't look at her.

"Then I'll just have to find some way around it. I've spent my whole life doing that, so it's not like it'll be a new experience."

She expected Marcus to put up more of a fight. When he simply dropped his chin and said, "Take Riph Raph with you. Maybe animals don't count," she worried even more. She needed to find the Augur Well as quickly as she could then get Marcus back to Earth.

"We are here," the knowledge illuminator said.

So far, nothing in Land Keep had been what she'd expected. But this might have been the biggest shock of all. The entrance to the Augur Well was a simple wooden door. Splintered and rough-looking with a worn leather pull, it could have been the door to a modest cottage or even the side entrance to a barn. The only unusual things at all were the clumsily inscribed images of a mouth and an ear that looked like they might have been carved into the door many years earlier by someone without much talent, maybe a child.

Kyja turned to the glowing cloud, confused. "What am I supposed to do?"

"Open the door," the tinkling voice answered with what sounded almost like amusement.

"That's all?"

"That's all."

Kyja studied Marcus, hoping he was going to be all right. "Maybe Riph Raph should stay with you."

Marcus and the skyte looked at each other and both shook their heads. "He'd just get in my way," Marcus said. "I'll read up on Trill Stones or something. Maybe by the time you get back, I'll be able to beat you."

"I wouldn't count on it." Kyja leaned forward and wrapped her arms around him. For a moment he resisted her. But finally she felt him hug her back, and a sense of warm relief filled her chest.

"Be safe," he said.

"I will." She turned to Riph Raph. "Hang on tight to my shoulder," she told him as she faced the door. Then to the illuminator, "Just pull?"

The knowledge illuminator flashed. "Just pull."

Taking the leather strap in her hand, she glanced back at Marcus, wishing there were something more she could say. She finally settled on, "Wish me luck."

"Good luck," Marcus said.

Riph Raph tightened his claws into the cloth of her robe. "Why couldn't I have been rescued by a girl who plays with dolls?"

Kyja pulled on the door, and everything around her disappeared.

CHAPTER 26

MR. Z

KYJA FOUND HERSELF STANDING in a dusty study filled with piles and piles of books. Shelves of them lined every wall of the small room. They were not the gold, leaf-shaped books from Land Keep, but tattered tomes with missing covers and broken spines that looked as though they had been literally read to pieces. The only visible piece of furniture was a large, wooden desk buried beneath more leather-bound stacks.

"Where are we?" asked a voice from behind her.

"Marcus?" She spun around and inadvertently knocked over a tall pile. Books clattered everywhere, including onto Marcus, who was sitting on the floor, his staff gripped in one hand.

"Watch out," he said, fending off several of the larger volumes with one arm.

"How did you get here?" Kyja tried to pull books off of him, while at the same time not upsetting any of the other tottering collections.

"Not sure," he said, pushing himself to his feet. "One minute I was watching you open the door, and the next minute I was here. Where's Riph Raph?"

Kyja realized she couldn't feel the skyte's talons on her shoulder. Had he been left behind?

"Quiet, you two," said a squeaky voice. "Things are about to begin."

Two large piles of books slid aside on the desk, and Kyja found herself looking at a tiny man with a blob of a nose and enormous red ears. The man was wearing a pair of gold-framed glasses too big for his face, a long, black coat, and a battered felt hat that looked dangerously close to falling off his head. He perched at the top of a tower of books that wobbled every time he moved.

As she watched, the man reached into the pocket of his purple vest and pulled out a horn no bigger than his pinkie. He put it to his lips and blew a surprisingly loud trumpet.

"Isn't this exciting?" the man said, putting the horn back into his vest and clapping his hands. "Ullr the challenger is a fine specimen, fleet and strong. But the champion, Váli, is a veteran of many battles, wily and trickilicious." Resting his chin in his hands, he set his elbows on the desk and stared at its wooden surface.

Marcus looked to Kyja, but she had no more idea than he did what was going on. Stepping carefully around the books, she and Marcus approached the desk. "What are you talking about?" she asked timidly.

"Hmm?" the man replied without looking up. "Sport, of course. Man against man. Beast against beast. Strength versus speed. Mind over muscle."

Marcus leaned across the desk to see two brown shapes no bigger than walnuts. "Are those snails?"

"Yes, yes." the man chirped. "Look at them go!"

Kyja glanced from one snail to the other. "They don't seem to be moving."

"That's what they want you to think," the little man said, tapping the side of his head and nearly knocking off his hat. "They're sizing each other up, probing for weaknesses. It's a thinking man's sport."

"And what sport would that be?" Marcus asked. As far as Kyja could see, the snails hadn't moved at all. In fact, she suspected at least one of them might be dead.

"Snail jousting, of course!" the man snapped. "The sport of kings and noblemen."

"Seriously?" Marcus leaned across the desk until the tip of his nose was almost touching the snails. "I don't see any lances."

"Lances?" the man leaned backward so abruptly his pile of books swayed like a tall tree in a high wind. He rubbed his glasses furiously with the sleeve of his coat and glared at Marcus as though he were crazy. "Do you have any idea what a lance would do to these beautiful shells? What do you take me for, a barbarian?"

"I thought if they were jousting . . ."

"*Lances.*" The man said, giving Marcus a stern shake of his head before returning to his snails.

"If it wouldn't be too much trouble," Kyja said. "Could you tell us who you are? I'm not sure we're in the right place."

"Who am I?" the man said, as though asking himself. "When most people ask *who* you are, they really want to know *what* you are. Are you famous? Are you powerful? Are you wealthy? Are you someone who can help them get what they want, do you stand in their way, or can you be dismissed out of hand?"

He looked left and right from one snail to the other as though watching an especially exciting tennis match. "Titles are quite useful that way, aren't they? How about Commander of the Fleet? No, too forceful. Master of All Things Inconsequential and General in Nature? Too stuffy. Merciful and Benevolent Ruler? Too self-serving. High Executioner? No." He shivered. "That won't do. How about Her Majesty the Queen? I've always favored that one."

Marcus twirled a finger beside his head, but Kyja gave him a quick elbow in the ribs.

"Actually, I was just wondering what to call you," she said. "I'm Kyja, and this is Marcus."

"You want a name? How unusual." The man scratched a thatch of sparse, gray hair. This time, he actually did knock off his hat. But as it rolled from his head, he caught it with the tip of his left shoe and kicked it into the air, landing the hat right where it had been. "How about Zithspithesbazith? It's actually quite fun to say and allows you to spit freely on whomever you say it to."

"I don't think I could pronounce that," Kyja said, unable to stifle a giggle.

"No? Why don't we stick with Z then? It has a certain letter-like quality to it."

"All right then, Mr. Z. We're looking for the Augur Well. I don't know if you could help us, but we opened a door and—"

"The Augur Well?" the man said. "Why didn't you say so in the first place?" He began searching his pockets. First his coat. Then his vest. Then his baggy pants. "I know I've got it here someplace."

After searching all his pockets twice, he looked up and gave a loud *harrumph*. "What was I thinking?" He took his hat off his head, fished around for what seemed like an exceptionally long time, and finally pulled out a large, old fashioned-looking brass key.

"Here you are," he said, handing the key to Kyja. "Down the hall

to your left. Third door on the right. But you know that, of course."
With that, he went back to watching snails.

"That's it?" Marcus asked. "We just take the key and open the door?"

"That's right," the man said, waving them away. "I apologize for the inconvenience. It's been quite some time since I saw a land elemental here."

"Um." Kyja glanced down at the key. Marcus shook his head vigorously and put his finger to his lips. But she spoke anyway. "We're not land elementals."

"What?" The man again very nearly tumbled from his perch. "Not land elementals, you say? Very odd." He craned his neck to look at the two of them. He put the large gold spectacles into his coat pocket and replaced them with a much smaller silver pair. He squinted at Marcus and Kyja for a moment before mumbling, "No."

Placing the silver glasses into his right pants pocket, he tried on a pair of black pince-nez with thick lenses and no earpieces at all, balancing them on his plum of a nose. "Not right either," he said. Over the next few minutes he tried a pair of tinted bifocals, a monocle, a magnifying glass, several different pairs of spectacles, and even his own fingers closed into two circles. Finally, he put the last pair into his hat, settled it crookedly on his head, and looked at Marcus and Kyja with no glasses on at all.

"That's the trick," he said. "Why, I say, you aren't land elementals at all, are you?"

"No," Kyja said.

"I'm afraid I'll need to take the key then." As Kyja reluctantly handed it back to him, he turned to Marcus. "It wouldn't have worked for you anyway, you know. The Augur Well, that is. In fact, it could have proved quite dangerous had you gone in unprepared."

"I'd be willing to take my chances." Marcus rubbed his hip fiercely.

"Yes." The little man nodded. "I see that. Quite the chance-taker this one. Probably gotten you into trouble more than once, hasn't he?"

"So?" Marcus said with a grimace.

"You, on the other hand," said the man, turning to Kyja. "You have to be pushed out of your normal routine. I'll bet you didn't head into this adventure of your own will." When she started to disagree, he held out a hand. "But once you get started, there's no turning you back. Stubborn to the marrow of your bones, you are."

"I'm not stubborn," Kyja said. "But we *will* get to the Augur Well."

"I don't imagine I could convince you to turn back, could I?" he said, looking from Marcus to Kyja.

Both of them shook their heads.

"Even if I said your path would force you to face things worse than you've ever imagined? Even if I said your chances of a messy death are far greater than your chances of success? Even if I told you the Augur Well is a far less accurate oracle than most would have you believe?"

"No," Marcus said.

"We have to go," Kyja answered.

"Very well." The man put back on his original oversized, gold glasses. "Go out the hall to your right, second door on your left. Or is it the first? Well, if you suddenly find your elbows locked in place and your backsides swelling uncontrollably, you've taken the wrong door. Not that it will do you any good at that point."

CHAPTER 27

THE LAGOON

GUY WAS A TOTAL NUT JOB," Marcus said as they closed the door behind them. They were standing in a narrow hallway lit only by a flickering candle on a small wooden table. The hallway had a dank smell to it, like wet stone.

"Something about him didn't add up," Kyja said.

"Are you kidding? Nothing about him added up. I once had a history teacher who ran around the room flapping his arms and shouting, 'That's something to crow about,' whenever one of us aced a test. Blake the Flake was crazy, but this guy is even crazier."

"It's not just that. He claimed he'd seen land elementals. But according to the knowledge illuminator, no land elementals have been seen in over three thousand years."

"Well, that explains him—I'd be bonkers too if I sat locked up in that room for thousands of years with only a couple of snails to keep me company. Someone should buy him a deck of cards or something. At least he could play solitaire."

"Maybe," Kyja said. "But I think there was more to him than he was showing."

"He told us to turn right." Marcus stared into the dark tunnel. It was impossible to see more than a few feet ahead. "Hope they don't mind if we borrow their candle." He reached for the metal candle-holder on the table, but as soon as he picked it up, the flame went out, plunging the hallway into total darkness.

"What did you do?" Kyja's voice asked from his left.

"Nothing. I just picked up the candle and it went—" As he set the candlestick back on the table, it relit. "Okay," he sighed. "That's one way to discourage people from borrowing."

"We'll have to feel for the doors," Kyja said. She took Marcus's hand in hers and began to run her other one along the left wall as they walked forward. "I hope Riph Raph's all right."

"Guess animals can't come after all," Marcus said, tapping his staff on the stone floor in front of them and trying to ignore the pounding in his head. "He's probably already trying to get that knowledge illuminator to find him some fish."

"Here's the first door." Kyja paused.

"Don't open it," Marcus said, remembering the man's warning. The guy was probably loony tunes, but that didn't mean Marcus wanted to take a chance on having his rear blow up like a balloon.

"That's another thing that doesn't make sense," Kyja said as they began walking forward again. "I was the only one who opened the door. Why did we both end up here?"

"Who knows? Maybe they figured you couldn't do it by yourself. Or maybe they needed someone devastatingly handsome."

"Maybe your ego was so big it got caught in the draft and pulled you in with it." Kyja stopped walking. In the darkness came a faint clunk as she knocked on the wall. "The second door."

"Open it," he said, reaching in the darkness.

"Wait." Kyja's hand went to his arm. "I'm not sure about this. Let's not go rushing in."

"What's to think about? The sooner we get this over with, the sooner we can move on to the next test."

"Maybe we should come up with a plan," Kyja said. "Maybe one of us should wait outside the door, just in case."

"Maybe we should stop talking and go in." Marcus was tired of plans. He was tired of feeling like everything he did was controlled by everyone else. He wanted to get to the Augur Well—whatever it was—find a land elemental, and get back to Earth. He limped to the door, felt for the rough, wooden surface with the palm of his hand, and pushed.

Kyja's fingers tightened on his shoulder as the door swung open. Nothing leaped out at them. Nothing happened at all. "Come on," he said, limping through the doorway.

"That was really dumb," Kyja said. "You can't just go running into things blindly."

"And you can't spend all your time worrying about what *might* happen."

Both of them stopped arguing as they stepped from the wooden floor and splashed into knee-deep mud.

"Where are we?" Kyja asked, rubbing her eyes at unexpected sunlight that nearly blinded them both.

Marcus squinted at stunted trees, high grass, and swaying reeds around them. "We're back in the swamp," he said. "Forget the Augur Well. Let's jump to Earth."

"I don't think this is the swamp. Listen."

Marcus tilted his head. "I don't hear anything."

"Exactly. I spent two days looking for you in the swamp. There were *always* buzzing insects and birds singing and frogs ribbeting. It was never quiet." She sniffed the air. "It doesn't smell like the swamp either. It's not stinky enough. I don't think we're really above ground at all. I think it's an illusion, like the stars in the cavern."

"Maybe you're right," Marcus said. "But now what are we supposed to do?"

Kyja studied the dense foliage around them. "What's that?" she asked, pointing to something glittering in the afternoon sun. She splashed through the mud to a knobby tree. Marcus limped slowly behind her, trying to catch his breath. When he got there, he saw a small golden sign embedded in the bark.

"'The gem of wisdom is obtained through the procurement of knowledge and the willingness to use it,'" Kyja read.

"Sounds like something out of a fortune cookie." Behind the sign, a small path led out of the swamp and up a grassy hill. "Oh, great," Marcus said, not looking forward to the climb.

"At least it's dry," Kyja said.

With Marcus leaning on her shoulder for support, they slowly made their way up the rise. As they reached the crest, a dark lagoon came into view. The lake was not much more than a stone's throw across, and it was roughly circular, bordered by large, square stones with symbols carved into them.

Wooden rafts floated on the water, aligned so they formed six circles, one inside the other—a little like a Trill Stone board or a target. Painted on each of the rafts in red, blue, green, or yellow were the same symbols carved into the stones.

"Is it some kind of game?" Kyja asked.

"I think it's a puzzle," Marcus said. "See how the raft at the center has six walkways coming out from it? And the rafts on the next row each have six walkways too. All of the rafts are connected."

As they started toward the lake, Kyja pointed to a brilliant, fist-sized green stone on the raft floating at the center of the circles. "The sign talked about the *gem* of wisdom. I'll bet that's it. That's what we're supposed to get."

"Makes sense," Marcus said. "You have to go from the outside rafts to the inside one. See, the symbols are a pattern."

He started toward the nearest raft, but Kyja stepped in front of him, arms folded across her chest. "Don't you remember what Mr. Z said? You take too many chances, and it's gotten you into trouble."

"Was that before or after he told us to call him 'Her Majesty the Queen'? Forgive me if I don't pay much attention to the opinion of someone whose idea of excitement is watching snails joust. Besides, he said *you* have to be pushed into everything. So how about we get this puzzle figured out already?" Marcus was anxious to get started. He'd always been good at puzzles, and this one didn't look too complicated.

Kyja gave a dubious look toward the dark water and walked to the edge of the pool. "What's this for?" she asked, picking up a coil of rope.

"Who cares?" Marcus said. Eyeing the rafts, he was pretty sure he had the puzzle figured out already. All you had to do was stay on the same symbols. Start with one, find the same symbol on another raft, and keep going until you made it to the center. If he started with the symbol that looked like one triangle on top of another, a path could get him there in only seven moves.

"At least tie this around your waist first," Kyja said, holding out a loop of rope to him as he headed for the rafts.

"What for?"

"In case you fall in. Can you even swim?"

"A little," he said, not wanting to admit he was a pretty lousy swimmer. One summer at the city pool, he'd managed to climb to the top of the high dive and nearly drowned after cannon-balling into the deep end. "What does it matter? Haven't you noticed? There are like a million rafts out there. I'm not going to fall. But even if I do, I'll just climb back onto another raft."

Kyja glared at him and held out the rope.

"Fine," he said, as she pulled it around his waist and knotted it tightly. "Just make sure you give me plenty of slack. I don't want to get pulled off balance."

"Be careful," Kyja said, letting out rope behind him.

"I won't need to," he said. "I'll be there and back before you even know I'm gone." This was going to be a piece of cake.

Despite his confidence, he gave the first raft a firm poke with his staff before stepping onto it. Just because the puzzle was fairly simple, it didn't mean there couldn't be hidden traps of some kind. When the raft felt solid, he cautiously stepped out onto it.

"So far so good!" he called, waving back at Kyja. Holding the rope with both hands, she wouldn't even wave. Her problem was over-thinking everything. If being disabled had taught him one thing, it was that life was full of dangers. You either accepted that fact and got on with living, or you ended up alone in your room, afraid to try anything that seemed the least bit hard.

From the raft he was standing on, there were three choices: left, right, and straight ahead. Since the only raft that matched the symbol he was standing on was straight ahead, that was the obvious choice. Again, using his staff first to check for traps, he stepped out onto the wooden walkway that connected the rafts. It wobbled under his weight, and for a moment he nearly lost his balance.

Feeling Kyja's eyes on the back of his head, he caught himself with his staff and shouted, "I'm fine!" The last thing he needed was her thinking he was in trouble and tugging on the rope. The key was to take smaller steps to keep from bouncing the walkway. Once he was within stepping distance of the second raft, he nudged it with his staff. He stepped onto the next raft—thinking how easy this was going to be—when all the rafts and walkways disappeared at once, plunging him into the lagoon.

"*Gawp*," he sputtered, swallowing a mouthful of water. He'd expected the lagoon to be as warm as the outside air, but the black liquid was so icy cold, it instantly numbed his body.

"Want me to pull you back?" Kyja called with a smirk, "or would you rather swim?"

With no warning, the lagoon began to bubble and churn all around Marcus. Something closed around his leg. Something else grabbed onto his wrist. Dozens of small, gray creatures looking like a mix between monkeys and frogs leaped out of the water, chirping and giggling wildly. One of them wrapped its arms around his neck. A second tried to pry the staff out of his hands. A third jumped on his back, grabbed his hair, and began shoving his head under the water.

"Help!" he screamed, choking and coughing. "Pull me back. Pull me b-a-a-c-k!"

CHAPTER 28

MIND OVER MATTER

WHAT WERE THOSE THINGS?" Marcus asked, rubbing his head. "It feels like they yanked out half my hair."

"They would have done a lot worse than that if it weren't for the rope."

"Thanks for pulling me to shore," Marcus said, grudgingly. "But if you're looking for an apology, you're not going to get it. If it were up to you, we'd still be standing outside the door trying to come up with a quote-unquote-*plan*."

"I'm not looking for an apology," Kyja said, feeling like she was babysitting Timton Goodnuff again. "What I'm looking for is for you to admit that acting without thinking isn't such a good idea. If you remember, *I'm* the one who figured out how to get you past the harbingers. So yes, I did come up with a plan—one that worked."

"Fine." Marcus squeezed the bottom half of his robe, wringing out at least a gallon of water. "What's your new *plan*?"

"I'm glad you asked," Kyja said. "While you were busy playing with your friends in the water, I was thinking about the rafts. You tried to stay on the same symbol. But what if the puzzle isn't about the symbols at all? What if it's the colors that matter?" As soon as Marcus had reached land, the rafts reappeared, and the creatures left to wherever it was they came from. She pointed to a raft about a third of the way around the pond. "If you start over there on that red symbol, you can go forward one, left two, forward one, right one, then straight in to the middle without leaving red."

Marcus visually followed the path she described. "Okay," he said, nodding slowly. "I can see that. Colors. I'm impressed."

Kyja shrugged, trying not to look too proud of herself. Let Marcus see that he wasn't the only one who could figure out puzzles.

"Go ahead," he said, waving his hand toward the water. "Show me how it's done."

"Well . . ." Kyja bit her lip.

"Oh, no." Marcus shook his head vigorously. "It's *your* plan. You try it. I'm not falling into the water with those swamp-monkeys again."

"But you're already wet. Plus, I'm not sure you could pull me out if I fell in."

"So you get to come up with the ideas. But I have to test them." He pushed himself to his feet and began limping around the lagoon to the raft with the red symbol. "I should have stayed with the kook to see which snail got to become knight or whatever."

"I think this will work," Kyja said. But did she? Or was she just trying to prove that her ideas were the best?

"Keep the rope tight," Marcus said, mumbling under his breath as he stepped out onto the raft.

"How does it feel?" Kyja asked.

"Like a raft." He gave her a baleful glare.

"I've got the rope," she called with what she hoped was an encouraging smile.

"Here goes nothing." Taking small, sliding steps, he made his way along the bobbing walkway and stopped just in front of the next raft. "Sure you don't want to come out and try it yourself?"

Kyja shook her head.

An inch at a time, he moved his foot above the raft. With a sigh even Kyja could hear, he lowered his foot to the next wooden surface. *Please,* Kyja whispered to herself. *Please let this work.*

Then Marcus was in the water again, and Kyja was pulling the rope as fast as she could while he screamed and jabbed at the monkeys with his staff.

"Okay. So it's not colors," Kyja said once Marcus had recovered from his latest "swim."

"Brilliant reasoning," Marcus said, his teeth chattering as he lay on the grass, trying to get warm. "I'm sure those creatures are impressed with your incredible intelligence." He rubbed his calf. "I think one of them bit me."

Ignoring his sarcasm, Kyja studied the rafts. If the solution wasn't symbols or colors, then what else could it be? "There has to be a pattern."

"Of course there's a pattern," Marcus said. "Unfortunately, we don't know what it is."

"I guess we could just keep trying until we figure it out," she mused.

"Oh, no. No, no, no." Marcus ran his fingers through his wet hair. "If you want to use trial and error, *you* be the guinea pig. You can see what it's like getting your head shoved under the water by those sea-chipmunks. I'm sure I could get you out eventually."

Kyja sighed. Trial and error didn't make any sense. There were

too many possible variations, and they couldn't try them all—
Marcus didn't have that much time.

What had the sign said? *The gem of wisdom is obtained through
the procurement of knowledge and the willingness to use it.* So far they
had procured the knowledge that stepping on the same symbols or
the same colors didn't work. What other knowledge could they "pro-
cure"? What about stepping on the same symbol *and* the same color?
A quick examination of the rafts soon dismissed that idea. She could
see only three sets of connected rafts with the same color and symbol, and they weren't anywhere near each other.

"They wouldn't send us out here if there wasn't some way to
solve the problem," she said. "What are we missing?"

Marcus yawned and rubbed his eyes. "What we're missing is the
fact that we were sent here by a lunatic. How do we even know he
gave us the right door? We could spend days trying to get the stone
in the middle of this lousy little pond, only to discover that it's just a
paperweight he left out here while he was collecting snails. Wake me
up when you decide to go back."

Go back? Hadn't he noticed there didn't seem to be a way to go
back? The door had disappeared as soon as they entered the swamp.
She wasn't sure there was any way out of this test besides completing
it. As far as she could tell, they were still underground so jumping
was out, and Marcus was getting sicker. He looked even more
flushed, as if his fever was rising. He couldn't afford to fall into the
lake again.

"Think," she urged herself. What were they missing? What was
the clue they'd overlooked? She stared slowly around the lagoon. The
rafts, the gem, the walkways, the rope, the stones—

The stones! Of course, why hadn't she thought of that first? The
stones bordering the water had the same symbols painted on the

rafts. That must mean something. One at a time, she examined the rocks—searching for any clue. At first they seemed to be as random as the rafts. Six symbols—two triangles, two squiggles that formed an X, something that looked like an open hand, a half-moon with two dots, three squiggles side-by-side, and a tree-like shape.

But then, she realized there was a pattern after all. The symbols repeated themselves—triangles, X, hand, half-moon, squiggles, tree—over and over all around the lake. The solution was about the symbols after all. The colors were just to throw you off. She hurried back to tell Marcus, but he was asleep—breathing in wet, heavy snorts. He needed to rest. She looked out at the rafts. If she could make it out to the gem and wake him up with it . . .

But what if she fell in the lake while he slept? She was a strong swimmer, but hundreds of those creatures could pull her down before she made it back to shore. Trying it alone was a bad idea. Sending Marcus out on the rafts in his condition was wrong, too. He couldn't take much more exertion.

What finally made the decision for her was the thought of how Marcus would react if she woke him to try again. *Great. Another one of your crazy ideas. Why do I always have to be the one to do everything?*

Silently, she slipped the rope around her waist and knotted it. She set the coil by Marcus. If she got into trouble, her screams would awaken him, and—she hoped—he'd manage to pull her out before . . .

But that wasn't going to happen. Repeating the symbols in her head—triangles, X, hand, half-moon, squiggles, tree—she moved to a raft with a pair of triangles on it.

"Here we go," she said, and walked carefully but quickly to the raft with the X. She didn't hesitate, but as she stepped onto the raft, she turned toward shore—prepared to swim with all her strength if she hit water.

Only she didn't. The raft stayed afloat. It worked. So far, she was right! "Yes!" she whispered, pumping her fist as she'd seen Marcus do so many times. She might be cautious, but she wasn't a coward, no matter what he thought.

Now she had to make a decision. There were six walkways lead-ing from this raft—five if you didn't include the one she'd just crossed. Two had the hand symbol. She tried to track where she'd go after that symbol and the one after, but it was too complicated, like a maze. Well, the only way to handle it was to try one and see what happened. Then she realized that maybe the colors weren't a trick. There could be a pattern to them as well as to the shapes. But if that was the case, then it was pure luck this raft hadn't disappeared beneath her.

It might be the time to wake Marcus. But if she could give him even a few more minutes of rest . . . She looked back at the first raft with red triangles. The one she was on had a blue X. The hands on the two rafts ahead of her were green and yellow. A fifty-fifty chance. Chance, that's what it was. But maybe Marcus was partly right. Sometimes—after you'd done your best to prepare—it all came down to chance.

"Riph, Raph, wand, staff," she repeated a rhyme from a game she'd made up as a child. "Horse, cow, somehow, close my eyes, and you . . . are . . . it."

"Yellow it is." She stepped onto the raft and . . . it didn't disappear.

She had both patterns now—red, blue, yellow, green, and tri-angles, X, hand, half-moon, squiggles, tree. Focusing on colors and symbols, she began trying to unravel the maze that would take her to the stone.

Two hours later, Marcus sat up with a groan and rubbed his eyes. "Come up with any brilliant ideas yet?"

He looked left and right, apparently searching for Kyja on the shore. Then he met her eyes and sat up with a gasp. "What are you doing out there?" he shouted, getting to his knees.

"Trying to figure out this stupid puzzle!" Kyja shouted back. "I know the pattern of colors and shapes, but I still can't get there." She was on the second-to-last circle. Four times she'd made it this far, but every time she'd been stopped by a dead end. "It doesn't work. There's no way to get to the last circle." She stomped her foot on the raft, making it shake and bob in the water.

Marcus spotted the rope next to him, and his eyes went wide. There was only a single coil left on the grass. Kyja had wrapped the rest of it around rafts and walkways—stretching out into the lagoon as she tried first one path and then another.

"What were you thinking?" he yelled. "Do have any idea what would have happened if you'd fallen in?" Taking the rope in hand, he began to shake loose the tangles and knots.

"I was taking a chance," Kyja yelled, giving the raft another kick. This whole thing was idiotic. She was hot and tired.

"A *crazy* chance," Marcus said. He looped the rope around and around his arm with sharp, angry snaps. "You could have been killed! Why didn't you wake me up?"

"You needed to rest." What right did he have to complain? She'd done it for him. And besides, he'd taken much worse risks than this. "Besides, I knew you'd just complain if I asked you to go out again."

Marcus stared at her, his mouth open. "I . . . when. . ?" He pulled the rope taut so it made a straight line between them. "All right, maybe I would have complained. But that doesn't mean I want you taking stupid chances."

"Stupid?" Kyja roared. *"Stupid?* You're the one that fell in twice. I've crossed every one of these stinking rafts without getting wet once. Don't call me stupid!" With that, she spun to walk to the next raft, but in her anger she missed the walkway.

"Hang on!" Marcus screamed, tugging at the rope as Kyja struggled for balance.

Tilting far out over the water, Kyja clung to the line with both hands. On his knees, Marcus started to slide. "Oh!" Kyja cried. She was too far into the lake. Marcus would never be able to get her to shore if she fell.

With a ferocious yank, Marcus pulled her, one-handed, to her feet—and something moved. Shifting her balance, still trying to keep from falling on the raft as it bobbed and swayed beneath her, Kyja looked out at the other rafts, then in toward the gem. The walkways. The walkways didn't align with the other rafts anymore.

"Do that again," she called to Marcus.

"Do what?" he asked, his face pale except for the angry red circles high on his cheeks.

"Pull the rope," Kyja said. "Slowly." Holding the rope tightly with both hands, she set her feet against the boards of the raft. As Marcus tugged, she felt herself dragged toward the edge of the raft, but she reset her feet and leaned further back. "Keep pulling!"

Almost imperceptibly, the raft began to move. She wouldn't have noticed it if she hadn't been watching the walkway. She glanced over her shoulder. The entire circle of rafts was slowly turning like the horses on a merry-go-round.

"Move to the left," Kyja called.

Seeing what she was doing, Marcus pulled himself to his feet, limped several yards to the left, and pulled again.

"A little more." The walkway was closer, closer, "Stop!" she yelled.

That was it! She ran across the walkway, past the blue half-moon, across the last walkway, and, kneeling down on the center raft, closed her hand around the gem.

CHAPTER 29

THE FAIRY

"W E'RE CLOSED," SAID MR. Z, balancing on his stack of books.

Marcus blinked. The lagoon was gone, and they were back in the dimly lit study. "Closed?" he asked.

"Mr. Z, it's Marcus and Kyja. We brought back the gem of wisdom," Kyja said, stepping around a pile of books and holding out the green stone.

"The gem?" Mr. Z looked up from a dog-eared volume and squinted at her.

"Take off your glasses," she whispered.

"What? Oh, yes, yes." He took off the gold spectacles, pushed them into the sleeve of his coat, and looked from Marcus to Kyja with a frown. "You two again, eh? Figured you'd have drowned by now."

"*Hoped* is more like it," Marcus said. "Next time you send us to a swamp full of lake-lizards, give us some warning."

"I have to admit, I felt sure at least one of you wouldn't make it back alive. Those willywogs are a brutal lot. Lost a wager on that one."

"A wager?" Kyja asked. "You bet one of us would get killed? With whom?"

"Myself," the man said, scratching his enormous right ear. "My right hand bet Marcus would drown his first time out. My left hand bet he'd make it. It's hard for me to keep track. The left hand doesn't know what the right is doing."

"That sounds strangely familiar," Marcus said.

"Could be." The man nodded. "Have we met before?"

"We got the gem of wisdom," Kyja said holding out the stone. "We passed the test. Can we go to the Augur Well now?"

Mr. Z took the gem, pulled his silver glasses from his pants pocket, and examined it closely. He breathed on the gem and rubbed it with the sleeve of his coat.

"Well?" Marcus said, leaning forward on the desk. Both of his legs were killing him, and his stomach felt like he was going to be sick soon.

"That's it, all right." Mr. Z set the stone on one of his book piles with a thunk. "Been looking for that everywhere. Pages flying all around without a good paperweight. Where did you find it?"

"Paperweight?" Marcus growled. "All that trouble for a stupid—"

Kyja cut him off with a kick to the ankle. "What about the key to the Augur Well?"

"Come back later," Mr. Z said, opening his book. "Maybe next week. I've got a lot of reading to do."

Marcus opened his mouth, ready to give this pipsqueak a piece of his mind, but Kyja held out her hand. "We don't have until next week. Marcus is really sick. We need to get to the Augur Well right away."

"My dear girl," the man said without looking up from his book. "As you can see, I am a very busy man."

"Busy?" Marcus shouted, slamming a hand on top of the desk. "The last time we were here, you were snail jousting. What happened to that?"

Mr. Z flinched at Marcus's outburst. His stack of books swayed far beyond what should have been possible without falling over completely. His eyebrows rose nearly to his hat. "Called on account of rain, if you must know."

"Mr. Z," Kyja said, "I'm sure you've got a lot of things to do, but we don't have much time. If you could just tell us what we need to do to get the key . . ."

Mr. Z produced a silk handkerchief from under his hat and blew his nose rather loudly into it. "Time is the one commodity no one can control." He pointed a runty finger at Marcus. "You can demand someone else's time with bluff and braggadocio. She can plead that she doesn't have enough of it. Yet the only time we can control is our own, and we waste most of that."

He put away the handkerchief, pulled a silver pocket watch out of his vest, and flipped open the cover. "Speaking of time, shouldn't you two be on your way?"

"On our way where?" Kyja asked.

Marcus groaned. He didn't have a good feeling about this.

"On your way out the door." Mr. Z flapped his hands. "Go! Go!"

"Go *where?*" Marcus said. "If this is another test, at least tell us what we're supposed to do."

With astonishing dexterity, Mr. Z leaped from his pile of books onto the top of the desk. "Hurry, now! You must help her. She's in terrible danger. It may already be too late."

"Help who?" Kyja said. But the man jumped to the floor and pushed them in front of him like a collie herding sheep.

"Which door do we take?" Marcus asked, trying to keep from stumbling over the stacks of books falling in every direction.

"Any door, every door. Go. Go!" With strength Marcus never would have expected, the man shoved him and Kyja through the door. Losing his balance, Marcus dropped his staff and put out his hands to brace his fall. But instead of landing in the hallway, he found himself sprawling onto a rough, stone floor.

"Help!" screamed a high-pitched voice.

Marcus scrambled to his knees. He was in a dark, stone cavern. For a moment he couldn't see anything. The voice screamed again. It sounded like a young girl in danger. "No, don't. Leave me alone!"

"Gurggooolah!" grunted a deep voice.

Spinning around, Marcus saw a crackling fire where the study had been a moment before. Standing beside the fire—silhouetted by the sunlight shining through the cave entrance—was a squat-trunked creature with a broad chest and shoulders nearly as wide as the creature was tall. It had three hairy, muscular arms. In one it held a wooden club tipped with sharp chips of rock. The second hand held a flaming log. With the third, it seemed to be trying to swat something out of the air.

At first, Marcus couldn't see what it was slapping at. Then, as his eyes adjusted to the light, he noticed a figure no bigger than a Barbie doll fluttering through the air. She looked in his direction, her eyes wide with terror. "Please, help me."

Marcus edged closer to the fire. Something was wrong with the creature's wings. She was trying to dodge the swinging paw of the three-armed beast to get past it and out the cave entrance, but she couldn't seem to maintain any kind of altitude.

As he watched, the creature caught her with the edge of its plate-sized palm and knocked her toward the dancing flames. She managed to keep from falling into the fire, but not before her wings crackled from the heat, trailing smoke as she dodged a blow from the rock-tipped club.

"The tribrac has a fairy," Kyja cried, grabbing Marcus's arm. "We have to do something!"

Marcus looked for some kind of weapon, but there was nothing in the cave. What would he have done with it even if there were? Beside him, Kyja scooped a handful of rocks and began firing them at the hairy creature that looked intent on crushing the fairy. One hit the monster's face on the bridge of its nose.

"Riggle gortog!" the creature growled, baring its brownish tusks. But it refused to be drawn from its prey, slapping the fairy again, knocking her to the stone wall.

"Use your magic!" Kyja shouted. "It's going to kill her."

The last time Marcus had tried to use magic, he'd been near the harbingers, and it didn't work. But now that they were gone, surely it would be all right. He reached for air to knock the monster back, but there was nothing. It was as if he'd never had magic in his life.

The creature reached down and with its thick fingers snatched the struggling fairy from the ground.

"Help her!" Kyja shook Marcus. "Use your magic now."

Marcus looked from Kyja to the fairy, whose struggles were slowing as the thick fist closed around it. "I can't," Marcus said helplessly. "My magic is gone."

Kyja stared at him open-mouthed.

He raised his hands. "I'm sorry. I . . ."

"Ayyeeeeeee!" the fairy screamed. She was dying, he knew it, and there was nothing he could do about it.

"No-o-o-o-o!" Kyja cried. She raced toward the beast, arms held out as if she would wrestle it to the ground by herself. Suddenly, Marcus felt a terrible heat rise inside him as if he'd swallowed hot coals. The fire burning beside the creature rose up from the logs with a life of its own and attacked the beast, setting its hair on fire from its thick head to its broad feet.

"Graklog! Gerr-r-r-lack," the monster shrieked as the fire raged around it. Dropping the fairy onto a stack of sticks and logs, it raced out the cave entrance, flames trailing after it.

Kyja dove to the ground and lifted the fairy from the wood pile gently in her palms. She cradled it against her chest, prodded it gently with one finger, and put her ear to its chest. The fairy remained motionless.

Kyja looked at Marcus and shook her head. "She's dead."

CHAPTER 30

WINDS OF CHANGE

WHAT JUST HAPPENED?" Marcus scooted across the floor to Kyja's side.

"We . . . let her die." Kyja's rage had banked itself to overwhelming grief at the sight of the motionless figure lying in her arms. No more than eight or nine inches tall, the fairy weighed less than a sparrow. Her two pairs of translucent wings—as light and fragile as tissue paper—were singed from the fire and crumpled against her tiny body by the monster's fist. Gently straightening the wings with the tip of her finger, Kyja felt her anger rise again at this senseless death.

"It's our fault," she said, tears flooding her eyes and leaking down her cheeks. She glared at Marcus. "Why didn't you tell me you didn't have magic anymore?"

Marcus drew back from the heat of her gaze. "I hoped that . . . I didn't want to believe . . ." He looked from the fire to Kyja and swiped a hand furiously across his own eyes. "Why didn't you tell me you *did?*"

"What are you talking about?" Kyja gulped, trying to keep from outright sobbing.

"Did you think I wouldn't figure it out eventually?"

Blinking until her blurred vision cleared, Kyja realized that Marcus was as angry as she was. He stared at her, his right fist clenched into a ball, his left hand squeezed together like the claw of a bird. She wasn't the only one that felt the horrible burden of guilt. She remembered the helpless feeling of watching the mimicker nearly kill Marcus shortly after they met because she had no magic.

"It's not your fault," she sniffled. "Besides, you nearly saved her with that fire."

"Stop it!" Marcus shouted. "Stop lying. It was you all along. With the bike on the trail. With the kids on the playground. And now here. Did you get magic at the same time I lost mine? Was it the snifflers? Is that why you didn't tell me?"

The bike? The playground? What was he talking about? Kyja shook her head, unsure what he wanted from her. "I don't have . . ."

Marcus pounded his fist on his hips, tears streaming down his face. "Why did you pretend *I* was doing it? Why did you let me think I was losing control? Why didn't you just say, *You're a cripple whose only thing going for him was that he had magic, and now that's gone too?* Be honest. I have nothing, and you have everything."

He wasn't making sense. Sure, Marcus was struggling with his magic, but he'd regain control over it in time. He had to. He was the one ordained to save Farworld. He had the mark on his shoulder to prove it.

So what did he mean about *letting him pretend he was doing it?* Didn't he understand that she, of all people, knew what it was like to have no magic? Once, for a brief moment she'd thought she did have it—at least a little—when she'd made a hairclip move. But it turned out it was Riph Raph, watching over her shoulder. He'd been the one who . . .

With a sudden burst of understanding, she realized what Marcus was saying. But that was crazy. She pointed where the fire had been. "You don't think *I* did . . . that?"

"Of course you did," Marcus blurted, his face red and contorted. "You made the fire rise up to save the fairy. You stopped the bike from falling when you lost control. And *you* were the one who created the wall of flame when the kids were picking on us."

"No, I didn't." Kyja shook her head. "Don't even joke about that kind of thing." All her life she'd wanted magic—more than anything. Having none had made her an outcast. Worse than an outcast. It had made people see her as infected, dangerous—someone to avoid on the streets and keep their children away from because whatever she had might be catching.

Only Master Therapass had accepted her—because he knew the truth. The Goodnuffs had taken her in but made her sleep in the barn, just to be safe. The only friends she'd had were adults. She'd dreamed about magic, begged for it, worked at it, prayed for it. But she didn't have magic. She never would. To think anything else could only lead to a disappointment too great to bear.

Marcus pulled a flaming stick from the fire. He jabbed the branch into Kyja's face. "Look out!"

"What are you doing?" Kyja screamed and jerked backward, raising her arm against the skin-crackling heat. The flames turned into a swirling vortex, shooting toward the roof of the cavern before disappearing with an audible *pop*.

"You did that," Marcus said, shoving the stick back into the fire.

"No, I didn't."

"Jaklah said the Keepers use snifflers to suck away magic from some people and give to others. Just my luck that they took away my magic and gave some to you instead. Maybe it was an accident when Screech attacked the sniffler right when we jumped."

Could it be? She *had* felt something when the sniffler attached its suckers to her skin, but she'd just assumed it was the revulsion of the attack. No, what he was saying was impossible. She was from Earth. She *couldn't* have magic.

Marcus wiped his cheeks and ran his fingers through his hair. "It took me a *whole day* to learn enough air magic to keep a stick from hitting me in the head." His pained grin looked more like a grimace. "You figured out fire magic without even trying."

She stared into the fire—willing it to grow, to move, to go out. Nothing happened. It was exactly how it had been when she'd spent hour after endless hour trying in Terra ne Staric.

This was stupid. Why get her hopes up again? The kids were right. She *was* a freak. Not for being immune to magic. But for trying to be something she wasn't—to fit in with the very ones who'd rejected her and teased her mercilessly.

I won't, she thought, gritting her teeth. *I won't try to be like them. I won't let them convince me I'm less than they are because I'm different.* She stared defiantly into the fire. A pair of eyes stared back. A head rose out of the flames, then a body with wings and a curling tail.

"Holy macaroni!" Marcus shouted, scooting backward.

Was *she* doing that? Had she created a flame creature? *Go up*, she thought. The imp flapped its flaming wings and rose into the air. *Spin around.* The creature gracefully pirouetted. She *was* doing it! She was using fire magic. She imagined a second imp. Instantly another appeared by the first. Then a third and a fourth. Four flaming imps zoomed around the dark cavern, diving and looping at her command.

She was doing *real* magic—powerful magic. It felt wonderful! For the first time in her life, she was seeing the world through a pair of eyes she didn't even know existed. The thrill of energy flowed through her body. If she wanted to, she could—

"Arghhh," Marcus groaned.

Kyja jerked her attention away from the imps to see Marcus curled in a ball, vomiting near the entrance to the cavern where he'd crawled. At once, the flame creatures disappeared, and with them the energy that had surged through Kyja.

"What's wrong?" she called, running to him.

"Sick," he groaned, motioning for her to stay back. "Just give me—" He threw up again, coughing and choking.

Kyja had been so caught up in the death of the fairy and in trying her newfound magic, she'd completely forgotten how sick Marcus was getting by the minute. "We have to get you out of here," she said.

Marcus rolled onto his back and wiped his mouth with the sleeve of his robe. "Don't know how we're going to do that. The test was to save the fairy. We failed."

Kyja looked at the lifeless figure still cradled in her arms and gently set her on a piece of bark. Had they failed? Was that really all there was to the test? There had to be some way to try again—another chance. A cold wind blew through the cave entrance, brushing her bangs back from her forehead.

What d-o-o-o y-o-o-o-u exp-e-e-ct? They're hu-u-u-mans.

Kyja looked at Marcus. "Did you say something?"

"Uh-uh," Marcus groaned, covering his eyes with his palm.

A warm breeze gently caressed her skin. It reminded her of summer days standing on the tower balcony in Terra ne Staric.

You have to admit, they-y-y-y tri-i-i-ed.

"Did you hear that?" Kyja looked around the dingy cavern and out the entrance.

"Hear what?" Marcus pushed himself up onto one elbow.

"I don't know. It sounded like someone whispering—but from far away, carried on the wind."

They both sat silently for a moment.

"I don't hear anything," Marcus said. "Probably just wishful thinking."

Had she imagined it? The words had been clear, but they didn't sound as if they'd come from human mouths somehow.

Again an ice-cold breeze swirled about the cave. *We shou-u-u-ld take her-r-r no-o-o-w. She's as good as gon-n-e.*

Not unti-i-i-l sunse-e-e-t.

Marcus sat up. "I heard something. Was that you?"

Kyja shook her head, listening intently. Like the wind soughing through the treetops, it was easy to miss if you didn't concentrate on it.

Why-y-y-y-y w-a-i-t? A wind—too cold for the summer day outside—licked at the flames of the fire. *It is ho-o-o-peless.*

"What is it?" Marcus asked. "Another monster?"

"I don't think so." Kyja didn't know what it was. And yet, this whole thing seemed vaguely familiar. What did she know about fairies? It seemed important to recall everything she'd learned about them in academy. Fairies lived in almost all climates. They gathered during the autumn and spring equinoxes, but spent much of their time isolated.

"Who's there?" she asked, peering into the late afternoon.

A breeze that seemed to carry the warm scent of flowers and fresh berries rattled the leaves of the trees. *They-y-y can hear us-s-s.*

Kyja tried to think. There was something significant about when fairies died, but she couldn't remember what. Dead fairies were never left to be eaten by animals—she knew that for sure. Something came for them—something gathered them home so they could receive a fairy funeral. Something to do with directions. Something that reminded her of the cold and warm breezes blowing through the cave.

"The North Wind and the South Wind," she said. That's what it was. When a fairy died, the North Wind and the South Wind picked up the fairy's tiny dead body and returned it to the birthplace of all fairies.

She-e-e-e has-s-s named us-s-s-s, blew the warm gentle breeze.

I told you-u-u-u we should not-t-t-t have stayed, chopped a cold blast.

She-e-e-e has-s-s named us-s-s-s, and we are hers to command.

Unsure of what she was doing, Kyja spoke. "Please, you must help us."

Must, must, must-t-t-t-t. Humans are so-o-o-o-o demanding.

An ice-cold gust cut straight through Kyja's robe, and she wondered if she'd said the wrong thing. But a warm puff of air tickled her ear.

What is it you desire, child?

Kyja held the dead fairy out in her arms. "She was killed by a tri-brac."

That is-s-s-s why we are here, chil-l-l-d. To return her to her own kind.

"But she can't die," Kyja said. "We were supposed to rescue her,

but we got here too late. Isn't there something you can do? Can you
. . . bring her back to life?"

No-o-o! thundered the Arctic North Wind.

Kyja's heart sank. Marcus, who had been propped up on one
knee with what looked like a trace of hope in his eyes, dropped his
head to his hands.

We can-n-n-not, sighed the South Wind. *But you mi-i-i-ight . . .
if-f-f-f you hurry-y-y-y.*

CHAPTER 31

HEART AND SONG

TELL US WHAT TO DO," Marcus said. His head pounded, and his muscles felt like they'd gone through a meat grinder. But he wanted to do something—*needed* to do something—to convince himself he wasn't as useless as he felt.

"She's not really dead?" Kyja asked.

She is de-e-e-ead, the North Wind said.

But she-e-e-e need not stay-y-y dead if you return two things.

Although their voices sounded the same in tone and pitch, Marcus imagined the North Wind as male—a thick, black cloud flinging around hailstones and blizzards. He pictured the South Wind as a warm breeze on a summer day—maybe somewhere in Georgia—that dried the sweat from your brow as you sat on a porch swing. He was sure she must be female.

"What are the two things?" he asked.

Her heart and her son-n-n-g, the South Wind whispered.

"Her *heart?*" Kyja asked.

Marcus pictured a beating organ stored in a bottle of formaldehyde. How could the fairy have been alive without it, and how could they get it back in her? The thought gave him shivers.

All fairies-s-s-s keep their hearts stored safely away-y-y-y, or they leave them in the possession of their true lov-v-v-e, for occasions such as this, the South Wind said. *It will look like a glowin-n-n-ng blue liquid in a tiny crystal jar with a glass stopper.*

That didn't sound too bad.

It will be hidden in her sanctum. On the peak of an un-scalable s-s-s-slope, the North Wind added.

Okay, maybe a little bad. "How are we supposed to climb a peak that can't be climbed?" he asked. "That's impossible."

Finding her hear-r-r-rt is the easy part, the North Wind blustered.

A fairy's song is her most sa-a-a-a-cred posession, the South Wind said. *She protects it with her li-i-i-ife, for it is her essence—her soul. Without it she-e-e-e becomes nothing.*

"Where does she keep her song?" Kyja asked.

Inside her. Her song is-s-s-s not a thing, although she may-y-y-y keep a symbol that represents it. To discover a fairy's song, you must know what she-e-e-e values above all e-e-e-e-lse.

"Wait," Marcus said. "You're saying we have to figure out what she loves? How are we supposed to do that? If you haven't noticed, she's not talking much."

You must see-e-e-e inside her, said the South Wind.

A cold rush of air sent bits of dirt, rocks, and other detritus skating across the cavern floor. *You mu-u-u-st return her song and her heart befor-r-r-re sunset.*

"Sunset?" Kyja looked out the entrance. "That's only a few hours away."

I told you it was ho-o-opeless.

"I'll get the heart," Marcus said. "Maybe I can find a crevice or something to climb up the slope. I'm good at wriggling through small spaces. You figure out the song. You're better at feelings."

Kyja only looked at him.

"What?"

"You're in no condition to climb a mountain."

"Don't tell me what I can't do," Marcus spat. He looked for his staff, but it was nowhere in sight. He must have dropped it in Mr. Z's study. He'd have to go without it. Ignoring the pain, he put one hand against the cave wall and pushed himself slowly to his feet. Digging his fingernails into his other palm, he took first one step, then a second. Agony shot from his ankle to his hip then up his spine with each faltering movement, but he refused to let it stop him. "I. Am. Fine."

On the third step, his leg gave out, and he fell face first to the ground—the air whooshing out of him as he landed on the stone floor. A spasm of coughing shook his body. When he looked up, Kyja was walking out the cavern entrance.

"Come back here!" he roared, balling his hands. "At least let me go with you."

"Once I get the heart, I'll help you find her song," Kyja said. Without a backward glance, she disappeared into a thick stand of trees.

Marcus crawled back to the fire and waited there, occasionally adding another log, sure that Kyja would realize her mistake and return. How could she climb a mountain by herself? She was scared of heights. What if she was attacked by wild animals? What if she needed help? But after nearly an hour had passed, he realized she wasn't coming back. Why would she? He couldn't keep up with her.

And now she was the one with the magic.

You are no-o-o-o-ot well? the South Wind asked after another racking series of coughs shook his body.

"No," he said, resting his head in his arms. Beside him, the fairy lay cradled in a piece of bark where Kyja had left her. He tried not to look at her. Seeing the pale, lifeless body just reminded him of his failure to save her.

You do not try to find her-r-r song while your frien-n-n-nd searches for her heart.

"What would be the point? Kyja will scale the peak, come back with the heart, figure out the song, and I'll sit here doing nothing." Just like she'd solved the puzzle while he was asleep. He could say anything he wanted about how smart he was, how brave, how strong. But the truth was, without magic, he was pretty much useless.

He looked outside the cave entrance. The sun was dropping lower in the sky. There couldn't be more than an hour or two before sunset. He looked back at the fairy. She didn't appear how he'd expected a fairy to look. No upturned nose or pointed chin. In movies, fairies were practically supermodels with wings. This one looked like an ordinary person, only smaller.

Fairies help the fores-s-s-st, the South Wind said. *They urge plants-s-s-s to grow in the spring, and show animal-l-l-ls where to find food during the long, hard winters.*

That surprised him, too. He'd always imagined fairies tossing pixie dust, the bells on the tips of their pointy shoes ringing as they flew around giggling and causing trouble. He didn't know they did actual work. "They must have powerful magic."

No. In fact, they-y-y-y have very little magic at al-l-l-l. That may be why the tribrac was able to cap-p-p-ture her so easily.

Marcus looked again at the tiny figure. How much courage would it take to patrol a forest full of blood-thirsty creatures, when even the smallest of them could probably rip you limb from limb?

"Do *you* have any idea what her song might have been about?"

No one kno-o-o-ows, except for her, the South Wind whispered. *You can only discover it by looking into her soul.*

Sorry, he thought to himself, *I left my X-ray soul-viewing glasses at home.* Still, he looked at the still figure and tried to imagine what she loved. The forest, of course, or she wouldn't have spent all her time flitting around the mountains. And animals, maybe. What would she sing about?

I've been working in the forest, all the live-long day? No, that was totally lame.

The problem was, all he could think of were jingles and sappy country songs, and he didn't think the fairy worried about cleaner dishes or spent lots of time in bars wondering why her ex-boyfriend left her for a younger woman with a nicer car.

"Why did she come here anyway?" he asked, touching the fairy's tiny cold hand. "Was it part of her . . . job?"

No, the South Wind sighed. *It would be much too-o-o-o dangerous.*

"Did the creature capture her outside and bring her here?"

I doubt th-a-a-a-t. In the open, she could easily elude a tribra-a-a-ac.

So she didn't come here because she wanted to, and she wasn't captured. What did that leave? As tiny as she was, the only reason she'd come here was if . . . if the tribrac had something she wanted badly.

He looked around the cavern. Lots of bones. A bed of smelly, dried grass. Shards of rock. None of that seemed to appeal to a fairy. But what if the thing she was searching for was hidden? Marcus couldn't climb a mountain. But maybe finding what the fairy had been looking for could help anyway. Sorting through the sticks and logs, he found a branch just about the right size to work as a crutch.

"Let's see what this tribrac was up to."

CHAPTER 32

HEART

KYJA EASED TO WITHIN THREE FEET of the icy chasm standing between her and the summit she'd been climbing toward for the last hour. Her stomach clenched. "There has to be another way."

There is no-o-o-o other path which will let you-u-u-u reach the peak before sunset. Frigid air swirled across the snow-covered ground, creating whirlwinds of ice biting at her arms and legs.

Chewing her lip, she stared into the drop. It was at least ten feet across and hundreds of feet down. The ground on both sides was covered with ice and snow. She couldn't possibly cross it. Even standing this close made her head swim.

She couldn't count on the North Wind for help. He'd been nothing but a nuisance the entire climb—blinding her with flurries of snow or rocking her balance with micro-bursts of cold wind. It was as if he wanted her to fail. Why couldn't the South Wind have joined her instead of staying with Marcus?

Thinking of Marcus brought back the guilt of leaving him. He was so sick. He shouldn't be alone in that dank cave. But what choice did she have? If she wasn't back with the fairy's heart in—she checked the horizon where the sun was sinking dangerously low—in an hour and a half at most, they would fail this test and lose their chance to reach the Augur Well.

If only she had Marcus's courage. He would take one look at this opening, tuck his staff under his arm, and jump. And the crazy thing was, he'd find a way to land on the other side. He was the kind of person who saw a challenge and immediately overcame it. She, on the other hand, needed to look at things from a dozen different angles—questioning herself about which was the best choice.

The only time she didn't hesitate was when she acted impulsively—out of emotion instead of logic. Like when she'd seen the fairy in the grip of the tribrac. She hadn't thought that through—hadn't considered that the creature would tear *her* apart. And she certainly hadn't known she had magic at the time. She'd just acted.

Was there any way she could do that now? Could she set aside all of her fears and doubts and let her instincts carry her across the chasm? Physical strength alone wouldn't be enough. She didn't have the muscles or grace to make that kind of a jump.

Which left magic.

Magic. The thought made her giddy and terrified at the same time. *She* had magic. The thing she'd longed for her entire life. Marcus was surprised she'd mastered it so quickly—without even knowing she was doing it. But it came as no shock to her. During all those years of studying, of seeing other students succeed while she failed, she'd known—*known*—that if she ever had the chance, she could do magic better than all of them.

She'd studied so hard, practiced so diligently, instinctively understanding how the elements combined and merged. Up until the point where she was asked to leave the academy, she'd mastered every part of magic—except actually having it.

And now that she possessed it, she was terrified she'd been wrong. What if she could finally use magic, but still failed miserably?

Time is-s-s-s pass-s-s-ing, the North Wind said. Whether he was happy about that, sad, or indifferent, she had no idea. But time *was* passing, and standing here wasn't going to solve anything. She needed air magic to get across—the most unpredictable of all magic, whimsical and light. Exactly the things she wasn't. Could she call on air magic when she was facing one of her greatest fears?

"You have to do it," she told herself.

A gust of cold wind blew at her back. Was that encouragement?

She set her feet and stared not into the chasm, but across it, to the other side, marking the spot where she would land. She began to rehearse in her mind what she would do, where she would jump, when she would use magic, and realized that was exactly the wrong thing to do. If she was going to succeed, she had to do it on instinct alone.

"For you," she whispered, and surprisingly she didn't see the fairy in her head, but Marcus. Tensing her muscles, she took three deep breaths, leaned forward, and ran.

Snow and rocks passed beneath her feet in a blur, but she wasn't watching them. Her eyes were fixed on the spot she'd jump from and where she'd land. Three steps, two, one. She set her foot to leap and her boot slipped on the icy ground. Flailing her arms, she tried to push off, but she had no traction.

She clumsily launched into the air. Her speed wasn't enough; she wouldn't reach the other side. She looked down. Icy rocks hundreds of feet below jutted up like spears. Fear surged through her body, and with it, desperation. Like a scream in the night, she called on air magic with every ounce of desire in her body. For a moment, nothing happened. Then a gust of air rose out of the chasm, lifting and pushing her. The thrill was intoxicating.

But would it be enough? She stretched out her arms, clawing for the other side. She was still going to be inches short. Her fingers would just miss the far cliff. Like a giant hand, a blast of arctic air slapped her forward. Her hands caught the edge, slipped, pulled. She was across, rolling on snow-covered ground. She'd made it!

Laughing and screaming like a little girl, she raised her hands and danced in the snow—her feet leaving a pattern of crazy circles in the white powder. She'd used magic under the most trying of circumstances. Maybe not perfectly, but well enough. Who knew how good she could become with practice? She held her arms out wide and shouted at the top of her lungs, "I. Have. Magic!"

Magic, magic, magic, her words echoed back to her.

The rest of the climb was surprisingly easy. Whether it was because she was unconsciously using magic or because she'd finally managed to set aside her fear, before she knew it, she'd reached the top of the peak. Standing on a granite outcropping several feet back from the edge—she hadn't lost her fear of heights completely—she stared in awe at the amazing view. Through the crisp, blue air she could see forever—hundreds of miles of woods, meadows, valleys and rivers unrolled before her eyes.

She could have stood there marveling at the majestic vista for hours, but the lower edge of the sun was nearly touching the horizon. "Where's the sanctum?" she asked.

A gust revealed a tiny rill in the fresh snow. Digging into the bank—using a small amount of fire magic to keep her fingers from freezing—she found a crevice in the rock below. It was a tight fit, clearly designed for a body much smaller than hers. But she managed to wriggle into the crack.

After the blinding light of the afternoon sun reflecting off the snowy ground, it took her eyes several moments to adjust to the dark opening. Finally she could see enough to make out the confines of a small cave. Unlike the tribrac's den, this cave seemed homey. Delicate shelves held shiny rocks, vases of flowers, a nest of fresh grass, and even a small, perfectly formed pinecone.

In the very back, Kyja saw something glowing blue. She reached out, and her fingers closed around a glass bottle no bigger than the tip of her thumb. It seemed to tingle in her hand. She looked around the rest of the room, searching for some hint to the fairy's song, but nothing stood out.

After struggling back to the surface, she checked the sun. It was now touching the surface of the horizon. She had half an hour at most before it set completely.

"Which is the quickest way back?" she asked.

The wind swirled for a moment before blowing straight down the side of a nearly sheer slope. It would have been impossible to climb, even with magic. But she might be able to make it down. Holding the bottle tight in her fist, she spread her arms for balance. She ignored the voice inside her head that told her she was crazy and raced along the side of the mountain.

Somehow, between air magic and the guidance of the North Wind that now seemed to be rooting for her, she made it to the bottom of the slope with only a few falls and no broken bones—and the crystal bottle intact. As soon as she reached the edge of the woods, she broke into an all-out run. Only a sliver of sunlight still showed in the western sky when the tribrac's cavern came into view.

Racing through the trees, the bottle clutched in her hand, she was nearly to the entrance when an ear-splitting roar echoed through the opening.

CHAPTER 33

SONG

MARCUS PRESSED HIS FACE to a crack so small he could barely get his finger in it. He had no idea how something as clumsy as the tribrac would hide anything there, but he'd looked every other place the creature might have stashed something important enough to tempt the fairy. "Can *you* see anything?" he asked the South Wind.

A warm breeze blew out from the crack. *Nothing but a set of lizard bones.*

"Terrific." Marcus hobbled to the fire and collapsed on the ground. That would make a great song—*Ode to a Dead Lizard.*

He rested his aching head against the cave wall. "Don't know why I thought I could do this anyway," he muttered.

If you have done your bes-s-s-t, i-i-i-i-t is all you can ask, the South Wind said.

"I *have* done my best." Not that it was much to talk about. He'd hobbled around the cave like a ninety-year-old man with arthritis, sifting through animal bones, bits of dried meat, and other things too disgusting to think about. Big deal. If *his* life were ever on the line, he hoped there would be someone better than him on the job.

Someone like Kyja.

She'd stare at the fairy, create some kind of psychic connection, and discover her song with hours to spare.

He didn't realize he'd spoken out loud until the South Wind asked, *Your friend?*

"Yeah, my friend," he said, staring gloomily into the fire. "She's good at thinking things through and understanding people's feelings—all that touchy-feely stuff. I've always been an act-first, think-later kind of guy. Maybe I'd have had an easier time on Earth if I'd have been a little more like her."

A small gust dried the perspiration from his sweaty forehead and kicked up the fire. *Perhaps-s-s-s you can cha-a-ange?*

Change. That was a laugh. He was always telling other people to change, when that was one of the hardest things for him to do. Of course, he knew why he had trouble showing his feelings. They'd been hurt too often. Every time he started to make a friend, he'd moved or the person turned against him. Or, in the case of Elder Ephraim, died. Eventually Marcus had covered himself in a hard shell. If you didn't feel, you didn't have to worry about getting your feelings hurt.

Could he change anymore even if he wanted to? Or had he become so fixed it was like he'd encased himself in concrete? The idea gnawed at him. He hated anyone telling him he couldn't do anything. So why was he telling the same thing to himself?

"What should I do?" he asked.

Put yourself-f-f-f in her pla-a-a-ce.

"Whose? The fairy's, or Kyja's?" He knew what Kyja would do.

She'd try to see things from the fairy's perspective. So he guessed the answer amounted to the same thing anyway.

Looking at the fairy's miniature features, he asked himself what she was doing here. What had drawn her? He gently ran a finger across the singed edges of her wings. They looked like they would go up in flames at the slightest heat. If he had wings like that, the last thing he'd do was go anywhere near a fire.

Yet, when Marcus and Kyja arrived, she'd been practically right in it, bobbing and diving around the dancing flames as if . . . as if . . . a chill ran through his body, chattering his teeth.

"Can you blow out the fire?" Marcus asked the South Wind.

He could have sworn he heard her laugh. A moment later, a hurricane-force wind snuffed out the burning logs like a child blowing out a candle. Quickly, he snatched up a thin branch and began sifting through the embers. Something glinted amidst the blackened chunks of wood. He reached to touch it, sure it would burn his fingers, but the tiny object was cool. It looked like blown glass—the sort of thing you saw people making in malls back home—and he wondered how it had survived the heat.

Tweezing it between his fingers, he blew away the ashes and sucked in his breath as he realized what it was. "A dawn chime," he whispered. One of the little purple flowers that sang every morning as the sun rose. Once, Master Therapass had told him that, according to Tankum—the man who saved Marcus's life at the cost of his own—dawn chimes were actually fairies who put down roots so they could be the first to welcome every new day.

Master Therapass had urged him to listen to their song and try to understand it. At first, he'd wondered if the old man was crazy. The dawn chimes' song sounded like just a bunch of notes. But the closer he listened, the more words he'd been able to make out. Later, after Master Therapass had been attacked by the Summoner, he'd actually thought he could hear the wizard's voice in their song.

"That's what you came back for," he said, holding the tiny glass flower in front of the fairy. "It must have been really important for you to risk the tribrac and the fire."

Could the glass flower have a song of its own? And was it possible to hear her song in it? Sweat dripped down his face as unnoticed as the shivers that were racking his body more and more. Gazing at the fragile purple petals, he tried to hear.

First there was nothing. It was so hard to concentrate. His mind seemed fuzzy. As he was about to give up, a single note seemed to issue from the glass, as clear as a stream running fresh from a mountain spring. Another note joined in, and another.

Something rustled around outside the cave entrance, but he couldn't lose his focus. This was the song—*her* song. Only it wasn't sung in human words, and it was going to take every bit of his concentration to understand it.

It was a song glorifying the sun. That much he got. Celebrating the change from darkness to light. But it wasn't just talking about day and night. It was talking about a battle between good and evil. The Dark Circle and . . . Sweat flooded out of his pores as he strove to understand.

There had been a battle between the Dark Circle and the fairies over a thousand years ago. An army of dark wizards attacked during the spring equinox, when the fairies were least expecting it. The battle raged for days. Some of the fairies gave in, allowing themselves to be turned from creatures of light to something dark and terrible. But the rest fought on—even though they knew they had no chance of winning, even as they saw their ranks slaughtered by the bloodthirsty horde. The music resonated in his soul as unnoticed tears streamed from his eyes at the bravery of the fragile but indomitable creatures.

At last, when all hope was lost, the last group of fairies—

Something growled only a few feet away. Marcus looked up—and into the eyes of a tribrac. It bared its fangs at him, roaring with rage when it saw what he was holding. He had to run. But if he did, he would lose the rest of the song. The fairy would die. He didn't know what made him do it. Maybe it was the fever. Maybe it was the song of the brave fairies still filling his heart. But on trembling legs, he rose to his feet, opened his mouth and sang the fairy's song.

He didn't do it well. It was hard to translate some of the words, and his voice was rusty, with none of the bell-like clarity of the dawn chimes. But he sang true to what was in his soul.

The tribrac should have killed him, but something in Marcus's voice seemed to hold it back. In his hand, the glass flower began to glow. Other voices joined his. First, it was only the South Wind, picking up the melody and words where she could. Then new voices added to the song. The dawn chimes were supposed to come out only when the sun rose, but one by one, they raised their purple heads outside the cave entrance and united in chorus. Their voices strengthened his, helping when he stumbled, correcting when he translated wrong. In his hand, the flower shined with a brightness that forced the tribrac backward.

He sang of how the fairies fought until no hope was left. How, at last, rather than surrender and be turned to creatures of dark magic, they put down their roots and committed to fight evil for the rest of their days as the flowers that glorified light every morning.

"Her mother was one of those," Marcus sobbed. With the last of his energy, he sang a tribute to the fairies who'd given their lives. He never saw the tribrac turn and run with a roar of frustration. Never heard Kyja scream his name. Never saw her pour the shining blue liquid into the fairy's mouth, or watched as the tiny creature sat slowly up, marveling at the field filled from end to end with purple flowers singing her song.

He had used the last of his energy, and before the song ended, he collapsed and passed out.

CHAPTER 34

THE LAST CHOICE

I HAVE TO SAY I'M ASTOUNDED," Mr. Z said. They were in his study for the third time. But something was different. The room was still filled with books, but the light seemed brighter, the books less messy. And the dust was gone, as if someone had tidied things up while they were away.

Kyja knelt on the floor, cradling Marcus's head in her lap. His skin was sickly white, and while a moment before he had been burning up, now his cheeks felt cold and clammy. His breathing was so shallow she could barely see his chest rise and fall. ""You have to help him. He's dying."

"He's sleeping now," the man said. "But he will expire soon if something isn't done."

"Then do it!" Kyja snapped.

Mr. Z seemed unexpectedly solemn. He wore none of his ridiculous glasses, and his hat was settled straight on his head. Even the stack of books he sat on looked solid. "That is up to you."

"What do you mean?" Kyja asked, holding Marcus's hand. "If this is another one of your tricks . . ."

"No trick." The man laced his fingers together, opened and spread them flat on the desk, then folded them again. "I'm completely sincere when I say I am astounded, amazed, flabbergasted. Less than three percent of the applicants make it through the second test. And none came to me with your inherent . . . weaknesses."

"Then give us the key," she said, choosing to ignore his veiled insult. She looked down at Marcus, running a hand over his brow.

"There is one more test."

"No!" Kyja shouted. "No more tests. He can't survive it."

"It's not him I'm worried about," Mr. Z said. Something in his voice made Kyja look up. "You've done an outstanding job on your first two. If I didn't know better, I'd think . . . But that's nonsense." He waved his hand, then pointed a finger at Kyja. "I am here to make you an offer."

"What kind of offer?" Kyja expected a trap, yet all she sensed from the man was sincerity.

"Don't take the last test. If you skip it, I will return your friend to full health and place you anywhere on Farworld you wish." He lifted the green stone from his desk and tossed it into the air, catching it in his palm. "I'll throw my paperweight into the bargain," he said with a raised eyebrow. "There are those who might consider it rather valuable."

Kyja narrowed her eyes. "Why would you do that?" The offer sounded too good to be true.

"Because I'm a sucker." Mr. Z pulled out his scarf and gave his nose a loud honk. "A sucker and a patsy. But surprisingly, I've come to, if not like, then at least *appreciate* the two of you. You seem almost . . . human, which I have to say is quite rare in humans. The truth of the matter is, there is no way to win the last test; you can only lose. I don't want to see you go through that kind of pain. So I propose to throw the competition now. I urge you to take this offer. I've never made it before, and I could change my mind at any moment."

Kyja looked for a loophole but couldn't see any. "And the land elementals?"

Mr. Z frowned. "What about them?"

"We need to find a land elemental so we can open a drift between Farworld and Earth. It's why we're here."

"I'm afraid that isn't possible."

"Why not?" she asked, her voice quiet. She thought she knew where this was going now. It was a choice she didn't want to make—couldn't be asked to.

"I do not control the land elementals," the little man said, folding his arms. "But as you may know, they have not been seen for some time. It is possible—even probable—that the land elementals no longer exist."

"But I thought . . ."

Mr. Z pulled out his pocket watch. "There is very little time left. Once you move to the last test, you're beyond my ability to help. Take my offer now. Save yourself pain you can't imagine. I have nothing against stacking the deck. I've done it on more than one occasion for myself. But the odds are not just stacked against you this time. You *will* lose."

This wasn't fair. Why was he asking it of her? If she said yes, Marcus would live. But what would he say when he discovered she'd given up any chance of opening a drift and returning him to the world where he belonged? If Mr. Z could be trusted, she was guaranteed to fail the last test. Then Marcus *would* die. And it might all be for nothing anyway if the land elementals were really gone for good.

"What kind of test is it?" she asked. "How do you know I'll lose?"

"The time for questions is over," Mr. Z said, urgency clear in his voice. "Make your decision now!"

She looked down at Marcus. What would he say if he was the one making the decision? She knew what he'd say. She squeezed his hand, looked the little man in the eyes and said, "I'll take my chances."

Instantly, she found herself standing in a bank of brilliant white fog. She held her hand in front of her face, but even when she touched her palm to the tip of her nose, she still couldn't see anything. It wasn't just fog then. It was like being in a pitch black cave, only in this case, it was pitch white. How could that be? If total darkness was a complete lack of light, was this the opposite? A light so complete it blinded?

"Marcus?" She knelt and ran her hands across the smooth floor until her fingers found his body. She put her hand to his chest and sighed with relief when it gently rose and fell.

"Why are you here?" The voice was neither loud nor soft, male nor female. It came from no single direction, but rather seemed to originate from the light itself. It wasn't demanding in any way or threatening, but Kyja felt her mouth go dry.

Reluctant to leave Marcus, she rose slowly to her feet. Her heart pounded. Mr. Z had promised she would fail this test—that she would lose no matter what. So why *was* she here? Dozens of answers raced through her mind. Because she needed to find a land elemental. Because she had to get to the Augur Well. To open a doorway.

To save Marcus. To save her world . . . and his. Because she had no choice. All of those were true except for the last.

The voice asked again. "Why are you here?"

"Because . . ." She licked her lips. "Because I chose to come."

"How did you get here?"

What kind of question was that? She had no idea how she got here. One minute she was standing in a room full of books with a strange little man, and the next minute she was here. That couldn't be what the voice meant.

How had she come all the way from sleeping in the Goddnuffs' barn—dreaming of learning enough magic to move a hairclip—to this? In her mind, she saw all the events that had brought her to this point—from the first time she saw Marcus in the aptura discerna to their decision to search for the elementals despite the fact that no one even knew they existed.

She remembered the times she couldn't make it on her own and Marcus had stepped in to help her, the times she'd seen him struggling and had known it was her turn to pull him up. She thought about the first test with the rafts and the crazy swamp monkeys. Marcus's impulsiveness had nearly got him killed. Her stubbornness hadn't let her consider different options. But her logic and his quick action had ultimately solved the puzzle. In the second test, they'd switched roles. She was the one taking chances, and he was the one thinking things through.

"*We* got here together."

"And what is it you desire?" the voice asked.

This question wasn't one she'd been expecting, and it made her anxious that she couldn't understand where things were heading. How could she keep from failing if she didn't even comprehend the test? All the time, Marcus was getting sicker and sicker.

"What do I desire?" she said, feeling heat rise to her chest. "I want to get to the Augur Well. I want to find a land elemental and return Marcus to Earth. I want to open a drift and do whatever we're supposed to do to save our worlds, then go back to being a kid. But most of all, I want to stop playing these stupid games!"

"Answer one last question, and you may leave," the voice said.

Like a flame being doused in icy water, Kyja felt the heat of anger replaced with cold dread. She remembered Mr. Z's words, *You* will *lose.* At that moment she wished desperately that she had accepted his offer.

"What will you pay?"

"I don't understand," Kyja said.

"There are those who are saved, and those who save," the voice said. "You have chosen to save both your friend and your world. You cannot be a savior without a sacrifice. What will you sacrifice?"

In the blinding white mist, Kyja shrugged. She was willing to pay whatever it wanted, but she had nothing to give. She had no money. What few possessions she'd had before were destroyed when the Thrathkin S'Bae demolished Goodnuffs' farm. Even the gold from Cascade and the rest of the Trill Stones were in her bag somewhere back in Land Keep. That must be what Mr. Z meant—there was no way she could pass this test because she had nothing to sacrifice.

"It's not fair!" she shouted. "I don't have anything to give."

"What will you pay?" the voice repeated.

What was the voice looking for? If she'd had gold she'd have given it already. Land, buildings, anything—wealth meant nothing to her. The only thing she'd ever really cared about was . . .

Sudden realization dawned on her, and her body went ice-cold. Mr. Z hadn't said she would fail—he'd said she would *lose.* Lose what?

"No," she whispered, her lips numb. There was only one thing she'd ever wanted in her life. Only one thing she'd cared about. Since she was a little girl she'd dreamed of it. Even though she said she'd given up hope, in the back of her mind, she'd always kept a tiny flame burning with the thought that someday, somehow . . .

And now she finally had it.

"No." She shook her head violently back and forth. "Not that. Anything but that."

The voice was silent.

This was too much to ask. If she'd never felt magic coursing through her, she could have given it up freely. But she'd had a chance to see what her life could be like with it. It was everything she'd imagined and more. And she was good at it. Maybe *better* than good! It was like giving a person who'd been blind all their life sight, only to ask for it back that same day.

"My eyes—take my eyes! Or take my hearing!" she shouted, balling her fists. "You can have my arms and legs. I'll crawl like Marcus if I have to."

She *couldn't* give up her magic. Not for Earth. Not for Farworld. Not even for Marcus. It was the only thing she'd ever owned in her life that meant something to her. She'd rather die than lose it now.

"I won't," she said, her entire body shaking. "I can't."

She imagined how proud Master Therapass would be to see how she'd mastered his lessons. Only when she pictured him, the old wizard wasn't beaming at what she'd accomplished. He was shaking his head, and his words returned to her.

The real power of magic lies within you. Who you are, what you do, and most importantly of all, what you may become.

Was this the only way then? Did everything have to be so hard?

Maybe the sacrifice really was just a test. Maybe she wouldn't really lose her magic if she *said* she was willing to give it up.

But she already knew the answer to that.

"What will you pay?"

Hot tears burned her cheeks as she lifted her head.

"I give . . . my magic."

CHAPTER 35

MOUTH TO EAR

IT'S DONE, THEN?" Kyja asked Mr. Z after she and Marcus returned to his study for what she hoped was the last time.

"I believe this is yours," he said, removing the brass key from his coat pocket.

Kyja took the key, hoping it would be worth what she'd paid for it, and knowing that, in some ways, it never could be. "Is my magic gone already?"

Mr. Z shrugged his shoulders. "Today, tomorrow. If not now, soon."

"It was all real, then? This room? The rafts? The fairy?"

"Haven't you learned by now? Everything is real to she who experiences it, and nothing is completely real to anyone else."

"Where's the Augur Well?"

"Left out the hall. First door on your right. Or is it the third?" he said, with a trace of a smile. "Remember, even an oracle can get things wrong sometimes. Or maybe we just misinterpret what we hear."

"Thanks for the advice." She picked up Marcus's staff and lugged him to his feet.

"Fairy . . . song," he mumbled, swaying.

"He's lucky to have you." The little man dabbed at his eyes with his scarf and blew his nose.

"We're lucky to have each other," Kyja said. "Will we ever run into you again?"

Mr. Z narrowed his eyes. "Would you want to?"

Kyja managed a small smile of her own. "I've never seen an actual snail joust."

"Then perhaps we will," the man said.

She started for the door, Marcus stumbling at her side, and turned back. "Who are you really, Mr. Z?"

But the man was gone.

"Figures," she murmured.

It wasn't a long walk to the first door on the right, but halfway there, Marcus seemed to wake up a little. "Where are we?" he asked groggily.

"On our way to the Augur Well."

"We passed, then?"

She felt a little of his weight lighten from her shoulder as he grew more steady on his feet. "We did. You were great."

"Were there any other tests?"

"One." Running her free hand along the wall, she felt the rough wood of a door. Halfway down, her fingers located a keyhole.

"Was it hard?" he asked. "I'm sorry I didn't help."

"Oh, you did." She shifted the key to her right hand and the staff to her left. "Do you think you can stand on your own?"

"I think so." In the darkness, she felt Marcus take the staff.

She reached toward the lock with the tip of the key, fumbled it for a moment, and finally slipped it into the hole. *Work,* she whispered to herself. She turned the key and heard an audible click.

"Should we make a plan?" Marcus asked.

In the darkness, she couldn't tell whether he was joking, but it didn't matter; she was done with planning—at least for today. She pushed the door open, and a flood of pink light filled the hallway.

They stepped through the doorway together and found themselves looking at a staircase winding downward. The walls, floor and steps were made of glowing pink crystal. Marcus groaned. "They couldn't have provided an elevator?"

She knew he was joking, but could see real apprehension on his face as he eyed the steep stairs. "I'll help you." Kyja put her shoulder under his left arm.

"I can handle it," he said, but didn't complain as she supported him one step at a time.

At last the stairs ended in an arched doorway so low Marcus had to duck to get through. As they came out the other side, he stared at the walls and frowned. "What is this?"

They stood in a circular room. Curved pink walls rose as high as Kyja could see, making it look like they were standing at the bottom of a well. But it was the first five or six feet of the walls that held her attention. Other than the opening they'd come through, the entire surface of the walls was decorated with a variety of crystal mouths and ears up to the height of the doorway.

Half the room was covered in lips, muzzles, bills, and beaks. There was what looked like an alligator jaw filled with glittering pink teeth, thick lips that looked like they might have been smiling if it hadn't been for the foot-long tusks curving out, a narrow beak that was at least eighteen inches long, and even something that could have been a fish mouth. The other half of the room had ears that seemed to belong to as many different species.

As they reached the center of the room, the arched door disappeared.

"I am the Augur Well," the mouths, muzzles, lips and beaks said as one. "Why do you seek me?"

Kyja glanced at Marcus and answered for them. "We come seeking knowledge," she said. Many of the ears seemed to move or flick as she spoke.

"You shall be granted one question," the mouths said. "But first, I will foretell of things to come. Things both good and bad. Things that may help or hinder, depending on how you use them. Things which may lighten your loads or burden your hearts."

"Okay," Marcus said, sweat shining on his forehead. "Go ahead."

At once the mouths began to talk, but it was impossible to make out what they were saying. All of them talked over each other. The voices echoed and bounced off the walls in a cacophony of noise.

"Can. You. Understand?" Marcus mouthed.

"No!" she mouthed back.

"Be quiet!" she shouted over the noise. The mouths kept chattering, screeching and howling words she couldn't make out.

Retreating from the assault of voices, they backed to the side of the room with the ears. The noise was still intolerable, but at least they could hear each other if they shouted.

"What are they saying?" Marcus yelled.

"I have no idea!" If she concentrated, she could make out a word here or there, but not enough to understand even a sentence. The noise sounded like a riot in a forest. Something brushed up against her arm. What looked like the ear of a mouse or some other small rodent quivered. All the ears seemed to be reacting to the noise in one way or another.

"Stay here!" she shouted.

Marcus nodded.

Dropping to the floor, where the sound didn't seem quite as bad, she found a fur-covered muzzle and crawled up next to it. She placed her ear as close to the lips as she could, trying to concentrate on its words. It was hard to make anything out, but the mouth seemed to be repeating something over and over. She tried to block out all the other noise and focus just on this one, deep voice.

"What . . . floats."

She got that much.

"What . . . floats . . . in . . . the . . . hair . . ."

Hair?

She tried again. "What floats in the . . . air." Not *hair. Air.*

Little by little, she got the entire message. "What floats in the air, burrows in the ground, wears away mountains, and creates life wherever it goes?"

It was a question. A riddle? She hurried back to Marcus and repeated the riddle. It took her several tries, but at last he seemed to understand.

"What floats, burrows, wears things down, and creates life," he repeated, his brow furrowed. "Water!" he shouted. Beside him a pointy ear glowed briefly for a moment.

Kyja looked back at the muzzle. It had stopped talking. "It's another puzzle!" she shouted, pointing at the silent mouth.

Marcus nodded. "Do we have to do all of them?"

She shrugged and motioned for him to stay by the ears while she listened to the mouths.

For the next hour they listened and called out answers. Some of the riddles were hard, while others were absurdly simple. But one by one, they answered them all. At first Kyja focused on listening while Marcus came up with the answers. Later they switched places. Early on, it was almost impossible to make out what was being said, and they had to yell directly into each other's ears. But as more of the mouths quieted, the task became easier.

At last they answered the final riddle from the last mouth—which looked like a bullfrog—and it closed with a wet-sounding *plop*.

"Whew!" Kyja sighed. "My ears are going to ring for a week."

"I know what you mean," Marcus said, dropping to the floor. "I feel like I can still hear all the voices shouting in my head."

"You have done well," the mouths spoke together. "Before you can truly hear, you must learn to listen."

"We hear you," Marcus said.

"Then listen well and remember."

Kyja stiffened. Would this be another situation where she wished she'd never come?

"Three will join you," pronounced a crystal bill. "One will reveal his true nature. One will cross far distances. One will break the bands of death itself."

"Betrayal will find you," spoke a tusked jaw.

"A key will provide great power and great danger," growled a furry muzzle.

"One of you has family seeking you," spoke a high-pitched feminine voice. Marcus and Kyja looked to each other wide-eyed.

"Dreams will speak to you," chirped a tiny beak. "But listen carefully, or be deceived."

"One of you is a thief," grunted the alligator mouth. "One of you is a liar."

"Old enemies-s-s will return," hissed what looked like a dragon.

"That is all," the mouths said as one. "You may now ask your question."

Kyja took a deep breath. She didn't understand most of what she'd just heard. What if the answer to their question was just as confusing?

"Go ahead," Marcus whispered.

Kyja swallowed. "Where can we find a land elemental?"

For a moment all of the mouths were silent. Then they spoke in unison. "You will never find a single land elemental."

A DARK PAST

Terra ne Staric

Dinslith turned on Dolan, his hands bunching the zentan's robe in anger. "Why have you locked up my master wizard?" he shouted. "You told me he was dead! You lied to me." He yanked the man toward him.

A sharp cracking sound split the air, and the high lord was thrown across the hallway in a flash of blinding blue sparks. The fingers he'd been holding the zentan with burned as though he'd just pulled them from a roaring fire.

"Do not lay hands on a *Keeper of the Balance!*" Dolan roared, rising to his full height so he looked down on the high lord. "Do not trifle with powers beyond you, or you may soon find the Balance no longer swings in your favor."

Dinslith gingerly touched his burned hands together. His protections as high lord should have blocked any damaging spells aimed at him within Terra ne Staric.

Exactly *what* he had allowed to enter the gates of his city?

Master Therapass let his eyes roam the round room beyond the bars of his cell as though seeing something no one else could. "When the Ishkabiddle invites the viper to dine, the Ishkabiddle must first understand what—or who—the main course will be."

Zentan Dolan's face tightened for a moment. Then he clasped his hands, bowed his head humbly, and released a deep sigh. When he looked up at Dinslith, his eyes were again calm. "I apologize, your Lordship. I'm afraid my temper got the best of me. I should have told you of the prisoner's capture. I was afraid you might interfere based on your friendship. But I did not lie. The man you knew as a trustworthy instructor and faithful advisor *is* dead. The pitiful creature in that cage has turned against you."

"Therapass against me?" The high lord wiped a palm across his damp forehead. He looked to the wizard. "Is this true?"

Master Therapass moved close enough to the bars of his cell for his face to emerge from the shadows. High Lord Dinslith sucked in a mouthful of air at the sight of his old friend's face. A ragged scar ran from just above the wizard's right eyebrow, across his forehead, and disappeared under his shaggy gray hair by his left temple. His cheeks had a sunken, hungry look to them, like Rashden's. But the old wizard's eyes flashed in the light of the flickering torch.

"Have I turned against you?" He tugged on the tip of his beard. "I am against any person or organization that sees fit to place one group of people below another. I am against anyone who believes it is their duty to redistribute power from the low-born to the high-born. I stand firmly against that creature claiming to advise you. But no, I am not against *you,* High Lord."

Dinslith looked from the wizard to the zentan. He felt trapped between two dangerous forces, and his head still buzzed from the force of the shock he'd received from the zentan. The wizard had been a friend and defender to the city all his life.

"You speak of betrayal," he said, eyeing the white-robed zentan. "Yet, I have heard no proof. If you feel Master Therapass is guilty of crimes against the tower, we will arrange a trial. Until then, I want him freed at once."

"That is not wise." Zentan Dolan's voice was soft but carried an icy edge to it that made the high lord uncomfortable. "Your— *wizard*—has not been honest with you. He has personally upset the balance of Farworld. Has he told you that thirteen years ago, he found the child destined to save our world? Has he told you how he sent that boy to another world called Earth, and then took a girl from that world, upsetting the balance of magic in both worlds and opening the way for the rebirth of the Dark Circle?"

He laughed at the shocked look on Dinslith's face. "Ask him to deny it."

Dinslith turned to Master Therapass. "Is this true?"

The wizard nodded. "I saved the boy from certain death at the hands of Thrathkin S'Bae and an army of Fallen Ones. I watched my best friend Tankum fall while protecting the boy from the Dark Circle. Sending the babe to Earth was the only way to preserve his life."

"But why didn't you tell me?" Dinslith asked, stunned that such important information should have been kept from him.

"Until I understood the situation more completely, it was far too dangerous to both the children and to Farworld to reveal their secret. I hoped the Dark Circle thought they were both dead. If word had gotten out that they were alive, it would have put them in extreme peril."

"So the old man says," the zentan snarled. "Yet for years, he withheld information vital to the well-being of Farworld and conveniently removed the only real threat to the Dark Circle."

High Lord Dinslith rubbed his pounding forehead with the tips of his fingers. He found it hard to think here in the dark and cold. It was almost as though the dank walls sucked away his concentration.

The zentan leaned close to the high lord. "If he speaks the truth, have him prove it. Have him bring the boy and the girl here so you may question them personally."

Dinslith nodded to Therapass. "If I free you, you must return the children to us at once. The fate of worlds is not something that rests upon the shoulders of one man."

Therapass's shoulders slumped as he gave a low sigh. "I cannot do that without putting them in extreme danger, High Lord. Even as we speak, they are pursued by the forces of the Dark Circle. If Kyja hadn't escaped Terra ne Staric when she did, she would have died at the hands of the Thrathkin S'Bae along with the rest of the Goodnuffs."

"Kyja?" the high lord asked. "The girl with no magic? What does she have to do with this?"

"Ask him where she is," Zentan Dolan said, his eyes glittering. "And why he will not produce the boy."

Therapass glared at the zentan then turned to Dinslith. "High Lord, you must trust me. Knowingly or unknowingly, the Keepers are serving the Dark Circle. Do you think it any coincidence that he arrived here the same day as the Thrathkin S'Bae? I dare not say anything more without forfeiting what little safety the children have. But if you set me free, I can help them."

"Help them?" Dolan sneered. "Or destroy them once and for all? You speak of fighting against the power of the Dark Circle. You accuse me of serving them. And yet it is you who cannot be trusted. Don't you think it's time you tell the high lord about your true bond with the Master of Lies?"

Dinslith looked from the wizard to the zentan, clearly confused. "What is he talking about?" he asked his old friend.

The wizard refused to look away from Dinslith's gaze, but in the light of the flickering torches, the high lord thought he saw something like pain cross the old man's eyes. Master Therapass ran a tongue across his cracked lips. "I have made mistakes in the past. And I have learned from those mistakes."

Grinning in victory, the zentan took the high lord's arm in his. "Your so-called *master wizard* claims to oppose darkness. He claims to have battled to save the child's life. But it is a lie. He tried to kill the child himself, and when that failed, he sent him as far away as possible, hoping no one would find the boy until it was too late. He says he fights against the Thrathkin S'Bae, but that is a lie as well. He is, in fact a dark wizard himself. He trained with the Dark Circle."

Dinslith felt as if he'd been slapped across the face. He turned a desperate gaze on the wizard whom he'd loved like a father. Could such a story be true?

"Did you . . ." He swallowed—a dry click sounding in his suddenly parched throat. "Did you do what he says?"

"I did everything I could to save Marcus. I would have gladly joined Tankum in giving my life, if it would have helped," the wizard said, his voice filled with pain, his eyes wet. "And yes, I once turned to the power of dark magic. It was a mistake I will regret to the end of my life. But I am not a dark wizard. I do not serve the Dark Circle. I have *never,* nor would I ever, do anything to put Farworld or this city in danger."

"Lies!" The zentan shouted. "You speak of equality, but you are the most power-hungry wizard of all. It was your thirst for power that drove you to the side of black magic. Your pride convinced you that you could harness that power without becoming corrupted. You show your dark side every time you turn into a wolf. Beast transformation is what allows the Thrathkin S'Bae to assume their snake form. Only through the corrupt magic of the Dark Circle is such a transformation possible."

The zentan pointed a thin, white finger at the wizard. "He has betrayed you, High Lord. Not only did he remove the girl from the city, but he also returned to steal something of great power from *you*. Allow me to use whatever means necessary to question him, and I will obtain the item."

High Lord Dinslith felt sick. His stomach burned, and his brains felt as though they were being sucked from his ears. "What is this item?" he asked dully.

For a moment the zentan didn't answer. Then he shook his head. "I don't know."

Dinslith turned to Therapass. "Give me some reason to believe you. If you have taken something from the tower, admit your crime and plead for the leniency of the court."

"I cannot," the wizard whispered. "I am sorry." He dropped his eyes. "Perhaps if I had a . . . a drink of water? My throat is parched."

The high lord waved his hand, and called out, "Guard!"

The zentan stepped forward. "Allow me." At the touch of his hand, the iron door swung open. Upon entering the room, he scooped a ladle of water from a dark wooden bucket. As Dinslith watched him cross the circular room to the cell, he thought for just a moment that something shimmered in the murky gloom. When he blinked, it was gone.

The zentan approached the cell cautiously and held the dipper to the bars. As the wizard's fingers closed around it, the zentan jerked the water away, spilling a small puddle onto the dusty stone floor. Dolan's lips curved in a mocking grin. "Not so fast. First tell me about the item you took. What does it look like? Is it a book? A charm?"

The wizard raised a bushy gray eyebrow. "I do not know whether you are a fool, a puppet, or both. But the fact that your master doesn't even know what he is looking for should concern you. Perhaps you should reconsider who you side with."

With a growl of rage, the zentan threw the ladle to the floor, sending the water splashing out of reach. "You fool!" he screeched. "You will tell me everything. And when you have nothing more to tell, you will pray that you did. But you will never leave this cell. Never!"

The zentan waved his hand, and this time High Lord Dinslith was sure he saw something shimmer in the air. Instantly the wizard fell to the ground, his body writhing in pain. A wet, smacking sound echoed through the small chamber.

"Come, my lord," the zentan said, closing the door, and pulling Dinslith back toward the stairs. "This is not something you need to witness."

The high lord nodded. For a moment he'd felt as if his stomach was turning inside out—as though some unseen beast was trying to lap up his very essence. But as they moved away from the room, the feeling dissipated.

"We have other matters to attend to," the zentan said. "At this very moment, a group of villagers are plotting your overthrow."

"Yes?" High Lord Dinslith nodded. If Therapass was a traitor, perhaps he didn't know his people as well as he thought. Perhaps he had been too lenient with them.

Caught up in their conversation, neither of the men noticed the way the wizard's eyes followed them as they walked down the hallway—the way he relaxed a little once they weren't looking, his pain not *quite* as intense as it had appeared a moment before. Or the way his hand went to the puddle, his fingers pressing against the damp floor and turning to let a few precious drops of water fall onto the petals of a tiny purple flower growing in the back corner of his cell.

PART 3

Return

CHAPTER 36

DUAL PURPOSE

"IT HAS TO BE A LIE," Marcus said as Kyja helped him up the stairs, pausing every few steps to let him catch his breath. "They can't all . . . be . . . gone."

Kyja was too devastated for words. She'd worked too hard, given too much, to have it be for nothing. Mr. Z had known what they were after. How could he have let them continue? Then again, he *had* tried to stop her. He'd given her the chance to have almost everything she wanted—her magic, Marcus's health, money—and she'd turned it all down for what now seemed to be no reason.

"Give me . . . just . . . a minute." Marcus said, leaning against the wall at the top of the stairs. Sweat soaked his hair and dripped down his face. His arms and legs shook constantly. He looked like he'd lost twenty pounds over the last forty-eight hours. How long had it been since either of them ate? She realized she had no idea how much time had passed since they started the quest for the Augur

Well. It felt like a week at least, but it couldn't have been more than a day.

"Any ideas?" Marcus asked.

Kyja shook her head. She didn't trust herself to speak, afraid she'd burst into tears if she did. She wanted to tell him what she'd done in the last test, how she'd thrown everything away, but she couldn't bear to.

Marcus pushed himself upright. "I say we go back to the tree and just start throwing those gold books everywhere. If we make a big enough mess, we've got to get someone's attention."

Something between a giggle and a cry forced its way out of her mouth. The idea of yanking every book from the stupid land elementals' tree and throwing them all into a big pile on the floor was so appealing she thought she must be going a little loopy. She giggled again then, without any warning, burst into tears.

"Hey, stop that," Marcus said. She felt his too-hot arm go around her shoulder and buried her face in his chest. "It's okay, we'll figure something out."

"It's not okay," Kyja sobbed. "I ru-ruined everything." Her face still buried in his chest, unable to face him, she told about the offer Mr. Z had made if she'd quit the test. When she got to the part where she'd turned it all down, she could barely get the words out through her sobs. "I . . . t-told h-him . . . I'd t-take my . . . ch-ch-chance-sss," she bawled.

For a moment Marcus was totally silent. Then he burst into tears too, his body shaking as badly as hers. Except he wasn't crying. He was *laughing*—laughing so hard that he bent over, clutching his stomach. Tears streamed from his eyes, but they were tears of mirth, not sadness.

"What's so funny?" she asked, wiping her nose with the back of her hand.

"That is *so* awesome," he said through a huge grin. It was the happiest she'd seen him in days. "That's exactly what I would have said if I was there. I mean, I was there. But, you know, if I'd been awake."

"You would have?" she sniffed.

"Heck, yeah. The little puke thought we'd give up for a one-way ticket and a measly rock? I hope you told him where he could stick his rock."

"But it turned out to be for nothing."

"No, it didn't," he said, wiping her tears away with his fingers. "It got us to the Augur Well."

"Which told us we'll never find a land elemental."

"So now we know. I'd rather find out early then search for the rest of the elementals, only to discover we could never complete the set."

Kyja hadn't considered that. "What about the drift?"

"We'll just have to find another way to make it." Marcus set his jaw. "You showed that we aren't quitters. I'm really . . . proud of you." He leaned quickly forward and Kyja felt his lips brush her cheek.

Was that a kiss? His face was burning up, but she felt shivers all the way to her toes.

"Let's, uh, get back to Land Keep," he said.

"Right," she agreed wondering if the red in his cheeks was all fever—and if she might be running a fever herself. Her face felt as hot as his.

They stepped through the door, and neither was surprised to

find they were back in Land Keep outside the door with the ear and the mouth scratched into it.

What looked like a bullet of blue soared out of the air and landed on Kyja's shoulder. "Where have you been?" Riph Raph cried. "I was scared to death. I thought . . . hey, why are you crying? And why is your face all red?" He looked Marcus up and down. "What ran over you? I've seen fish that looked better than that—after I ate them."

"Good to see you, too," Marcus sighed, knuckling him just behind his ears.

"You haven't seen the bag with the food in it, have you?" Kyja asked.

"Sure. It's right over there." Riph Raph waggled his ears and ducked his head. "I might have had a little taste while you were gone. Just to make sure nothing went bad."

Kyja attacked the combination of Earth and Farworld food as if she'd just returned from a hundred mile hike. Marcus slowly picked at his—nibbling a little here and a little there, but not actually eating much of anything.

"You have to eat," Kyja said. "You have to keep up your energy so we can get you out of here."

"I'm trying. I just don't have much appetite." He peeled the plastic off a cheese stick, took two bites, drank a few swallows of water, and lay on the floor to rest.

"What happened in there?" Riph Raph asked, gnawing on a piece of dried meat. "One minute I was on your shoulder, and the next, it felt like something swatted me into the air."

"We just had a couple of tests," Kyja said. "And we met a weird little man in a room full of books."

Riph Raph snorted and looked at Marcus, who was snoring softly. "Why did you take him instead of me?"

"I didn't," Kyja said. That still bothered her. Why didn't she go alone? It didn't seem like an accident. Not that Marcus wasn't helpful. In fact without him, she never would have made it to the Augur Well. How would she have reached the gem of knowledge if he hadn't been there to pull the rope? She never would have had the time to find both the fairy's heart and song by herself.

Looking back on their journey, it almost seemed as if both of the first two tests had been designed specifically around the strengths and weaknesses of her and Marcus. Mr. Z had mentioned her stubbornness and Marcus's tendency to take chances. And it was both because of and despite those weaknesses that they'd solved the raft puzzle.

What if her being forced to take chances and face one of her greatest fears while looking for the fairy's heart was intentional? What if she was supposed to learn from Marcus's strengths while he learned from hers as he searched for the song? Could it be they were intentionally sent too late to keep the tribrac from killing the fairy?

Even the third test required one of them to sacrifice for the good of the other. Could she have raised the courage to give up her magic if Marcus hadn't been there and in danger? But why design a test that could only be completed if . . .

Her mouth dropped open as the pieces of the puzzle came together in one bright flash of understanding.

"Wake up!" she shouted, shaking Marcus's shoulder.

Marcus opened his eyes. "What's wrong?"

"Nothing's wrong. In fact, everything is absolutely wonderful! Knowledge illuminator!" she shouted. "Where are you?"

The glittering cloud floated down from the tree. "I am a knowledge illuminator. What information may I—"

"Take us to the doors of eternity," Kyja called, cutting her off.

Marcus pushed himself up to his elbow as the floor began moving them toward the upward spiraling ramp of the tree. It seemed to take all his strength, but if she was right, she knew he wouldn't need to hold on much longer.

"I think I know how to find the land elementals," she said, bouncing on her toes with excitement.

"But the Augur Well said we never would."

"No," she said as they neared the first branches. "That's what we *thought* it said. But Mr. Z warned me. He gave me a hint, even though I didn't know it was a hint at the time. He said that even oracles can get things wrong sometimes, or that maybe we just misinterpret what we hear. The Augur Well wasn't wrong. At least not about that. It answered exactly what we asked. But we asked the wrong question."

Marcus pressed a hand to his forehead. "Maybe it's just because I'm sick. But I still don't get it."

Kyja looked for the top of the tree, eager to reach it so she could test her theory. It had to be right; there was no other explanation, and yet her stomach was a bundle of bouncing balls. "We asked the Augur Well where we could find *a* land elemental. It said we would never find *a single* land elemental. What we *heard* was that there were no land elementals. But that's not what it said."

Marcus wore a look of incomprehension.

"Think about it. Why did you and I get pulled into the tests together? Why wasn't Mr. Z surprised that both of us were there? Why did the tests require two of us to work together and learn from each other? Why did we have to get past our own weaknesses and draw on the strengths of each other?"

"Because there were supposed to be two of us?"

"Exactly!" Kyja said. They were almost to the top of the tree now. The black inverted pyramid was in sight. "When the Augur Well said we would never find a *single* land elemental, it wasn't saying there were *no* land elementals, just that there we'd never find *one* by itself. They come in pairs. They're a team. That's why the tests required two of us."

Marcus slowly grinned. "Okay. I get it. Two. That makes sense. But what does that have to do with the door of eternity?"

"Not the door of eternity," Kyja said, her heart pounding. "The *doors* of eternity. When we saw them we thought it was one door with two sides—one silver, one black. We went through one side and then through the other. We didn't realize there is no such thing as *a* land elemental. Only *land elementals,* plural. There was one thing we never tried with the door."

Marcus's eyes lit up. "We didn't try opening both sides at the same time!"

CHAPTER 37

LANCTRUS-DARNOC

"YOU'RE SURE THIS WILL WORK?" Marcus asked from the silver side of the door.

"No, but I hope so," Kyja's voice answered from the black side. "Because if it doesn't, I'm out of ideas."

Marcus gripped the knob, its metal surface sweaty beneath his fingertips. "What's the . . ."

"Plan?" Kyja laughed. "I count to three, and we both pull. After that—*if* something happens—we'll make it up as we go."

"I like it." Marcus dried a hand on his robe and took the knob again. "Ready when you are."

"One . . ." Kyja counted, "two . . . *three!*"

Marcus pulled. Half of him expected to feel Kyja tug at the same time. When he didn't, he stumbled and nearly fell over backward. Only his grip on the knob saved him.

"Come on in!" Kyja called. Her voice no longer seemed to come from the other side of the door. It sounded far away, like an echo.

Marcus stepped through the doorway. A sharp sense of vertigo hit him, as if he'd looked down into a well, only to see clouds floating across a blue sky. He was in what looked like a large silver bowl, standing at the base of a black pyramid. At the top of the pyramid, two circles were joined at ninety-degree angles. Above that, a pair of silver ramps wound upward, with branch-like walkways and gold leaves.

"We're standing on the ceiling of Land Keep, aren't we?" he asked, gripping his staff tightly with both hands. He'd never been scared of heights in his life. But looking up—down—at the top of a tree he knew to be hundreds of feet tall terrified him. Finally he understood how Kyja viewed heights.

"Either that, or the ceiling was really the floor all along." Kyja walked around the corner of the polished black pyramid with apparently no fear at all. Riph Raph, however, seemed to share some of Marcus's concern. He clung tightly to Kyja's shoulder, silently eyeing the immense tree above them.

Marcus found he did better if he didn't look up. Instead, he studied the pyramid. "Do you see any kind of entrance?"

"Not from over here," Kyja said.

Somehow Marcus didn't think knocking would be the way to go this time. But what were they supposed to do now? Fortunately, he didn't have long to ponder. A glittering, golden cloud floated down from the tree branches.

"You knew about this all along?" Kyja asked.

The cloud flashed. "I'm sorry; the information was not accessible."

"But it is now," Marcus said.

"What information may I help you locate?" asked the tinkling voice.

"We would like to speak to a—I mean *the*—land elementals,"

"They are listening," the cloud said.

Marcus gulped. He looked at the tall black pyramid. Was that where they were? "H-hello," he stammered.

"Only land elementals are allowed through the doors of eternity," a deep voice thundered from the general direction of the pyramid. "How did you get here?"

"We reached the Augur Well," Kyja said.

"Humans may not seek the Augur Well!"

"*We* did." Marcus wiped a hand across his hot forehead. "We passed all the tests and Mr. Z gave us the key. Doesn't that at least make us *honorary* land elementals?"

The pyramid was silent for a moment, as though considering this information. When it spoke again, it sounded a little less hostile. "We must consider this. What do you call yourselves?"

"I'm Kyja," Kyja said with a curtsy.

Marcus gave an awkward bow. "And I'm Marcus."

"Why do you seek us?"

Kyja motioned for Marcus to lift the sleeve of his robe. Feeling the awkward embarrassment he always had when showing the mark, he revealed the brand on his arm to the pyramid. Ridges of scar tissue he'd had as long as he could remember formed the image of two creatures doing battle inside an elaborately designed circle.

One of the creatures was part snake, part dragon—with a long, serpent body, a mouthful of wicked teeth, great wings, and sharp talons. It was locked in combat with a creature with the head of a boar, the tail of a fish, and the body of a bird with feathered wings. Two pairs of horns sprouted from the bird-boar-fish's head, and a pair of human arms held a flaming sword in the air. The serpent's talons locked on the front of the bird's throat, while the tusks of the boar were closed on the snake's writhing body. According to Master Therapass, this symbol marked Marcus as the person who would either save or doom Farworld.

Kyja explained. "He was sent to Earth to keep from being killed by the Dark Circle. I was sent to Farworld in his place. The only way we can return to our own worlds is to open a drift."

"A drift would require the cooperation of elementals of land, air, water and fire," said the voice. "Such a thing has never been done."

"That's why we're here," Marcus said, figuring he might as well get to the point. "We need one—or, I guess, two—land elementals to help us."

"We already have the assistance of a water elemental," Kyja added.

"Oh, and you might want to do something about your harbingers," Marcus said. "The Dark Circle turned them into monsters, filled the entrance to Land Keep with mud, and blockaded the exit tunnel. There are a thousand or so people stuck just outside the doors to the library right now."

The pyramid thundered. "Is this true?"

"Yes," tinkled the knowledge illuminator.

"It has been long since land elementals left Land Keep," rumbled the pyramid.

"Over three thousand years," Marcus added.

"Perhaps it is time to examine the world firsthand again."

Through bleary eyes, Marcus watched a layer of shiny, black material peel itself from the pyramid. *A moth,* he thought as a pair of glossy, black wings rose into the air, flexed, and flew several feet away, landing gently on the edge of the silver bowl.

A pair of heads appeared between the wings of the "moth" and Marcus wondered if he was experiencing some sort of fever-induced dream. One head looked like a lion with a thick golden mane. The other was a ferocious-looking dragon with yellow eyes and shining black scales. The creature perched on a pair of heavily armored black legs as its paws clutched a silver scepter.

The lion-dragon flapped its wings and bright colors flowed over the shiny black of the pyramid. The colors weren't just the typical patterns of a butterfly's wings, but what looked like crags and valleys, trees and streams. Focusing became hard for Marcus—if he looked too long, he could lose himself in the landscape that changed each time the wings flapped.

"Come," roared the lion head.

"Forth," finished the dragon.

Another layer of the pyramid peeled itself off and flew across the bowl to land beside the dragon. It also had two heads—a hawk and a rabbit. A pair of talons jutted from its torso as it balanced on furry white feet.

Another layer peeled off and flew across the room, and another, and another, until the pyramid was completely gone and the entire rim of the silver bowl was filled with two-headed land elementals.

Were each of these a pair of creatures that sought out the Augur Well together? An image appeared in his mind of himself and Kyja attached together between a pair of color-changing wings. Maybe he wasn't quite so anxious to become an honorary land elemental after all.

The last elemental to form had the heads of a beautiful red fox and a boar with long, curving tusks and a ridge of black bristles above the thick shelf of its forehead.

It had red and white forepaws and stood on a pair of bristly, brown-hoofed feet.

"Showoffs," Riph Raph said. But Marcus noticed he said it quietly enough that none of the land elementals could hear.

"A council of Land Keep is called," roared the dragon and lion heads in unison.

"A council," repeated the other land elementals.

"Land Keep has been defiled. We must restore the library to its former status."

"Aye," called all the heads.

The dragon head nodded. "So be it."

"Kyja-Marcus seek our aid in opening a drift between Farworld and Earth," the lion said.

"The creation of a drift has never been attempted," said a wrinkled head that looked like a turtle except for its long curved beak.

"So we keep hearing," Marcus muttered. Kyja put her finger to her lips and scowled.

"We are knowledge gatherers," said the rabbit.

"And teachers," said the hawk.

"This-s-s drift is none of our concern," hissed a pair of heads that looked like great angry lizards. Their black eyes fixed on Marcus and Kyja.

"We do not know if opening a drift is possible. Even *our* knowledge of this is limited," said the fox and the boar. "If such a thing can be done, the knowledge gained would be most valuable."

The dragon and lion heads both nodded and turned to Marcus and Kyja. "You have reached the Augur Well, Kyja-Marcus. As such, you are granted honorary land elemental status, and with it comes certain rights and privileges. Who will volunteer to help them?"

"If this-s-s is-s-s to be, we will go," said the lizard heads.

"No," said the lion. "I do not wish you two to leave. Lanctrus-Darnoc, you are the youngest. Will you go?"

Marcus crossed the fingers on both hands. With curiosity, Kyja looked at what he was doing, shrugged, and crossed hers, too.

"We will," said the silky voice of the fox.

"Yes," grunted the boar, baring its long, upward-curving tusks in what Marcus hoped was a smile.

The dragon nodded slowly. "Very well. Lanctrus-Darnoc may join you for as long as they desire."

The lizard heads muttered something to themselves—their long tongues flicking in and out.

Kyja grinned at Marcus, eyes shining. He gave her a thumbs up. Somehow they'd managed to get both water *and* land elementals to join their cause. They were halfway there.

He should have been ecstatic. Instead, he felt exhausted. As the stress from the past few days lifted from his shoulders, he dropped to his knees. The room felt as if it was slowly rotating on an off-center axis.

"Lanctrus-Darnoc," rumbled the voice, "Return Land Keep to its previous state. Re-open the library. Join Marcus-Kyja for as long as you are needed."

The silver bowl gave one last spin, the creatures around it a blur of wings and faces. Marcus passed out.

CHAPTER 38

FRIENDS

WHEN KYJA WALKED OUT of the tunnel from Land Keep, struggling to drag Marcus beside her, no one in the cavern noticed. Working in the gardens, preparing food, none of the prisoners gave her a second glance. It wasn't until Lanctrus-Darnoc flew out behind her that people looked up in alarm.

"What is that thing?"

"It must have killed the boy!"

"Don't worry!" Kyja called out. "They're land elementals. They're here to help you."

Most of the people still fled the gardens, running back to the safety of the stone buildings.

"How could this happen?" said the land elementals, looking at pitiful plants struggling to grow, the cracked stone floor, the general grime.

"It's a travesty," said the fox half, which Kyja had learned was Lanctrus.

"Someone should be held accountable," said Darnoc.

The land elementals flapped their wings, which changed colors with each movement. The grime disappeared, returning the stone to a pristine white. The cracks in the rock repaired themselves. The brook, which had been small and silt-filled, now gushed clear and full. The gardens filled with a variety of plants, fruits, and grain.

"Look at the harbingers!" shouted a bent woman with short black hair. "They're changing."

"They're . . . they're beautiful!" cried the man beside her.

"They look like fairies," whispered a girl a few years older than Kyja. Tears ran down the girl's cheeks as she stared in wonder and amazement.

Kyja couldn't see them any more than she could earlier, but she imagined the clawed horrors turning into beautiful, winged helpers.

"Do we go back up the stairs?" Kyja asked the land elementals as she watched the people stare in wonder at what had happened to their prison. They pointed, laughed, and shook their heads in wonder.

"A gretak will clear the exit," Lanctrus-Darnoc said.

Kyja heard a scraping sound and turned to see what looked like a ten–foot-tall worm or caterpillar crawling across the stone floor. It headed straight for the collapsed tunnel and began chewing its way through the rock.

"You're back," a boy's voice said to Kyja.

She turned to see Jaklah and another man staring at her, Marcus, and the land elementals.

"We are," Kyja said. "And now you're all getting out of here. This place is going back to being the library it was made to be instead of a prison."

"Is that a . . ."

"They're land elementals," Kyja said. "Jaklah, this is Lanctrus-Darnoc."

"G-good to meet you," the boy said, clearly trying to master his fear.

"Could you help me carry Marcus?" she asked.

"Of course." Together, Jaklah and the man he was with lifted Marcus's unconscious body, which could not have weighed much at all.

"He's sick," the man said, touching Marcus's forehead. "Would you like me to see if I can help him?"

"No," Kyja said. "Once he gets out of here, I can take him to a place where he'll get better."

The three of them started up the tunnel the gretak had carved out. A few people peered into the opening, and several followed cautiously as the land elementals continued their work repairing the cavern.

After a long but gentle climb, Kyja stepped from the tunnel, blinking at the bright light. It felt good to have the warmth of real sun on her shoulders. She looked around and thought they were somewhere on the edge of the swamp. Thick groves of moss-covered trees and bushes grew in puddles of stagnant water, but the smell of decaying plants was overpowered by the sharp, salty aroma of the sea.

Behind her, Jaklah and the man carried Marcus out and stood in the sun, blinking. Many more streamed out behind them. Several of the oldest looked around fearfully, as though the idea of so much open space was too much to handle after all their years of captivity. Kyja looked for the gretak, but the giant worm had either burrowed back underground or disappeared into the trees.

"What about the Keepers?" Jaklah asked, lowering Marcus's unconscious body to a dry patch of grass.

"They don't know you're free," Kyja said. "By the time they find out, you should be far away."

"You are mistaken," said a silky voice.

Kyja spun around to see a man in a silver robe, sitting astride a white horse. She instantly recognized him as the Keeper who'd attacked her.

With a sneer, he eyed the group standing just outside the cave entrance. Eight men in crimson rode out of the trees to join their leader. "An unexpected pleasure. I was told I might find the boy and girl here. But to find so many of you just waiting to be scaled is a treat indeed."

"Go down!" called the people at the front of the crowd, trying to push their way back into the tunnel.

"Leave them alone," Kyja cried.

The Keeper smiled as he reached for the silver coil at his side. "Call out the snifflers," he said to his men, then nodded at Kyja. "I'll deal with this one myself."

"Just try it," Riph Raph snarled from his spot on her shoulder.

The man on the leader's right raised a black, crescent-shaped horn to his mouth. Before he could blow it, an arrow flew from the trees, knocking it from his hand. Another arrow pierced his chest, and he fell from his horse. Before Kyja even knew what was happening, two more men dropped to the ground. Each had an arrow shaft sticking out of his body.

"Shield yourselves!" the Keeper shouted. Instantly, glowing blue clouds surrounded them.

A man stepped out of the trees—the arrow in his bow aimed at the leader's chest. A quiver filled with many more arrows was strapped to his back. Kyja almost didn't recognize the archer. The last time she'd seen him, he'd been nothing but skin and bones. Now he looked strong and healthy.

"Rhaidnan!" Kyja shouted, with unexpected joy. "What . . . ? How . . . ?" The last time she'd seen him was before she and Marcus entered Water Keep, after they escaped from the unmakers' cavern. He'd flown home to his wife and children on the back of Zhethar, the frost pinnois.

"You rescued me from the unmakers." He smiled without taking his eyes off the Keepers. "You didn't think I'd rest until I returned the favor, did you?"

"You have made a grave mistake," the Keeper in the silver robe said, eyes tight with fury. "The penalty for attacking a Keeper is a very slow and painful death."

"I've been threatened with worse," Rhaidnan said. From the trees and grass around him, another ten men appeared, each with drawn bows. Kyja recognized most of them—they were from Terra ne Staric. One was Breslek Broomhead, her next-door neighbor from when she'd lived with the Goodnuffs. Flickers of red light danced around the tips of the men's arrows. Caught between the archers and the Keepers, the prisoners from tunnels pressed against one another like a flock of frightened sheep.

The leader laughed. "You think your arrows are a match against us?" His remaining five horsemen rode up to his side.

"They won't be alone," said a voice from behind them. Screech shambled out of the woods holding a wand that looked as if it had been clumsily mended.

The Keeper's eyes widened. "What are *you* doing here? You should be with the unmakers."

"That is done," Screech said.

Kyja looked from the cave trulloch to the man in the silver robe. How did they know each other?

"No matter," said the Keeper. "All of your magic combined is not enough to stop us. You will be just one more dead body left to rot."

"Is your magic stronger than ours?" a voice asked, one Kyja recognized at once. Figures of water took shape one by one, rising out of the murky water on one side of the woods, and at their head stood a man with spiky white hair and wearing a blue robe.

"Cascade!" Kyja grinned.

"Or ours?" At the mouth of the tunnel, people moved aside for a large figure emerging. It rose into the air, wings slowly beating. The boar head grunted, baring wicked tusks. The fox head seemed to grin.

"And don't forget about me," Riph Raph said. "I am flying death."

"What is this?" the leader growled, looking around at the gathering group. His horse pawed anxiously at the ground.

"Let me introduce you to my friends," Kyja said with a smile. She pointed to Rhaidnan and his fellow archers. "These are some of the best hunters from Terra ne Staric, the greatest city in all of Westland. And this is Screech, a cave trulloch who managed to escape a mountain full of unmakers and follow me all the way here. Cascade is a water elemental. And Lanctrus-Darnoc are land elementals. I think they want to talk to you about what you've been doing with their home."

"And me," Riph Raph piped up.

"*Elementals?*" the Keeper said, his eyes going from Cascade to Lanctrus-Darnoc. "That's impossible."

"No, it isn't," Kyja said. "But it's more difficult than you might think." She glared at the leader and his followers. "You and your creatures are disgusting. Nothing gives you the right to take away people's magic. Nothing!"

"Considering the circumstances," said the fox part of Lanctrus-Darnoc, "it might be wise for you to notify all Keepers of the Balance that their services are no longer required in these parts."

"Doing so might keep you alive," agreed the boar.

"I'll count to ten," said Rhaidnan. He raised his bow.

"One," Riph Raph called, snapping his tail. "Two."

Before he reached three, the Keepers were gone.

CHAPTER 39

GOING BACK

ONCE THINGS HAD QUIETED DOWN, Kyja asked Rhaidnan, "What are you doing here?" She sat on the grass, cradling Marcus's head in her lap. She had to get back to Earth soon, but first she needed to understand what was happening in Terra ne Staric.

The hunter squatted nearby. A few of the people from Land Keep had returned to the safety of the cavern, but most had followed a nearby road leading to Aster's Bay and points beyond. The rest of Rhaidnan's archers were scouting to make sure the Keepers were really gone.

"I'm afraid I have bad news," the hunter said. He looked carefully around as though afraid someone might overhear. "Terra ne Staric has been taken over by the Keepers."

"No!" Kyja thought she'd seen the last of the Keepers of the Balance. "How is that possible? Why didn't the guards stop them? Why don't High Lord Dinslith and the Masters do something?"

Rhaidnan ran a palm across his stubbly chin. "I'm afraid most of them have joined the Keepers. Zentan Dolan, head of the Keepers, arrived right about the time you left. Somehow he managed to convince High Lord Dinslith that most of the city was plotting to overthrow him. The other Master Wizards are either siding with Dinslith or rotting in prison. A few of us think Dolan is working directly with the Dark Circle."

"We have to do something," Kyja said.

"I'm not sure anything *can* be done . . ." He plucked a piece of grass from the ground and began to shred it.

"There's something else?" Kyja asked, sensing the hunter was delaying.

At last he nodded. "Master Therapass has been captured, locked in a separate cell of the tower prison. They say he took something from the tower right after you left—something the zentan wants. I spoke to a guard who believes the zentan is torturing Therapass with . . . with a pair of unmakers."

Kyja stared at Rhaidnan. Master Therapass in prison? Part of her was relieved he was alive at all, but another part of her remembered how Rhaidnan had looked after only a month of being used by unmakers. And Rhaidnan had been a healthy man in the prime of life at the time of his capture. Master Therapass was old. He couldn't take that kind of treatment for long.

"We have to go to him," she said. "Just let me get Marcus back to Earth until he recovers, then we'll ride back with you."

"No," the hunter said. "You can't go. That's the reason I'm here. The wizard was afraid you and Marcus would hear what had happened and try to rescue him. You can't do that; it's too dangerous. But he gave me a message for you. Therapass wants the two of you to stay as far away from Terra ne Staric as possible. It's the only way to keep you safe."

"He might be right," Riph Raph said.

"But what about *him?*" Kyja demanded.

Rhaidnan bowed his head. "All of the men who came looking for you have put their lives and the lives of their families in danger. We'll return to Terra ne Staric as quickly as we can. Hopefully no one will notice we've been gone. There are still some people loyal to Therapass—perhaps forty or fifty. We'll wait and watch. If a chance presents itself to fight Dolan, we'll take it. If not . . ." He shrugged. "We may have to take our families and go to the Border Lands."

Terra ne Staric abandoned? Master Therapass left to the Dark Circle and the unmakers? She couldn't allow that. Marcus wouldn't either. "How long will it take you to reach the city?"

Rhaidnan rubbed his lip. "We should be able to make it in three days—four at the most."

"Marcus and I will meet you outside the city at sunrise in four days," Kyja said. "Gather everyone who opposes the Keepers."

"Haven't you listened to anything I've said?" Rhaidnan shouted, driving an arrow from his quiver into the ground with his fist. "The *last* thing you must do is return to the city. If the Keepers discover you're there, they'll stop at nothing until you are captured or dead."

"Dead is bad," Riph Raph said waggling his ears. "And captured isn't much better."

"They're not counting on us having the help of Cascade and Lanctrus-Darnoc," Kyja said. "Maybe we can't free the city, but there's got to be a way to free Master Therapass."

"You think the elementals will help you?" Rhaidnan asked, nodding slowly.

"We can ask," Kyja said.

"Then there might be a way." Moving to a patch of dirt, the hunter drew a map with his arrow. "Trying to breach the tower itself is suicide. But an underground river runs directly under the west gates and passes within a few feet of the dungeon. If your friends could get us that far, we might be able to reach him."

"We'll find a way to get there," Kyja said.

The hunter put a hand on her shoulder. "Therapass was smart to send us to you."

"I owe him everything I have," Kyja said.

Rhaidnan stood. "We'll leave tonight. Meet us in four days where the Goodnuff house used to be. No one goes near the ruins."

It was a fitting place to return—a reminder of what the Dark Circle had done to her, and what they would continue to do if they weren't stopped. Letting Marcus rest for a moment, she called over Cascade and Lanctrus-Darnoc. The elementals gave each other a wide berth, eyeing one another with obvious suspicion.

Kyja explained about Master Therapass and what she wanted to do. "Will you help us?"

Lanctrus-Darnoc nodded both its heads, eyeing Cascade. "We are not warriors, but we may be able to help you reach the river. We make no promise what the water elemental will do."

"*If* the land elementals manage to reach the river without damming its flow with rocks and dirt," Cascade said, "I can help you reach the dungeon. But you will owe me a favor."

"Anything," Kyja said. "Can you meet us in four days outside Terra ne Staric?"

Both water and land elementals agreed they could, although they were clearly uncomfortable about working with each other. She explained where the Goodnuff farm had stood outside the western gates, and that they would meet at sunrise.

Marcus awoke to a cool hand on his burning face. "Wake up."

"Principal Teagarden?" he groaned. It felt like Chet and the rest of his gang had finally managed to push him down the stairs. Every bone and muscle ached, and his ears wouldn't stop ringing.

"No," said a girl's voice. "It's me."

He opened his eyes, and for a moment had no idea where he was. This wasn't the Philo T. Justice Boys School, and it certainly wasn't Arizona. Then he remembered. "Kyja?"

"Yes," she said, sounding relieved. "I'm pushing you back to Earth now. But I need you to be awake so you can pull Riph Raph and me with you. Do you understand?"

He tried to make sense of what she was saying, but it was so hard to concentrate. "Pull?"

"Yes." Kyja propped open his eyes with her fingers. His brain seemed to burst into flames.

"Ouch. That hurts."

"I'm sorry. But I need you awake. Can you hear me?" She poured a small trickle of water down his throat. It felt blessedly cool.

"I can hear you," he said. "We're going to jump. But do it quick. Don't know . . . how long . . . awake."

"Okay," Kyja said. "We're going now. One, two, three."

Something jerked at his stomach, and he knew he was going to be sick. He was falling. He wanted to close his eyes and fall forever, but he needed to remember something. What was it? *Pull.* He needed to pull. He didn't know what, but he reached out his arms and pulled anyway. Something caught, slipped for a moment, and finally caught again.

Then he was lying on the ground vomiting.

"I'll be back," a voice said from far away. "Just rest. You're going to be okay."

"A turtle," cried another voice. "How can I be a turtle?"

"Rest," Marcus murmured to himself. Rest sounded very, very good.

Sometime later, a burbling roar woke him. He jerked as a hand closed around his arm, sure that he was being attacked by a terrible beast.

"It's okay," Kyja's voice said. "Stop struggling. It's just me."

He opened his eyes. "Where are we?"

"On Earth," Kyja said. "I bought another bike from a guy who lives on a farm just down the road."

"Can't ride a bike," he muttered. He could barely keep his eyes open.

"You can ride this one." Kyja laughed, pulling him to his feet and practically carrying him out of the grove of trees where he'd been sleeping, to the edge of a narrow, country road. When he saw what she was pulling him toward, he tried to jerk away again.

"No. You can't ride that."

"Sure, I can," Kyja said. "The man who sold it showed me how." She led him around the side of an ancient-looking motorcycle and pushed him into the attached sidecar.

"You need . . . a license," he moaned, as she tucked a helmet over his head and strapped him in.

"Then just pretend it's a dream."

He tried to argue. But before he could, he was asleep again.

CHAPTER 40

THE DREAM

FOR MARCUS, THE NEXT THREE DAYS were a blur of movement, sleep, and occasionally waking up to eat or use a restroom.

For Kyja it was a time of wonderment and adventure—a time to discover her home world. No two meals were the same. She tried Chinese food (sweet and sour pork and wontons were her favorite), Mexican (where she scalded her mouth on a habanero pepper, drank a pitcher of water, then tried it again just to see if it was just as hot the second time around), barbeque (where she ate so many ribs she felt sick the rest of the day), and house specials ranging from jambalaya to meatloaf and gravy.

It took her a few hours—and a hundred-mile detour in Arkansas—to figure out how to read a map. But once she worked it out, she realized she would need to travel across Texas and New Mexico to get to Arizona. That's where Marcus was from, and she suspected it might be in the general area of Terra ne Staric for when they'd need to jump back to Farworld.

She stuck mostly to frontage roads and smaller highways after a biker group, who called themselves Steel de Muerte, explained her bike and hack were not built for freeway driving. The bikers were fascinated by her story of Farworld, and although she didn't think they believed she really came from another world, they made her an honorary club member and gave her a leather jacket. She promised to bring them all back robes if she was ever in the area again.

Every day was a learning experience. Some things she learned the easy way—like jumping rope with Dhala and Bethany, two friendly girls, outside a Whataburger in Abilene, Texas. Other things she learned the hard way—like nearly being flattened by a fast-moving semi before figuring out how stoplights worked. She saw everything from Earth that she could, from a group of men and women line dancing in Seminole, Texas, to a brief tour of the Carlsbad Caverns.

She constantly made sure Marcus got enough rest and ate well. It was good to see him gaining weight again, and by the second day, his fever was almost completely gone. She never forgot why she was going to Terra ne Staric or stopped worrying about Master Therapass. But that didn't keep her from absorbing every experience she could in a world that didn't shun you because you had no magic. And it didn't stop her from thinking about what the Augur Well had said—especially the part about one of their families looking for them.

After the first few minutes of watching Kyja drive the old motor-cycle, Riph Raph disappeared into the sidecar and spent most of his time hidden inside his turtle shell.

By the end of the third day, she and Marcus were camped out-side Lordsburg, New Mexico, a small town near the Arizona border.

Kyja sat beside a fire several hundred feet off the side of the road, while Marcus rested in a sleeping bag. The night sky was perfectly clear and filled with millions of stars, none of which glittered above Farworld. She wondered what it would be like to live under this sky all the time.

"How close are we?" Marcus asked.

"We'll be in Phoenix tomorrow." Kyja added a few more sticks to the fire. The sun had gone down, so the desert air had quickly developed a chill. "Are you hungry? I've got apples, half of a beef sandwich, and these really yummy black crackers with white cream between them called aureas."

"Oreos," Marcus corrected. "I'm fine. But I'd get rid of the sandwich. They go bad pretty quick in the heat."

"Bad?" Kyja asked, picturing the sandwich growing teeth and attacking people.

"It'll make you sick. There aren't any preservatives in a sub sandwich like there are in the cookies."

"I'll take an apple," Riph Raph said, poking his head out of his shell. "And an Oreo. And another Slim Jim if you have any left."

"Oink, oink." Marcus pushed up the tip of his nose.

Riph Raph blinked his leathery eyelids. "Try carrying your house around on your back. It's not as easy as it sounds. Besides, I haven't spent the whole trip sleeping like you."

"That's right. *You've* only slept nine-tenths of it," Kyja said, handing over the food. She studied Marcus in the fire's flickering illumination. "You know, I haven't heard you moaning in your sleep once since we got here."

Marcus looked silently back at her.

"If you don't want to talk about it, that's fine. I just thought you'd want to know that you only seem to have the nightmare in Farworld."

Marcus pulled the sleeping bag back up around his shoulders as he sat looking into the fire. "If we're going to Terra ne Staric, I guess it's time to talk about it. It's just—I don't understand it myself, and I guess I'm afraid of what it might mean."

Marcus pulled a small branch from the fire, drawing patterns in the night with the glowing end. "Did I ever tell you I used to dream about you—before we ever met?"

"Warn me before you start that kind of talk, so I can throw up," Riph Raph said, pulling his head back into his shell.

Kyja felt blood rush to her face and was grateful for the darkness. "You might have said something like that just after I pulled you to Farworld the first time. But I was so surprised by your being there, I don't think I paid much attention to what you said."

"Well, it's not like it sounds. It's just . . . I was so unhappy with my life. I had no family, no friends. I guess *you* can understand that. The rest of the kids in the schools I went to either felt sorry for me, were afraid of me, or wanted to beat me up. I think the ones who wanted to beat me up were the easiest to deal with. At least they said what they were thinking."

Kyja understood far too well.

"Anyway," he continued, poking the stick into the fire again, "whenever I got feeling really lonely or sad, I'd pretend there was a world I could go to. A world where no one cared what I looked like." He waved a hand out at the barren desert landscape. "I imagined a world different from all of this, where everything was green—where trees talked, and fish flew, and cows told jokes."

"Farworld," Kyja whispered.

Marcus nodded. "Farworld. Only I didn't know I was seeing a

real place. I thought it was all in my head. It's funny—I called it *Farworld* because it was as far away from my life as I could picture. But I've never asked why it's really named Farworld. What is it far from?"

"I don't know," Kyja said. "I've never really thought about it. Maybe we could ask Master Therapass if—I mean *when*—we free him."

"Well, that's the thing. I was pretty out of it there at the end. But according to Rhaidnan, Master Therapass is in the dungeon, right?"

"Yes, under the tower. It was never used much when I was there. But Rhaidnan says it's practically overflowing now." Kyja unzipped her sleeping bag and wrapped it around herself like a blanket. She didn't know whether it was the thought of her home being controlled by the Keepers of the Balance or the cold night air, but goose bumps covered her arms.

Marcus went on. "The last dream I had about Farworld—right before I met Bonesplinter for the first time—was about the tower," Marcus said, his voice so soft that Kyja had to lean forward to hear him. "I was standing on the balcony of the tower, listening to the dawn chimes singing, looking at a crystal-clear river."

Kyja had spent many hours standing on the tower balcony, looking down at the Two Prong River, wondering what she would do with her life.

"In the dream, everything was perfect. You were there watching it all with me, although I thought I was imagining you at the time. But then it all went wrong. Thick, dark clouds covered the sky. The flowers sank to the ground. Even the huge trees of the Westland Woods wrapped their branches around themselves as if they wished they could run away from whatever was on the tower." Marcus closed his eyes for a moment before going on.

"I turned to find you. But Bonesplinter was there instead. He was the one who'd caused the change. He lifted me up and threw me off the tower. Then I woke up and saw him right there in the school. It was the most terrifying dream I'd ever had."

A cold breeze whipped at the fire. In the distance, a coyote howled, and another answered. "Are you having that dream again?" Kyja asked.

"No, it's worse." Marcus shrank within his bag, almost disappearing inside it like a caterpillar enclosing itself in a dark blue cocoon. "I'm climbing the tower stairs, trying to reach something on the balcony. My legs ache, and I keep stumbling, but I know I'm going to be too late. I know someone else is looking for the same thing I am. They're ahead of me, and I have no chance to get there first.

"When I finally reach the balcony, the weather is clear. The flowers are singing. And I think, *maybe I'm not too late after all.* But as I step out onto the white stone tiles, it happens all over again. The flowers disappear. The trees cower away. The sky turns black, and rain begins to fall so hard I can barely see a thing. I turn around, knowing the person they fear is right behind me. He's been waiting all along."

"Who is it?" Kyja asked.

Marcus swallowed. "Me. It's *me* they're afraid of. When I turn around, I realize I'm the only one there. I'm dressed in a black cloak. Blue fire crackles across my staff. I've found whatever it is I'm looking for, and all of Farworld knows what I'm going to do with it. I'm not there to save the world—I'm there to destroy it. Somewhere in the distance I hear laughing. It's the Dark Circle. They know I'm about to do their work for them."

"That's crazy!" Kyja said. Her voice was far too loud in the quiet desert night, but she didn't care. *This* is what had been eating at him—what he'd been afraid to tell her. Had he really convinced himself that he was part of the Dark Circle's plan? "You'd never betray Farworld. It's just the Dark Circle trying to confuse you. Why would you believe that for a second?"

"It's not the Dark Circle," Marcus said, his voice muffled from inside his sleeping bag.

"Of course it is," Kyja said. "Who else would want you to think something like that?"

"There's something I've haven't told you," Marcus said. "Do you remember the morning we left Water Keep? When we listened to the dawn chimes?"

"I guess." She vaguely remembered pausing just before they got on the sailboat.

"At first I could only hear the song. But the more I concentrated, the more I could make out something else. Hidden deep within the chimes' song, it was as if I could hear another voice calling to me. I thought I recognized the voice. It sounded like . . . Master Therapass."

"Therapass?" Kyja sat up straight. "Master Therapass has been trying to contact us, and you never told me? How could you let me think . . . that he was dead?" After everything she'd done to help Marcus, why wouldn't he tell her that the person she loved most in the world was still alive? It felt like a betrayal.

Marcus stayed quiet so long, she thought he wasn't going to answer. When he finally did, the words sounded as if they were being pried painfully out of his throat one at a time. "At first I couldn't understand what Master Therapass was saying—or if it was really his voice at all. I didn't want to get your hopes up for no reason. Then, once I could understand . . ."

He sighed long and deep. "The reason I didn't tell you is the same reason I didn't tell you about the dream. Haven't you figured it out by now? Why I only have the nightmare when the dawn chimes sing? It's Therapass. He's the one—the one who's telling me I'm going to destroy Farworld."

CHAPTER 41

TANKUM HEARTSTRONG

MARCUS REFUSED TO TALK about his dream anymore that night, or even the next day—focusing instead on getting back to Farworld. It took them three tries before they'd located a place on Earth that jumped them to within walking distance of Terra ne Staric. He wasn't surprised at all to find the final spot was in the Southern Arizona desert—less than five miles from Saint Demetrius' Monastery where he'd been found as a baby.

"This is it," Kyja said after they'd walked about twenty minutes.

For a moment, as Marcus studied the knee-high grass, randomly scattered boulders, and lack of any buildings, he thought they'd stopped in the middle of an empty field. It wasn't until he looked carefully around that he noticed broken boards strewn among the weeds, shattered trees, and a deep crater that looked like a bomb had gone off.

Kyja led him to a partially collapsed stone wall—the only thing still standing. "This is where they lived. Mr. and Mrs. Goodnuff and . . ."—she swallowed—"and the baby, Timton."

Even Riph Raph seemed sad. Although he was probably just hungry again.

"Maybe we should go somewhere else," Marcus suggested, noting a farm not too far away.

"No." Kyja wiped a hand across her eyes. "I'm all right. It's just seeing it like this for the first time since I left. It brings back memories."

Crouching beside the ruined house, he looked up at the walls surrounding Terra ne Staric and beyond them, the tower. At the sight of the imposing white building, his heart began to pound. "Maybe I should stay here."

"Brawk, brawk," Riph Raph said, flapping his wings and strutting around the ground like a chicken.

Kyja studied Marcus. The night had begun clear, but dark clouds were blowing in from the east, and the air felt as if it would rain soon. For a quick moment, two of the three moons showed through an opening in the overcast sky, and Kyja could see the worry on his face. "Whatever Master Therapass is trying to tell you, it's not that you're a traitor."

"How do you *know?*" Marcus met Kyja's eyes for a moment before returning them to the tower reaching toward the gray sky like an accusing finger. *She* hadn't had the dream—hadn't felt an entire world loathing and fearing her.

He couldn't imagine any circumstances under which he'd ever lay a hand on this place he'd dreamed about since he was a child. But why else would the wizard send him that message? Why would the Dark Circle not send Thrathkin S'Bae to pursue him? "The Augur Well said betrayal would find us. That one of us is a thief and a liar. It had to be talking about me. It's the only answer that makes sense."

"That doesn't make any sense at all," Kyja insisted. She ran a hand along the cold stone of the ruined wall. "But I think I know who the betrayer might be."

"Who?" he asked as a drop of cold rain spattered on the back of his hand.

"In the swamp, when I was looking for you, Cascade warned me to be careful of Screech. He said Screech had hidden reasons for helping us."

Of course Screech had hidden reasons. He wouldn't have tracked them down just to say hello. "I knew we shouldn't have trusted him."

"Trusted whom?" asked a voice.

Marcus turned to see Lanctros-Darnoc standing behind him. It was the first time he'd seen the land elementals since he passed out. Even without the fever raging in his head, he still thought the creature was an imposing sight.

"Who do you not trust?" Darnoc, the boar, asked.

"Go ahead," Marcus said, when Kyja hesitated. "If they're going to help us, they should know."

"It might not be anything," Kyja said. "Cascade warned me to be careful of Screech, but I don't think Screech would do anything to hurt me."

Lanctrus nodded slowly. "The water elemental again. Perhaps it is wise to be wary of others. But be careful of rushing to judgment." The fox looked directly at Marcus. "Be especially careful of how you judge yourself."

Marcus thought that was interesting advice considering how the land and water elementals seemed to distrust each other. His focus quickly changed when the land elementals waved their wings and a ball of tiny glowing insects appeared in the air, lighting the night like a lantern.

"Cool," Marcus said, his attention diverted from the tower. "How'd you do that?"

"Simple land magic," the boar said. He showed Marcus how to do it until Marcus was able to summon a lantern of his own. Darnoc was right. It was easy.

"There is much more we can teach you if you're willing to study," Lanctrus and Darnoc said together. "Land magic is the magic of teaching. We would be honored to share our knowledge."

"That would be great," Marcus said.

"Put out those lights!" Rhaidnan appeared like a ghost.

"How long have you been there?" Kyja asked as Lanctrus-Darnoc dispelled the lanterns of insects.

"Long enough to make sure you weren't followed. Things have gotten worse since we last talked. A dozen more Keepers have arrived, and the guards are actively searching for anyone plotting against Zentan Dolan." Even in the darkness, the stress on the hunter's face was clear. "And long enough to hear your concerns about the trulloch."

"It's probably nothing," Kyja said.

"In the last three days, four of my men have disappeared," Rhaidnan's eyes roamed from the city walls to the nearby farm, across the empty field, and back again. "Four more are too scared to help us any longer. I'm afraid to let my family leave the house. There are traitors everywhere. If you have suspicions about someone, I need to know it."

Kyja nodded. "I understand." Rhaidnan whistled softly. Five more men rose from the grass less than fifteen feet away. "Have any of you seen the trulloch?" he whispered.

"He hasn't arrived," said a fat man with a thick moustache.

"Tall thing like that would be hard to miss," said Breslek Broomhead, the man who lived at the next farm over.

"What about the water elemental?" Rhaidnan asked.

"He could be anywhere," Lanctrus-Darnoc said.

"Or he could be right behind you," Cascade replied.

The land elementals spun around, clearly annoyed at being surprised.

"I've been scouting the city," the water elemental said. "Not playing tricks with bugs. There are at least forty Keepers in and around the tower."

"And three unmakers," said a tall figure that materialized just behind Breslek. Screech gave the man a black-toothed grin. "I'm easier to miss than you might think."

Rhaidnan snorted in disgust. *"Apparently."* He motioned to his bewildered hunter, who stared at the trulloch as though suspecting he was some kind of illusion. "We're all here. Gather the rest of the men. There's no telling how long this cloud cover will continue, and we need every bit of help we can get. Meet us just outside the west gate."

He turned to Marcus and Kyja. "We'll stay off the road until we reach the gates. Two of my men are on guard duty. They'll let us inside while your friends access the underground river. According to my reports, Therapass is still alive. But he won't be much longer. Tonight might be our last chance to rescue him."

Marcus glanced toward Kyja before planting his staff in the tall grass. "It might be better if I stay here."

"No," Kyja said.

Not far away, thunder shook the night. Rhaidnan scowled. "Marcus, what are you talking about?"

"I think I should stay away from the tower," Marcus said, not wanting to explain why. "Besides, I'd just slow you down. And I don't . . . I don't have anything that could help you."

"Not true," the hunter said. "I have very limited man power. I can barely guard both of you together. Separate, there's not a chance."

"You have to come," Kyja said. "Master Therapass would want you there. *I* want you there."

Marcus looked at the city walls with a feeling of dread. In the past—before he lost his magic—he'd occasionally been able to sense danger before it happened. He no longer had that ability. But he still sensed that if he entered the tower, something terrible would happen. Even so, he soon found himself following Rhaidnan and his men, pausing every so often as one of the hunters gave an update.

By the time they reached the west gate, a steady drizzle was falling. Marcus and Kyja were soon soaked, and Riph Raph wrapped both of his ears around his head.

"Who's that?" Marcus whispered as they approached the statue of a fierce-looking warrior.

"Tankum Heartstrong," Kyja whispered back.

Marcus stopped and stared, no longer conscious of the pain in his hip, or of the falling rain. This was the man who, along with Master Therapass, had found him as a baby—the man who'd saved his life. He'd battled an army of Fallen Ones while the wizard had opened the doorway that sent Marcus to Earth to evade the reach of the Dark Circle.

In his mind, Marcus had always pictured Tankum as a valiant fighter. Master Therapass told how his friend had continued to battle with one of his blades broken and blood pouring from dozens of wounds. The man on the pedestal looked like everything the wizard had described. With a thick mane of hair down to his shoulders, heavily-muscled arms, and a sword in each hand, he appeared ready to fight anything that crossed his path.

What Marcus hadn't expected was the intelligence that showed clearly in his eyes. Or the crooked smile, as though the warrior found humor even in the heat of battle. Holding one sword in front of him and the other over his head, he looked surprised that he had to fight at all. As if he'd rather settle things over a glass of ale and a few good jokes, but understood that some people or creatures were too foolish to understand when they were outmatched.

Marcus would have liked to stay longer, studying the face of the man who'd sacrificed himself so a child he didn't even know could live. But Rhaidnan was tugging at his arm.

"It's time to go through," Rhaidnan whispered. Standing outside the gate, Marcus counted between twenty and thirty men. The hunter eyed Cascade and Lanctrus-Darnoc. "You two stay outside until we get through the gate. Once we're inside, I'll whistle for you. I assume you can get in on your own?"

Lanctrus-Darnoc nodded, but Cascade looked around anxiously.

"Where's the trulloch?" Rhaidnan asked.

Marcus looked for Screech, but he was nowhere to be found.

"I didn't see him leave," Kyja said.

"Come on." Rhaidnan pulled Marcus and Kyja. "Let's get inside." He gave four sharp raps on the gate, and a small door set into it swung open. Two guards waved them in.

"Stop!" Cascade called. "It's a trap."

Marcus, who'd stepped halfway through the door, saw a group of men suddenly rise up from hiding just inside the city entrance.

"Keepers!" screamed a man beside him. "Fall back!"

Marcus turned to run, but a hand closed around his arm, and a gleaming blade pressed against his neck.

"I'm sorry," whispered Rhaidnan. "I can't let you leave."

STRATAGEMS

The Dark Circle

Surrounded by darkness, the master sat staring into a low, stone bowl filled with a blood-red liquid that bubbled and churned. He touched a finger to its surface, and a pale face appeared, its mouth a frustrated, downward slash.

"Have you found it?" the master asked.

"No," Zentan Dolan said from the bowl, clearly agitated. "I told you I'd contact you if and when—"

The master clenched his fist; instantly the zentan went stiff. The tighter the master squeezed, the harder the zentan's teeth bit into his lower lip, piercing the flesh.

"Do not forget who brought who here. As long as you remain in the form I created for you, I am your master." He unclenched his fist, and the zentan slumped, licking the blood from his lip.

"It would help, *master*," the zentan said slowly. "If you told me exactly what it is I am looking for."

The master chuckled softly. "You'd like that, I'm sure. Just remember, if you ever want to get back to where you came from, you will do as I say. Have the boy and girl arrived?"

"Yes," the zentan said. "Just as I—*we*—planned. I hope they're worth the cost. I lost several good Keepers convincing them the hunter could be trusted."

"They are worth all of your Keepers combined. Be sure not to let them out of your grasp, or I will cause you more pain than you can possibly imagine. Take special care with the boy. I believe Therapass has hidden it in such a way that only the chosen can find it. It is exactly the kind of thing the old fool of a wizard would do. And if the boy managed to get his hands on it, he could cause great harm to both of us. He will lead you to the item, but do not let him touch it under any circumstances. Do you understand?"

"Yes." The zentan looked over his shoulder as if someone had come into the room behind him. "They're here. I must go. What of the wizard?"

"We've spent enough time toying with him," the master said, his face a mask of fury. "I would like to be the one to personally snuff out his life for his actions, but that is not possible. As soon as you have the boy, kill Therapass. Make it as slow—and painful—as you possibly can."

The zentan smiled with grim delight. "As you wish."

The master touched the liquid again; another face appeared. "Master!" The man looked up with a pathetically eager smile, the long scar that ran from his jaw to his temple quivering. "Everything is ready."

"No one has spotted you?"

"No. There is no one for miles—nothing but empty, ugly space. We are all in position."

"Do not lay a hand on them when they arrive."

"N-no, of course not."

The master pointed a finger at the bowl, and the Thrathkin S'Bae flinched. "You have failed me twice before, Bonesplinter. Do not fail me again."

"I won't." The dark wizard trembled. "You said that if I succeed, you will give me . . ." He licked his gray lips. "Power."

The master touched the liquid that now looked more than ever like boiling blood. The face in the bowl disappeared. The master smiled, his eyes gleaming. "More power than you can imagine."

This would prove to be an interesting night. He could rid himself of two adversaries at once, assuring his plans with Farworld could go forth uninterrupted. Then he would learn more about the girl and how he could use her to expand his dominion in the world called Earth.

He laughed softly, lifted the bowl to his lips, and began to drink.

PART 4

Battle for the City

CHAPTER 42

ZENTAN DOLAN

FOR A MOMENT, KYJA COULD ONLY stare at the blade Rhaidnan held to Marcus's throat, waiting for it to change into something she could understand—waiting for the situation to turn out to be a mistake.

"I'm sorry," Rhaidnan said again, but the knife remained pressed against Marcus's skin.

Beneath the light of flickering torches mounted along the walls, men rose from either side of the cobblestone street, removing the shimmering gray cloaks they'd been hiding under. They closed in a half circle. Another group surged down the steep hill that led to the base of the tower and over the footbridge that crossed a small creek. Kyja counted between fifteen or twenty of the crimson or gray robes. Most of them were citizens of Terra ne Staric. Had they all sided with the Keepers?

"Why?" Kyja asked Rhaidnan. She'd known him most of her life. She'd cared for his children so his wife, Char, could find work when he was captured by the unmakers. And she and Marcus had saved his life.

A tall man, with skin so pale it seemed to glow, stepped across the bridge. Even if he hadn't been wearing the only white robe in the crowd, Kyja would have known he was the leader of the Keepers by the looks of awe bordering on terror as the others cleared a path for him.

"Welcome," he said, holding out his long-fingered hands. "I am Zentan Dolan. As you can see, we've been expecting you. I'm sorry the weather hasn't been more accommodating for our guests."

"Tell you what," Riph Raph said. "Why don't we just all go to our homes and try this again when the weather's better?"

"Do you always hold your *guests* at knifepoint?" Marcus asked.

"Of course not," the zentan said. His gray lips lifted into a narrow smile. "I must apologize. Mr. Everwood is under a bit of stress at the moment. I've tried to explain that weapons are no longer necessary here, but some are slow learners. Put the knife away, Rhaidnan."

"Not until you show me my family's safe," he growled. "Where are they?"

"I said, put the knife away." The zentan spoke quietly, but Rhaidnan's fingers snapped open, and the blade dropped to the cobblestones. The hunter's body jerked and spasmed like a puppet tossed about by some unseen hand. "Perhaps I should leave your lovely wife and two perfectly charming children with the unmakers for a few more days to teach you a little respect?"

"N-no," Rhaidnan gasped, his face straining and twisting as his body continued to jitter. "Pl-please."

So that's why he had betrayed them. "Leave him alone," Kyja said. Rhaidnan had been nearly killed by the unmakers. The idea of Char and his children being put through the same torture must have nearly driven him mad.

Zentan Dolan looked at Kyja with a frown that appeared every bit as phony as his earlier smile. Rhaidnan's muscles relaxed and he nearly fell. "I'm sorry," Dolan said. "That was quite inconsiderate of me—especially in view of the poor man's earlier . . . *experiences.* Return his family to him at once."

There was a bustle from the tight circle of Keepers. A tall woman with long, blond hair was pushed into the street. A length of cloth had been placed over her eyes, and her hands were tied behind her back. She stumbled; Rhaidnan ran forward to catch her.

"Char!" he cried, pulling away the blindfold and fumbling with the knots around her wrists. "Are you all right?"

"I'm fine." She blinked in the torchlight. "Where are the children?"

"Daddy!" A girl who was the very image of her mother rushed forward and threw her arms around her father's legs. Rhaidnan lifted her and covered her cheeks with kisses as tears of relief streamed down his face.

On her heels came a boy whose head reached nearly to his father's shoulder. He glared at the ring of Keepers around him as though he wanted to fight each of them personally. "Father," he nodded, trying to look brave.

Then he saw Kyja, and his grimace changed to a grin that made him look like the nine-year-old he really was.

"You're back," he shouted.

"Kyja?" Some of Char's fear seemed to melt away. "When did you get here? How . . ." She looked from Kyja and Marcus, who stood with their backs pressed against the city wall, to the zentan and his circle of Keepers. The beginnings of her smile disappeared. "What's happening?"

Rhaidnan met his wife's eyes for a moment but had to look away. He squeezed his daughter in one bear-like arm and curled his other arm around his son's shoulder. "We need to leave."

"Your husband has been a great help to me—and to his city," Zentan Dolan said to Char. "He has revealed traitors among his fellow citizens, returned these children to where they can be properly . . . looked after, and saved his family. I consider him a hero. You should be grateful."

Char's steel-gray gaze went from Rhaidnan's knife lying on the ground to her husband's face. "No. I don't believe it. My husband would never betray his friends." She started toward Kyja, but Rhaidnan reached for her arm.

"I didn't have any choice. We—"

Char pulled her arm from her husband's grip. "What have you done?" She looked at Kyja with pleading in her eyes. "This has to be a mistake. The man I love would never do this." Char started toward them, but the Keepers instantly grabbed her.

"Get his family out of here," Zentan Dolan said.

"Leave them alone," Rhaidnan roared as the Keepers closed around Char and her children.

"No!" Char screamed. "I'm not going anywhere without Kyja."

"It's all right," Kyja said. She understood what Rhaidnan had done and why. But over the roar of the Keepers struggling with Char and her husband, she didn't think anyone heard.

"Tell me you didn't," Char cried to her husband as she was pulled away, struggling and clawing. "Tell me!"

Just before Rhaidnan disappeared into the crowd, he met Kyja's eyes and opened his mouth as if he wanted to say something. Before he could utter a word, he was dragged away into the darkness.

"Open the gates," Zentan Dolan ordered. Eight men lifted the metal crossbar and cranked the handles. As the gates swung slowly open, the rest of the men from Rhaidnan's group were herded forward by more Keepers and at least thirty city guards.

"You see?" The Zentan laughed. "More traitors. Just as I told you." He moved to one side as another figure stepped into the light.

Kyja's heart sank when she saw who it was. "High Lord Dinslith," she whispered. He looked smaller than he had the last time she'd seen him, his body frail and bent, his eyes dull. Weaker, too—as if the presence of the Keepers had drained him of both strength and authority. "Why have you let these monsters take over the city?" If the high lord heard her words, he ignored them.

"These men came to break out the wizard who organized the entire rebellion," Dolan said, his eyes glittering merrily.

"Therapass?" Dinslith muttered.

"Therapass." The zentan nodded and laid a hand on the high lord's shoulder. "Final proof that he is no longer a friend to you or to Terra ne Staric. I will have him executed immediately—with your permission, of course."

"No!" Kyja looked to the men who had come with her, but they all stood with shoulders slumped, eyes fixed on the ground. She turned to Marcus. "We have to do something."

"You might have these men fooled," Marcus said, limping forward to face the zentan. "But we've seen what you did to Land Keep. We know what you really are." He looked to the guards. "In a month or two, this entire city will be just another one of his prisons. How many people's magic have they taken already?"

Inspired by Marcus's bravery, Kyja stepped up to his side. She pointed past the bridge, where a flagstone path wound up a steep hill to the base of the tower. Bordering the path were the statues of Westland's most famous wizards and warriors—men and women who represented everything Terra ne Staric stood for. The line stretched from Varthlik Verblan—the wizard who originally founded Terra ne Staric—at the base of the tower to Tankum Heartstrong outside the gate.

"Look at these statues," Kyja called, trying to meet the eyes of those she recognized. "What would those men and women think if they knew who you'd turned their city over to?"

The statues swiveled their heads and glared—showing clearly what they thought. It didn't seem to matter. As Kyja searched the crowd, they either glowered at her, or more often, turned away. They were too late. The city was already beaten.

"You're mistaken," Zentan Dolan said. "We are not here to take over your city. We were invited here to be of aid by your own high lord. It is only by his will that we stay." He turned to High Lord Dinslith. "Do you wish us to leave?"

Her eyes pleading, Kyja stared at the man who had led the city since before she was born. He rubbed a shaking hand across his wrinkled cheek and without looking up said, "No. I want you to stay."

"Fine," Kyja snapped. "The rest of you may be beaten. But we're not."

Marcus spoke up. "Maybe you forgot that we didn't come alone." Outside the gate, men moved quickly aside as two figures appeared out of the rain. Cascade walked side by side with Lanctrus-Darnoc, who flew a few feet off the ground toward Marcus and Kyja. The land elementals stretched their wings wide as the water elemental tossed a glittering ball of water from one hand to the other. It was the first time Kyja had seen them so close together.

"Elementals," whispered someone in the crowd.

"They're real," murmured another.

"That's right," Riph Raph said, bobbing his head. "Now my friends and I are going to teach you a lesson, dough face."

"Give us Therapass, and we'll leave the city along with anyone who wants to join us," Kyja said. For the first time, the men they'd come with looked up with expressions of hope on their faces.

Despite the elementals, the zentan threw back his head and laughed. "I don't think so."

CHAPTER 43

STANDOFF

MARCUS LOOKED IN CONFUSION from Cascade and Lanctrus-Darnoc to the zentan. A man with his experience must understand how powerful elementals were, yet there was no sign of fear on Dolan's face.

"I apologize for laughing," the zentan said, dabbing at his eyes with the back of his hand. "It's just that I assumed all-powerful elementals would be so much more . . . *imposing*. Instead I find a butterfly and a fish. Ahhh, perhaps you'd better return to your homes before someone mistakes you for dinner and puts that pig on a spit."

"I'd like to see *his* head on a spit," Darnoc said, bearing his tusks.

"You would be mistaken to judge the power of an enemy by their looks," Lanctrus-Darnoc told the zentan.

"Would I? Would I, indeed? Then show me your great power. Display the wonder of your land magic. Wasn't your plan to burrow a tunnel to rescue the wizard? That should be simple enough." He waved his hands. "Dig away. I am prepared to be amazed."

"Stand back," Lanctrus said to Kyja and Marcus.

The two backed away as the land elementals flapped their broad wings and a deep-throated rumbling began under their feet. Marcus planted his staff and leaned into it as chunks of dirt and rock ripped loose from the ground and flew to the side of the road.

As soon as the land elementals began tunneling, Zentan Dolan raised his arms and called out, "Now!" Around him, all the other Keepers raised their arms. Marcus felt something like electricity fill the air. Overhead, lightning flashed, and the clouds began to swirl. A rush of wind, stronger than anything Marcus had ever felt, knocked him backward.

The dirt that had been piling up beside Lanctrus-Darnoc's tunnel, rose in a funnel of swirling debris and was thrown back into the hole. Dirt and rocks coming out of the ground collided violently with what was being sent back. The land elementals kept tunneling, but every time they seemed to make some headway, the Keepers increased their efforts and threw more dirt back where it had come from.

Marcus cupped his hand over his nose and mouth. It was impossible to see through the swirling cloud of grit, which sounded like a pair of freight trains smashing repeatedly into each other.

At last the crashing stopped, and the air began to clear. Coughing at the dirt, Marcus strained to see what had happened. Little by little, the falling rain cleared away the dust. The hole was gone—and in its place sat a low mound of dirt and rocks.

"That's not good," Riph Raph said, edging behind Marcus.

"Is that the best you can do?" Zentan Dolan smirked.

"It is pointless to continue the effort," Lanctrus-Darnoc said.

"What about you?" the zentan asked Cascade. "Care to test your water powers against the Keepers of the Balance?"

Cascade lifted his ball of water. The clouds seemed to rip open. Marcus ducked his head as a torrent of water poured down. But it never reached him. Instead, the water poured waterfall-like into the stream, raising it nearly to the footbridge. Six glittering water dragons rose from the rushing water. Their scales gleamed like diamonds as they lifted their wings, roared, and prepared to charge the Keepers.

As before, the zentan raised his arms in the air, as did the rest of the Keepers. A column of fire shot down from the sky. For a moment, the dragons seemed impervious to the heat, though Marcus was forced to drop face-first to the ground to keep his skin from being roasted. Then, one-by-one, the dragons began to disintegrate. Steam rose in billowing clouds from their backs.

The dragons moved in stuttering steps toward the zentan, and Cascade pulled more water from the stream to rebuild them. It was no use. As fast as water replenished the creatures, the fire evaporated them until the air felt like a sauna. Sweat soaked through Marcus's robe, but it was clear that the Keepers' strength matched that of either of the elementals.

"Had enough already?" the zentan taunted when Cascade lowered his ball and the last of the dragons disappeared.

"It would seem our power is equally matched," Cascade said.

"Equally matched?" the zentan laughed. "You haven't seen a tenth of my power."

Marcus turned to Kyja. Was it time to give up and jump to Earth? He knew Cascade and Lanctrus-Darnoc would be safe without them, but how could they desert Master Therapass and the people of Terra ne Staric—everyone who had supported them?

The zentan seemed to read his thoughts. "Thinking of running, coward?"

"It might be best," Lanctrus-Darnoc said. "We will do what we can here."

"They will not be able to harm us," Cascade said.

"We'll never run," Kyja said.

They couldn't run out on Master Therapass, but maybe they could use a trick that had worked for them before. "Remember Water Keep," Marcus whispered.

Kyja nodded.

The walls of Water Keep had seemed impenetrable. But by jumping to Earth, walking forward, and jumping back, they'd been able to get into the city. Maybe the same trick would get them into the tower.

"Take them!" the zentan shouted.

"Now," Marcus said. He felt the Keepers' hands grab at him, but he slipped through their grip, turning and falling. As he reached back for Kyja and Riph Raph, he thought he heard the zentan's laughter.

Landing on the rocky desert soil, Marcus could still hear the laughter. He opened his eyes and looked into a face he remembered all too well. The man standing before him grinned—the scar that ran from the base of his jaw to his right temple, twisting like a snake.

"Okay, bad plan," said Riph Raph, who was a shivering green rock lizard.

"Surprise," the man said, his silver eyes gleaming. He lifted his forked staff, and fire jumped between its prongs. Marcus turned to run and bumped into Kyja, who was staring at another Thrathkin S'Bae. It was a trap. They were surrounded by dozens of the wizards of the Dark Circle.

"Thought you lost me?" Bonesplinter said. "We've known where you were all along. We could have taken you any time we wanted."

Marcus searched for some way out. But there was none. The

Thrathkin S'Bae reached for his throat, and he felt himself falling again—back to Farworld.

"Welcome back," the zentan said as Marcus, Riph Raph, and Kyja got to their feet. "I trust your trip was an educational one."

"What do you want?" Kyja asked.

"She sees reason!" The zentan chortled and the rest of the Keepers echoed his laughter. "What I want is quite simple. The pathetic worm who calls himself a Master Wizard stole something of value from High Lord Dinslith. I've kept him alive in the hopes he would see the error of his ways and reveal its location. Now that you are here, I can finally kill him. You will tell me where it is—and if you do, perhaps I will let you live."

"We have no idea what you're talking about," Kyja said.

But do we? Marcus wondered. Master Therapass had gone back to the tower when he'd sent the two of them to the Westland woods. He'd never explained exactly what he'd returned for. What if he'd hidden whatever he'd taken within the tower? Could *that* be what the dreams were about? If so, revealing the location of the item could destroy Farworld.

"I think you know where it is," the zentan said, his eyes boring into Marcus. "Should you fail to tell me, I will kill each of the men you brought with you, one by one. Then I will kill their wives and children while you watch them beg for their lives. Finally, I will kill the two of you, slowly and painfully. Your deaths will last weeks, and before they are over you *will* break. The decision is yours. Tell me now—or tell me later."

Marcus felt his will slipping away. What choice did they have? He thought he could stand to lose his own life if he had to. But could he watch innocent children be killed because of him? He turned to Kyja and saw the same uncertainty on her face. They'd been too cocky, walking into the Dark Circle's trap without thinking things through. It was the story of his life. But this time his arrogance would hurt many more people than himself.

"I believe you are still underestimating your adversaries," Lanctrus said, as though teaching a student. Her dark fox eyes glittered, and her muzzle wrinkled in a smile.

"What are you blathering about?" The Zentan threw his hands in the air. "I thought you'd realized you were outmatched."

"Not outmatched," Cascade said, the amused smile back on his face as he met Lanctrus' gaze. "Just outnumbered."

"Outmatched, outnumbered. What difference does it make?" the zentan asked. "Either way, your magic is no match for mine."

"Maybe not directly." Darnoc grinned, his tusks glittering in the torchlight. "But apparently, you've never heard of a flank attack."

For the first time, the zentan looked taken aback. He turned to his second in command. "You told me they were alone."

"Th-they are," the Keeper said, shrinking back from his leader. "There's no one else out there except the trulloch, and we'll track him down soon enough."

"Enough of these games," the zentan said, his arrogance returning. "There is no flank attack. You brought no others with you."

"We had no need to," Lanctrus-Darnoc said. "They were here all along."

What were the land elementals talking about? Who was the *they* that had been here all along? If this was a bluff, Marcus thought, it would be a short-lived one.

Lanctrus tilted her head in an oddly human gesture. "Your magic is indeed powerful. But you wield it as a weapon. You see only black and white, sword and shield. That is your strength, but it will also be your downfall." The land elementals stretched their wings, and Marcus heard a sharp crack behind him.

He spun around and peered through the west gate. At first he couldn't understand what had made the sound. Then he realized something was missing. What was it?

A figure moved in the darkness. A pair of Keepers flew through the air, landing face first in the dirt. A tall, broad-shouldered shape bulled its way through the crowd. Just before it stepped into the light, Marcus realized what was missing: the statue outside the gate was gone—its pedestal stood empty.

"Tankum," Kyja breathed as the warrior stepped into the clearing and stopped. He was still made of stone, yet he moved like a living person.

"Nice work," the statue said to the land elementals. "Gets kind of old standing up there all the time." He stretched his arms above his head with a groan of pleasure—massive marble biceps bulging as his twin swords gleamed. He looked at Marcus and nodded. "You've grown some since the last time I saw you, kid. Any good with a sword?"

"What is this?" the zentan howled.

All the way along the path to the tower, stone wizards and warriors climbed down from their pedestals, greeting one another with shouts and calls of recognition.

Tankum clanged his swords together—the sound ringing through the night—and the rest of the statues turned to face him. He winked at the zentan. "Looks like the numbers just evened out."

CHAPTER 44

THE DUNGEON

KYJA WATCHED TANKUM—amazed to see the statue she'd passed every day as a child come to life—when a fireball exploded halfway up the tower hill. Someone—she couldn't tell who—raised a battle cry, and suddenly the sound of steel meeting steel split the air.

Bodies hurled at one another as stone wizards and warriors charged down the slope into the Keepers, who attacked back with blasts of fire. The zentan shouted for his men to form ranks, but Cascade calmly lifted the glittering orb in his hands, sending bursts of water that extinguished the torches, plunging the city into a darkness lit only by blasts of magic. All hope of an organized battle was lost.

An explosion shook the ground, and Kyja fell against Marcus.

"This way," a familiar voice spoke into her ear. Somehow, Screech was at her side. His cold fingers closed around Kyja's wrist and lifted Marcus completely into the air. All around them spells flew and weapons collided. The battle ranged from the side of the hill into the city streets, but the trulloch guided them with unerring accuracy through the tumult.

"Over there," Kyja said, spotting a metal gate. It was locked, but she knew she could squeeze through the rusted bars because she'd done it before—several months ago, the last time she'd been in the city. Marcus had more difficulty getting through, but the trulloch easily folded his long limbs and twisted his shoulders as though he were made of nothing more substantial than tissue paper.

"How did you find us?" Kyja asked once they'd reached the relative safety of the tall hedges beyond. "Can you see in the dark?"

Screech held out his broad hands. "One of the few benefits of being a trulloch."

"Where did you disappear to before?" Marcus asked.

"The night," the trulloch answered enigmatically. "It was too late to warn you when I realized the Keepers were waiting."

"Either that, or you were part of the trap."

Obviously, Marcus didn't trust Screech. Kyja wasn't sure she trusted him either. She hadn't forgotten Cascade's warning that the trulloch had motives of his own for helping them, or the fact that the Keepers had recognized Screech back at the swamp. But this was the third time he'd come to their aid.

"Do you know where Cascade and Lanctrus-Darnoc went?" she asked him.

"I'm here." The water elemental appeared from a puddle of rain water. "The land elementals are supporting the statues in battle."

"We have to get to Therapass," Kyja said.

Marcus looked up at the tower with either fear or fascination. "How? There's no way we can reach the underground river with all that going on."

Kyja pointed to the path winding past a low, stone wall. "That leads to a back entrance into the kitchen. With the battle as a distraction, we might be able to sneak past the guards."

"What about the unmakers?" Marcus asked. "Rhaidnan said there were at least two guarding Master Therapass's cell."

"I sense three," Cascade said. "But I can't tell exactly where they are. They are difficult to see, even for a water elemental."

"Can you help us get past them?" Kyja asked.

The Fontasian shook his head. "Unmakers are creatures of shadow, so normal magic does not affect them. That's why the zentan is using them to guard the wizard."

"Maybe I can help," Screech said. "Do I smell apples?"

"Yes." Kyja pointed past the hedges. "The orchard is just over there. But what do apples have to do with anything?"

"Don't tell me you're hungry at a time like this," Riph Raph said. "Although if anyone has a few spare fish, I could eat them."

"Did you ever notice a certain smell when the unmakers were near?" Screech asked, ignoring the skyte.

Kyja tried to remember. She'd been encased in ice when they were first captured and later, she'd been running for her life. But Marcus nodded at once.

"I remember. They had a moldy smell but sweet too. Like . . ." he looked up at Screech. "Like rotten apples."

The trulloch nodded. "They love spoiled fruit even more than emotions or magic. If we brought a couple of bushels to the dungeon, I might be able to distract them long enough for Cascade to open the lock."

"Let's do it," Kyja said. She started up the trail but stopped when she saw that Marcus hadn't followed. He was still staring up at the tower. "What's wrong?"

"Nothing." He shook his head. "Just thinking."

"Well, stop thinking and start walking." She could barely keep from breaking into a run. The zentan had said Master Therapass was going to be executed. Who knew how long they had? Minutes?

The rotten apples were even easier to come by than she'd expected. A big stinking pile of them sat just outside the pig pens, and several empty bushels were stacked nearby. She and Screech quickly loaded a basket each.

"Are you okay?" she asked Marcus.

"Sure," he said pulling his gaze away from the tower. "Why wouldn't I be?"

He hadn't helped load a single apple, and he seemed lost in another world. Kyja leaned closer, "Are you still worried about the dream?"

He paused for a moment as if pondering her question before answering. "Surprisingly, no."

She sensed he wasn't telling her the whole truth, but she'd have to wait until later to ask more. Holding the basket to her chest, she led the group up a stone passageway slippery with mud and damp hay.

This was the back entrance to the kitchen, used for delivering slaughtered animals and fresh produce. Bella, the head cook, had taken her this way to escape the tower what seemed like a lifetime before. Back then, Kyja had no idea what the Dark Circle was. She knew Marcus only as a face in the aptura discerna.

She hoped to find Bella in the kitchen, but when she reached it, the big room was empty. Normally good smells filled the air here no matter what time of night or day. But even though magical torches burned on all the walls, the place had a deserted feel to it, as if no one had cooked here for days or weeks. It smelled of spoiled meat and rotted vegetables. Bella would never have left her kitchen like

304

this. Had something happened to her? Kyja hoped her friend hadn't been punished for helping her escape.

"This way." She gestured to the group and passed the stairs she used to take to reach Master Therapass's study for her magic lessons, avoiding the front entrance to the tower. It always had at least two guards. She cut through the back of the dining hall.

"The pig sties looked cleaner than this," Riph Raph said.

If the kitchen had normally been clean, the dining hall had *always* been immaculate. Kyja couldn't remember a time when the long, wooden tables weren't polished to a golden honey-like gleam. Silver candlesticks provided a warm glow over the whole room, while china and goblets were laid out for the next royal meal.

But now the room looked as if a group of wild animals had been let loose in it. Wine had been splashed across the tabletops. Chunks of meat were strewn across the floor, and fruit splattered the walls.

Unwilling to see the tower in this kind of condition, she hurried from one hallway to another until they were one turn away from the door to the dungeon.

"If there are guards, they'll be just around this corner," she whispered.

Screech held a finger to his lips and eased around the wall. A moment later, he returned. "They are gone, but the door is locked."

"Leave that to me." Cascade led them around the corner and stopped in front of the door. He put his eye to the keyhole.

"Can you open it?" Kyja asked.

"Splash and spray," he said. "You humans ask the most foolish questions." He held out the blue globe. A finger of water slid into the lock, and a second later, the globe and water froze solid. He turned the "key," and the lock opened with a click.

Kyja paused before going through the door. She'd been in the dungeon only once—helping Bella take dinner to a man accused of killing another over a woman they both loved—but the memory of the cold walls and dark cells had stuck with her.

"Maybe Cascade and I should go alone," Screech said.

"No," Kyja said. "We're all rescuing Master Therapass. Right, Marcus?" Kyja turned for Marcus's confirmation, but he was gone.

CHAPTER 45

THE TOWER

WHILE STANDING BESIDE the animal pens as Kyja and Screech loaded rotten apples into baskets, Marcus's eyes had kept slipping toward the upward jutting spire of the tower—his mind returning to the dream, trying to understand it, to decode it. More and more, he was coming to believe the zentan was right in assuming Master Therapass had taken something. Whatever he'd removed was hidden somewhere up there. Part of him wanted to run away screaming in terror at the recollection of how Farworld had trembled before him in his nightmare.

But another part of him wondered what was so powerful that it could make an entire world fear *him*—a kid with his magic stolen, a leg that barely held him up, and only one good arm. And if the item was that dangerous, why had Therapass bothered to hide it at all? Why not destroy it? And why send him the dream? It was almost as if the wizard *wanted* Marcus to go into the tower—as if he was tempting him to see what it might hold.

Whatever Marcus found there—if he found anything at all—he'd never use it against Farworld. Of that much he was certain. But if the item was that powerful, could it be used for good instead of evil? Could it be turned *against* the Dark Circle? Maybe that's what Master Therapass was trying to tell him. He could hear the battle raging below as the Keepers fought the stone wizards and warriors—as citizen fought citizen for control of a single city. Who knew how this battle would end? And the next? And the one after that?

Soon the battles would spread; they'd fight over more than cities. The Dark Circle was getting stronger. Farworld was crying out in pain at what was being done to it—and that pain echoed through Marcus's body. What if he could use the item in the tower to stop all the battles at once—gaining victory over the forces of darkness without raising a sword?

Should he go or stay?

Look for whatever it was, or leave it where the wizard had hidden it? Every time Marcus tore his gaze away from the structure, which reminded him more and more of a skeletal finger reaching into the darkness, he resolved to stay outside. Then his gaze would drift back, and again he'd start to wonder.

Torn between fear and desire, he followed Kyja into the stone passageway. As soon as he set foot in the tower, his worries began to disappear. As he walked across the hay-strewn floor, an odd separation of mind and body occurred. With each step, the pain in his hip diminished until it felt as if he were no longer moving his legs at all, but merely floating forward.

They reached the kitchen, and Kyja crossed through an arched doorway with Cascade, Riph Raph, and Screech. Instead of following her, Marcus found himself turning down another hallway lit by flickering torches. He passed door after door, but none of them interested him. Whatever he was looking for was not behind any of them.

An icy fist—half-horror, half-grieving acceptance—slammed into his stomach when he looked up and saw the spiraling staircase. He'd been meant to come here all along. Just like he had in his dream, he climbed the stairs one by one. Through the tower windows, the fighting continued below, but the sounds seemed farther away—less urgent. He didn't know if it was because of his distance from the battle or because the item called to him with greater and greater urgency the closer he got to it.

He had no idea how many steps he climbed or how long it took him. Somewhere in the back of his mind, he was aware of sweat streaming down his forehead, of his limbs trembling as he pushed his body far past what it should have been able to withstand. But all of that was unimportant. The only thing that mattered was what was waiting for him—calling him, singing to him as he'd sung to the tribrac. Only this song was not about fairies and brave battles. It was much simpler.

Come to me. Find me. Make me yours.

The song pulled him like a noose tied around his neck. He followed with no more hope of stopping it than he had of stopping gravity.

When he felt the cold night air blowing down the stairs and realized he was nearing the balcony, he made one last desperate try to think for himself. This wasn't *like* the dream, this *was* the dream. Lightning flashed outside, and thunder roared, growling like a wild animal. If he stepped onto those wet stones, he'd see exactly what had been in his dream—a world terrified—of him.

A voice shouted his name from somewhere down the staircase. He understood he didn't have to do this; he could still turn back if he wanted to and end this nightmare. He could wait for Therapass. The wizard would know what to do.

Except, somehow Marcus was already standing on the balcony. While he'd been trying to decide what to do, his feet had made the decision for him.

I am the door, the voice in his head sang at a fevered pitch. *Open me. Open me. Open-n-n-n.* The air shrank around him, crackled blue and spread. He was the key, and by coming here, he had opened a lock meant only for him. He stepped through.

———— ◦•◦ ————

At first Kyja thought Marcus was lagging behind again. He'd seemed strangely remote ever since they entered the tower, as if his thoughts were somewhere else. But as she retraced her steps to the dining room, then all the way to the kitchen, she realized he was really gone.

"What does it matter?" Riph Raph groused. "He probably got distracted by a coat of arms or something. We don't have time to waste."

"He's right," Cascade said. "The guards may return any minute. The Keepers will discover you've escaped and come looking for you."

"The unmakers are active." Screech shuddered. "I can feel them."

Kyja knew all those things, but it wasn't like Marcus to just wander off. "I don't understand," she said. "Where would he have g—"

Her eyes opened wide. She *knew* where he'd gone—she should have realized it as soon as she noticed him missing. "He's heading for the balcony."

"In the rain?" Riph Raph flapped his ears. "He's even dumber than I thought. He'll get soaked up there, and the view has to be terrible."

Kyja slapped at the skyte. "He's not going there for the view. It's his nightmare. He goes to the balcony, and then something awful happens." She turned to Cascade and Screech. "I need you to free Master Therapass yourselves."

"Of course," Screech said.

"Do you want me to go with you?" Cascade asked. "I sense something powerful waiting above."

"No. I need you to unlock Master Therapass's cell. As soon as you do, send him to the balcony. I think he knows more about whatever's up there than anyone. Riph Raph, fly up to see if Marcus is there yet."

"I'm unchained lighting," Riph Raph shouted, shooting into the air.

Kyja pushed the bushel of apples into Cascade's arms and ran for the stairs. How could she have let this happen? She knew Marcus was upset about entering the tower, but she'd been so focused on freeing Master Therapass that she'd completely forgotten about his nightmare.

"Who's there?" a guard called as she passed the entryway, but she raced into the kitchen—the quickest way to the stairs—without looking back.

She was sure she could catch up to Marcus once she reached the stairs—there was no way he could make it to the balcony without stopping to rest a few times. But each time she stopped to listen for him and call his name, no answer came. At the halfway point, she was gasping for breath, but still couldn't hear the familiar tapping of Marcus's staff.

Had she missed him somehow? He couldn't possibly have come

this far so fast in his condition. Maybe he hadn't gone up the stairs at all. What if he'd gone back outside the tower to wait? She'd nearly decided to turn back when she caught the first faint sounds of someone climbing the stairs above her.

"Marcus!" she screamed, her voice echoing. The only answer was the rolling crash of thunder.

A bedraggled Riph Raph flew down the narrow staircase, water dripping from his wings. "He's already on the balcony," the skyte called. "I tried to stop him, but it was like he couldn't hear me."

Kyja raced up the stairs again, sweat pouring down her face. She was almost to the top. "Marcus, stop!"

Cold air blew her hair from her face. She could hear the *tap, tap, tap* of wood on stone. With the last of her energy, she raced up the final stairs and ran to the balcony door. Marcus stood outside. Water poured from the sky in a torrent, slicking his hair to his head and turning his blue robe black. He didn't seem to notice. His eyes were fixed on a shining column of white light. Floating in the middle of it was what looked like a gauntlet. Purple and silver sparks leaped from the armored glove as it slowly turned.

"Stop," Kyja cried. Whatever that thing was, it seemed to have Marcus hypnotized. She had to keep him from reaching for it.

She stepped out onto the balcony to tackle Marcus if she had to. But before she could reach him, a figure moved behind her. Seeing the motion, she turned, but something heavy hit her on the back of the neck, and she collapsed to the ground.

CHAPTER 46

INNORIS A'GENTORAN

I N SOME ATTIC CORNER OF HIS BRAIN, Marcus sensed he was not alone on the balcony. That knowledge was rendered trivial by the power of what floated before him. Encased in a pillar of white light so bright it seared his eyes and burned the thick black clouds overhead, a gauntlet blazed with a violet splendor as though composed of millions of tiny amethysts. Sparks of purple and silver shot from its surface as it pulsed with the rhythm of his heart.

Instinctively, Marcus understood it was meant for him, that it had been placed here in anticipation of his arrival. By whom or by what, he didn't know—and didn't care. His appearance had drawn it from its hiding place. He reached his hand into the light; the brightness raced up his arms and over his body until he glowed like a beacon, burning in the night.

He stretched forth his hand, and a purple flicker jumped from the gauntlet to his fingertip. Energy surged through him as if he'd just been wired to a generator of enormous potential. Strength flowed through his limbs, and every hair on his body stood at attention. Yet he'd felt only a tiny spark. What sort of power might the gauntlet itself hold?

Be careful, a voice warned in his head. But he couldn't be careful. He couldn't have pulled back now even if his life depended on it. And it very well might. No human body was meant to have this kind of power. He pushed his hand forward, slipping it into the gauntlet.

The glove closed around his fingers, fitting his hand every bit as perfectly as he knew it would.

"How does it feel?" asked a voice from behind him.

Marcus turned to see Zentan Dolan standing in the doorway.

"How does it feel to hold the power of a world in your hand?" The zentan stepped forward, his eager face illuminated by the light shining from Marcus's body. With the strength of the gauntlet flowing through him, Marcus understood two things.

He realized that despite having a human form, Zentan Dolan was not human. And he understood where the Keeper got his magic.

The zentan's pale face broke into a smile. Thousands of glowing violet lines radiated from his body into the darkness. Each line pulsed and glowed in faint imitation of the gauntlet.

Marcus watched the violet lines. "Those all lead to people you've scaled, don't they? You're drawing their magic from them."

"Of course."

Marcus looked out over the balcony. He wasn't surprised to see all of the Keepers with violet lines extending from them as well. "Did you give any of the magic away to others, or was the whole rebalancing concept a scam?"

"A scam?" the zentan frowned. "No, not at all. I promised magic would be rebalanced from those who couldn't use it to those who could. I did exactly that.. As it turned out, I am the one best equipped to use it."

"What about the people you promised magic to? Didn't they wonder why their power never increased?"

The zentan laughed aloud, his guffaws echoing into the night. "That was the beauty of it. They thought they *were* more powerful. They thanked me for increasing their magic. Said they felt better than they had in years. And the few who didn't ended up with the harbingers—at least, until you came along."

Marcus flexed his fingers inside the gauntlet the tiniest bit. Somewhere in the distance, a mountain shifted on its foundation. He shivered. What could he do if he *waved* his hand? Sink cities, reshape landscapes, move continents? "What *are* you?" he asked Dolan.

"Does it matter?" the zentan answered, and Marcus realized it didn't. Dolan's eyes glittered like steel in the night. "Do you understand what you have?"

Marcus nodded slowly. "This gauntlet is what you've been trying to find. It's what you've been searching for."

"Innoris a'Gentoran—the Hand of Life. It's why I came here in the first place. Not just to this city, but to this world, over two hundred years ago. It was stolen from me."

Marcus was afraid to move for fear of what he might do with the power without meaning to. Wearing the gauntlet was like being a giant in a world of ants. One wrong move of his wrist might cause tornadoes, hurricanes, or tidal waves. He looked from the glove to Dolan. "It does what you've tried to do with the snifflers—it takes other people's magic—doesn't it? Except it draws on the magic from all the people in the world at the same time."

"That . . . and so much more," the zentan said. "Those elemental friends of yours think *they* control magic. But the real control is the power to bend magic to your will. I can show you how to use it. I can teach you."

Now it was Marcus's turn to laugh. "You mean, take it from me? I don't think so. "

"Not until you're ready to give it up. I've waited over two hundred years to find it. What are a few more? I swear I won't touch it until you are finished with it."

Marcus knew the zentan was telling the truth—did wearing the Innoris a'Gentoran grant him the ability to tell when someone was lying? On the other hand, he knew he wasn't getting the whole truth. "As soon as you got your hands on it, you'd destroy me."

"Why would I do that? I don't care about you or your world. The only reason I'm here is to get what was taken from me. I'll help you accomplish anything you desire. Then, when you're finished shaping this world after your design, I'll take my property and leave. You have my word." The zentan's eyes glittered as he spoke with a silky voice. "I can show you how to destroy the Dark Circle."

Marcus blinked. "Is that . . . possible?"

"Look inside yourself. You know it is."

Marcus closed his eyes, allowing the power of the gauntlet to flow through him, and for the first time, he really *saw.* All his life he'd assumed he was seeing everything there was to see. But his eyes were limited; they showed him only what was on the surface, a tiny fraction of what was really there. Through the Hand of Life, though, he could see underneath.

Not just inside rocks, trees, and animals—although he saw those, too—but he could see their relationships. How a falling rock caused an avalanche that moved a stream that undercut a bank that toppled a tree that hit a woodcutter, causing him to lose a limb that cost him his wife, who met a man that started a battle that led to a war that . . .

The interactions between one thing and another were endless— everything shaped the things around them. He saw them all— cataloging them through the eyes of the woodcutter and his wife, the bark of the tree that fell, the flake of the rock which caused the avalanche, all at the same time. Even more than that, he realized how he could *reshape* the events. With no more than a breath, he could restore the man's limb. His wife would never have left.

And the war that costs hundreds of lives between two cities would never have taken place.

It wasn't as if he would need to go back in time, because now he could see time as just another relationship—as flexible as all the others. At first he thought maybe this was the way Cascade saw, and his temper flared as he wondered why the water elemental had never shared this with him. But then he realized that what he saw and felt was beyond what any creature or elemental experienced.

His gaze fell on an army of Fallen Ones far to the north. He traced them back to the Summoner who'd raised them, which led to an army of Thrathkin S'Bae marching toward a border town, which took him back to the lair of the Dark Circle itself, and the creature who led it. For a moment, Marcus felt himself slipping into the creature's head and gasped with surprise. He'd assumed the Dark Circle wanted to destroy Farworld. But that wasn't their intention all.

It wasn't *destruction* the Dark Circle wanted but . . .

"The scales have fallen from your eyes." The zentan nodded. "What will you do about it?"

"I have to stop them," Marcus gasped.

Zentan Dolan held out his hands, palms up. "What's stopping you?"

"I don't know how," he admitted. He no longer needed to close his eyes to see, but there were too many relationships to keep of track of—too many variables changing every time he considered an option. Killing the creature that headed the Dark Circle was easy. But another would take his place. Even if he destroyed all of them— the Fallen Ones, the Summoner, the Thrathkin S'Bae, that would only stop things for a century or two. Like cutting off the heads of a hydra, the Dark Circle would rise again no matter what he did.

"Perhaps you're looking at it from the wrong direction," the zentan said.

"I don't understand." Marcus shivered.

"There's one relationship you've overlooked."

What was Dolan talking about? No matter what Marcus did, the Dark Circle would keep coming back. They were only going to get more powerful. And if he and Kyja continued on their course, they were playing right into the Dark Circle's hands. The only way he could stop them would be—

Inside the gauntlet, Marcus's hand clenched, and thunder ripped through the sky like a fiery sword. The relationship was so obvious, he didn't see how he'd missed it. He couldn't stop the Dark Circle no matter how he attacked it. Farworld was inherently vulnerable—like an egg before a snake.

If he couldn't stop the snake, maybe he could change the egg into a hawk. He could make Farworld so powerful that nothing could damage it.

The way to do that had been right in front of him all along. Master Therapass had been more right than he had known. There was a link between Marcus and Farworld, a link more powerful than even the wizard realized.

"To save Farworld, all I have to do is . . . heal myself."

CHAPTER 47

WEAKNESS

WAS IT REALLY THAT SIMPLE?

With the new vision the glove provided, Marcus studied his body and cringed at what he saw. Again, he realized, the wizard was right. The injuries the Dark Circle inflicted on him when he was an infant should have killed him. The only reason they hadn't was because of his tie to Farworld—a tie that for some reason he feared to examine too closely.

"The doctors tried to repair my bones and tendons," he murmured, running the gauntleted hand gingerly across his limp left arm. "But no matter how many surgeries they performed, no matter how much physical therapy I went through, it would never heal completely. Because . . . because the injuries aren't just physical."

He shuddered as he realized what Master Therapass had meant when he said his wounds couldn't be healed with normal magic. "It's like the Dark Circle put some of what they're made of inside me. The doctors couldn't fix my body because a part of me is just as corrupt as the Dark Circle." The thought of the darkness living and even growing inside his flesh made him want to vomit. It was like discovering a nest of maggots squirming and breeding just under his skin.

"Then burn it out," the zentan said. "Cleanse yourself of the darkness and cleanse Farworld at the same time."

"Yes." Marcus nodded. That was the only way. Even with the power of the Innoris a'Gentoran, he could not completely repair the damage. Like a cable rusted from the inside, there would always be inherent weakness in his body. The only way to heal himself was to burn everything out—tear it away and rebuild from scratch.

"It will hurt," Marcus murmured. He didn't mean it would hurt him, although he knew his pain would be so exquisite, it might come very close to killing him. But the cleansing would hurt Farworld, too.

"Of course it will hurt," the zentan said, his voice oozing with contempt. "It *should* hurt. Perfection requires sacrifice, and you are far, far from perfect. Look at yourself. Look at Farworld. Both of you are disgusting."

Marcus looked at himself—his pathetic arm, his misshapen leg. The sight made him gag. Weakness and frailties filled him like poison polluting a stream of crystal water. He looked at the world around him. It was no better. At the first sign of the Keepers, Terra ne Staric had folded in on itself. People were afraid, and the Dark Circle preyed on their fears. The fact that he'd ever considered himself capable of saving himself—never mind all of Farworld—was pathetic.

"If you are afraid of a little pain," Dolan said, "you don't deserve to be cured. Give me the Hand of Life and stay here, wallowing in your inadequacies. You and this world deserve each other." Zentan Dolan reached for the glove. Marcus jerked it away.

"It's mine!" he shouted, rage boiling inside him. He *was* weak. He *was* inadequate. His entire life he'd felt powerless. Locked in a wheelchair or crawling like a bug on the floor, he'd been dependant on others. But that was about to change. Holding the gauntlet high above his head like a lightning rod, he reached for all the power available to him. Magic was everywhere—in adults, children, animals, plants, rocks. Even the ground itself contained magic. All of it flowed to his hand like water down a hill.

Wind spun around him in a frenzied tornado. Lightning bolts struck at the glove and added to the magic. As the power came, Marcus felt himself expanding, growing in the darkness. He felt as tall as the zentan—taller. His head seemed to reach the top of the tower and beyond. The stones of the building trembled beneath his weight, and the very ground strained to hold him up. He felt taller than the tallest mountain, looking down on the world he was about to save.

People cried out in terror as their magic was pulled away from them. Forests moaned, their roots clutching the ground for purchase. Boulders shook, and plants flattened themselves against the ground. Still he kept taking magic. He needed all the power he could get to rebuild himself and Farworld. Let them complain for the moment. They would thank him afterward, when they understood.

Somewhere far underground, a gray face looked up in surprise. The leader of the Dark Circle raised his hands in fear, the gold ring on his finger blazing—the ring with the same symbol as Marcus bore on his shoulder.

Marcus took his magic too, laughing at the pitiful coward. "You did this to me. You caused this pain. Now you can feel it yourself."

Clenching his fist into a flaming ball of white, molten lava, Marcus looked down at his powerful body and prepared to purify both himself and Farworld.

A single voice whispered, "Don't."

———◄◆►———

Kyja came to slowly. Cold water pounded against her arms and legs, but something warm and scratchy caressed her cheek.

"Wake up," a voice said, and despite the freezing rain, she thought she was back in the Goodnuffs' barn. How many times had she woken to Riph Raph licking her face or pulling her hair?

"A few more minutes," she mumbled, rolling over.

"You don't have any more time." A flash of pain shot through her head and neck as she moved. Riph Raph nipped at the lobe of her ear. "Wake up."

"Ouch." She touched the back of her head, and another flair of agony shot up her spine to her skull.

"Come on," the skyte said, tugging at the front of her robe. "We have to get out of here. He's gone crazy."

Kyja opened her eyes and instantly wished she hadn't. Wind-lashed rain stung her skin, lightning glared, and the stone floor seemed to seesaw beneath her, making her stomach lurch. Where was she? The last thing she remembered, she'd been racing up the stairs, looking for—

"Marcus!" She pushed herself to her elbows, ignoring the pain in her head and the churning in her stomach. Something was happening at the edge of the balcony. Her first thought was of Marcus's dream. Thunder crashed just the way he'd described it. Gales slapped her robe against her body and whipped her hair across her face. Rain fell in such heavy sheets that it was impossible to see clearly. In the middle of it all, a figure stood with his arm raised to the storm.

Clutching the balcony wall for support, she pulled herself up. The wind threatened to knock her over the side, but she had to find Marcus. The huge creature at the end of the balcony was some kind of monster. Purple light encased it like a bloody, second skin. The figure throbbed with a dark energy that made her skin tingle. Evil seemed to seep from it like a putrid gas.

"We have to go," Riph Raph shouted over the storm. "Can't you feel it? He's sucking all the energy into himself. He's going to explode."

She *could* feel it. This was what Marcus had warned her about. Whatever the monster was, *it* was the betrayer of Farworld. Not Marcus. But where *was* Marcus? She searched the balcony and found a second figure. Zentan Dolan stared at the creature with rapt attention.

She opened her mouth to warn Marcus—wherever he was—to get away, when the creature threw back its head and laughed. "You did this to me!" it shouted toward the night, sparks of energy shooting from its hand. A blade of lightning sliced through the sky, illuminating the monster's face. Kyja stumbled backward.

"No," she said, shaking her head in disbelief. The creature had Marcus's face, but it was twisted, pale. It *couldn't* be him; it was the very embodiment of darkness. And just as he had predicted, the entire world drew back from him in terror and revulsion.

This wasn't Marcus. This ravening creature couldn't possibly be the boy she was such close friends with. Unaware she was doing it, she staggered forward on numb legs—eyes searching for some semblance of the person she knew.

"Are you crazy?" Riph Raph screeched, pulling at her hair and flapping his wings in a vain effort to lead her back to the stairs.

"Not you. Not you. Not you," she said, without realizing she was speaking.

The creature clenched its fist, sending out a burst of light that nearly blinded her. Holding her hand to block the light burning her retinas, she understood what was about to happen. Marcus was about to destroy Farworld.

In despair, she whispered, "Don't."

CHAPTER 48

SACRIFICE

KYJA FEARED IT WAS TOO LATE. Heat seared her skin as she squinted against what looked like a miniature sun. The balcony was lit up as if it was the middle of the day, and the whole world seemed to stop.

"Do it," the zentan said, his face locked in a blazing grin. "Burn it all."

The creature that couldn't be Marcus—but had his face—raised its hand, then hesitated. "Kyja?"

Zentan Dolan spun around, his eyes meeting hers. "Stop your meddling," he hissed. "This is none of your business." He raised his fist to strike her, but his arm stopped midair as though frozen in place. The veins in his neck bulged as he struggled to move; something was clearly holding him back.

Kyja thought she knew what it was. "Marcus?" she asked softly. "What are you doing?"

At first the creature said nothing. She wasn't sure it could hear

325

her—or that if it did, it understood who she was. Standing in front of this glowing figure raging with dark energy, she felt as though she were in the presence of an insane god.

Then it spoke. "Cleansing." The voice wasn't Marcus's. It shattered the air like thunder.

"Cleansing what?" she asked, afraid of what his answer would be.

"Myself," came the answer. Revulsion radiated from the figure in a cone of icy cold.

On her shoulder, Riph Raph shivered and whispered, "Don't make it mad."

Kyja ignored both Riph Raph and the zentan, who was furiously glaring at her, still unable to move. This wasn't Marcus she was talking to. But somewhere inside it, Marcus still existed—at least, she hoped he did. She had to get through to him before he destroyed both himself and Farworld.

"What are you cleansing yourself of?"

"Weakness."

That was it. That's how they'd gotten to him. He'd always been afraid of being weak, the same way she'd always been afraid of having no magic. But if she'd learned one thing over the last few days it was that shortcomings weren't always what they seemed. "Master Therapass warned us that we shouldn't be too anxious to get rid of our weaknesses. He said sometimes they turn out to be our greatest strengths."

"Wrong!" the creature roared, making the light flare. Both Kyja and Riph Raph flinched. "The Dark Circle preys on weakness. The only way to stop evil is to purify the world so the evil can never get a foothold."

"So this isn't just about you," Kyja said, knowing she was risking the creature's anger, but also knowing it might be the only way to reach Marcus. "It's bad enough that you want to remake yourself, but now you want to remake everyone else as well. Remember what the land elementals said about judging others . . . and judging yourself."

"It's for their own good," the creature growled. But she thought she sensed the smallest crack—that maybe Marcus was within reach.

"Did you ask *them* what they thought of your plan?" she asked. "Did you ask if they wanted to be perfected? Or did you take what they want into consideration? It only seems fair to ask if you're stealing their magic to purify them."

"Stealing? No." This time she was sure she heard Marcus's voice. He sounded miserable and lost. Beneath his rain-soaked hair, his eyes had a glazed stare.

She pressed on. "What else would you call it? You're no better than the Keepers. What gives you the right to decide what's best for everyone else? You've never taken anything that wasn't yours." Kyja stepped forward. The light in the creature's fist seemed to dim just a little. "Why start now?"

"Don't listen to her!" the zentan shouted. "She talks about stealing. But *she's* the thief. She wanted magic so much, she stole yours."

The creature turned its head. Kyja thought she heard it say something that sounded like *line.*

"That's true," the creature roared. The globe of fire in its hand flashed so bright Kyja had to close her eyes. "You stole my magic just like the Keepers stole theirs."

"No. I didn't." Kyja shook her head. But . . . *had* she? Hadn't it seemed just a little *too* convenient that Marcus's magic disappeared about the same time she got hers? Didn't a part of her always think that having magic was too good to be true? She must have suspected, but her happiness at having what she'd always wanted kept her from considering its source too closely.

"No one cares where power comes from, as long as they have it," the zentan said to the creature. "Stop wasting time and do what you have to do. There's no place for *weakness.*"

The creature raised its fist; Kyja swallowed hard. "Maybe I did steal your magic," she said, her face burning. "Maybe I'm the thief the Augur Well talked about. But I didn't do it on purpose. I wanted magic so bad that I didn't worry about where it came from or whether having it was right or wrong. But isn't that exactly what you're doing now? You're taking what you want without weighing the cost. I know how you feel about your injuries." She blinked away tears. "I wanted magic as much as you want to be strong. But I gave up *my* dream for Farworld. Can't you?"

"She's lying." The zentan said.

"I'm not. Giving up my magic was the third test. Marcus, you were unconscious, so you never knew about it."

The creature stood silent. Like listening to someone far away, Kyja heard the sound of her own voice saying, *I give . . . my magic,* as though Marcus were replaying the scene.

Little by little, the light began to fade. "You gave it away?" This time the voice was clearly Marcus's. "Why didn't you tell me?"

She shrugged. "It wasn't as important as getting you healthy. Once you were all right, there didn't seem to be any point."

The glowing globe winked out, leaving Marcus—not the creature—standing in a purple glow. Slowly, he lowered his fist.

"Don't be a fool," the zentan said. Now free of Marcus's hold, he slipped his hand into the pocket of his robe. "If you quit, you'll never defeat the Dark Circle."

"Maybe not. But if I do defeat them, it'll be by my own power."

"*Our* power," Kyja corrected.

"Our power," Marcus repeated. He held the gauntlet before him as if seeing it for the first time. "This provides the power the snifflers use to steal magic." He turned to the zentan. "What would happen to you if it were destroyed?"

"Enough! You are not worthy of the Innoris a'Gentoran. You are as weak as the rest of this world. They deserve whatever comes to them, and so do you." The zentan pulled a blade from his robe. Flames leaped and danced on its slick dark surface. He pointed it toward Kyja but spoke to Marcus. "This is flazite. One scratch, and your blood turns to fire. Give me the gauntlet, or your friend is dead."

Marcus raised the gauntlet as if about to use its power again, but Kyja shook her head, her rain-drenched hair clinging to her cheeks. She'd seen what the glove did to Marcus, how even a little power from it changed him. "Don't use it again. It's too dangerous."

Marcus searched her eyes. "But I don't have magic without it."

"Maybe if you destroy it, my magic will go back to you."

"I can't take that from you," Marcus said. Kyja smiled. "I already gave it away. Besides, I think the Keepers have relied on others' magic too long. I don't think they can survive without it."

"She'll die first," the zentan said.

Kyja met Marcus's eye and nodded ever so slightly. "Now!" she shouted and dropped to the ground. Riph Raph flew from her shoulder, blowing a fireball to distract the zentan. But even as Marcus slammed the gauntlet to the stone wall, shattering it into a million glittering pieces, Kyja knew it was too late.

The zentan's hand was a blur. The blazing light of the flazite blade tracked her to the ground. Its aim was true. She watched it fly straight at her, knowing she was about to die and hoping Marcus would be able to complete their quest alone.

She didn't see the figure leaping from the doorway until he dove, stretching out his powerful body to intercept the knife meant for her. With an explosion of fire, the blade entered his chest.

"Rhaidnan!" Kyja screamed. The hunter collapsed to the ground, his face a mask of agony.

Without the magic of all the people he'd stolen it from, the zentan howled in rage and pain. His skin seemed to shrivel and melt. But Kyja cared nothing of that. She wrapped her arms around Rhaidnan. "Marcus, *do* something!"

"Too . . . late," the hunter said. His skin had turned a bright red, and smoke leaked from his eyes like burning tears. Rain drops sizzled against his cheeks. "So sorry," he whispered through gritted teeth. "Tell . . . tell Char . . . I . . . didn't dis-a-ppoint."

"Never," Kyja whispered, tears streaming down her face. "You never disappointed me or her."

"Made . . . children . . . proud." Flames burst through his robe, forcing Kyja to back away. But before Rhaidnan disappeared completely in a pyre of flames, she saw him smiling.

CHAPTER 49

REUNION

L EANING AGAINST THE BALCONY WALL, Marcus felt as if he'd just returned from a long trip. His head ached, and it was hard to concentrate. He could remember putting his hand into the gauntlet and seeing so many amazing things. But exactly what he'd seen was beginning to fade. Overhead, the clouds cleared away—the storm seemingly ended by the destruction of the Innoris a'Gentoran—and light from all three moons washed over the balcony.

Looking down, he was not surprised to see the battle appeared to have ended. Villagers wandered the streets in confusion as the guards relit the torches. With the power of the Hand of Life destroyed, his magic was back, but all the aches and pains—and weaknesses—returned as well. He guessed he'd have to live with them after all.

He found his staff a few feet away and stumbled on wobbly legs to Kyja's side, where she stood weeping over what was now no more than a pile of ashes. "My fault," he croaked.

"No." She squeezed his hand. "Rhaidnan did what he had to—to restore his honor." She turned to glare at the crumpled body of Zentan Dolan. "It's *his* fault." She looked like she wanted to kick him, but the zentan himself was little more than a dried husk—his body shriveled like a piece of fruit left out in the sun.

He was like a vampire, Marcus thought. *Kept alive by sucking away the strength of others.* And Marcus had come close to becoming the same thing. The pull of the power had been so great. If Kyja hadn't stopped him, he might have destroyed Farworld, thinking all the time that he was curing it.

"We need to check on Master Therapass," Kyja said.

They started toward the staircase, when Riph Raph spoke up. "Hey, you two. I don't think this guy's completely dead."

Marcus heard what sounded like a newspaper crinkling in the wind, and turned to see the zentan's body moving. His arms and legs—really no more than leather-covered sticks—writhed on the ground as though he were trying to get up. His eyelids flapped open and closed like window shades over his empty, black eye sockets.

"That's disgusting." Kyja wrinkled her nose. "He can't be alive. It has to be some leftover magic."

But Marcus wasn't so sure. He didn't remember most of what happened after he put on the gauntlet, but he did remember realizing that the zentan wasn't human. "Stand back," he said pushing her against the wall.

The zentan's body began to shake. His skull banged against the ground—teeth chattering. His chest swelled as though he were trying to breathe—once, twice—and then, with the sound of a dried squash cracking, ripped open. Wet, black gore poured from the dead man's body. The glistening puddle pulsed on the stone floor.

"What is it?" Kyja asked.

Marcus shook his head. His body felt drained, but sensing something was about to happen, he readied his magic anyway.

Out of the slime rose an obsidian demon with shoulders as broad as Marcus was tall, a horned head with a dog-shaped snout, and two tentacle-like arms that ended in coiled whips. At least twelve feet tall, the demon towered over Marcus and Kyja. Its legs—each as big around as tree trunks—ended in sharp hooves that struck sparks from the stones as it stomped against the balcony floor.

"Ahhh," it groaned, flexing its muscles. "It feels so good to be free of that limiting human body."

"Time to go," Riph Raph called.

Before Marcus could take a step, one of the demon's tentacles slashed through the air, slamming him against the wall. His staff clattered across the balcony, and a burst of agony raged through his good arm.

"Heal yourself now!' the demon roared.

"Leave him alone!" Kyja shouted.

She ran toward the demon, but it wrapped an arm around her and held her over the edge of the balcony. Hanging hundreds of feet in the air, she screamed and struggled in its grasp.

Riph Raph flew at the demon, hissing and blowing fireballs, but the demon slapped him away without even a glance in his direction.

"Shall I drop her?" the demon asked Marcus. "Break her like you broke the Innoris a'Gentoran?"

"No," Marcus said. "Let her go. She didn't do anything to you."

"On the contrary," the demon said, "she ruined something I have spent over two hundred years working for. A quick death is too good for her."

The demon set Kyja back on the balcony. "You watched as what *I* wanted was destroyed. Now you can watch as I destroy your friend. I'll do it slowly so you don't miss a thing."

With Kyja safe on the ground, Marcus blasted the demon with a gust of air magic. It didn't seem to affect it at all. "Is that the best you can do?" The creature sneered. "Killing you will be far too easy."

"Maybe you'd like more of a challenge," said a voice from the stairway.

The demon spun around as Tankum Heartstrong stepped onto the balcony. The stone warrior pulled his twin swords from the scabbards on his back. "Your Keepers were too easy. I got to use only my fists on them. It's time I wet my blades."

"Go back to your pedestal before I reduce you to rubble, statue." The demon looked away disdainfully. It stepped toward Marcus, and Tankum charged.

So quick Marcus never saw it coming, the demon snapped its left tentacle, whistling through the air at Tankum. The warrior raised his sword to meet the attack, but the strength of the blow knocked him backward. Instantly the demon struck again with its other arm, this time aiming higher.

Tankum ducked the second arm, spun around, and stepped inside the attack. He swung both swords at once at the demon's neck. With surprising agility, the demon pulled away, but the right blade nicked its chest.

Unhurt by the cut, the demon kicked its hoof, hitting Tankum in the side of the head. "Had enough fun yet?" the demon taunted as Tankum shook off the blow. "Quit now, stone head, and I'll let you wet your blades on the girl."

"I'm just getting started," Tankum said. He feinted left toward the demon then swung his right sword in an overhand blow. The demon countered with a strike of its own, but the warrior was waiting for it. In a blur of movement, he brought up his left blade and sliced off the tip of a tentacle.

Dark, green gore oozed from the tip of the severed limb and smeared the end of the blade.

Tankum held out his bloodied blade, taunting the demon as he called it forward with his other sword. "Come and get more, dog face. If I'm going to clean one blade later, I might as well clean them both."

With a cry of rage, the demon attacked with both arms. Tankum fought back, but it was impossible to fend off all the demon's blows. A quick snap caught him on the back of his leg, sending him stumbling. Another wrapped around his left wrist, nearly pulling the sword from his grip.

With blindingly quick strokes, Tankum fought back. His blades flew so swiftly, they were only a silver blur in the moonlight. Man and demon moved about the balcony in bounds and leaps—striking and parrying, ducking and feinting.

Marcus tried to help, but his magic wasn't strong enough to affect the battle. All he could do was stay out of the way, cradling his broken right arm to his chest. Master Therapass had told him how strong and fast Tankum was, but seeing it for himself took his breath away. Every time the demon seemed to have Tankum cornered, the warrior found a way out of it. His swords moved as though they were part of his body.

He managed to hit the demon several times, drawing blood on more than one occasion. But for every blow that connected, the demon struck twice. Tankum didn't bleed, but pieces of him chipped away at an alarming rate.

Ducking a particularly fierce attack, the demon opened its mouth and sprayed something that looked like acid on Tankum's left arm. Smoke rose from the stone, and his sword fell to the ground. Before he could retrieve it, the demon struck at his right wrist. Stone cracked, and the sword slipped from his grasp.

In an instant, the demon wrapped the soldier in both arms and lifted him over its head like a child. "Time to see if rock can fly," the creature boomed, walking toward the edge of the balcony, sparks flying from its hooves with each step.

"Don't!" Kyja screamed. She ran toward the demon, but there was nothing she could do. A second before she reached it, a blast of blue flame struck the demon on the side of the head, sending it spinning. It stumbled backward and Tankum dropped from its arms, hitting the ground with a thud.

A bent figure limped onto the balcony, his long gray beard swaying with each step. The figure raised an arm, and another blast of fire rocked the demon. It roared in pain, shaking its massive head.

"Looks like I have to get you out of another predicament," Master Therapass said, a crooked grin splitting his seamed face.

"What are you talking about?" Tankum said, getting to his feet and retrieving his swords. "I'm always the one getting you out of trouble."

"Haven't I told you a hundred times, magic over might?" Therapass said.

"And haven't *I* reminded *you* just as many that your magic wouldn't be here if not for the might of my swords?"

With a howl of rage, the demon charged both men. Tankum met the charge with his blades raised. The demon spit a cloud of acid, forcing Tankum to backpedal.

"Too much for you?" the demon howled, battering the warrior with one strike after another, sending chunks of rock flying through the air.

"Try hitting what you can't see," Therapass said. He raised his staff, and a fog of gray smoke surrounded the demon's head.

The demon whirled, teeth bared. "Time to finish you off, old man." It lunged toward the wizard, snapping its arms like bullwhips. Therapass blocked the first two swings with his staff, but a kick from the demon's sharp hoof got past his defenses and sent the wizard flying across the balcony. Blood streamed from Therapass's shoulder.

Tankum stepped in front of the demon as it tried to finish the wizard off. With one sword held cross-wise in front of him and the other behind his back, he whirled toward the demon. The spinning blades hacked at the creature's arms, leaving no opening for it to strike back.

"Now who's saving who?" he called to Therapass.

"Just letting you feel useful," the wizard called, pulling himself to his feet.

Forced backward by Tankum's attack, the demon snarled something that sounded like, "Trigrk gra."

Eight black globes rose from its chest and flew at Tankum. He caught the first with his sword, shattering it into a thousand tiny drops that hissed as they landed on the ground. The second globe hit his right leg, burning a deep crater into it before he could slap the orb away with the edge of his sword.

"A little help here!" he shouted, trying to keep track of the six remaining balls.

"Right behind you," the wizard said. He raised his fist and sent a handful of ice bolts that shot the globes out of the air.

The wizard and the warrior attacked and parried with the demon, combining strength, cunning, and more than thirty years of fighting, back to back. But despite their best efforts, the demon held them off at every turn. Though green gore flowed from at least a dozen cuts and burns, none of them showed any sign of slowing the creature.

But Master Therapass was beginning to weaken. Fighting against the unmakers appeared to have taken its toll.

"Let's finish this thing off," he gasped, shooting a ball of fire at the demon's feet. "So you can buy me dinner."

"I always buy dinner, you miser." Tankum blocked a tentacle and attacked with a reverse spin. Even *he* looked like he couldn't hold out much longer. Huge chunks of stone had been torn from his chest and legs, and he could barely move his left arm.

The demon struck again. This time, Tankum's response was too slow. The creature's tentacle hit his left arm and ripped it completely off in a shower of dust and rock. Tankum's sword fell to the ground.

"No more playing," the demon growled. Focused on Tankum, it never saw Kyja as she darted forward and lifted the heavy sword from the ground. She slipped under its guard and slashed at its unprotected ankles.

With a howl of rage, the demon lunged for her.

Using the trick Lanctros-Darnoc had taught him, Marcus summoned a swarm of glittering green insects that flew into the creature's face, stabbing at it with venomous stingers.

As the demon swatted them away, Tankum dropped to his knees and pushed Kyja to safety.

The demon looked down, and Therapass blasted it from above with a bolt of lightning. At the same time, Tankum lunged up, driving his sword into its stomach.

Gurgling in pain, the creature tried to pull the blade out, but the warrior twisted it, driving it deeper. With a howl of agony, the demon opened its mouth and lowered its head to bite Tankum.

Therapass stepped forward, his fist glowing bright red as he slammed it into the demon's face. It screamed, raised its tentacles high into the air, and exploded in a spray of black goo.

"Mine!" Therapass and Tankum shouted together.

Therapass looked at Kyja with a sardonic grin. "You saw the whole thing. Tell this rock head that I finished the demon off."

Tankum winked at Marcus. "The poor old fool's eyesight is failing. Explain to him how I landed the killing blow."

Marcus and Kyja looked at each other wide-eyed and both burst into laughter.

CHAPTER 50

GRAEHL

KEEP YOUR BALANCE NOW. Lean more to the left. Find your center. Pivot."

Following Tankum's advice, Marcus put more of his weight on his left leg and turned. They were in the small practice arena behind the tower. Tankum had been completely healed by Lanctros-Darnoc, and Marcus was feeling better as well. All around them, men and women sweated as they trained in the hot afternoon sun. Most of them practiced with swords much bigger than the one Marcus was using—but a few swung maces or shot arrows at practice dummies.

"Can you feel it?" Tankum asked.

Marcus nodded. The leather grip of the half-size sword felt good in his hand, and the weight no longer seemed like it was going to topple him over any minute. "But I'm not sure I can swing without falling."

The warrior hefted his own curved scimitar. "That's where magic comes in."

"But I thought only wizards used magic."

Tankum winked and looked over his shoulder as though making sure no one was close enough to overhear him. "We let the spell-tossers think that so they don't get cocky. But just because they can't swing a sword without cutting off their noses doesn't mean a warrior can't enhance his skills with a little extra something. Watch closely."

He swung his blade—which must have weighed ten times that of Marcus's—so quickly it was nothing but a blur. Now that Marcus was looking for it, he could see how the warrior enhanced his balance and speed with bursts of air and land magic.

"Think you can do that?" Tankum asked.

"I think so." It came down to cutting wind resistance on the swing while strengthening his stance and arm through land magic. Concentrating on the balance, he whispered, "Air and land, foot and hand," and swung the sword. The power and speed of his swing were so great he nearly fell over, but the extra land magic kept him upright.

"Very good!" Tankum said, beaming at his pupil. "Keep that up, and we'll make a soldier out of you yet."

"He'd make a better scholar," said Lanctrus-Darnoc, who were watching from just outside the arena. "Although you've got a lot more studying to do."

Marcus turned and realized Kyja was watching from the other side of the arena wall. "Did you see that?" he called.

"Very impressive," she said.

"You should try it yourself."

Kyja shrugged.

Marcus puffed up his chest. "Maybe it's more of a guy thing."

"Are you going to let him get away with that?" Riph Raph squawked.

Kyja rolled her eyes and vaulted the wall into the arena.

Marcus hoped she didn't embarrass herself. Sword fighting was trickier than it looked. "Don't get down on yourself if you don't pick it up right away. It's harder without magic."

"I'll try not to do too badly," she said, strapping on a padded leather practice vest and helmet as though she'd done it before.

He handed her his sword, but she waved it off, calling to one of the female weapon masters, "Yhuleana, throw me a one-and-a-half handed claymore."

The athletic-looking woman pulled a sword more than twice as big as the one Marcus had used off the rack and tossed it into the air. Kyja caught it smoothly in one hand. She flexed the blade, tested the balance, and said to Tankum, "Care to spar?"

"Love to." Tankum grinned.

"You might want to stand back," she told Marcus.

Unable to keep his jaw from hanging open, Marcus stepped a few feet away and watched in amazement as Kyja and Tankum battled toe-to-toe. Tankum was stronger. But even without the benefit of magic, Kyja was amazingly quick and dexterous. She moved like a humming bird, stepping outside the warrior's range before darting inside his swings. More than once her sword threw off sparks as she made contact with Tankum's stone body.

At the end of fifteen minutes, both were breathing hard. "Well done," Tankum said, ending the bout by holding his sword at his chest and bowing. "I would gladly fight with you at my side."

"Wow!" Marcus said. "That was incredible. Where did you learn to fight like that?"

"A guy thing?" Riph Raph blustered. "She's beat you at Trill Stones and sword fighting. She's tougher and smarter than *you'll* ever be."

Hiding a smile, Kyja bit her lip and gave her sword and vest back to the weapon master. "What do you think I did while the other kids were practicing spells?"

"You humans are full of surprises," said Cascade, who continued to make a habit of randomly appearing out of nowhere. Today he wore a hat, leather vest, and a pair of woolen britches instead of his usual blue robe.

"What's up with the outfit?" Marcus asked.

"I thought dressing like a human might help me understand them better," the water elemental said. "But mostly, it just itches." Cascade nodded toward a thin man with a small beard standing a few feet away. "That gentleman's been watching you both for quite some time now. It might be worth your while to go meet him."

"Who is he?" Marcus asked. Something about the man looked familiar, but he couldn't say exactly what.

"Go over and find out," Cascade said.

Marcus and Kyja approached the man, who seemed embarrassed to be noticed. He looked as if he might flee, but at the last minute, licked his lips and stood his ground.

"Hi. I'm Kyja, and this is Marcus," Kyja said.

"I . . . I know." The man bobbed his head and tried to shrink in on himself in a way that seemed very familiar. He kept his head cocked toward his chest as though he were used to looking down on people, even though he wasn't all that tall.

"Do I know you?" Kyja asked. "I do, don't I?"

"Well,"—the man shrugged—"we have met before. But I looked a little different back then."

Marcus was sure *he'd* never met this man, but Kyja's eyes lit up as her mouth formed an O of surprise. "Screech!"

What was she talking about? Marcus looked from Kyja to the

man. Screech was a cave trulloch at least seven feet tall. This human couldn't be more than five ten. But there *was* something about him that looked a little like the snaggletoothed creature.

The man swallowed—his Adam's apple bobbing up and down on his whiskered throat. "I suppose I should have told you before. But it was a little complicated, considering the circumstances."

"What happened to you?" Kyja asked. "Who turned you into a human?"

"Actually, it was the other way around. You see . . ." He licked his lips and looked at the ground. "I used to be a Keeper."

"A Keeper?" Marcus growled. He knew they shouldn't have trusted him.

The man nodded, his eyes still fixed on his feet. "One of Zentan Dolan's top aides. For a long time, I believed he was right that giving magic to the most powerful was the best way of keeping balance in the world."

Marcus felt his face burn and found himself looking at the ground too.

"I thought that way until I talked to some of the people who'd been scaled," Screech continued. "That's when I realized more good gets done by normal men and women engaging in everyday acts of kindness than by all the most powerful people combined. Once I discovered that, I tried to tell the others. A few of them listened to what I had to say, until . . ."

"Until Zentan Dolan found out," Kyja said.

"That's right." The man looked gratefully up at her. "He turned me into a trulloch and sent me to work for the unmakers. He used them to torture information out of people as well as to breed more snifflers. I knew if I didn't obey, I'd be fed to the unmakers next."

"So you let them kill other people to save yourself," Marcus said. "You would have let them kill us if we hadn't escaped."

The man pulled at his long, scruffy hair with both hands as though the pain helped him deal with his guilt. "I can never make up for that. But I am grateful to you two for helping me escape. And for killing the zentan and breaking his spell. I'd like to assist you with the rest of your search. If you'll let me. I know you have no reason to trust me."

"And we have lots of reasons not to," Marcus said. "You came this far just so you could get turned back to a human."

"You don't owe us anything," Kyja said. "I'm just glad you aren't with those horrible creatures anymore. But if you want to help us, we'd love to have you."

Marcus scowled. Mr. Z was right. Kyja was the most stubborn person Marcus knew once she made a decision. And he still didn't trust Screech as a man or a trulloch. He glanced back at Cascade, who was watching them with his annoyingly amused smile.

"What do we call you?" Kyja asked.

"My human name was Graehl. But I'm thinking maybe I should just stick with Screech. To remind me of what I was."

"No," Kyja said. "I like Graehl better. We all have things we need to forget. We've all made mistakes."

She didn't look at Marcus, but he couldn't help thinking about what nearly happened in the tower. Maybe the land elementals were right. Maybe he *was* too quick to see the worst in others—and in himself.

"Yeah," he said. "We have." He stuck out his hand. "Nice to have you with us . . . Graehl."

The man smiled for the first time since they'd met. He took Marcus's hand. "Nice to be here."

"I hate to interrupt," a guard said. "But are you Marcus and Kyja?"

"We are," Kyja said.

The guard jerked a thumb toward the tower. "Master Therapass would like to meet with you in his study."

CHAPTER 51

THE PLACE BETWEEN

MASTER THERAPASS'S STUDY looked like something had recently exploded inside. Boxes, crates, and baskets were scattered everywhere. The shelves—normally covered with everything from animal skulls to bottles of sparkling powders and mysterious liquids—were either empty or in complete disarray.

"Hello?" Kyja said, sticking her head through the doorway.

"Bring that box of books over here," the wizard said without turning around.

"Does it always look like this?" Marcus whispered.

"No," Kyja whispered back.

"Usually it's worse," Riph Raph said with a shudder.

"Be quiet." Kyja found a wooden box filled with a disorganized array of leather-bound tomes and carried them across the room. "Where would you like me to put these?"

"What?" the wizard spun around and blinked. "Oh, it's you. I thought it was the people I requested to get this place in order. Just set them over there with the goat cheeser."

Kyja had no idea what a *goat cheeser* was, so she just pushed aside a dusty, stuffed fish with scales peeling off and set the box on a shelf.

"Did you get robbed or something?" Marcus asked, looking around at the mess.

"So it would seem." Therapass threw his hands in the air. "Apparently when I was locked in the dungeon, a few other wizards decided my study and possessions were free to whomever wanted them. If I find out who took my fossilized bat livers collection, I'll string them up by their nose hairs. It's going to take me weeks to get this place back in shape."

"You asked to see us?" Kyja asked, brushing the dust off her hands.

"Yes, yes." The wizard held up something that looked like a blue hourglass filled with glowing sparks. He turned it one way and then another before muttering, "I have no idea what this is," and tossing it back into a box. "Sit anywhere you want."

Kyja and Marcus looked around the room for a seat, but there was only one chair, and it quickly scuttled across the floor to catch Master Therapass as he collapsed backward into it. They each settled atop a wooden crate.

"Now then," the wizard said, tugging on his beard. "I understand you've had a few adventures since we parted company."

"That's the understatement of the century," Riph Raph said.

"Quite a bit has happened," Kyja agreed.

"Well then," the wizard said, leaning back in his chair and lacing his fingers in front of his chest. "Tell me all about it."

Kyja looked at Marcus. Where to start? "I guess the first thing was when Marcus and I jumped to Earth."

"Really?" the wizard said.

For the next hour and a half, Kyja and Marcus took turns relating all the things that had happened to them—from the unmakers to the Fontasians, to Water Keep and Land Keep, the snifflers, the harbingers, the Keepers, Cascade, Lanctrus-Darnoc; finally ending with the zentan and Innoris a'Gentoran.

The wizard seemed particularly interested in the water and land elementals. He asked several questions about Land Keep and the tree of books, muttering, "I'll have to visit it at my first opportunity." He seemed very impressed with how they'd handled the tests on their way to finding the Augur Well and asked several times to repeat exactly what it had told them.

He laughed aloud at their description of Mr. Z. Kyja saw what looked like recognition in his eyes and asked if he knew the little man.

The wizard only smiled and said, "I might. I might."

"What was that demon you and Tankum fought on the balcony?" Kyja asked once they'd finished telling their story.

"An excellent question," the wizard said. "You mentioned the snifflers and the unmakers. I believe your water elemental friend explained how they are creatures of shadow."

"Yes," Kyja said. "But what does that mean?"

Master Therapass stroked the tip of his beard. "Shadow creatures are not from this world."

"You mean they're from Earth?" Marcus asked.

"No, they're not from there, either."

Kyja wrinkled her brow. "If they're not from Earth or Farworld, where are they from?"

Therapass leaned back. "You mentioned that when you jumped

349

from the snifflers to Earth, you seemed to get stuck for a moment. That you heard something coming toward you?"

"You mean the in-between place," Marcus said. "The gray area."

"The *between* place, yes. I have long suspected that between Earth and Farworld is a third realm. Another world, if you will. When I opened the doorway that sent Marcus to Earth, I sensed something there. It is a place of shadows—shadow creatures. The Dark Circle has apparently found a way to tap into that world. I have good reason to believe the demon hidden within the zentan's body was from that shadow world, as are the snifflers and the unmakers. Their magic is extremely dangerous. It is imperative that they all be captured or destroyed."

"Is that where the Hand of Life came from?" Marcus asked.

At the name, Therapass raised his eyebrows. "Oh, is that what the old snake called it? More like the Hand of *Death*. Yes, it, too, came from the realm of shadows."

"The zentan said it was stolen from him," Marcus said. "He said he came here looking for it."

"That was a lie," Master Therapass said. "I have no doubt he lusted after it once he realized what it was. But creatures of shadow cannot leave their realm on their own. They must be summoned. The demon arrived here long before the Innoris a'Gentoran. I'm sure the Dark Circle brought him here the same way they brought the gauntlet."

"So how *did* the gauntlet get here?' Kyja asked.

"The Dark Circle reached into the realm of shadows and took it. I'm not sure how. It was merely a powerful artifact there, but *here* they thought it would allow them to rule all of Farworld."

"Why didn't it?" Marcus shivered. "They could have controlled all magic with it."

"They couldn't use it completely," Therapass said. "It was beyond their abilities."

Kyja sensed the wizard was avoiding something. "If the Dark Circle had it, how did it end up here in the tower?"

The old man pushed himself out of his chair with a groan and limped across the study. He lit a fire in the big stone fireplace, changing the flame from blue to green to red, and back to blue again.

"Master Therapass?" Kyja got up from her box.

The wizard paced slowly around the room, touching objects at random. "When I was much younger and much more foolish, I heard a rumor that the Dark Circle had obtained a device of such great power that whoever owned it could do anything they wanted. I also heard that no wizard had been able to use it. Being vain and prideful, I thought that if I could get my hands on the device, I could be the one to unlock its mysteries."

"But you would have used it for good," Kyja said, clasping her hands in front of her chest.

"So I told myself. But the truth was, I allowed myself to be blinded by the promise of power. I told myself I was only seeking after it for the greater good of man, but I allowed myself to be seduced by the very evil I was fighting against. And I joined the Dark Circle."

"No!" Kyja gasped. That wasn't possible.

The wizard clenched his fists. "I don't know what might have happened had I been able to use the Innoris a'Gentoran. It wasn't until I realized its power was beyond my reach as well that I came to my senses. I stole it and brought it here, telling myself that such had been my plan all along. It wasn't until I sensed the power of shadow on Zentan Dolan when he arrived here with High Lord Dinslith that I realized the gauntlet might no longer be safe."

Marcus shook his head. "Why didn't you just destroy it when you realized it was of no use to you?"

"I couldn't," the wizard said, waggling a finger in the air. "At the time I didn't think anyone could."

"So you hid it," Kyja said.

"I hid it in a place I thought would be completely safe—right under their noses, but hidden in such a way that only one person besides myself could find it."

Marcus got slowly to his feet. "Me."

"You," the wizard said with a nod, returning to his pacing. "If something happened to me, I knew that an item of such power should only be left in the hands of the person destined to save Farworld. Even if I knew you couldn't use it either."

Marcus hesitated. "But I did use it."

"Yes, you did. It was only once I was in the dungeon that I realized you would be able to. I tried to send you a warning through the dawn chimes, but the pull of the Innoris a'Gentoran was too strong."

Marcus blushed and stared at the floor. "When I was wearing it, I thought I was stopping the Dark Circle once and for all by making everyone on Farworld too perfect to be tempted by them."

"Instead you would have become the master of darkness yourself," the wizard said. "By trying to force everyone to meet your image of perfection, you would have damned them to eternal servitude with you as their master. You would have been as corrupt as the Dark Circle."

Marcus jerked as if he'd just remembered something. "When I was wearing the gauntlet, I saw something. I think I was in the head of the Master of the Dark Circle."

Therapass stopped pacing and stared at him. "What did you see?"

Marcus shook his head. "I don't remember exactly. It's all sort of fuzzy now."

"Try," the wizard said. "Concentrate."

"I'm trying," Marcus said, squeezing his eyes shut. "I was surprised. I thought the Dark Circle wanted to destroy Farworld, or take it over. But they didn't, at least not right away. They wanted . . . they wanted . . ." He pounded his fists against his legs. "I can't remember. It's all a blur."

"It's all right," the wizard said. "Maybe it will come to you later. If not, this much gives us something more to consider. As with Trill Stones, the more we know about the enemy's strategy, the more likely we are to defeat it."

"What happens now?" Kyja asked. "We still need to find the air elementals and the fire elementals."

"Yes." Master Therapass tugged at his beard. "But there are several things to be taken care of first. Our city is in shambles. High Lord Dinslith is no longer fit to rule. I have been asked to take his place."

"You're going to be the new high lord?" Kyja asked, grinning ear to ear.

"I've been asked to be, but I don't think I'll accept the position. I have too much to do. I've asked Breslek Broomhead to take it instead. He was one of the few wizards to stand against the Keepers, even at the possible danger of his family."

"What about Rhaidnan? Who will take care of his wife and children?"

"As his first order as high lord, Breslek will declare Rhaidnan a city hero for sacrificing his life to save you and Marcus. His statue will be added to Terra ne Staric's greatest wizards and warriors. His family will be well cared for."

"What's going to happen to the other wizards and warriors?" Marcus asked. "Will they go back to being just . . . statues again?"

"For the time being, no. I have asked Tankum if he would consider leading a small army consisting of the other stone wizards and warriors to search out and destroy all of the unmakers and snifflers, and to make sure no Keepers remain. The stone warriors should be somewhat immune to the power of the shadow creatures, so it is a good assignment for them. Lanctrus-Darnoc have agreed to join them. Their power will keep the warriors and wizards from returning to their previous state."

Kyja nodded. It would be good to know the snifflers and unmakers were gone once and for all. "Will Cascade stay with us?"

"I've asked him to go on a special mission important to humans and Fontasians alike. Until I know more, his operation will remain a secret."

"So it's just Kyja and me going to look for the other elementals?" Marcus asked.

"There will be others to help you," the wizard said. "But I am afraid you will need to postpone searching for the other elementals for a few weeks—or possibly months. For a time, Marcus, I must ask you to remain on Earth."

Marcus looked up in shock. "Why?"

The wizard clenched his staff. "Haven't you wondered why you could use the Innoris a'Gentoran when no one else could? Why you were able to destroy it?"

Marcus shrugged. "Because I'm the one who's supposed to save Farworld."

Master Therapass shook his head. "The gauntlet was not created in or for Farworld."

"Then why?"

"After I hid the gauntlet, once I was locked in the dungeon, I had a chance to study the unmakers. I sensed something in them I had only sensed twice before—in the zentan and in one other place."

"What are you saying?" Kyja asked, a chill running up her back.

"The realm of shadows is a place we know very little about. As you have seen, it contains creatures that can wield great power here on Farworld. Ordinarily those beings of shadow would not pose a threat unless they were summoned here. They should be unable to harm you as you pass from Earth to Farworld and back. The fact that they not only sensed Marcus's presence among them, but actually hunted him down, combined with the fact that he was able to use the Innoris a'Gentoran, worries me a great deal."

Marcus raised his hands. "I don't understand. What does that mean?"

The wizard looked Marcus in the eyes. "I'm sorry, but the only thing I can conceive of to explain this is that you must have a special relationship to the realm of shadows."

"What kind of relationship?"

"I'm afraid I must conclude that one of your parents was a creature of shadow."

CHAPTER 52

GOOD-BYE

I CAN'T BELIEVE YOU HAVE TO GO." Kyja folded her arms across her chest. "This totally stinks."

Marcus couldn't help smiling at all the Earth slang she'd picked up. At the same time, he was doing everything he could to keep from crying as they stood just outside the ruins of the Goodnuff farm. Being away from Farworld and his only friends for weeks—or months—was going to kill him.

"Maybe you could occasionally jump me back without anyone knowing," he suggested. "Just to say hi and tell me what's happening."

"I can't," Kyja said. "You'd have to jump to get me back to Farworld, and Master Therapass insisted that jumping's too dangerous until we understand more about the realm of shadows. Once you're here or there you're safe, but . . ."

"I know. I know. Jumping across is the most dangerous because my body is there." He'd hoped their experiences with the Augur Well had convinced her to be more of a risk taker. Apparently, not everything had changed.

"I wish you could stay here a few days longer," she said. "But Master Therapass think it's best if you leave before the Dark Circle has a chance to recover."

Marcus nodded glumly. "Did you manage to pry anything out of Cascade about his secret mission?"

"Not yet. But I'll keep snooping."

"I still don't trust him completely. He always has that odd little smile. And he didn't come up to the balcony to help fight the demon after he freed Master Therapass from the dungeon."

Kyja picked a long blade of grass and poked Marcus in the chest with it. "Scree—I mean Graehl, said they were both keeping the unmakers occupied so Master Therapass could get away."

"Yeah, well, I don't know that I trust Graehl much either. He didn't tell us what he was really up to before. Who knows if he's telling us everything now?" Marcus kicked a rock buried in the ground and looked at the mountains where the sun was beginning to rise. All around them, small purple flowers began to raise their heads in song.

Marcus listened to their beautiful music, relieved that the song no longer included images of him destroying Farworld. He wondered if one of the dawn chimes might be the mother of the fairy they'd saved.

"I guess it's time for you to go," Kyja said, blinking quickly.

Marcus wiped his eyes with the back of his hand. He thought about trying to convince her to wait a little longer, but he already knew what she'd say. Master Therapass wanted him on Earth well before sunrise. By now Bonesplinter and his army of Thrathkin

S'Bae would undoubtedly be on their way back to Farworld to regroup after their latest failure.

Therapass was hoping the motorcycle was still there and that Marcus could manage to somehow get it moving with only one good arm and leg—even if it meant driving the whole way in first gear. But if not, Marcus would have to crawl the couple of miles to the monastery where he was supposed to stay until it was safe to bring him back to Farworld, and the desert heat could be almost as deadly as the dark wizards.

"Do you really think Therapass is just guessing that the monks will let me stay with them?" he asked. "Or do you think there's something about the monastery he's not telling us?"

"I think there are a lot of things he's not telling us," Kyja said with a shrewd smile. "But the good thing about me staying in the tower is that I'll have plenty of time to poke around while you're gone."

"I'll do the same there."

"And you have your books," Kyja added.

"Right." Marcus hefted the pack of books and scrolls Master Therapass had given him to study. It was heavy. If he had to crawl, he'd have to leave it with the motorcycle until he could come back for it later. But between the magic books, the histories, and what little there was on elementals, it would give him plenty to study while he was stuck on Earth.

"Master Therapass said I can use the Aptura Discerna to check up on you now and then," Kyja said.

"Just make sure it's not first thing in the morning or right before bed. I'd rather not have you peeking at me while I'm getting dressed or going to the bathroom or something."

They both giggled at the thought. "I promise to keep my eyes closed until Master Therapass says you're decent."

Marcus sighed. There was so much to think about, so many things happening here. He knew being stuck on Earth, with no idea what was occurring on Farworld, would drive him crazy—even if he did have the books and scrolls to keep him busy.

"See you later, fish breath," he said to Riph Raph.

The skyte looked up from licking his talons as though he hadn't even realized Marcus was there. "Haven't you left yet?"

"I'll try to figure out a way to send you messages," Kyja said.

They both stood awkwardly, looking anywhere but at each other. Then as if on cue, each stepped forward and wrapped their arms around each other. After a moment, Marcus pulled back, not sure of what he was going to say or do. Kyja leaned forward and kissed him softly on the lips.

Before he could say a word, the tugging sensation pulled in his stomach, and he was falling. He opened his eyes to find himself sitting by the side of a narrow dirt road in the middle of the Arizona desert. A few feet away, the motorcycle was waiting.

He touched his lips softly, as though afraid that whatever was on them might rub off, and shook his head. "Wow."

UNLIKELY ALLIES

The Dark Circle

Cold lines of sweat trickled down Bonesplinter's face as he knelt on the floor of the antechamber. He did not wipe them away. Clutching his staff crosswise before him, the Thrathkin S'Bae tried not to think of what lay ahead. But beneath his black robes, his heart thudded with the knowledge that the remainder of his life could be measured in minutes.

The walls and floor of the hexagonal room were highly polished black stone with tiny flecks of silver. Occasionally the flecks shot out blue arcs of fire that sparked and crackled up the walls to the domed ceiling high above, like seeking fingers.

Is that how death would come? Blue flames wrapping around his neck and cutting off his breath so he couldn't even cry out as they burned his life away?

His eyes strayed to the deep grooves running from each corner of the room and down to a small bowl at the center. His fingers tightened around his staff, but he dared not raise it. Even if he hadn't known how close he was to Fein Ter'er, the inner sanctum of the Master, he could feel bands of energy raging invisibly about him as if he were kneeling at the edge of a hurricane. He understood instinctively that the moment he so much as lifted the staff, dark magic would rip his body to shreds.

They had failed again to capture the boy. That much he knew, although not how or why. It wasn't his fault this time. His men had been exactly where they were supposed to be—had done everything they were asked to do. He couldn't be blamed.

But the master wouldn't see it that way.

Yet even here, with shame making the thick scar on his face burn, and his death only minutes—perhaps seconds—away, he couldn't help feeling magic flowing wildly around him and imagining what it would be like to take control of it. To hold in his fist the power, to call up almost endless armies of the dead, to raise and destroy kingdoms, to move the very mountains beneath which he knelt.

Above his head, something crackled and flared. A bolt of blue lightning struck the ground beside him, and the Thrathkin S'Bae hunched his shoulders, waiting for the next blow that would undoubtedly take his life. But the blow never came. When he dared raise his eyes, a figure sat on a throne, where the room had been empty only a moment before.

"Master," Bonesplinter whispered, returning his gaze to the floor. He hoped the end would come quickly but feared it would not.

After a moment, when nothing had happened, he dared to raise his eyes again. He'd never seen the Master of the Dark Circle in person—only a hand or eyes in the darkness—and hoped to gain a glimpse before he died. But even that wish seemed too much to hope for. The gem-encrusted throne was clearly visible: blood red with veins of black. Outstretched claws twisting up from the arms and legs looked like some creature in mortal agony.

Two eight-legged dogs perched at either side of the throne, so thin their bones pushed against their black fur. Their red eyes watched him hungrily, as though only waiting for their master's word to tear the Thrathkin S'Bae limb from limb.

The figure in the throne was not so easy to see. Though only a few feet away, it seemed to swim in and out of focus—a shadow within a shadow. For a moment, Bonesplinter thought he could make out a dark face, gray lips straining over long, yellowed teeth. But a moment later, the face disappeared like swirling smoke, to be replaced by a young woman with achingly beautiful features and a tongue that flicked out from between her red lips like a viper's.

Trying to make out the figure made Bonesplinter's head ache. He satisfied himself with concentrating on the wrinkled, gray hands that gripped the arms of the throne. On the right hand, a gold ring glimmered. He had kissed that ring only a few months before with hopes of reestablishing himself with the Master—reclaiming a position of power. Now those hopes were crushed.

"I am old." The voice speaking from the shadows sounded neither male nor female. It could have come from a child or an ancient. It could have come from something not human at all—a dragon flushed with razing an entire city or the crimson-stained steel of an executioner's blade.

Bonesplinter had no idea how to respond, so he said nothing.

"Do you have any idea what the difference is between life and death?" the figure asked between sharp intakes of air.

This was it. This was the moment. Bonesplinter tensed his

muscles, wondering what direction death would come from. He licked his lips and managed a hoarse whisper. "No."

The voice laughed cruelly. "It's a riddle all men solve eventually. I've helped hundreds discover the answer. Thousands. I myself have nearly solved it more than once."

The figure shifted in its chair and sighed deeply, as though remembering. "I think the distance might not be as far as most think."

Bonesplinter screwed up his courage, his limbs trembling, and managed to choke out, "I . . . failed you, Master."

"Yes, yes." The papery gray hand waved in the air as though brushing off a bite-me fly. "Failure and death. All men must taste both in their lifetimes." Along each of the walls, pulses of energy raced upward in zigzagging patterns, exploding loudly overhead as they clashed together. "I do not wish to taste either!" The voice—now hard as stone—roared. "Is that too much to ask?"

"No!" Bonesplinter quailed, his pulse racing.

"No." The voice grew soft again, and along the walls, the energy dropped back to its previous levels. "Do you believe there are worlds within worlds?"

Confused, Bonesplinter nodded dumbly. He had no idea what the Master was talking about, but the fact that they were still talking inspired a faint sliver of hope.

If the Master saw him at all, he seemed to pay no attention, but went on talking. "The foolish believe they see things as they are. But the truly wise understand that nothing is as it appears. Life lies within death. Success within failure. You have seen Earth and Farworld. Perhaps even sensed a link between the two. But there is another world more powerful than both."

Bonesplinter waited silently, trying without success to understand what the Master was saying.

"I have tried to kill the child three times," the Master finally said. "Perhaps it is not his death I must seek at all, but his failure. As death lies within life, so perhaps the child's failure lies hidden within his success."

The figure shifted again, and Bonesplinter felt a sudden, intense aching at the center of his brain. He looked up to see two yellow eyes staring at him from within the shadows. "Why do you think the boy seeks out the elementals?" the voice demanded.

Bonesplinter felt as though his head was splitting in two. "To return to Farworld," he moaned. "It's the only possibility."

"Perhaps," the voice agreed. Bonesplinter felt sure the veins in his head were about to burst. "He hopes to return to his own world and the girl to hers. But it is not that simple. The scales are not so easily balanced. The wizard knows that—which leads me to believe he is not telling the children everything. There is something he knows that I must understand. But I have allies he is not aware of."

The burning inside Bonesplinter's skull stopped, and it was all he could do to keep from collapsing to the floor. The Master's attention had been turned elsewhere. In a haze of pain, the Thrathkin S'Bae looked up to see a section of wall slide open. The master's assistant—a creature with the body of a twisted human and the head of an owl—stepped through the opening. In its mold-coated arms, it carried a small, curved dagger, a cage, and a box made of polished, black wood.

The creature handed the dagger and the cage to the Master. Both dogs sniffed curiously at the cage, but when the creature shuffled to the center of the room and opened the box, they pulled back snarling and whining.

Bonesplinter watched as the creature lifted a bleached white skull from the box and placed it near the bowl-shaped opening in the floor where the trenches met. He'd never seen anything like it. The skull had thick, curved horns similar to a ram or a goat, but instead of growing forward or around to each side, the horns curved up and then back into the skull again as if it had somehow succeeded in goring its own brain. A single eye socket lay black and empty in the center of the skull's forehead.

As silently as it had arrived, the owl creature picked up the box and disappeared from the room, leaving the door open a crack. Bonesplinter watched as the Master's gray hands lifted the cage. Something round and furry squeaked inside the thin bars, which looked suspiciously like they were made of bones. As the Master unlocked the cage and reached inside, Bonesplinter recognized the animal—an ishkabiddle. At the sight of the ball of fur, the two dogs nearly went wild.

"Soon, my pets, soon," the Master whispered. He raised the curved dagger into the air. As he brought the blade down, the ishkabiddle seemed to sense what was happening. At the last second, it jerked in the Master's hands, the blade barely nicking it on one side. The Master lost his grip on the furry creature, and it dropped to the floor.

Instantly the two hounds pounced on it, jaws wide, twin tongues slavering. But the ishkabiddle was too quick. Pink feelers rose from its head and shot out a cloud of tiny gray specks that blinded the dogs momentarily. Before the hounds could react, the ishkabiddle scurried past them with surprising speed and escaped through the still-ajar door.

"Too slow!" The Master cackled as the frustrated dogs pawed

open the door and raced into the hallway beyond. "Success and failure."

The Master turned back to Bonesplinter. "I promised you power," he said.

Bonesplinter looked up, his heart pounding. "Y-yes," he stammered. This had to be a trick. The master was going to kill him; he was sure of it. But a glimmer of hope refused to go out. Perhaps the master recognized that he'd done everything he'd been asked to do. Could he have been called here to be rewarded instead of punished?

What do you desire? a deep voice asked. At first Bonesplinter thought it was the Master speaking, but then he saw that the eye socket at the center of the skull was no longer empty. Orange light danced and flickered from within it, as if a fire burned inside.

"I seek a gift," the Master whispered, holding out the knife with both hands.

What do you offer? the skull asked.

"The blood of an innocent," the Master said. He held the dagger above one of the grooves in the floor. For a moment, Bonesplinter thought the blade was bare. Then he saw a single drop of the ishkabiddle's blood roll down the tip of the dagger and drop into the groove. At the center of the room, the fire inside the skull grew brighter, flashing orange in the darkness.

The tiny drop of crimson flowed down the groove in the floor until it was only inches from the skull. Then, like a snake striking, a long, black tongue unfurled from inside the skull's mouth and lapped up the drop.

At once, the blue light that illuminated the ceiling turned red, forming a small, intense ball of light that looked like a bloody moon. A cold wind appeared from nowhere, chewing and clawing at Bonesplinter's clothes and face, filling the room with the sound of terrifying laughter. The floor trembled beneath his knees, and he clenched his teeth, waiting to be struck dead.

Do you hunger? the skull asked, its voice echoing off the close walls.

Dropping his staff, the Thrathkin S'Bae leaned back, pressing himself against the wall. Was the skull talking to him now—sensing his desire for power?

Do you hunger?

The question repeated itself—pounding like a sick heartbeat, somehow making itself heard above the storm raging through the room. The cold wind froze the sweat on Bonesplinter's face and arms.

Do you hunger? the skull asked again.

With a terrible groaning, the stone walls cracked and broke. Unimaginable power tossed him about the room. Slivers of black stone, ripped away by the swirling air, cut his skin. He knew he couldn't last much longer. Whatever was in the room with him could destroy him without even noticing.

Do you hunger?

"Yes!" he cried pressing his hands to his face. "I hunger. I do. I want power!"

At once everything stopped—the sudden silence as shockingly loud as the chaos that had preceded it. The Thrathkin S'Bae shuddered with dread and terror.

Then you shall have it. The skull's eyes flared.

The Master held out his hands. "A gift for you, my faithful servant."

Bonesplinter looked up. The master's gray hands held something out to him. Still sure he was about to die—that this was some sort of trick—he got to his feet and stumbled forward. The Master offered a circular band of metal so big Bonesplinter could barely hold it. A smaller link was attached to the front. It looked vaguely familiar. He tried to remember where he'd seen it before.

"You shall have more power than you've ever dreamed of," the master said, then laughed a gurgling chuckle. "Of course, such power requires sacrifice."

Suddenly, Bonesplinter remembered where he'd seen this kind of ring. It was a collar. The kind he'd seen chained to the neck of a Summoner.

Summoners were some of the most powerful creatures known to man. The master had owned two until one was destroyed by the water elementals. No one knew exactly what magic was used to create them, but rumors claimed that deep inside the creatures lived the warped souls of those who had once been human, now twisted and defiled until nothing could stand against their dark rage.

His fingers went cold, and he dropped the collar to the ground. "No. Please, no."

Something dark and wet slithered from the hole at the center of the skull's forehead. Evil radiated from it in waves, crushing and terrible. It rose into the air, hovering halfway between ground and ceiling. The dark wizard dropped to the floor, stretching his arms out. "Please, kill me instead."

"I hunger."

Bonesplinter looked back in terror. This voice had not come from the skull, but from the dark thing floating in the air. The skull had not been talking to him at all. It had been talking to this thing. This abomination. *It* was what hungered. And what it hungered for was . . . him. It began to hum softly as it wrapped itself around the Thrathkin S'Bae from head to foot, muting his screams.

"How do you like your power so far?" the master said, watching as the creature that had once been Bonesplinter writhed and twisted in agony on the floor.

The owl-headed assistant returned again, carrying a stone bowl filled with a bloody liquid. It set the bowl on the arm of the throne.

On the floor, the creature continued to spasm and moan. It was already beginning to turn red—dark pustules rising on its back where wings would form once months of continual torture transformed it into the powerful creature known as a Summoner.

"Take it away," the master said.

The assistant picked up the collar, and led the gibbering creature that had been Bonesplinter out the door.

As it left, the lights in the room went out, leaving only the glow of the red liquid. The master touched his finger to its surface and three faces appeared.

"Are you ready to do my bidding?" he asked.

The faces looked back at him from the bowl. One was a water elemental, the other, two land elementals.

All three nodded. "Yes."

DISCUSSION QUESTIONS

1. The melankollia tree makes Marcus focus on his own problems so much that he doesn't realize Kyja is in danger. How does only thinking about your own problems keep you from seeing what is happening with your friends?

2. Marcus buys a charm that turns him into a dog. He is surprised by how differently he sees the world as a dog. If you could temporarily be turned into an animal, what kind of animal would it be? How do you think the transformation might affect the way you look at the world?

3. The Keepers believe magic should be taken from common people and given to the rich and powerful. Do you think this is a good idea? Why or why not?

4. The land elementals built their library in the form of a giant tree. Why do you think they might have done that? If you could create your own library, what would it look like and why? What kind of books would you keep in your library?

5. Mr. Z tells Marcus that he often takes chances which can get him into trouble. He tells Kyja that she tends to be very cautious and stubborn. Which describes you best? Why can that be good and bad?

6. In order to save the fairy, Kyja has to become more like Marcus and take a chance. And Marcus has to become more like Kyja as he tries to understand the fairy's feelings. If you could be more like someone else, who would it be? What might that experience teach you?

7. The fairy's song is about her mother giving up her life rather than joining the Dark Circle. If you had a song, what would it be about?

8. Marcus has the chance to change Farworld by using the power of the gauntlet. Would you change the world if you had a tool like that? What if changing the world meant that other people would lose the ability to make their own choices? Why do you think Marcus chose not to use the power of the gauntlet?

9. Marcus wants to have a healthy body more than anything. Kyja wants to have magic. But they both give up their dreams to help save Farworld and Earth. If you could change one thing about yourself, what would it be? Would you be willing to give up your greatest wish if it would help save Earth?

10. Marcus almost destroyed Farworld. Master Therapass joined the Dark Circle in search of power. Screech was a Keeper. What did each of them learn from their mistakes? Have you ever made a mistake? What did you learn?

ACKNOWLEDGMENTS

I t's only been a year since *Water Keep* came out, but it feels like much longer. My only daughter got married, my oldest son accepted a position that will take him away from home for two years, my little guys aren't so little any more, and I'm writing full-time. Fortunately some things stay the same. I still have great editors, great friends, and the best family ever.

As always, thanks to my incredible critique group, the Women of Wednesday night, who continue to rock the literary world. Thanks to my early readers, Kathy Clement, Tyler Clement, Mom and Dad, Mark Savage (who is introducing Denmark to *Farworld* one reader at a time), Austin, Mrs. Staheli's English classes, and everyone else who gave me their feedback.

Thanks to Lisa Mangum, Chris Schoebinger, Annette Lyon, and everyone else who edited, marketed, sold, and made *Farworld* look good. Brandon Dorman is the most talented artist an author could ask for. His covers and illustrations really make the story come to life.

A special thanks to James Dashner, author extraordinaire of *The 13th Reality* series and the upcoming *Maze Runner* trilogy. He is a great friend and inspiration, even if he pays for lunch about as often as Therapass pays for dinner. (Okay, maybe a little more.)

And, of course, thanks to my family who keeps me laughing every day, who make it a joy to be home, and who understand when I get lost in faraway worlds. Nick, Jake, Scott, Erica, and Big Nick, you guys are great. Jen, I can't imagine a life without you by my side.

And last of all, thanks to you, the readers. Since *Water Keep* came out, I've visited more than 250 schools, and 100,000 students. I've received more than 1,500 e-mails. Each and every reader who says "hi" or tells me how much they like *Farworld* makes my day all over again. When I am asked why I write, the answer is always, "You!" Thanks for joining me on the ride. Drop me a line and say "hi" at scott@jscottsavage.com.